Rhubarb, Strawberries, and Willows

Sylvia Barnard

 FriesenPress

Suite 300 - 990 Fort St
Victoria, BC, V8V 3K2
Canada

www.friesenpress.com

Copyright © 2021 by Sylvia Barnard
First Edition — 2021

All rights reserved.

No part of this publication may be reproduced in any form, or by any means, electronic or mechanical, including photocopying, recording, or any information browsing, storage, or retrieval system, without permission in writing from FriesenPress.

ISBN
978-1-03-911168-4 (Hardcover)
978-1-03-911167-7 (Paperback)
978-1-03-911169-1 (eBook)

1. FICTION, ROMANCE, HISTORICAL, 20TH CENTURY

Distributed to the trade by The Ingram Book Company

Dedication

To the Memory of the forty-eight passengers who lost their lives in the Spanish River Train Disaster on January 21, 1910, near Nairn Centre, Ontario, Canada.

To the valiant efforts of Conductor Thomas Reynolds, Brakeman Morrison, Mrs. Linall, and others who worked tirelessly to rescue and treat the trapped and injured.

Table of Contents

Prologue	ix
Rhubarb	**xiii**
Chapter One	1
Chapter Two	11
Chapter Three	23
Chapter Four	31
Chapter Five	39
Chapter Six	53
Chapter Seven	65
Chapter Eight	75
Strawberries	**85**
Chapter Nine	87
Chapter Ten	101
Chapter Eleven	115
Chapter Twelve	123
Chapter Thirteen	129
Chapter Fourteen	139
Chapter Fifteen	149
Chapter Sixteen	157
Chapter Seventeen	165

Chapter Eighteen	173
Chapter Nineteen	183
Chapter Twenty	189
Chapter Twenty-One	197
Chapter Twenty-Two	205
Chapter Twenty-Three	215
Chapter Twenty-Four	223
Chapter Twenty-Five	239
Chapter Twenty-Six	253
Chapter Twenty-Seven	261
Chapter Twenty-Eight	273
Chapter Twenty-Nine	285
Willows	**297**
Chapter Thirty	299
Chapter Thirty-One	313
Chapter Thirty-Two	327
Chapter Thirty-Three	341
Chapter Thirty-Four	351
Chapter Thirty-Five	359
Chapter Thirty-Six	369
Chapter Thirty-Seven	379
Ballad of the Spanish	387
Author's Notes	389
Acknowledgements	391

Rhubarb, Strawberries, and Willows

Prologue

THE TORONTO DAILY STAR

TORONTO, SATURDAY, JANUARY 22, 1910

FIRST SURVIVOR'S STORY, MAIL CLERK TALKS TO STAR

One Car Telescoped—Remained on Bridge and Burned Cremating Passengers—Other Half Dropped Into River—Shrieks of Injured and Dying—

Terrible Details of Tragedy

Special to The Star
Sault Ste. Marie, Jan. 22—Three big dray loads of rough boxes are ready to receive the bodies of upward of two-score victims at the scene of yesterday's Canadian Pacific wreck at Spanish River. Your correspondent interviewed William Dundas of Ottawa, mail clerk on the ill-fated CPR train wrecked yesterday at Spanish River. He tells the following graphic story.

"We left Nairn Centre at 12:42 and nothing unusual was noticed until we reached the bridge at Spanish River. When about half a train's length from the bridge, I felt the train pulling in a very ragged manner behind, and I knew a portion of the train behind me was off the track."

"For a distance, the train pulled on; then I felt the air brake applied. I kept to the train when I felt her pulling up, and directly we were slowing down. On the other side of the bridge, I jumped."

Burned on the Bridge
"Immediately the second-class car jumped the track. It struck an upright of the bridge and telescoped. The first part remained on the bridge and burned while the other half simply leaped out into the stream with the other two coaches behind it."

"The broken car took its victims with it. Those in the first half were burned, while those in the second half were drowned. The few rescued from the burning car were terribly injured, and I doubt if they are still living. The dead taken from the half which jumped to the river were removed and numbered ten."

"Directly I jumped from the train, I looked about to render some assistance. There were only two women to be seen. The shrieks of the injured and dying could be heard, but I could not see anyone. There were only the three of us to do anything. The remainder were on the other side of the bridge and could not get across. After escaping the sinking dining car, Conductor Reynolds, ignoring his own terrible bruises and cuts, joined in the rescue. Mrs. Linall, one of the two women, set up a hospital in the sleeping car. She was assisted in bathing and bandaging the injured by the other woman survivor whose identity remains unknown. The telegraph wires were all torn down, and it was evident that relief could not be summoned by wire. It was five miles to the village of Nairn. Three unknown loggers came upon the site soon after the event. Two joined in the rescue. The third ran the distance to deliver a report of the wreck at the Canadian Pacific station at Nairn. We worked and did all we could for five hours before assistance reached us.

Went Clean Through Ice

"What was worst of all was our helplessness. When the two coaches leaped into the river, they went through the ice like bullets and did not break the ice for more than a foot on each side of them."

Rhubarb

RHUBARB

Chapter One

The knots in my neck unraveled as I drove through the granite rock cuts crowned with birches, pines, and poplars. Out of habit, I checked for moose in the passing pothole lakes and swamps as I drove up Highway 69 to Sudbury. The wind sucked the gritty tones of Pat Benatar out of my VW bug's open convertible roof.

"Yeah, go ahead, fire away!" I yelled.

Every day of the past two months while living with my mother in Toronto, I'd heard how irresponsible I'd been for breaking up with Rick without telling him about the baby. Never once did she think it might be a mistake to marry a man with alcohol and anger issues. Yesterday was the last straw. She threatened to call Rick herself and tell him he was going to be a father. This morning, I packed everything I owned into my car and headed north. I didn't need him. I didn't need her. The baby and I could live on the trust fund left to me when my dad was killed in the mine. And I had Gran.

A few kilometres west of Nairn Centre, five hours after the start of my journey, I crossed the Spanish River Bridge on Highway 17. Turning right on Dumont Road on my final kilometre, my car kicked up a wake of dust from the gravel surface. I slowed to inhale the fresh scent of green as I passed through the tunnel of saplings pressing up against the road's edges. Coming out of a tight S-curve, I threw my hands in the air and let out a whoop of joy at the acres of meadows spreading below me on the flood plain.

Gran emerged from the small grey bungalow as I pulled in. I walked into the warmth of her embrace, inhaling the scent of pines and sunshine from her long grey ponytail.

"So good to see you, Katie," she whispered against my hair.

She kept hold of my hand as we walked shoulder to shoulder up the quarried stone path and onto the screened back-porch. I gave Gran's hand an added squeeze before she disappeared into the house to make tea.

"How was your trip?" she called from the kitchen.

"Great. Not much traffic north of Barrie." I turned at the clink of the tea tray as Gran set it down. "What happened to one of the weeping willows?"

"It split right down the middle in a wind storm last week. I stuck a branch from it into the ground and, if you look closely, you can see there's a new tree already growing in its place."

"I didn't know they grew naturally up here."

"They don't. The first Dumonts planted the three original trees along the bank in the 1880s. Every time one comes down, we replace it with a cutting." Gran sat in her rocking chair. I continued to stand by the screen wall.

We savoured a moment of silent camaraderie over our cups of strawberry tea. My great-grandfather, Jean-Pierre, had divided the Dumont family holding into three riverfront portions, leaving two smaller plots to his two daughters, Rita and Cécile, and the bulk of the holding with its forests and house to his son, Jacques—my grandfather.

Gran said I had the slim Dumont build and inquisitive blue eyes. I knew my wide smile belonged to my father, Greg Walker.

"See much of tante Cécile and tante Rita?" I gestured toward the two small cottages set along the line of the ridge above the flood plain.

"No. Cécile's son, Daniel, drops in from Espanola for a cup of tea and a chat when he cuts the grass or plows the snow. Maybe we'll see them at Christmas."

I settled on the porch swing beside Gran's rocker. My eyes dropped to my lap. "I'm keeping the baby."

"Mmhmm," Gran said.

"These last months with my mother were a disaster. She's against me having a baby on my own. Keeps pushing me to marry Rick." My frustration burst like steam from a kettle. "Why can't she believe in me, celebrate me being my own person? You'd think we were still living under Queen Victoria."

Gran waited.

"And what's her fascination with living in Toronto?" I was up and pacing around the porch now. "Lively was our home." I threw my hands in the air. "Six months after Dad's accident, she sold everything and fled to the big city like some star-struck teenager."

"Katie, your mother was devastated. Every face she saw reflected her sadness. Every place she went reminded her she was alone."

"But she's left me without a home." I winced at the whine in my voice. "I hate Toronto. It never seems to have enough oxygen. I know you're supposed to grow up, but shouldn't you always be able to go home?"

"You know you'll always have a home here, sweetheart. Your last name may be Walker, but you're a Dumont through and through."

A tear escaped down my cheek. "I can stay here?"

"As long as you want." Gran's face glowed with warmth.

I flung my arms around Gran's neck. My inner spring uncoiled for the first time in weeks.

She gently pushed me back, the steel in her blue eyes meeting mine. "But you do need to tell Rick about the baby."

I opened my mouth to protest.

Gran held up her hand. "Let me finish. I understand you don't want to marry him, but—"

3

"Marry him? I don't even want to see him."

"That may be, but this baby is not yours alone. Rick deserves the opportunity to be involved. Think about what your life would have been like without your father."

I stood at the screen and watched a line of fluffy baby Canada geese, bookended by their parents, march single file across the riverfront lawn. Where would I have been without my dad? He'd taught me to be true to myself and not worry about what other people thought. If he were here right now, he'd be celebrating the upcoming birth of his grandchild, not pushing me into a doomed marriage. I sighed. "Okay, Gran. I'll call Rick next week."

Gran came to stand beside me. "You know, Katie, sometimes life'll put you on a path you didn't choose. That's when you treat it like rhubarb, dip it in sugar and turn the bitter into sweet."

"Hmm. I like that."

"I have fresh-picked strawberries and rhubarb just waiting to be made into a crisp for the Nairn Centre Canada Day Strawberry Social tomorrow."

"I'll help."

* * *

June danced into July. Gran and I spent our days tending the vegetable gardens, making jams from the wild berries we picked, and reading on the porch. At night, the terrors of motherhood chased away my sleep. What kind of mother would I be? How would I protect this new life? I knew nothing about babies, about molding a new person. As if reading my thoughts, that was when the little guy would decide to roll. I loved tracing his progress by the little elbow points tracking across my abdomen. He'd only settle when I sang to him and rubbed his head, or maybe that was his bottom. Either way, my fears would dissolve. We would find our way together.

Rhubarb, Strawberries, and Willows

On an outing to Sudbury one Sunday afternoon, Gran and I took in a play at the Bell Park Amphitheatre. It brought to life the challenges and joys of daily life in the 1880s as revealed in the journals of two women settlers living in Northern Ontario. Inspired, I decided to try my hand at writing. It'd help pass the time while I waited for the baby to come.

One day, as I was poring over yellowed maps in the Espanola Library, an attractive woman of about my mother's age approached me.

"Excuse me," the woman said, hazel eyes shining, "I've noticed you're here almost every day, working with these old documents. Are you a writer?"

My eyes widened. "Um . . . I'm researching for a play. So . . . I guess you could call me a writer." My voice rose at the end.

"Lois Maxwell." She extended her hand.

"Kate Dumont Walker."

We shook hands.

"I assume it's historical." She gestured at the pile of documents I'd spread across the counter.

I nodded. "I'm looking for a pivotal event in Nairn Centre's history to bring to life. Maybe one day, it'll be performed in the town park."

Lois smiled and tossed back her curly dark brown hair. "Great idea. If we don't know where we've come from—"

"Then how can we figure out where we're going?" I put my hand over my mouth. "I'm sorry."

She laughed. "Precisely. I've done some acting, so if you need help with the script . . ."

"Have you done anything I might know?"

"Maybe you've heard of Miss Moneypenny from the James Bond movies . . . *Casino Royale*, *The Spy Who Loved Me* . . . ?" Lois grinned.

I felt the warmth flooding my face.

"Or the TV show *Adventures in Rainbow Country*?"

I nodded, open-mouthed.

"Played the mother."

"Oh, my God. I'm sorry. I didn't recognize you."

She chuckled and waved her hand. "So what event are you looking at?"

I handed her a copy of the newspaper report I'd found that day. "One of World's Worst Railway Wrecks", printed in the *Toronto Daily Star*."

Lois scanned the copy. "I've never heard of this disaster. Mind if I read with you?"

For the next hour, Lois and I sifted through news articles, maps, sketches, and journals to piece together the events of that terrible day.

It was after four o'clock when Lois glanced at her watch. "Wow! Time really flies. I need to get home and let Lulu out. She's probably sitting with her legs crossed, poor dog."

"Thanks for your help." I smiled.

Lois tilted her head. "Would you like to meet at Richardson's Cafe for tea next week?" Her smile quivered uncertainly. "People are friendly here, but they all have their own lives."

I nodded. "I'd love to. How about Tuesday afternoon?"

"Sounds great. Bring your research." Lois grinned as she grabbed her purse and headed out the door.

The article continued to burrow a home in my brain as I walked up the Riverhouse path. A *V* of honking Canada geese landed like float planes on the river. Yellows and reds were already interjecting within the deep green of the conifers as the poplars, birches, and maples signalled their descent into the dark days to come.

I dropped onto the porch swing. "Gran, have you ever heard about the 1910 train derailment on the Spanish River?"

Gran's eyes narrowed. "I've heard talk of it." She shifted in the rocking chair.

Rhubarb, Strawberries, and Willows

"One of the worst train disasters in Canada, and it happened just a few miles from here. Imagine, they believe up to eighty people either drowned or burned. I can't get it out of my mind."

"How horrible. Explains why they rerouted the track a few years later." Gran seemed to be rocking a little faster.

Staring out at the river, images of my grandfather and his sisters as children throwing stones into the water were so real I chuckled aloud.

Gran followed my gaze. "What's so funny out there?"

It wasn't unusual for me to see people and events from the past unfold as an overlay on the present, like living in layers of history. "I was imagining *Grand-père* and his sisters playing along the river."

Gran tilted her head, brow slightly puckered.

"It's like . . . wait a second, I'll be right back." I pushed myself up and waddled down the hall to my bedroom. Minutes later, I propped a framed James Lumbers print entitled *City Limits* on the swing.

Gran leaned in. "The log cabin and the maple are solid." She peered closer. "Is that a horse and wagon under the tree? They're so faint, they look like phantoms. Look, there's two ghost people sitting in the wagon. Amazing. Where did you find this?"

"In the gift shop of the Massey Area Museum the day I was reading settler women's journals. It kept calling to me from its easel in the window." I paused. "It's how I see things sometimes."

"Oh, my." Gran's mouth continued to move, but my attention was absorbed by the sound of the train crossing the river bridge. Even the baby had ceased its constant gymnastic routine. " . . . promise me. Do you understand? Kate, Kate . . ." The warmth of Gran's hand on my hip pulled me back to the present as the train sounds faded into the distance. Punctuating my return to awareness, the baby gave me a sharp elbow in the back.

Gran's expression was etched with alarm.

"What were you saying?"

Gran grasped my hands in hers. "No hikes out to the site of the old railway bridge. Promise me your wilderness excursions are over until spring."

"I hear you, Gran. No more bush walks."

* * *

All morning, I'd been pacing from the front living room window overlooking Dumont Road and through the open kitchen, straightening the yellow placemats on my way past the pine harvest table. Standing at the back French doors, I bounced four-month-old Amelia gently against my shoulder, her baby breath tickling my neck.

A shadow moved over the pristine snow between the willow trees on the riverbank below me. Squinting, I made out the ghostly figure of a tall, slim man, the fringes on his tan hide jacket swaying in rhythm with his mukluks as his snowshoes churned over the snow. He turned toward the house and brushed impatiently at the chestnut curls against his fair, cold-reddened cheeks. I gasped.

"Kate, is something wrong?" Gran asked.

"Is someone living in tante Rita's or tante Cécile's cottage?"

"No, why?"

"I thought—" The sound of the whistle and the clickety-clack of the wheels against the track as the morning train crossed the river bridge a kilometre away absorbed my attention. Baby Amelia tensed against me until the sound faded into the distance.

"Kate!"

Turning at the sound of my name, I met Gran's eyes. "That train sounded so close." I forced a smile and nestled Amelia into her cradle beside Gran.

"They always sound closer in winter." Gran's expression softened. "Now, what were you saying?"

"I thought I saw someone down by the willows." I turned to find the snowy field vacant and undisturbed. "I think I'm going stir crazy."

"It can't be very stimulating, being stuck indoors with a baby and your old Gran for company."

"No, it's not you. I love our days together, but I miss my weekly tea and research talks with Lois. The fall whizzed by with the family gatherings at Thanksgiving and Christmas. Now, January feels as if it's going on forever. I can't remember the last time I got out on my snowshoes." Amelia's even breathing signalled she'd given in to her morning nap.

Gran's eyes brimmed with understanding. "I think something else is bothering you, too."

"I miss my friends." My eyes slid from her gaze. When I looked back, she was still staring at me. My hands fidgeted in my lap. "I guess I'm envious. I was supposed to be at teachers' college with Maggie, Julia, and Louise right now." A heavy sigh escaped me. "It's not that I don't love Amelia, but . . ."

Resting her knitting in her lap, Gran reached out to grasp my hand. "But you feel like you're missing out on your career?"

I nodded. Her hand was warm, smooth.

"I know this isn't how you scripted your life, but give it time. You'll get to your teaching career soon." She gave my hand a squeeze, let go, and tucked her hair behind her ears. "Why don't you get out for a walk now? Go on. Take your chance while Amelia's asleep."

As I bent to plant a grateful kiss on her cheek, Gran grasped both my hands in hers. "Stay away from the river. It's deceptive at this time of year." A cloud of concern flitted across her eyes.

"I will."

When I headed out the door, snowshoes in hand, Gran was rocking Amelia's cradle in front of the wood stove with her foot, in rhythm with the click of her knitting needles. I crossed the river on the Trans-Canada Highway, and then snowshoed into the woods. This was what I needed—crisp air filling my lungs, bright sunshine sparkling off the fresh snow. I threw up my arms and shouted, "Woohoo!" into the infinite blue sky. My cheeks were soon tingling as I strode through the powdery snow. My promise to Gran to stay away from the river briefly tickled my conscience, but it was such a perfect day for snowshoeing. What would be the harm?

Since the railroad track was rerouted in the 1920s, the path of the old track has been used by hunters, loggers, and campers, keeping it easy to navigate. It was flanked by a reception line of evergreen trees standing like elegant ladies dressed in their snowy white gowns. Birds flitted among the bare birch branches. Squirrel and rabbit tracks littered the snow, and I even crossed several deer trails. Soon, I was singing "The Ballad of the Spanish," a song I was writing as part of my play.

> *Up north of Biscotasi*
> *The mighty river is born*
> *Through rock cuts, ov'r lowlands*
> *Her southward path is worn*

The trail ended at the site where the previous railway bridge had crossed the river. The old piers continued to stubbornly part the waters, even though they'd lost their purpose decades ago when the bridge had been removed and the track rerouted. If I stared at the space between the piers, would the bridge appear in my mind? My thoughts were pulled into the sound of the whistles as the one o'clock train crossed the current bridge, running parallel to the highway about half a mile behind me. A tremor rose through the soles of my boots, up my legs. Suddenly, it was as though the train were driving through me, as if I were the track, as if the locomotive pushed into my chest. I fell backward into the snow.

The screech of metal wheels on rails and the desperate screams of people filled my head. I blacked out.

RHUBARB

Chapter Two

I came to. The roaring in my ears subsided. I forced myself to stop gulping air.

"Okay, Kate." My voice cut the silence. "Focus."

My eyes squinted in the sun reflecting off the snow. How long had I been lying here? Long enough for the cold to seep through my down parka and snow pants. My snowshoes were still attached to my feet. Apparently uninjured, I pulled myself up using a nearby branch. I was still in the clearing of snow-covered evergreens on the granite outcropping above the river.

Why had I passed out? How could there have been a train? The tracks had been gone for decades. And those screaming people?

I let go of the branch. Whirling around, I searched for the bridge piers. Instead, I found the inky waters coursing unimpeded between banks scalloped with ice. No sign of my snowshoe tracks on the trail. "Breathe, Kate."

I needed to get back to the Riverhouse. Amelia would be waiting for her afternoon playtime. Surrounded by her toys on the floor, I'd been teaching her to roll over and push herself up on her elbows. How could Rick have called her a *problem*? After the hurt and anger at his response to my letter telling him about our coming child, I was left with sadness for Amelia that she'd never know her father, and relief knowing I'd done the right thing in breaking off our engagement.

Imagining my baby's open arms, I strode forward, hands swinging to restore circulation. I pictured Gran sitting in her rocker when I came through the door. She'd say something like, "Ah, there you are. You're looking much brighter. I find a good walk through the forest is the best remedy for cleaning the soul." My mouth was already watering at the imagined aroma of her homemade pea soup simmering on the stove.

Why couldn't I hear any traffic sounds ahead? Unease ticked down my spine. The watery winter sun was sinking when I broke through the trees. Where were the highway and rail bridges that crossed here side by side? The river rushed through the open granite-walled gap as the moon rose. How was I going to cross? A howl echoed in the empty twilight.

Cold reason forced me to keep marching north along the river. Within minutes, the smell of smoke pulled my attention to the opposite bank. In the dim light, I made out the outline of a log cabin sitting in the place where the Riverhouse ought to be. A yellow glow from its two front windows illuminated the covered veranda. In place of Gran's studio, there was a barn. No sign of Dumont Road. No sign of Gran's car. Gran! She must be out of her mind with worry. I brushed tears from my frozen cheeks.

Uncontrolled shivering pushed aside my bewilderment. "You're not going to solve this tonight." I had to find shelter to survive. My best hope was to break into one of the summer cottages on this side. I might even find materials to light a fire. Then, in the morning, I'd find my way home. Buoyed with this plan, I struck out upstream along the embankment.

The snow gathered the crisp light of the full moon, silhouetting the trees and rocks like cardboard cut-outs. Movement generated warmth throughout my body until even my toes and fingers uncurled, but nothing could release the icy grip the fingers of fear had wrapped around my mind.

Over my ragged breathing, I picked up the distant sound of male voices punctuated by the hiss and spit of a campfire. My pace increased as I made my way toward the raucous laughter. Maybe they'd know where the bridge was.

A mitten-clad hand grabbed me from behind, smothering my mouth and nose. I tried to jerk free.

"*Calme-toi.* Don't make a sound!" my captor whispered fiercely. His rough beard chafed my cheek.

I tried to scream. No sound escaped the muffling. I flung myself sideways in a desperate push for freedom. A resounding crack, smoked-meat breath, white-hot pain. Black.

* * *

Soft, steady crackling broken by sudden louder snaps resolved into the flicker of a brisk fire. Shadows twirled over the low log ceiling above where I lay on a bed.

"Ah, there you are," said an accented male voice. "No, no, don't be afraid," he added as I shot backward on the bed. I gasped, pulling my knees to my chest and wrapping my arms around my head at the exploding pain.

"Your head, it hurts, *n'est-ce pas*? You hit it against the tree."

I moaned as my fingers found a tender lump and a small raw opening.

"Drink this. Good for pain. Food will be ready soon."

I gazed for a moment into deep-set eyes the colour of moss before accepting the cup. The man's moccasins scuffed back across the hard-packed dirt floor.

The scent of willow bark wafting from the enamel cup transported me—Gran would give me this same tea for a headache. I pictured her pacing from window to door. Quelling the shaking in my hands, I sipped while assessing my surroundings—moss-chinked log walls, fieldstone fireplace, my red parka standing out next to the long deer-hide jacket hanging from a dowel behind the only door—too far to risk. My captor's linen shirt stretched taut across his back as he stirred something in the fireplace. My mouth flooded with saliva at the scent of cooking meat. Who is this man? This place looks as if it came out of the 1800s.

He turned. "Hungry?"

My nod reignited the throbbing. He pulled two tin plates and cups from the plank shelf mounted above a rudimentary washstand. Gesturing toward a rough-hewn wood table under the single window, he then turned to fill the cups from a small metal bucket suspended over the fire.

I emerged from under the lush bear hide, sock feet hitting the floor. Never taking my eyes from the man's back, I tentatively stood up, only to pitch backward onto the bed as the room spun. I felt the bed compress beside me under the pressure of the man's weight, the warm imprint of his enormous hand supporting my back.

'Don't touch me!"

"*Ben*, find your own way." He rose abruptly, picked up the bread and butter from the wooden worktop, and settled himself at the table.

Pushing myself up, I wobbled to the empty seat. We sat across from each other, silently consuming the rabbit stew. "Eat slow," he said in response to my increasing pace. When we had both eaten our fill, he replenished our cups.

Avoiding his gaze, I caught my wavering reflection in the window. My finger slid over its undulated surface.

"Thank you, monsieur," I murmured, trying to smooth over my earlier roughness. "Who are you? Where am I?"

"*De rien, mam'selle.*" He extended his hand. "My name is Abraham Obey."

"Catherine Dumont Walker." Rough calluses brushed my palm.

"So, Mam'selle Dumont Walker, why were you out in the forest alone after dark?" His caterpillar eyebrows climbed his forehead.

"My baby daughter and I live with my grandmother on the river, near here. I was snowshoeing and lost track of time. Then, in the dark, I became disoriented and couldn't find the bridge to get back."

"Bridge? There's no bridge here." He leaned forward. "Perhaps you were approaching the logging crew to offer them comfort?"

"What do mean *comfort*?" I leaped to my feet.

"Mam'selle, please, sit."

I was closer to the door now, but I'd never get my boots on in time. I sat.

"A young woman approaching a group of rough men in the night, dressed to reveal your assets. It is not unusual to think . . ."

"What's wrong with the way I dress? I was bundled up like a snowman. They wouldn't even know I was a woman."

"Even though you dress like a man, your shape is unmistakably a woman."

I pulled my sweatshirt closer around me and crossed my arms over my chest.

"Do you know what a group of drunken loggers would do to you, stumbling into their camp alone?"

"I suppose you expect me to be grateful for rescuing me?"

He made a dismissive gesture with his hand.

We stared into the fire for a while.

"Are you familiar with this area, monsieur?"

He nodded. "I have trapped here all winter."

"Have you seen a grey-and-white bungalow? It's about half a mile north of where the rail and highway bridges cross the river."

He shook his head. "There is no railway here. And what is this highway and bungalow?"

"You know, a highway—*une autoroute*. And a bungalow—*une maison à une étage*."

Abraham responded with a Gallic shoulder shrug, hands open with palms upward.

"No matter." I gave him a placating smile. "I'm sure I'll find the house in the morning. I'd appreciate it if I could curl up in front of your fire tonight?"

"Of course you'll stay the night, in the bed."

My eyes widened.

"Don't worry," he hurried to add. "I will sleep by the fire. In the morning, we'll find this bungalow of your *grand-maman*."

"*Merci*, Monsieur Obey."

"Come, let's warm ourselves by the fire. Wrap this blanket to replace your skirt."

"I didn't have a skirt. My jeans are perfectly warm, thanks."

"Please. I am not comfortable faced with your . . ." He gestured toward my hips.

"Fine." The warmth of the blanket did feel cozy. "I need . . . ah . . . to relieve myself," I said, heading to the door.

"No, no. It is far too cold." His words stopped me before I could reach for my coat and boots. He pulled an enamel night pot from under the bed. Damn. Following his pointing finger, I ducked behind the drying rack where my snow pants hung next to the fire while he busied himself clearing the table. When I finished, he settled himself by the fire.

Having exhausted all hope of escape, I joined him. Igniting a taper, Abraham drew deeply on his pipe. "Dumont, eh? We have Dumont settlers near our farm—near Fort Garry, in Manitoba. Do you know Gabriel Dumont by chance?"

"Dumont is my grandmother's married name. She's actually a Robitaille Métis. Her ancestor was a voyageur who settled with his Indian wife in Penetanguishene."

"*Sa si boon. Ki nishitohtayn chiin?*"

I stared at him, giving my mind a moment to process what he'd said. "Okaaay. I think you said 'that's good'? I've heard Gran say that, but I have no idea what the rest was."

"I asked if you understood. So you've heard Michif?"

Rhubarb, Strawberries, and Willows

I nodded. Huh, so that's what Gran was speaking. We mostly spoke French, but sometimes she'd throw in strange phrases.

It was as if I'd released a dam. Abraham poured his story into the cabin. He spoke with bitterness of the English settlers who had moved into Manitoba right after they'd created their Dominion—arrogant white occupiers, he called them, who built their homes and farms on land that had belonged to his forefathers.

Leaning in conspiratorially, he elaborated, "*Ben*. Just now my father is accompanying a group of our elders to Montana. They'll bring Louis back, and we'll show the *maudits Anglais* they cannot push around the Métis!"

"Louis?"

"Ah, you have heard of Riel? He helped us in '70 against the government, and he'll help us again with Gabriel Dumont at his side." A rosy flush suffused Abraham's face. "They forced us west once. This time we will hold at Batoche."

"Monsieur Obey," I said, "What year is this?"

"1881, of course."

There it was. Since that afternoon, I had been skirting the obvious. The old bridge footings were not rising out of the river. The Trans Canada seemed to have vanished into thin air. The only thing I could do now was try to gather as much information as I could. "Then why are you here instead of helping mount the rebellion?"

"My father sent me here to find land. In case something goes wrong, we need a safe place to move our families. My oldest brother is in Batoche protecting our mother and our new lands. My second brother defends the lands of our heritage on the Red River."

I looked at him. He seemed to believe what he said. "How did you get here?"

"I followed the route of my ancestors, *les coureurs des bois*." Abraham rose and crossed to the dowels behind the door. "*Regarde. Ma ceinture fléchée et ma tuque.*" I ran my palm over the intricate arrow pattern of the woven sash and fingered the red knitted hat.

17

"They remind me of who I am, even if I must hide them under my clothing."

"Beautiful." I stifled a yawn.

"Time to sleep. You have had a difficult day."

I crawled back under the bear rug. The weight of missing Amelia and Gran, and the confusing encounter with Abraham consumed me. Could it be 1881? If so, how could I be here? But his cabin, the way he lived. With no possible resolution in sight tonight, I consoled myself by devising a plan to get home until I dropped into an exhausted sleep.

* * *

Erasing the frosted lace with my hand, I peer through the window at a distorted image of Gran rocking Amelia in her arms. I punch my palms repeatedly against the glass. I call their names. They can't hear me. They don't see me. I scream.

I awakened and turned into the pillow to muffle my sobs. Abraham scuffed across the room to sit beside me.

"Leave me alone." I pushed his arm from my shoulders. "It was just a nightmare, *un cauchemar*. I'm worried about my baby girl."

Abraham nodded, "*Je comprends*. I miss my wife and children and pray each day for their survival." He sighed deeply. "Enough. Now it is time to eat."

I sat hunched in the chair while Abraham prepared our meal of porridge, sumac tea, and bread drizzled with maple syrup. I choked down a few spoonfuls of porridge.

"Let's begin at the spot where I found you," Abraham declared.

Bundled against the cold, we stepped out into a northern winter day, where the sunlight exploded like fireworks against an infinite blue sky.

In response to Abraham's glances at my snowshoes, I offered, "My mother sent them to me from Toronto. They're lighter than my old ones."

"They're made of metal?"

"Yes, aluminum. And the straps are nylon, so the snow doesn't cake."

"What is a nylon? We don't have them at home. Can I hunt them here?"

"No." I covered a smile. "Nylon doesn't come from an animal. It is a man-made material."

Another Gallic shrug.

Soon we were moving through the trees in a companionable rhythm. Above the chirp and chatter of birds and chipmunks, Abraham's husky voice drifted back to me singing, "*Auprès de ma blonde*" under his breath. I joined in, and soon the forest rang with our two-part harmony:

> *Auprès de ma blonde, qu'il fait bon, fait bon, fait bon.*
> *Auprès de ma blonde, qu'il fait bon dormir.*

We marched our way to the river, occasionally stopping for Abraham to collect a rabbit and reset a snare. The sun was already past midday when we were standing on the same embankment where I'd stood the previous evening. Snow tumbled on my head from an overhanging branch as Abraham shifted his weight against the red pine.

"This is the right place. But Gran's bungalow should be where that cabin is." I pointed further downstream. "The highway and railway bridges should be right there, side by side, crossing the Spanish." Adrenaline prickled my fingertips. This couldn't be happening. I turned and started walking south.

Abraham was beside me in a flash. "Where are you going?"

"I've got to go back to where I blacked out yesterday so I can figure this out." My voice rose higher. "I have to figure this out. I have to find Amelia and Gran!"

Suddenly, Abraham dropped to the ground. I followed his lead.

"Quiet," he whispered, lips against my tuque-covered ear.

I remained still.

Voices floated on the air above the ice-choked river. We crawled back to the shelter of a tree leaning over the embankment. Two men clad in deer hide coats hanging to their knees and wearing traditional Indian mukluks had emerged from the cabin. One of them laughed and gestured toward the north. Rabbit fur peeked around the cuffs of his hide gloves. We strained to catch the men's conversation, but the edges of their words blurred like melting snowflakes.

The cabin door opened again, and a young woman stepped onto the veranda carrying a wriggling bundle. "Papa, papa!" When she put him down, the little one wobbled unsteadily toward the two men. Both woman and child wore furs.

"It's a family, Abraham," I whispered, struggling to stand.

He pushed me back into the snow. "Listen. That logging crew is near."

Sitting back against the tree, I focussed through the birdsong to pick up other sounds. The people across the river had moved into their barn. Then I heard it—men's angry voices, the periodic *thunk* of an axe into a tree as they blazed their trail. Their outlines materialized on and off between the trees as they moved along the river, parallel to our route.

"How we gonna get over this river? We bin lookin' for days." The short, wiry man whined.

"*Oui.* I say we set a crossing here and get back," replied his robust companion with a French accent.

"Not yet. It's too flat over there." *Thunk.* The clean-shaven leader kept moving forward.

"*Mais la distance,* she is getting too far from camp."

"Yeah. Mr. Campbell ain't gonna be happy with a tote road way out here. This is bull."

"*Ben.* We should find ourselves some nice company in Nelsonville before we return to camp."

"Now you're talkin'. Three months is a long time with just these." The man waggled his fingers in the air.

"Keep moving, lads, if you want your pay when we get back to camp." *Thunk.* The three men seemed unaware of our presence as they continued south.

The forest wrapped us once more in its snowy silence. "Let's go further downriver, Abe."

"Look, *le soleil,* she is already low, Mam'selle. It will be dark soon."

"Then will you take me to Nairn Centre?"

"*Ben,* I don't know this Nairn Centre. Tomorrow we'll go to Nelsonville. Safest to return to my cabin, now." He turned and headed back along our track.

I stared out at the river. Images left me immobilized. Abraham's cabin . . . the way people dressed . . . the cabin instead of Gran's house. Could this really be 1881? What happened when I blacked out on the river bank? Reluctantly, I turned and followed Abraham's fur hat bobbing along our trail, pinning my hopes on finding the answers the next day in Nelsonville.

Chapter Three

Each day, I followed Elisabeth Schroeder's short, matronly frame around the cookery, fulfilling her directions in silence. At night, memories marched across my mattress, stealing my sleep—Amelia's laugh, Gran's smile—images and moments I didn't want to remember yet feared to forget. While I'd learned to keep my head low to avoid hitting the beams, I hadn't yet reconciled myself to the fact that I was actually living in 1881.

The evenings were the hardest. Designed as a bedroom and sitting room for the cook, the tiny space now housed three sleepers. The rough log walls of the twenty by twenty foot hut compressed Elisabeth, her twelve-year-old son, and me into a tight knot in front of the fire.

Tonight began like every other. While mother and son chatted, I stared into the fire, waiting for the moment I could retreat behind the gingham curtain which delineated my corner. I hugged myself into the warmth of the sweater I'd knitted using the leftover wool I scrounged from Elisabeth's collection. A rough lumberjack shirt beneath the sweater rubbed a century from my skin. My fingers followed the seams of irregular rag patches, cobbled together to create my floor-length skirt.

"*Nein,* Mutti. Not *dis*. Put your tongue between your teeth and blow *this*."

"Zzzis"

"This"

"Dis. Ach, Paul, zis is reeducoulous."

"Ridiculous, Mutti." Paul's impish grin lit his blue eyes.

She flapped her hand. "Come, Paul, enough. Five times five."

"Mutti, do we have to?"

"You are going to make a living with your brain, not your body, my son. Five times five."

"Twenty-five."

"Five times ten."

My thoughts bounced to the rhythm of the mental arithmetic drill. I saw myself strapped to a toboggan, jouncing through the snow, carried into a dim room, dropped by the fire. I heard Abraham's whispers through a dark tunnel, felt the cold cloth on my hot forehead. Broth. Commands to open my eyes, sit up, eat.

The crackle of paper as Paul smoothed a page on his skinny knee snapped me into the present.

"Look, Mutti, Mr. Parker gave me this news sheet this morning. It tells about the railroad coming to Sainte-Anne-des-Pins. He said the railroad will come to Webbwood too."

"*Ach das ist doch verrückt!* Why would anyone put a railroad through this bush?"

"Maybe it's not crazy. Here."

Elisabeth's nose almost touched the page. She handed it back to her son. "It is too dark. Ask Mr. Parker tomorrow."

Paul's eyes glistened with tears. "Mutti, he said I should read it for myself. He called me a dummy because I can't read English."

I reached across Elisabeth and grabbed the news sheet.

Paul stared at me. "You can read?"

"*Gott sei Dank.* Thank goodness." Elisabeth murmured.

I began reading aloud, "Montreal syndicate rescues Macdonald's dream of a transcontinental railway. On the twenty-first of October, 1880, a new syndicate was appointed to build the transcontinental

Rhubarb, Strawberries, and Willows

railway." Skimming the document, I summarized, "Okay. It goes on to talk about the contract and who's building it. He's appointed a renowned railway executive by the name of William Cornelius Van Horne to oversee the construction."

"It still sounds crazy," Elisabeth declared. "Who wants to travel that far? I've heard it's just flat land and Indians out West."

"Well, according to this, it's so raw materials can be transported for manufacturing in the East. I think it's because the politicians want to stop the United States from taking over the West."

"Kate, will you teach me to read English?" Paul's eyes were wide with hope.

"Of course, if it's okay with your mother." The words caught in my throat. I bent double, consumed by a choking cough.

"Paul, get Miss Kate some water and bring me the honey pot with a spoon. Relax, Kate." Elisabeth stroked my back. "It's been weeks since you spoke. Your voice is . . . I don't know the English word . . . like when metal gets eaten by water."

"Rusty, Mutti." Paul handed me the water. "*Bitte*, Mutti, can Miss Kate teach me? I promise I won't take time away from my work."

"*Ja*, Paul, Kate can teach you. Now, here, Kate, this will take the rust off."

"How long have I been here?" I croaked as the honey worked its magic.

"Well, let me see. Abraham brought you on January twenty-fourth, and it is March already, so five weeks maybe."

"He was supposed to take me to Nelsonville."

"You were vomiting and crazy with fever. Abraham knew Paul and I worked in one of these camps in winter. He tried three before he finally found us."

"Mr. Abe boarded with us last spring, helping us clear stumps from our land in Webbwood," Paul explained. "He showed me how to sharpen the blades on our plow. Then one day, he said he had to find his own land."

25

"Abraham is a good man, so of course I said yes when he asked me to help you, Kate." She fixed me with a look. "Your silence has not made it easy for me with Mr. Campbell."

"I'm sorry, Elisabeth. Thank you for all you've done."

"It's all right. If I need something, the camp boss will give it to me. Everyone knows that Elisabeth Schroeder's cookery is the best. Men line up to be hired into the Spanish River Lumber Company Camp." She stood. "*Nun*, time for bed. We have eighty-five hungry men to feed at dawn."

Paul kissed his mother on the cheek and awkwardly shook my hand before disappearing behind the curtain into his corner.

"Elisabeth, thank you for not giving up on me. How can I ever repay you?"

"*Ach*, Kate." She rose to go to her own corner. "If you teach my son to read and write, you will give me the world."

* * *

"Are the eggs ready, Kate? It is almost dawn," Elisabeth called from across the cookery.

"All scrambled. And the ham is fried and stacked, too."

"Good. Let's get these plates laid out."

Paul dealt tin plates across the wooden counter that separated the cookery from the eating area of the long dining hall. I followed, spooning a generous serving of eggs onto each while Elisabeth added slabs of ham.

"Paul, go ring the gut hammer, then make sure there is plenty of bread, jam, and butter on the tables. I need to finish the lunch. Once you have everything on the tables, you can refill coffee. Now, *schnell, schnell*, everyone!" Elisabeth clapped her small hands.

An army of Paul Bunyans—tall, short, broad, lanky, all bearded—emerged from the low bunkhouses as Paul struck the large metal triangle hanging outside the dining hall. Each man grabbed a

Rhubarb, Strawberries, and Willows

heaped breakfast plate and a cup of coffee before settling at one of the long wooden tables. Within minutes, all eighty-five were seated. The rhythmic scrape of fork on metal plate supplanted all conversation. I circulated through the hall, plopping more eggs and ham on plates raised into the air. At the call, "All Aboard!" the men filed out. The rhythmic scrunch of Gold Seal boots on packed snow accompanied their progress across the square in the centre of the camp. The last four men hefted the metal buckets of venison goulash and linen bags of freshly baked buns from the counter, depositing them on a waiting sled. Lunch would be heated over a fire at the worksite.

Elisabeth joined me at the window as we watched the laden sleds disappear into the forest.

"Quiet bunch."

"Too much talk, not enough eat. Not enough eat, not enough trees cut. Not enough trees cut . . ." Elisabeth accompanied each phrase with a turn of a hand, right, then left, palm up.

"Unhappy camp boss."

I jumped at the voice behind us. "Oh . . . good morning, Mr. Campbell." He stood close enough for me to count the purple veins on his bulbous nose. I took a step back.

"Good morning, Kate. So nice to finally hear your voice. I was beginning to doubt you had one."

"Yes. Mr. Campbell, I'm afraid I haven't been very gracious." I kept my eyes downcast. "Thank you for allowing me to stay."

"Keeping the cook happy makes my life easier. Now, come and sit for a moment, Kate. I'd like to hear more about what you were doing alone out in this wilderness."

"The tradesmen will be here soon for their breakfast . . ."

"Elisabeth, I'm sure you can spare Kate for a few moments?"

"Of course, Mr. Campbell."

I watched Elisabeth's receding back over my shoulder as Mr. Campbell's smooth palm guided me by the elbow to his private table. His chair creaked as he lowered himself, arranging his belly to droop between wide-spread thighs.

"Now, who sent you here?"

"My mother."

"Your mother sent you into the woods alone?"

"No, sir. I mean, she . . . um . . . sent me from Toronto to check on my grandmother. We'd heard she was ill. I got lost on the way."

"And I'm to believe you travelled alone? Why wouldn't your father come, or your husband?"

"My father is dead, and I don't have a husband." I pressed my damp palms against my thighs.

Mr. Campbell raised one eyebrow. "What is your grandmother's name? This is my third season, so I know most of the settlers in the area."

"Evangeline Dumont."

"Hmm," Campbell's eyebrow dropped. "Only Dumont on the river is an engineer from Montreal. Built a nice place above the flood plain two years ago a few miles south of here."

"My grandfather's name was Jacques. He passed almost ten years ago."

"Maybe a relation? Dumont I know lives with his baby son. Indian sister and brother from upriver help him out most days. Heard his wife died in childbirth."

"Thank you. Maybe I'll visit him, try to learn more." I braced to stand.

Mr. Campbell leaned across the table, pinning my hand. "What do you think of our camp?"

I sat back down. "I don't know . . ." I muttered in confusion. "It seems very efficient." My eyes darted around the room. The tradesmen and clerks were at their table, eyes downcast, heads tilted to catch our conversation.

"How so?"

"Well, the blacksmith's and handyman's shops, the stables and warehouses . . ."

"Go on."

"I suppose having services on site is good for productivity."

"Productivity? Where would a young woman get such lofty concepts? What do you think, Parker?" Mr. Campbell addressed his young assistant at the adjacent table while keeping his steely eyes locked on my face.

"Perhaps she's a spy, sir, from one of those fly-by-night companies that poach our logs."

Mr. Campbell narrowed his eyes. "A spy?"

"Or, more probably, Miss Kate is simply parroting what she's heard others say." The scrawny, rat-faced Daniel Parker pushed his spectacles further up his nose. "It's surprising how much you can hear when you lurk in doorways in Toronto."

"I happen to have a university degree, and I have never lurked anywhere."

Elisabeth materialized at my side as my chair clattered to the floor. "Come, Kate, it is time to make the pies for tonight's dinner." She gripped my arm, hauling me away from the group. "Please excuse us, sir. Paul is bringing out your breakfast and coffee."

Once out of earshot, she jerked me round to look into her flushed face. "Kate, I don't know where you come from, but you are not there now."

"Where I come from, women are considered equal to men."

She glared at me. "Ever since my husband was killed, I have had to work *and* create a home. I do not care about equal. I care about survival and providing a good life for my son." She released my arm. "Please, for all our sakes, keep quiet. Now, prepare the blueberries and fill these pies. We need to get them in the oven for dinner tonight."

I gathered the sun-dried blueberries from their woven bark baskets, watching them plump as I ladled them into the pot of steaming water. Tossing the berries in a sugar-and-flour mixture and tucking them into their waiting pastry beds, I came to regret my behaviour. I needed to leave before I did more harm. It was time to figure out how to get back home.

Paul returned to the kitchen, his skinny arms weighed down by dirty plates and cups. "The men have finished their breakfast. Mr. Campbell said the camp men don't need lunch today. He's taking them all out to the work site. They'll eat out there with the lumberjacks."

"Good. Now, do the dishes, and be careful when you pour the hot water."

An empty camp would give me the perfect opportunity to escape.

RHUBARB

Chapter Four

The clack of the metal latch as I closed the door exploded like a gunshot through the deserted camp slamming my back against the snowy log wall. I'd left Paul phonetically sounding his way through Mr. Campbell's old newspapers after his first reading lesson. Elisabeth was dozing by the fire, head bent over her knitting. I waited. Neither came out to investigate.

Under a leaden sky, I circled behind the buildings, snowshoes pressed against my chest. Beyond the firmly packed surface of the central square, I fastened my snowshoes and plunged into the forest. Virgin powder wafted in my wake. The men would be cutting and hauling logs to the riverbanks for the spring breakup. I set my course through the trees, parallel to their sled trail.

"Follow the river, return to the bridge piers site, recreate the 'jump,' get back home," I muttered my mantra under my breath. My legs churned against the friction of the snow pants beneath my skirt. The dingy blanket I'd taken from my bed covered the telltale red of my parka.

In less than thirty minutes, the ring of axes warned of the activity ahead. "Timber!" A tree crashed through its neighbours' canopies. *Whumpf!* It dropped in the snow near me. I'd arrived at the work site. Plenty of daylight left.

I froze at the sound of Mr. Campbell's clarion voice resounding above the cacophony. "Parker, make note of this location for our departure point in the spring breakup. Mr. Dumont, what obstacles can we expect in this section of the river?"

I ducked out of sight behind a brush pile left by the trimmers.

"Well, Monsieur Campbell, three narrow points in the river will cause jamming." I'd heard that voice before.

Peaking around my shelter, I picked out the camp boss talking to a tall, athletic man, the same man I'd seen in the yard of the log cabin at the Riverhouse site. I stared harder. Was it the same one I'd watched from Gran's house walking past the willows the morning before my jump?

"And just above my property, there is a broadening where the river slows. You'll need to string a boom. If the logs go astray in the shallows there, you will lose them to the mud and reeds."

"Parker, do you have all that? Parker!" Campbell whirled to find his men examining the snow. "What are you lot looking at?"

"We found some strange prints over here, sir."

"All kinds of animals make this forest their home. Now, keep up."

"But these aren't animal tracks, sir. They're snowshoes, but . . . you might want to take a look."

Deciding not to wait around for the outcome, I moved deeper into the woods.

I ran until ice crystals burned my lungs. Soon, snowflakes filled the air and crusted my eyelashes. Clumps of snow dropped on my shoulders as the trees swayed in the rising wind. I leaned against a white pine to catch my breath. My snowshoe prints were filling in before my eyes. I'd lost sight of the river. My impulse was to keep moving, but in what direction? Recalling my father's advice to seek shelter and wait out bad weather, I crawled into the cavern created by the bent boughs at the base of the tree. My head filled with the scent of slow pine sap as daylight surrendered to blackness in the cracks between the branches.

"Want to go home," I cried through chattering teeth. I took refuge in my catalogue of joyful images, letting my thoughts drift on the moaning wind.

"Miss Kate!"

I jerked out of my stupor.

"Miss Kaaate!"

I struggled to my knees. "I'm here!" I called, pushing my way out through the snow-laden boughs.

A lantern light swung dimly through the swirling snow.

"Here!" I yelled, waving my arms.

"Gus, she's over here!" The speaker materialized out of the snowy darkness. "Miss Kate, are you all right?"

"Lars?" I recognized the crystal blue eyes, aquiline nose, and blond beard.

The short, broad figure of Gus appeared beside him. "Don't cry, Miss Kate. You're safe now." My rescuers were two of the friendliest lumberjacks in camp, always ready with a kind word and an offer to help. The storm had turned them into abominable snowmen.

I wiped at the tears freezing on my cheeks. "What are you doing out here?"

"Mrs. Elisabeth said you went out for a walk this afternoon. When you didn't come back, Mr. Campbell asked for volunteers to search for you."

"And you volunteered?"

"We all did. Now, come. Let's get back. Can you walk?"

I tried to stand. "My feet are numb."

"We can take turns carrying you. It's not far." Lars knelt with his back to me, and Gus helped me clamber aboard. As we set off, my snowshoes swayed against my back to the rhythm of my rescuer's stride.

* * *

It had been three days since my failed escape, and Elisabeth still wasn't speaking to me. Mr. Campbell was the last to leave the dining hall. "Thank you for a delicious dinner, Elisabeth." His look hardened. "Glad to see you up and about, Kate. We won't have any more walks, will we?"

"No, Mr. Campbell," I murmured.

"Good night, then, ladies."

"Good night, Mr. Campbell."

Elisabeth and I worked side by side, preparing the kitchen for breakfast while Paul washed the dinner dishes. With our work completed, we returned to our room for the evening ritual of sitting by the fire. Paul was writing down the recipes for the food his mother prepared in the camp cookery to practice his written English. He followed her around the kitchen all day, noting the ingredients, the quantities, and the processes as she made the various dishes. In the evenings I helped him transcribe his notes.

"Did you really get lost, Miss Kate? Mr. Parker says you ran away."

"Paul, never mind what others are saying. It is none of your business."

"But, Mutti . . ."

"I was searching for my grandmother, but I got lost," I said.

"Bed now, Paul."

"*Gute Nacht,* Mutti." Paul dragged his hide slippers along the plank floor. "Goodnight, Miss Kate."

Once we were alone, I tried to break through Elisabeth's silence. "My grandmother does live south of here on the river . . . in 1981." My hands clamped the seat of my chair. Why had I just blurted that out?

Elizabeth stopped knitting.

"I know it sounds crazy, but it's the truth." Elisabeth had put her job on the line for me; she deserved the truth. And saying it out loud made it real for me. "I've been living with her while I had my baby.

One day, I somehow jumped a hundred years back in time. That's when Abe found me."

"Hmph." Elisabeth looked up. "That's quite a story."

At least she was talking to me again. I leaned forward. "I'm sorry. I didn't mean to cause you problems with the boss."

"I don't care about what you meant to do." She threw her knitting into her basket. "*Mensch* Kate! You need to wake up. Wherever you came from, this is your world now."

"You don't understand. I miss my daughter. I had to do something."

"Don't tell me what I don't understand. Klaus and I fled to this country so our children wouldn't grow up in fear. You think you're the only one who's lost a child?" Elisabeth sat back in her chair, her shoulders rigid.

"Elisabeth, I had no idea."

"Influenza. The pain has been my comrade from the day I watched the life leave my little daughter. It is like dragging a heavy load." Elisabeth's hands clenched tightly in her lap. "I understand."

I saw my pain in Elisabeth's eyes before she bent to pick up her knitting. "I'm sorry," I whispered. "Elisabeth, why can't I leave? Mr. Campbell doesn't own me. I should be free to go any time I want."

Elisabeth shook her head. "Women do not wander alone in the wilderness. He will lock you up next time and hand you over to the Mounties at the end of the season."

"But that's not fair! I haven't broken any laws."

"*Ach*, who ever said anything about fair?" Elisabeth looked directly at me, her knitting in her lap. "Look, the work of the fallers and trimmers is ending. The camp will be broken up, and the lumberjacks will move into the towns to do what men do after being out here for months. We will all be taken out in the wagons, and you can go where you wish."

"How long until then?"

"Not long. Maybe a week or two. Listen to the men talk. They know it is coming."

Sylvia Barnard

* * *

That Sunday, I listened. On their day of rest, the lumberjacks usually did their laundry, mended clothes, and slept. On this particular Sunday, the men grouped around fires, reminding me of my days camping with my dad on McFarlane Lake. Lars and Gus invited Elisabeth, Paul, and me to join their circle. Their talk was filled with the upcoming migration into Nelsonville, or Sainte-Anne-des-Pins. The smoky air billowed with the dreams of hard men putting meaning to their struggle to build a better life.

Mr. Campbell circulated among the groups, recruiting men to work the river drive at the end of April. "The company will provide you with boots and equipment. Those who don't want to burl the logs can push them from the banks into the river and work the rapids to break up jams."

Lars joined in. "*Ja*, I have worked the drive. I saved enough in just three years to build my family a real house this summer."

"What's the pay?" called Joe from the back of the group surrounding Mr. Campbell.

"How do we sign up?" asked a smaller man whose name I didn't know.

"Log riders make three dollars per day," Campbell responded. "All others make a dollar fifty. Food and bunk are included. You need to bring blankets and make your own way to the head of the drive."

"When do we sign up?"

"Before you leave, or I'll be in Nelsonville at the lumber company shack two days before the river drive begins. Everyone who wants to work will be signed up, but if you want to ride the logs, you'll need to show you know how to burl."

This was met with discontented grumblings.

"I've seen too many men get a leg crushed or worse. It slows us down."

Most of the single men immediately approached the boss to sign up.

Elisabeth and I remained in our place, watching Paul poke a stick into the fire.

"Did you ever cook for the river drive?"

Her eyes filled with sadness. "*Ja,* the first year we moved here. Klaus and I did not get our plot until it was too late to plant, so we spent the fall building a cabin and clearing the land. Then in the winter, we boarded the children *mit* . . . with . . . a Mennonite family, and we worked the winter camp and the river drive."

"It must've been hard leaving your children behind."

"We knew they were with a good family. We made lots of money, and that summer, Klaus was able to build our barn. We planted potatoes, turnips, and carrots and continued clearing more land. The next winter, Klaus worked the cutting season while I stayed home with the children." Elisabeth's shoulders drooped. "That was the winter my Lilli died."

I reached for her hand and warmed it between mine.

"It was a wet spring. Klaus persuaded me he should do a river drive while we waited for the land to dry. I was afraid."

I nodded.

Elisabeth hung her head. "My Klaus was one of those men Mr. Campbell talked about. He was caught by one leg between the logs. When they came apart, he dropped into the water. They found his body three days later on the riverbank."

Wordlessly, I reached out and hugged her. Seeing the distress in Paul's face, I stretched out my arm to him.

Elisabeth pushed back first. Straightening her cape, she held her hands to the fire for warmth. "That is why I do not want Paul to work in lumbering. Thanks to you, Kate, he will make more of himself."

"What's this I hear, Elisabeth?" Mr. Campbell had overheard Elisabeth's last statement. "Paul isn't coming back? I was hoping to have him start on the trimming crew next cutting season."

"Oh, we will be back next year, Mr. Campbell, but Paul will never work on any crew," Elisabeth announced. "Soon we will stay on our farm and sell you our vegetables. We will send fresh baking to the camp each week on the railroad when it comes."

"Interesting idea," Campbell mused.

"My Paul will work in an office." Elisabeth draped her arm around her son's shoulders and pulled him to her. "Maybe one day he will be your boss." Elisabeth ended with a smile.

"My, you have big dreams."

"With respect, why shouldn't she have dreams?" I felt my fists balled at my side. "Because she's a woman? Or because she's an immigrant? We are all immigrants to this country, Mr. Campbell, and Elisabeth is a strong, determined woman."

"Ah, Kate." Campbell shook his head. "I don't suppose you're planning to return next year?"

I shook my head.

"I didn't think so. Shame. You are a puzzle—an attractive woman with an education in need of a husband. You'll never get one until you learn to hold your tongue."

I swallowed my retort.

Mr. Campbell turned back to Elisabeth. "You and Paul will be very welcome back to my camp any time. I wish you a prosperous farming season." Then, with a nod of his head, he added, "Good day, ladies," and walked back to his office. Elisabeth and I watched until his office door closed, and he was out of our view.

"Some advice, Kate?" Elisabeth raised her eyebrows, only continuing once I nodded. "Okay." She winked as she used my word. Then her eyes looked earnestly into mine. "God places us where we are for a reason. Figure out why He has placed you here. Otherwise, you will always be visiting, not living."

RHUBARB

Chapter Five

True to Elisabeth's prediction, four days later, the felling season came to an end. In one day, with the help of several lumberjacks, we packed up the remaining food and scrubbed the wooden work surfaces and grills. Men who were accustomed to wielding axes were set to work pushing brooms, shovelling horse stalls, and packing wagons. Everything that could rust, rot, or attract wildlife was removed, leaving the vacant log buildings ready for the next season.

At dawn the next day, Paul rang the gut hammer for the last time. Out of habit, the men ate in silence, washing down the bread and cheese with the last of the coffee.

"All aboard!" They filed out to the waiting wagons, nodding their heads and murmuring their goodbyes as we stood by the door.

"I hope you find your grandmother." Paul hugged me before clambering into the wagon going to Webbwood. The men shuffled along the bench to make space for the boy.

Elisabeth held my hands. "I pray God keeps you safe, Kate."

"Thank you, Elisabeth, for everything you've done for me." I pulled her into my arms.

"Last call!"

Elisabeth stepped back. "We are in Webbwood if you need us."

I swallowed hard as one of the men helped my friend up onto the seat beside the driver. Snowshoes wrapped in a blanket across my back and an old hide sack over my shoulder, I skittered my way across the snow and mud square to the Nelsonville wagon. Gus and Lars made space for me between them.

"Walk on." The wagons moved off, bouncing through frozen ruts and sinking into muddy potholes. The horses snorted and steamed under the strain of moving twenty men and their packs over the rough terrain. I tucked my sack and blanket-wrapped bundle on the floor between my legs. Pines darkened the track. And as we wove our way around ice-crusted boulders in the chill damp, I was thankful for the warmth of the tattered jacket Lars had draped over my shoulders. "You keep it, Miss Kate. I won't be logging anymore." My jeans and snow pants, hidden under my skirt, kept my bottom warm.

Soon, heads drooped and bobbed with the wagon's rhythm. Chickadees called their name as they flitted among the naked birch branches, gaining purchase where the sun had melted the frost. Occasionally a blue jay screeched his objection to our presence. The scent of rising pine sap softened the musk of rot from swamps beginning to thaw. The moaning cow sound of a rutting moose echoed in the distance. The timeless familiarity lured me to believe I could be back home, riding through the forest on *Grand-père*'s wagon to the sugar shack. If all went according to my plan, I'd be back there tomorrow. I drowsed.

"Lunch break."

I jolted awake. The skin on my face came alive at the touch of early spring sunshine. We'd left the dense forest behind. Keeping my back to the line of twenty men urinating at the edge of the forest, I spread the bread, venison, and cheese that Elisabeth and I had prepared for each wagon on one of the benches. When they ate their lunch, I slipped behind the root ball of a fallen tree, lifted my skirt, pulled down my multiple layers, and squatted.

"All aboard!"

The wagon rolled more freely over the well-drained tote road. The men began to talk. Eyes closed, I pulled in the lumberjacks' conversations floating around me, like surfing the dial on my car radio.

"First thing, I'm findin' myself a nice bottle." The speaker smacked his lips.

"For me, it's a woman." Laughter.

"Sainte-Anne-des-Pins's the place for that."

". . . soft bed. Gonna sleep for a week. What about you, Lars?"

A pause where I could almost hear him smile. "Tonight I'll have my wife in my arms."

"Lucky bugger."

And I'll be holding baby Amelia with Gran's arms wrapped round us both, I thought.

Someone at the back of the wagon was singing under his breath. Those near him joined in, and soon a choir of male voices carried us along. I swayed in time to the music, imagining the lives that were unfolding beyond the solid green screen—mother squirrels suckling their young, bears stretching and yawning, raccoons chattering instructions at their adventurous kits. Wide pastures suddenly opened on both sides as we rounded a bend.

"Papa! Papa!" Two children—a boy, pulling a smaller girl by the hand—ran toward the wagon.

Lars and Gus were on their feet. "Wilhelm! Hilda!"

The children's heads bloomed with dandelion-yellow curls as they threw their hats into the air. The wagon erupted with good wishes and slaps on the back.

"Goodbye, Miss Kate. I hope you find your way." Lars shook my hand, and Gus held my eyes for a moment before nodding his head in farewell. The two men descended into the welcoming arms of their children. In the distance, I spied two small cabins, a large barn, and several low huts for chickens and rabbits. Two women stood in front of their homes, shielding their eyes with their hands. They reminded me of old sepia photos of settlers I'd seen at the library. My stomach lurched as one of the women propped her baby against her shoulder. Stick to your plan, and you'll be reunited with your baby, too. I sat straighter, shoulders squared, ready for action.

"Walk on." Everyone settled.

The homecoming scene was repeated several times before Nelsonville came into sight in the afternoon sunshine. Six homes in a row—all log, two double storied, four with verandas. Opposite the six, a seventh house sported two doors, one adorned with a plain, wooden cross. Beside it, there was a long, two-storey building with a sign swinging from the veranda—General Store: Proprietor, John Hall. A modest beginning for the Nairn Centre I knew. I recognized two of the houses. They still stood in my time.

The horses stamped their feet, protesting the driver's command to stop. Several men disembarked. These were the regulars who worked the camps each year and had standing arrangements for room and board with the local families.

At the signal to walk on, the horses broke into a trot, eager to get to their warm stable and a meal of oats. I clutched the side rail to keep my balance as the wagon swung in a large circle in front of the Spanish River Lumber Company's compound. Long narrow buildings sported garage-door-style openings into a stable, warehouse, and repair shops. Beyond, I glimpsed a flat field littered with shacks barely larger than outhouses. These were available for men coming off winter camp while they waited for spring breakup.

"Mr. Campbell will have a room for you in the company house, Miss Kate." The driver pointed to a two-storey white clapboard standing alone to one side.

"Thank you, but I'm leaving early tomorrow. Don't want to disturb anyone. A clean stall in the stable would suit me fine."

"As you wish, miss." The driver doffed his hat and directed me to a fresh stall before unharnessing the horses. I snuggled into the warm straw and nibbled from the food pack Elisabeth had pressed on me that morning. I was so close now. How was I ever going to sleep? Images of Gran sitting by the fire overwhelmed me, Gran bouncing

Amelia on her lap as she sang her French folk songs, walking the floor when the baby was teething. Hang in, Gran. I'm coming. My eyelids drooped.

* * *

Soft nickering. Crunchy chewing. My equine roommates were awake. Gathering my belongings, I was soon underway in the early dawn light. Memory told me it would take a few hours through the woods to get to the bank above the old railway bridge piers where my jump had taken place. I imagined Amelia's sweet baby smell. Would I feel the silkiness of her hair against my cheek today? I would. I had to. If I let doubt and fear plague me, I'd never make it to the river. I stuffed my skirt into my snow pants to give me free movement as my snowshoes sank through the crystallized snow. The crunch underfoot took me back to the last time my dad and I had skied together. He'd warned me of corn snow treachery, icy pellets in the morning that transformed to gravelly soup under the afternoon spring sun's caress. My cheek had been rubbed raw as the sodden top layer forced a sudden deceleration that my body couldn't accommodate, and I'd pitched headfirst down the slope.

The sun was still climbing when I stood on the bank, squinting at the wavelets lapping against the ice flows. I was in the right place. Finches and grosbeaks joined the chorus of chickadees, just like the last time. I squeezed my eyes shut, willing to hear the roaring in my ears, listening for the sound of a train. Nothing.

I swallowed a lump in my throat, backtracked along the trail, and repeated my approach, this time singing "The Ballad of the Spanish." No train.

I waited until the sun was beyond the noontime position, turned to face the river and squeezed my eyes shut. No roaring.

I even tried lying on my back in the snow. I screamed into the clear blue sky. I dropped to my knees and sobbed. For several hours,

I recreated the conditions of my jump over and over until birdsong was replaced by the hoot of a snowy owl and the yip of coyotes. Would I never get home? Wrapping my blanket around me, I sank to the frozen ground, my back propped against a tree. I didn't even watch the constellations blink to life one star at a time.

* * *

I jerked upright at a sharp kick to my shins, eyes blinking in the bright sunlight.

"He's up, sir," proclaimed the kicker, who'd jumped back out of reach.

My clearing had been taken over by a group of men.

"All right. Give him some tea and bread and leave him be, James," directed a disembodied male voice.

I remained seated under my tree, my blanket firmly wrapped over my tuque-clad head. James approached, offering bread and a steaming cup. I kept my gaze on the ground and rounded my shoulders into Lars's old jacket. James set the food down near me and backed away.

Through glances from the tops of my eyes, I counted four men. The one they called James, a slight youth of no more than eighteen, paced around our clearing identifying animal tracks aloud. Two other men, one squat and robust, the other tall and broad shouldered, worked on the edge of the bank, constructing two platforms made of six-inch diameter logs. All three cast suspicious stares my way. The man who had directed James remained bent over a wooden table propped in the snow.

Keeping my face in the shadow of the blanket, I consumed the bread and strong tea with my mittened hands. Abraham's warnings about groups of men in the wilderness terrified me. I had to keep my true identity hidden.

James helped the builders lash one log platform on top of the other, logs perpendicular.

"Raft's done, sir," announced the taller man.

"We need to measure the distance from here to that granite shelf over there for the bridge." The leader pointed across the river. Wordlessly, the three men slid down the sloped bank. The shorter man balanced the paddles across his shoulder, the taller one slung a coil of rope over his forearm, and James came up the rear pulling the raft. It was no bigger than a double bed.

"So, what are you doing out here all by yourself?" The leader remarked in smooth, cultured tones.

I shrugged my shoulders.

"Cat got your tongue?"

I didn't respond. My heart beat double time, making me feel short of breath. Could I outrun four men on legs stiff from sleeping in the snow?

"Well, let's leave it at that for now." He returned his attention to the document on his table, and I turned to the river. James floated the raft at the river's edge as the shorter man settled himself on it, paddle poised. The taller one handed one end of the rope he carried to James, flung the coil onto the raft, then, balancing on one foot on the rough surface, he pushed it into the flow. The two men perched precariously on their knees, the short one paddling forward while the taller one used his paddle to clear a path through bobbing chunks of ice. The youth played out the rope from shore. Upon reaching the opposite side, the short man steadied the raft against the rock while his fitter partner scaled the twenty-foot granite face.

Seeing his men in place, the leader directed, "All right, James. Climb back up the bank. Leo, feed him the slack."

The men moved with the smoothness earned from repetition.

"Now, Leo, mark the rope, and count the knots. Herb, bring the raft back over here."

The leader packed up his equipment, storing writing and measuring implements in a leather satchel slung over his shoulder and folding the wooden table into a compact package for carrying. "Now, my mute friend, on your feet. You'll join our party until I can find somewhere safe to leave you."

I continued to stare at the river. My plan to return to this spot was the only thing that had kept me going over the past few months. This man was not going to stand in my way.

James loaded packs and tents onto the raft. The short man drove his paddle deep, his powerful shoulders propelling the full raft to the other side where he passed the cargo to the taller man.

"Listen. You either come with us willingly, or I'll have those two men there tie you up and carry you."

I jerked my head round. If they touched me . . . I fixed the man with my hardest blue glare and stood my ground.

"Mr. Van Horne, we're ready," called James.

Mr. Van Horne? Could this be the William Cornelius Van Horne mentioned in the news sheet? He did say something about a bridge. A gentleman, maybe?

"So, what will it be?"

My mind raced. They would get me across the river. I could walk to the Riverhouse. Maybe if I was on the property I could jump forward . . . Keeping my eyes downcast and the blanket over my head, I rose and preceded Mr. Van Horne down the bank. Herb ferried him and his materials across the river while James and I waited our turn.

"I'm James, from Callander. You got a name?"

I ignored him.

"My first time on a crew. What do you do?"

I kept my eyes on the river.

"Just tryin' to be friendly." James offered his hand. I turned away. "Don't have to be rude," he snarled.

Rhubarb, Strawberries, and Willows

Herb arrived. We scrambled onto the raft. I sat in the middle, while James took on ice clearing duties in the front and Herb paddled us across. On the other side, Herb dismantled the raft, shoving the ropes into his pack for use at the next crossing, leaving the logs on the bank.

"That's it for the river for now. We'll meet her again just before Webbwood," Mr. Van Horne announced. The river to our backs, we trudged northwest through the forest for the remainder of the day. From time to time, we stopped for the men to take measurements under Mr. Van Horne's direction. I avoided eye contact, sheltered my face under the blanket, and held back from the group.

Once we made camp for the night, I gathered firewood while Herb pitched two white canvas prospector's tents. James laid out strips of salt pork and bread in a frying pan. He let out a whoop of glee as Leo materialized out of the gloom, two rabbits hanging limply from his hand.

Within minutes the two skinned creatures were skewered and suspended over the glowing fire. James counted to himself, turning the spit a quarter turn each time he reached thirty. Leo whittled, letting the curls of wood drop into the fire, and Herb maintained a watch on the perimeter where firelight met blackness around our camp. Each occasionally cast glances at where I'd established myself, a large red pine at my back, cocooned in my blanket. The kerosene light silhouetted Mr. Van Horne on the wall of his tent as he poured over his table.

My mouth watered as the aroma of roasting rabbit filled our clearing. James approached Mr. Van Horne's tent. "Dinner's ready, sir. Do you want me to bring your plate?"

"No, son. I'll join you at the fire. Please provide some food to our friend as well."

"Yes, sir."

With a nod of thanks, I accepted the plate of roasted rabbit wrapped in pork strips accompanied by fried bread slices. It wasn't what I'd been hoping to eat tonight. I'd hoped for Gran's pea soup. I hoped to see what foods Amelia had graduated to during my absence. Regardless, my stomach rumbled with relief as I swallowed the tender, pork-moistened meat.

The men consumed their meal with gusto. Swiping the backs of their hands across their greasy mouths, each disappeared in a separate direction into the darkness. Upon his return, James cleaned the plates. Herb stacked several full logs in a log-cabin pattern in the fire, then they disappeared into their tent.

"So, my young friend, you'll join me in my tent."

I vigorously shook my head no and patted the ground.

"It's too cold out here. I'll do you no harm." Mr. Van Horne held open the flap of his tent. "Now, come along." He stared me down. Steel glinted from his eyes in the firelight. I did his bidding.

"You can move those packs and make yourself comfortable on that side." Turning his back, he returned to his worktable.

The yellow glow from the kerosene lantern wafted warmth across my cold cheeks. I mounded the packs up to create a wall down the middle of the tent. Under the shield of my blanket, I struggled out of Lars's jacket, spreading it to block the cold of the semi-frozen ground. I turned in time to see Mr. Van Horne exit the tent, pulling the flap shut behind him.

I craned my neck to see the chart fixed to Mr. Van Horne's tabletop. It looked like a map. I was tracing my finger over the proposed route for the railway track when Mr. Van Horne whispered behind me, "What do you think?" I leaped sideways. He grasped my wrist to prevent me from falling.

Once stable on my feet, I retreated to my enclave.

"So you can read a map. Not common up here in this Godforsaken landscape." He patted the cot. "Come and sit."

I chose to sit on one of the packs instead.

"All right. Good to be cautious, but I won't hurt you."

I stared into my lap.

"Could we do away with this charade . . . miss?"

Gasping, I launched myself into the tent flap. Van Horne grabbed my ankle and jerked me backward, my hands sliding across the ground. He flipped me over onto my back, pressing my shoulders against the dirt.

"Stop!" he hissed. "I'm trying to protect you from those men in the next tent."

I went limp under his pressure. "How do you know I'm a woman?" I sputtered.

The creases at the corners of his eyes deepened. "By the way you move, my dear. Do you know who I am?"

"You're William Cornelius Van Horne. You've been hired by Prime Minister Macdonald to oversee the route for the transcontinental railway," I spit back.

His eyes widened at my explanation. "Thank you, madam. Please, do me the favour of explaining yourself. Who are you?"

"I'm Catherine Dumont Walker. Why are you out here surveying? Don't you have people to do that?"

"Certainly, we have surveyors, but Northern Ontario is challenging with its rocks and swamps. I feel more confident doing the work myself." He adjusted his coat. "Honestly? I get so bloody bored in offices. I miss the snow on my face, the scent of awakening earth."

A whistling snore from the other tent stilled us.

Silence restored, he asked, "What brings you to be wandering alone in this bush, Miss Dumont Walker?"

"You can call me Kate." I gave him the same story I'd recounted to Mr. Campbell, watching him for any reaction. No wrinkled brow. No disbelieving tilt to his head.

"When the lumber camp closed, I resumed my search. I was trying to find a way across the river when you found me."

"You would have looked in vain. Only way across is by boat."

"So you're planning to build a rail bridge back there?"

"Yes. It's the most stable location."

"Mr. Van Horne." I moved to the map.

"You can call me William."

"William, have you thought about routing the bridge over this point?" I placed my finger where both the railway and the highway crossed the river in my time.

"Interesting. But with logs transported on the river, we need piers, not trestles. Banks are too high there, making a pier unstable. I wonder . . ." His tall frame bent over his plans, lost in drawing the alternative proposal.

It seemed the conversation was over. Returning to my corner, I snuggled into my blanket. If he changes the location, will it change history? I drifted off to sleep before I could puzzle out the answer.

The next morning, the men rose with the sun and packed up the camp while drinking coffee and munching on hardtack. In a quiet moment, William directed I maintain my ruse in front of his men, something I'd already intended to do. I trudged along mutely, my blanket and my false persona both protectively wrapped around me until twilight, when William called a halt to the day's work. The three men set up camp. That night, we made do with salt pork, bread, and my contribution of Elisabeth's cheese.

Once the other three were snoring in their tent, William and I spent a quiet hour in conversation.

"In the morning, we'll start by taking some measurements at the location for the river crossing which you suggested. Then we'll turn straight west to Webbwood before the muck of the spring thaw traps us in these woods."

"You've been most kind, William. In the morning, I'll be on my way to my grandmother's home, about a mile north of here on the river."

William's gaze hardened. "It would be reckless of me to abandon you now. My dear wife, Lucy, would never forgive me. You will travel with us to Webbwood where you and I will make our way to Toronto on the steamer."

I took a breath. Under the unruly beard, bushy eyebrows, and rough wilderness clothing beat the heart of a well-educated gentleman. He was accustomed to being in charge. "That's kind of you, William, but there's no need for you to delay on my account."

"No need for concern, Kate." His mild manner belied the tense twitch in his jaw. "I'm obligated to report progress to our investors in Toronto, and it will be my pleasure to escort you back to civilization." He held up his hand. "Now, get some sleep. We have a long walk tomorrow."

Recognizing we'd reached an impasse, I returned to my sleeping corner and curled myself into my blanket. The man was a puzzle. He seemed genuinely caring, so how could he condone using underpaid Chinese labourers to build the railway out West? Would he lose sleep in the future when so many lives would be lost? Not my problem. He thought the discussion was over, but there was no way I was leaving the river. I knew it was irrational to believe I would turn the bend and magically find Gran's house, but the only hope I had was to stay in this area.

RHUBARB

Chapter Six

The sun was already high in the sky by the time William called a halt. The men sank where they stood. That morning, we'd pushed south around a swampy mess of low land, the remains of last year's cattails clattering in the breeze. While the others had moved ahead on their snowshoes, mine remained hidden under the lumberjack coat. I slogged through knee-deep snow, feeling my boots suck into slushy mud underfoot. Once on solid ground, William turned us on to a northwest loop to intersect with a distant ridge. The men hacked through young trees packed so densely that, in some places, there was no sky. Our final climb to the higher ground had put us under a canopy of mature birches.

I leaned against a tree and inspected our glade. If this were 1981, we'd be standing on the highway. The Riverhouse lay to the east. There was little undergrowth and only a few inches of corn snow. It would be easy going. Maybe if I hung back, I could melt away without notice.

"Up, men," William called. The men hoisted their packs.

Leo began leading the men west.

"No," William said. "East."

"Sir, Webbwood's this way." Leo pointed. Herb and James nodded agreement.

William turned and started walking away. "We're backtracking to the river." Leo and Herb hung their heads and followed.

"Why we goin' back? Stupid old man," James muttered to himself. Seeing the others disappearing into the trees, he yelled, "Wait!" and ran past me to catch up, feet slipping over stones slick with frost. So much for continuing on my own.

I'd been right—it was an easy walk. The sun was in mid-afternoon position when we arrived at the granite narrowing I'd suggested to William. The men began taking their measurements. I waited until they'd climbed down the rock face to the water's edge. Pretending to search for a place to relieve myself, I walked into the woods. Once out of sight, I broke into a run, snowshoes jouncing on my back. By my reckoning, the small homestead Abraham and I had seen while searching for Gran's house was only a kilometre upriver. Claude Dumont's home, according to Mr. Campbell.

I'd had only a few moments head start when the sound of crashing through the forest erupted behind me. William had been the only one still above the river. I heard cursing. It was James.

My heart hammered against my ribs in rhythm with my pounding feet as I dipped under low-hanging spruce bows, leaped over snow-covered logs, and battled sharp branches and raspberry canes that grabbed polyester threads from my snow pants. But I forged on, gulps of icy air inducing a milkshake-like brain freeze.

Finally, the side of the little barn came into sight between the trees. Breaking into the homestead clearing, I hopscotched through the lacework of rivulets in the courtyard of semi-frozen mud. Smoke drifted from the chimney of the log cabin.

"Stop you stupid mute!" James yelled.

Skittering along the wall to slip through the barn door, I stopped. I'd be trapped. Instinct took over as I turned into the cover of trees, darting from one massive pine trunk to the next, making my way around to the back wall of the cabin. I was crouching against the corner of the building, eyes on the courtyard, when James burst through the trees. Bent over, gasping for air, he was joined by Leo. My heart sank. I'd jumped over soft mud and melting snow, but my tactics were no match for Leo's tracking skills. James let out a whoop as both men followed my footprints to the barn door.

Bouncing on tiptoes, I turned and drove deeper into the forest. Got to get away. Where can I go? Back in the woods alone, I could collide with another group, a hungry bear, or rutting moose. But if I complied with William's plan, how would I ever get back to my own time? No, I had to stay in the area.

From behind me came the sound of pounding on a door. James was yelling. Soon the men would realize I hadn't taken refuge in the homestead and they'd be back on my trail.

Turning, I could still make out faint indications of my tracks. Wherever I spotted a footprint, I carefully retraced my steps. After about forty backward steps, I climbed onto a granite outcropping beside the path, crawled across its sun-warmed surface, and slipped into the sanctuary of dense undergrowth.

I ducked my head under the dense junipers as James's voice drifted to me on the breeze.

Through the boughs, I made out bits of their shoulders on the other side of the rock. "He's gone down to the river, ain't he? Why's Mr. Van Horne want him back so bad anyway?"

"Shut up, James." The larger silhouette dropped out of sight. "Come on." The glint of Leo's silver-tipped fur hat moved toward the river.

I stood. Shoving my snowshoes and hide bag under the bushes, I clambered over the rock. I was hit broadside—James had leaped from behind a shrub and tackled me.

"I got him, Leo!"

"Get off!" I yelled, struggling to break free. My flailing hand closed around a loose stone. I struck James in the back of the head. Heaving his limp body to one side, I sprang to my feet, spitting chips of muddy ice.

"Gotcha," Leo grunted, pushing me backward. The back of my head thumped into the tree trunk, blurring my vision. Incessant high-pitched ringing filled my ears. Leo's brawny forearm threatened to cut off my windpipe as it pegged me to the tree. I went rigid as his other hand roughly prodded under my jacket and made contact with my breast. "I knew it. Van Horne wants his whore back."

I kneed him. Missed his groin. His hip crashed into my pelvis, shooting an electric jolt down both my legs, and I hung, helpless, over his forearm.

"Stop, or there'll be more." His hand groped through the layers of my clothing. I gasped at the touch of his cold hand against my skin. I wanted to scream, but his forearm squeezed my throat. He fumbled one-handed to open his trousers. The stench of his putrefying gums wafted under my nose. Digging his fingers into my hip, he forced me around. Rough bark grazed my cheek. The forearm pressure returned, now to the back of my neck. With one tug, my snow pants were down over my buttocks.

"What you doin'?" James asked groggily.

Leo froze. "Damn mute tried to run off."

"He ain't no mute. He was screamin'. Hit me in the head with a rock."

"Get the rope. We need to get back to camp." As James dug through his pockets, Leo whispered, "So you thought you could fool old Leo?" He eased the pressure. "Get yourself sorted."

I pulled up my snow pants and adjusted my jacket.

James produced the rope.

Leo leaned in to me as he secured my wrists in front. "I'll be seeing you tonight." With a jerk on the rope, he forced me to stagger down the path toward the cabin. James brought up the rear, occasionally prodding me in the small of my back with a stick until our little party was skirting the homestead on the property I knew so well in another time.

"Can we stop? I need water," I croaked in as low a tone as I could produce.

"Me, too. I'm gonna get some from that squaw." James marched across the yard toward the porch before Leo could stop him. He pounded his fist on the cabin door.

"*Je peux vous aider?* Can I help you?" A tall man strode toward us from the barn, pulling a grey tuque over his chestnut curls. I swallowed a gasp. It was the same man I'd seen walking across our yard that morning at Gran's.

Before Leo and James formulated a response, I stepped forward, "*Bonjour mon oncle, Claude!*" I used my new voice. The man's brow furrowed at my use of his name. "I've been searching for you and grand-maman, but these men captured me." I yanked the slack from Leo's grip and held up my wrists. *Please help me*, I mouthed. Our heads swivelled at the step of a young woman emerging from the cabin. Her raven braids hung to the waist of her beaded deer-hide dress, and her complexion glowed like sunlight through honey. She glanced from Claude to me. She couldn't have been more than sixteen.

"Ah, Tekakwitha, are these the men?"

"*Oui Monsieur Claude. Les deux*," she said, pointing to James and Leo. After a hushed interchange between Claude and the young woman, Tekakwitha re-entered the cabin.

"Gentlemen," Claude said, "I understand you visited our compound earlier today?"

James cleared his throat. "Yes, we were—"

"And I believe you spoke threateningly toward Tekakwitha."

Leo maintained a stony expression, but James jumped in, "That squaw made the brat scream! She even slammed the door in my face."

Claude's fist flew so quickly I only saw the movement as he brought it back. James lay flat on his back on the partially frozen mud, rubbing his jaw.

"That child is my son. Now, get off my property."

Leo pulled James to his feet, loosening his grasp on my rope. "I apologize, monsieur. He is young and foolish."

I jerked the rope out of Leo's hands and backed away.

"She's just a dirty . . . ," muttered James.

Leo pushed him toward the path that led back to the spot where William and Herb were working, then beckoned to me. "Come."

I backed away.

"You," Claude said, pointing at me. "Go." He gestured toward the two stairs leading up onto the porch.

"Come." Leo repeated.

"Sir, my nephew will not be accompanying you. His grandmother is waiting to see him."

Leo's face flushed red, chest pushed forward. "Mr. Van Horne expects us to bring him back."

"Well, sir, I suggest you tell Mr. Van Horne that this young man has found his way home, and the Dumont family are grateful for his safe return. Now, off my land."

Leo raised his chin and looked at me, then at Claude. In response to Claude's glowering deep brown glare, Leo lowered his chin, turned, and motioned for James to follow him.

Claude held his position, relaxing his stance only after they disappeared into the forest. With a flick of his knife, he cut my bonds.

"Thank you for your help, Monsieur Dumont." I massaged my wrists. "I'll be on my way."

"How do you know my name?"

"Mr. Campbell from the Spanish River Lumber Company."

"And how do you know him? Who are you?"

"I'm Catherine Dumont Walker." I returned to using my normal tone.

Claude's eyes widened "*Enchanté, Mademoiselle.* Best you come in." He walked past me toward the door. I stared at his back. Alone in the cold woods? Taken to Toronto by William? After a moment, I followed Claude into the warmth.

He stoked the fire, then moved to the sleeping area in the corner of the single room. I stood uncertainly by the door, blinking in the dim interior. Blankets were tacked across the two windows.

"Take off those clothes and warm yourself," he directed over his shoulder.

I eased off my snow pants and shook out my skirt over my jeans. Once I'd removed the remainder of my outer clothing, Tekakwitha gestured for me to sit at the table in the centre of the room, where she'd set out tea and biscuits. My hand caressed the table top's velvet finish. She glided in silent moccasins across the packed dirt floor to join Claude. His head was tilted toward the child, attentive to its breathing. Tekakwitha tucked the cream coloured blanket adorned with the familiar Hudson's Bay indigo, red, green, and yellow stripes around the toddler's body. This must be the child I'd seen that day Abraham and I watched from across the river.

"He seems cooler, and his breathing is easier." Claude stroked the blond curls back from the child's forehead.

"*Oui,* Monsieur Claude. The fever has broken."

"Should we wake him to eat?"

"*Non,* he needs sleep. When he does wake, he can have some broth from the stew. I have plumped some dried blueberries that he likes so much."

"Thank you, Tekakwitha. How did you know what to do?"

"Nokomis."

"Thank your grandmother. She has taught you well." A shy smile drifted across Tekakwitha's lips.

My gaze wandered the room. The fieldstone fireplace with pot hooks and cooking grate dominated one wall, a mismatched padded settee, rocking chair, and wingback chair forming a semicircular gathering in front of it. The kitchen space occupied the opposite wall—washbasin on the wooden worktop and a floor-to-ceiling pine cabinet. Given the utilitarian decor throughout, I wondered what story the floral quilt on the double bed in the corner could tell.

Stamping on the porch. A young man stepped quickly through the door. I recognized him as the one who'd been speaking with Claude that day months ago when Abraham and I had spied on them from across the river. His eyes covered the room in one blink, skipping over me without reaction.

"Shh! Ma'iingan. The baby's sleeping." Tekakwitha admonished from the corner.

"J.P. better?" Ma'iingan whispered.

"Yes."

"Good. We must go now."

I stared at the handsome young man, as tall as Tekakwitha was petite, his eyes a soft brown. A thick black braid brushed his shoulder blades beneath his trapper's hat.

Tekakwitha picked up the stewpot from the kitchen worktop and hung it in the fireplace.

"What's the rush today?" Claude asked.

"Wind's up. Snow's coming. We need to get home before the storm."

While Tekakwitha pulled on her fur-lined leggings, Ma'iingan reported to Claude. "Saw a survey crew on the south edge of the narrows this afternoon. Measuring across the granite cut."

My ears pricked up.

"I followed tracks up behind the cabin. Looks like a fight. Found these." Ma'iingan produced my blanket bundle and hide bag from behind his back.

"That's mine." I rushed across the room.

Ma'iingan stepped back, hands up.

"Ma'iingan, this is Catherine Dumont Walker. She was brought into our courtyard today by two of the men. Where's that crew now?"

"Gone. Headed west."

I returned to my seat, belongings clutched to my chest.

"Monsieur Claude, if the baby starts to cough, give him some honey water. He'll be fine by morning."

"*Merci. À demain.*"

The brother and sister stepped out into the now swirling snow, pulling the door closed behind them. A cold current rushed over my feet.

Claude returned to his son. I stirred the pot of venison stew with the wooden spoon, then moved the pot to a side hook, allowing it to simmer, away from direct heat.

"Come." Claude moved to the table, gesturing to the chair I'd vacated. "Let's have some tea before it gets cold." The sweet smell of sumac floated above the table as Claude filled our cups and placed a blueberry biscuit on each of our porcelain plates. "We'll save the plain ones to go with our stew tonight." I held each bite of buttery biscuit in my mouth until it melted. Mmm. Just like Gran used to make when I was a little girl. I blinked away tears.

Claude sat back, cup held between his hands as if to warm them. "So, how do you know Mr. Campbell?"

I explained that Abraham Obey had brought me to the camp when I became ill because he knew the cook and her son.

"I know Abe. Good man. Helped him register his land claim southwest of here." He studied me for a moment. "What were you doing with him?"

I ignored the implication. "I was lost in the woods while looking for my grandmother's home. Abraham found me."

"Your grandmother. A Dumont?"

"Yes, Evangeline Dumont. But she was born a Robitaille. She married my grandfather, Jacques."

"Hmm. Thought I knew all the Dumonts in the area. Where's their homestead?"

"Near here, on the river." I gestured vaguely south.

He leaned across the table. "You sure about that?"

"I'm beginning to think I may have the wrong spot." I laughed nervously. "I got pretty turned around."

"Must be south of the rapids. I don't know people down there," he mused.

I nodded. "So, Tekakwitha and Ma'iingan. Mr. Campbell said they work for you?"

"Yes. Tekakwitha takes care of Jean-Pierre so I can work my land and logging business. Ma'iingan helps with heavy work, when he isn't on his trapline or repairing canoes for the lumber company. They live with their grandmother a short distance upriver." He pushed his chair back. "Now, that stew smells delicious. Over supper, you can tell me how you came to be captured by that railway surveying crew."

Jean-Pierre gave a small cry. Claude was across the room in four strides. I moved the stewpot into the middle of the fire to heat it through. A weak cry was followed by a mucus-filled cough. Claude murmured reassurances while I crossed to the kitchen worktop, spooned honey into a cup from the jar, and stirred in a some hot water from the pot on the fire. Claude sat on the double bed with his son on his lap while I offered the little boy spoonfuls of honey water. Soon, his breathing eased, and he leaned against his father's chest, big blue eyes fixed on me.

"Maybe some broth," I suggested. At Claude's nod of agreement, I dipped broth from the stewpot and mashed a carrot and potato into a slurry, aware of Jean-Pierre's eyes following my movements around the cabin. His mouth automatically received every spoonful of slurry his father offered him while I set the table and ladled stew into bowls. The cup empty, the child dozed as his father placed him back into his bed.

Over supper, I answered Claude's questions about my time with William Van Horne's crew, sticking close to the truth.

"Those men thought you were male." His relaxed gaze never wavered from my face.

"Yes, and I felt it was safer not to correct them."

"And they didn't see their mistake?"

"You were surprised when I told you my name was Catherine."

"It wasn't Catherine that surprised me. It was Dumont. *Je regrette mais*, I think at least one of those men saw through your disguise."

I rose abruptly. Pouring hot water into the basin, I busied myself washing the dishes. Behind me, I heard Claude's moccasins scuff across the dirt floor. Sneaking a peek over my shoulder, I watched as he tucked the blanket around his sleeping son. My breath caught in my throat as he brushed the child's hair back and planted a kiss on his forehead. My fingertips ached to caress Amelia's downy head.

Dishes cleared, I joined Claude in front of the fire. The wind threw icy snow against the glass window panes. The fire huffed and puffed like a dragon catching its breath in rhythm with the chimney downdrafts. I hoped William and his crew had made Webbwood before the storm. He'd been stubbornly controlling, but he was acting in what he believed to be my best interests. I didn't want anything bad to happen to them.

"How old is your son, monsieur?"

"Three years next month."

A couple years older than Amelia. Would I ever see her turn three? My eyes, blurred with tears, lit on the pinks and greens on the double bed. "That quilt is beautiful. Such a unique pattern."

"It was my wife's, for our marriage." I recognized the flicker of loss in his brown eyes. "She died in childbirth."

"I'm sorry, monsieur."

"Please, call me Claude. And may I call you Catherine?"

I paused. "*Oui*," Best to leave Kate in 1981. How was Gran explaining my disappearance?

Jean-Pierre stirred, then settled.

"I should go. May I stay in your barn overnight?" I stood and turned toward the door.

"It's not safe out there, especially in this storm. Please, wait a moment." Something in the velvet tone with its underlying iron caused me to stop and turn around. Each day over recent months, I had donned the armour of my invented persona, confident that once I arrived at this particular spot, I'd find a way out. Standing in the silent reality of that room, gazing at this man, hope deserted me. Tears slipped down my cheeks.

Claude was pulling several quilts out of the cedar blanket box. "You can sleep in the bed while I sleep here." He settled himself with his back to me on the floor in front of the fire.

"Thank you." Shaking off my feelings of defeat, I moved to the double bed, ran my hand gently over Jean-Pierre's forehead, folded the quilt to one side, and lay down.

I awoke to bright sunlight streaming through the open curtains of the cabin windows. Bacon and coffee spiced the air. Two bright blue eyes stared at me from under a mop of blond curls.

"*Bonjour.* You must be Jean-Pierre." I laughed as the bright curls bobbed in time to his enthusiastic nod.

"*Oui,*" he replied. "*Je m'appelle J.P.*" He tapped his chest.

RHUBARB

Chapter Seven

The storm had blown itself out overnight. Morning sun glinted off the snowdrifts in the courtyard between house and barn. Two shovelled pathways broke the surface of the snowy waves, one leading to the barn, the other to the outhouse. Claude came up behind me as I stood by the window, fresh cold still clinging to him. He handed me a steaming cup. The scent of coffee, thinned with a hint of chicory, filled my head.

"I doubt we'll be seeing Tekakwitha for the next few days," he said. "The river is ice-packed, and snowshoes are useless on this wet snow."

"Papa, *j'ai faim*." Jean-Pierre tugged his father's pant leg. Claude pulled a chunk of bread from the loaf on the table and handed it to his son.

"Catherine, would you mind taking J.P. out to the barn to collect the eggs and feed the chickens while I finish making breakfast?"

Interesting. He didn't assume I would cook.

"Chickens." Jean-Pierre began pulling his fur-lined mittens, knitted tuque, hide leggings, and jacket from the hooks. I helped him dress, and we headed out the door.

Standing in the middle of the barn, I was surprised at the warmth. Straw dust danced in beams of sunlight streaming from the high windows across from the double door. It smelled fertile, safe, not unpleasant. Jean-Pierre began chattering to me, pointing out the wagon, the garden tools hanging against one wall, and the tack storage bay containing saddles and harnesses under the left hay loft. Pulling me by the hand, we crossed the rough plank floor to the stalls under the right loft.

"*Celui-là, c'est* Beau." The beige gelding offered his nose for petting.

"*Et là, c'est* Étoile. *Regarde,* she has *une étoile* on her *nez.*" The dark brown mare remained aloof in the back of her stall but turned toward us so we could admire the white star on her nose.

"*Bonjour,* Crème," Jean-Pierre called to the black and white cow as he led me to the last corner where about a dozen chickens were confined in a wire enclosure. I gathered the eggs and placed them into the basket while he scooped seed from a bucket and flung it across the ground like a painter flicks paint on a canvas. I'd have to talk Gran into chickens for Amelia.

Ready to exit the barn, Jean-Pierre stretched his arms up. "*Prends-moi, ma tante?*"

I scooped him up on one hip. Egg basket outstretched from the other hand, I felt like a gymnast on a balance beam. "Your papa was right, J.P. This snow is impossible." Stopping to soak in the sun, I set the egg basket in the snow and hiked the little boy a little farther up my hip. "*Écoute,* J.P."

Jean-Pierre looked at me.

God, his eyes are the same blue as Amelia's. I pulled him a little tighter to me. "Hear the river sizzling? It sounds like frying pork strips."

Jean-Pierre tilted his head, then shrugged just as I'd seen his father do.

I chuckled.

A few more steps, and I set the child onto the porch.

He burst into the cabin, shouting, "*Papa,* the river is frying pork."

Claude turned from the fire with the cast-iron frying pan in his hand, brows raised.

"The sound of the ice chunks scraping against each other," I explained.

He grinned, then set the pan on the hearth and rushed to the door, arms up, fingers curled like bear claws. "*Monsieur Ourson* wants your clothes." He flung the little boy into the air and turned him upside down, holding him by the legs as he pulled off his mukluks.

Jean-Pierre shrieked. "*Encore, papa!*" Father and son performed a routine of flips and twirls, outdoor clothing flying in all directions. I laughed until my sides hurt. *This'll be a great game to play with Amelia when she's a little older.* I felt the smile leave my face.

"Get your slippers, then come to the table. Breakfast is ready." Claude set his son on his feet.

I turned to unpack the egg basket.

"Waaaaa!"

I almost dropped the eggs as I pivoted to see what was wrong.

Jean-Pierre was standing in the sleeping corner, face scrunched. "*Mon lit,* papa?"

I'd been so involved in the bear game, I hadn't noticed the changes in the room. The double bed had been turned and pushed against the wall. There was no sign of the trundle. A gingham tablecloth hung around the opposite corner.

Claude went to his son. "J.P., you're going to sleep here with me." He plopped him on the bed, then pulled the curtain to reveal the trundle. "*Et voilà, ma tante* Catherine is going to sleep here. You don't mind if she uses your bed, do you, *mon gars?*"

Jean-Pierre's face lit up, then he ran to pull me across the room, gesturing that I should test out my bed.

"Maybe, she'll stay for a few days until Tekakwitha can come back?" Claude posed his question keeping his eyes down as I scooped meat and eggs onto the tin plates on the table.

He was right about not being able to travel. I felt safe and comfortable here compared with taking my chances in the woods. "Okay," I said.

A smile flitted across Claude's mouth.

"Okay," Jean-Pierre repeated.

My fingers smoothed the little boy's curls, and I dropped a quick kiss on the top of his head as we settled around the table.

The scrape of a shovel and the swish of snow became the soundtrack for the remainder of the morning as Claude cleared the porch and the entire courtyard. I was preparing lunch when he came back in.

"Papa, *regarde.*" Jean-Pierre greeted his father at the door, holding up a straw horse I'd twisted for him. "*C'est Étoile.*"

Claude put a full milk bucket on the kitchen worktop and crouched beside his son. "It looks just like her." He made neighing sounds, and Jean-Pierre imitated him. "Want to help me bring in firewood?"

"*Oui.*"

"*Bon,* you stand by the door. Open it when I kick it with my boot." He began ferrying armloads from the woodpile beside the porch to the bin inside. Each time he exited, Claude tickled his son, tousled his hair, or made an animal sound. Jean-Pierre giggled in delight. My cheeks ached from smiling. I admired the way Claude made everyday activities into a game and an opportunity to learn. Jean-Pierre would never know his mother. *I won't let that happen to Amelia, I vowed. That sadness that never quite clears from Claude's eyes will never cloud mine.*

After lunch, Claude worked in the barn. Jean-Pierre napped while I put to use the kitchen skills I'd learned from Elisabeth. Finding Claude's larder stocked with dried beans and molasses, I set the beans on a quick soak over the fire. A further search through the kitchen's pine cupboard produced flour, sugar, lard, and baking powder. I prepared a blueberry pie, set the beans to baking in molasses and smoked pork, then kneaded dough for buns. As I worked, I sang under my breath, refreshing all the French kids' songs Gran had sung to me when I was little—"*Frère Jacques,*" "*Sur le Pont d'Avignon*," "*Chevaliers de la Table Ronde.*" My mother had been adamant in her plan to raise me English. Fortunately, my father won most of their hushed late-night arguments concerning their differing goals for their only child, freeing Gran to teach me my Franco-Ontarian heritage.

Working here in the kitchen for a few hours, I felt like myself. It could almost be Amelia napping nearby.

* * *

Three days of late-March sunshine opened the river and brought Ma'iingan and Tekakwitha back to us.

"Ma'iingan, can you help me with the beams for the saw shed today?"

Tekakwitha and I watched from the door as the two men snowshoed down to the riverbank. The supple grace of the youth contrasted with the power of Claude's broad shoulders.

I turned to Tekakwitha as we closed the door.

Her eyes dropped to her feet. Her hands fidgeted against her tan hide skirt. Tears spilled down her cheeks.

"Tekakwitha, what's wrong?" I drew her to the table. The material of her tunic was soft under my fingers. Could it be rabbit skin? A blue and white chevron pattern was stitched across the chest and around the cuffs. "Your tunic is beautiful. Did you make it?"

She nodded. "Nokomis showed me how."

Jean-Pierre came running from where he'd been playing in front of the fire. "*Regarde, c'est Étoile.*" He held up the straw horse.

"Why don't I make us some tea," I said and motioned her to stay in the chair while I went to the kitchen worktop.

Once the tea was ready, we moved to the settee by the fire where Jean-Pierre had returned to his handmade wooden toy barn. The young woman kept her eyes fixed on the little boy while she sipped her tea and responded with nods and brief statements to my attempts at conversation.

Suddenly, her face crumpled. "Nokomis is very sick." The girl's shoulders shook with sobs.

I rested a hand on her arm. "I'm sorry."

"Ma'iingan is going to tell Monsieur Claude that I can't come anymore." She raised her tear-stained face. "I want to be with Nokomis, but what will happen to J.P. and Monsieur Claude?"

My eyes wandered around the room. Claude and I had found an easy rhythm over the last three days. There was still so much snow. I took a deep breath. "Monsieur Claude will understand. In the meantime, perhaps you can show me the chores you do for him?"

I passed the remainder of the day in a crash course on settler survival. Tekakwitha smiled as she observed my cooking and baking skills. Her eyes widened with surprise at my awkward efforts with the butter churn, and she took over completely when it came to pasteurizing the milk. There was an ample supply of laundry soap and cleaning products, so we agreed lessons in how to make them could wait until they were needed. I didn't share my expectation that I'd be long gone by then.

Once Ma'iingan and Tekakwitha had left at dusk, Claude set the table while I served our meal of chicken, mashed potatoes, and carrots.

"This is delicious." Claude cleared his throat and put down his fork. "Ma'iingan told me about his grandmother. I suppose Tekakwitha told you she can't come anymore?"

I nodded.

"I know this is a lot to ask." His brow wrinkled. "But could you stay until I can find someone to help with J.P.?"

I'd anticipated this request, so why was I hesitating?

"This isn't a good time to travel." Claude leaned across the table toward me. "The forests are getting muddy. Bears are a danger until the berries ripen."

Where was I going to go? I looked at Jean-Pierre carefully spooning his supper, mostly into his mouth. From here I could visit my jump site. I met Claude's earnest brown gaze. "*Oui.*"

He smiled and gave a slight nod.

I cleaned up after supper while Claude tucked Jean-Pierre into bed. Then we met for our tea in front of the fire.

He sat with his legs stretched ahead to warm his sock-clad toes on the hearth. "You're an excellent cook."

"Thank you. I learned from Elisabeth." I gave a short chuckle. "I'm still working out the quantities though."

"No problem. There's plenty of room in the outdoor freezing box."

We each sank into our own thoughts. I conjured Amelia and Gran's faces in the coals. Did Claude search for the image of his dead wife? I gave him a sidelong glance, and my breathing quickened as my eyes travelled the length of his long, lean frame. What would his callused hands feel like on my skin? *Stop it. You'll be gone soon.*

Claude reached his hand to the arm of my chair.

"Don't you get lonely out here all alone?" I whispered.

He turned his body to face mine. "We're always alone, aren't we? No one can experience what anyone else is thinking or feeling. They only know the parts of us we let them see." His gaze moved past my head, his eyes clouded. A snap in the fire brought him out of his reverie and back to my face. "Friends and family make our journey less lonely."

A small sound of agreement escaped me. What a sad way to consider life. I glanced sideways, briefly admiring his profile in the firelight. Poor man, to be carrying so much pain. Suddenly his head swivelled and his eyes met mine before I could look away. Embarrassed, I concentrated on keeping my breathing even. My hands clenched in my lap.

A log crumpled in the fire, sending sparks up the chimney. He stood. My eyes followed his back as he selected two hefty logs from the freshly-stocked woodbox. After setting them gently on the glowing embers, he turned, and, with slow deliberation, came to stand in front of me. His hands reached for mine. Under the pressure of a gentle tug, I was on my feet, the heat of his thighs against mine. His hands dropped to circle my waist, his head tilted downward to find my lips with his. My fingers danced through the silkiness of his shoulder-length curls. Wordlessly we tumbled to the floor, hands pulling frantically on clothing until skin touched skin.

Hours later, I woke to a chill on my back. In the dim glow of the fire's coals I picked out Claude's silhouette curled around Jean-Pierre on the bed. I arose and slipped behind my curtain, pulling the covers tightly around me. What had I done?

* * *

Morning sun bathed my face. I stretched my arms and legs, feeling as languid as a cat.

"*Bonjour, ma tante Catherine.*"

I cracked my eyes. Jean-Pierre stood beside my bed, blond curls forming a bumpy halo in the sunlight streaming through the window behind him. I sat up. "*Bonjour, mon gars.*" A quick glance over his shoulder revealed an empty cabin. "Where is your papa?"

"Work. He said to stay by your bed until you woke up."

Each of the next four days began the same way. No matter how early I awoke, I'd find Jean-Pierre waiting by my side and Claude gone. The chimney on the riverside shed belched smoke and the hum of the steam saw played a backbeat to my mounting confusion and regret. Blocks of squared railway ties ran the length of the riverbank ready for pickup later in the month by the lumber company's barge. At meals, we moved around each other like a Mozart minuet. Evenings were laden with silence in front of the fire. We only spoke when Jean-Pierre was around.

In another time, I would have confronted Claude, but I was stuck here until the forest dried. Did he see our sex as breaking proper social behaviour? Maybe he saw me as a loose woman now. Did he feel guilty as if he'd cheated on his dead wife? Or maybe he just hadn't enjoyed it.

On the fourth evening, I decided to behave as if it had never happened. "J.P. and I went for a walk behind the cabin today. There's still so much snow in the bush."

"Hmph."

"I guess the sunlight can't get through the branches."

"Uh-huh."

This wasn't going well. "Will the river drive run even if there's still snow?"

"*Oui*. As long as the river is open."

"Maybe I'll go then."

He looked up briefly, shrugged, and returned his gaze to the fire.

"When we came back from our walk, I let J.P. play in the courtyard. Suddenly, the chickens started squawking and screaming in panic."

He looked up.

"I tore out of the house and ran to the outdoor pen. When I skidded around the corner of the barn, J.P. was chasing a chicken around the yard, waving his toy hatchet in the air."

A smile tickled Claude's mouth.

"He called, 'I'm getting dinner, *ma tante*,' and lunged at the chicken. He fell face first." I snorted.

Claude guffawed.

"When I got to him, he was back on his feet, hugging a muddy chicken against his chest." I was laughing now. "His hair dripped goopy mud and ice. The only part of him that was clean were his teeth shining through the brown dirt."

We laughed. We looked at each other. And then we took a breath and laughed some more. I'd put us back on the path to our earlier safe rhythm.

RHUBARB

Chapter Eight

Two weeks had passed, and while Claude and I had once again become comfortable around each other, there had been no repeat of our passion. And no amount of standing on the land of my grandmother had induced the jump that I hoped would bring me home. Perhaps it would happen as unexpectedly as it had the first time. I couldn't lose hope.

In the meantime, I went through the motions of life. Once the spring drive had ended and the waters were free of logs, I canoed upriver weekly with Jean-Pierre to visit Tekakwitha and Nokomis. Jean-Pierre would call out in greeting when he spied the one room log cabin nestled on a grass plateau above the riverbank. When the canoe grounded, he'd rush up the rocky path straight into Tekakwitha's waiting arms. On her good days, Nokomis sat on the porch, face tilted to the sun, her complexion like the soft nap of worn tan leather. Jean-Pierre made her laugh, holding his hands on his head, fingers spread like antlers when he described the moose swimming right in front of our canoe. On her difficult days, he curled up beside her and napped while she slept. I imagined Gran and Amelia spending their days in much the same way.

Tekakwitha taught me a new skill on each visit—like hanging berries in paper bags suspended from the clothesline for a few days after they've been sun-dried to stop them sticking together in storage, or piling potatoes in well-ventilated boxes covered with a dark cloth for several weeks to toughen their skin before storing them.

When Claude shot and butchered a deer in August, I paddled to Tekakwitha to learn how to preserve the meat in our round stone smokehouse. I found her sitting in the shade of the old oak beside the cabin, surrounded by small mounds of herbs, while Nokomis dozed in a twig chair on the porch. Jean-Pierre spent a few moments stroking Nokomis's hands before fetching the collection of straw animals Tekakwitha kept for him in the cabin. He settled next to us on the ground, enacting a convoluted story of an encounter between a cow and a bear.

"Never smoke fish and meat at the same time," Tekakwitha advised. "The meat will take on a rotten fish flavour."

"Do I put the meat on racks?"

"No. Spear it with the hooks and hang it in the smoke. Use hickory or maple." She reached for more plants from one of the mounds and left them in her lap. "I know how babies are made." Tekakwitha spoke softly. "Nokomis explained it, and I've watched the animals."

I smoothed the lines of surprise on my forehead, and remained silent.

Her brow furrowed, then cleared, then furrowed again. "But what does it feel like to be in love? How will I know if I love a man?" Her eyes searched my face in hope of answers.

Was this what it was like to be an older sister? I took a deep breath and plunged in. "Have you met someone?"

"No. I want to, but then I get scared. Nokomis warned I must strive for love and not be distracted by desire ."

"Desire can be the beginning of love." I took a breath, then plunged in. "You'll feel happy, excited when you see him, and think about him when you're not together. You'll want to feel his skin, memorize his scent. The touch of his work-hardened hands will take your breath away."

She listened as if she were keeping mental notes. "That is not love?"

"It can be, but when it's only desire, you'll start to see his flaws, and you'll want to fix him." I felt my jaw tighten, an image of Rick lurching drunkenly to the kitchen for another beer flitting past. "When you find you can't change him—and believe me, you can't—then you'll end up hating him."

"And when you love someone?"

I smiled. "When you love someone, you feel relaxed around him. You feel safe. You can be yourself."

"But you don't desire him?"

"Yes, you do, very much. The difference is, when you see he isn't perfect, you'll still want to be with him, just the way he is. Loving and being loved is a hard thing to do." I looked off onto the river. "Through his eyes, you see yourself like you've never seen yourself before. In his eyes, you can see forever."

Tekakwitha's face relaxed. "So you and Monsieur Claude . . . ?"

"What about me and Monsieur Claude?" I sat rigid.

Tekakwitha's fingers fidgeted in her lap. "Um . . . that day last week when Ma'iingan helped Monsieur Claude?"

"And you showed me how to harvest honey. What about that day?"

She raised her head. "When he was around you, his eyes sparkled with little gold bits, same as when he looks at J.P. And every time you looked at him, your face glowed like you had a light inside you." Her lower lip trembled.

I pulled her into my arms. "It's okay. Monsieur Claude and I are friends who are helping each other out right now." How many times had I heard those words from my friends? How many times had I said them? But this time, it was the truth. It had to be. I had somewhere else to be.

A few weeks later, on a brilliantly-coloured September morning, Tekakwitha and Ma'iingan stopped by our dock to say goodbye. On her deathbed, Nokomis had instructed the siblings to return to their community. As the children of the chief, it was now their time to fulfill their father's will and lead their people.

* * *

The chill autumn wind whipped the waves into whitecaps as I paddled alone to the clearing where the bridge piers should have been. With each dip of the paddle, the voice in my head mocked, "It's been eight months."

The poplar and birch trees along the bank had transformed from the fuzzy green buds of May through to deep green summer foliage. Now, they stood naked, the last of their yellow leaves tossing on the waves. Amelia turned a year old last week. She wasn't a baby anymore. Would I even recognize her?

I hunched my shoulders under the clouds of steel pressing down from the north. Snow sky. "I'm trying, Amelia. I'm trying," I whispered.

I pulled the canoe onto the sandy beach where Van Horne and his men had launched their raft, and then I stood in the exact spot where I'd lain upon my arrival in January. The moss underfoot had lost its summer springiness. The soughing of wind through pines filled my head. Taking a deep breath, I squeezed my eyes shut and willed the roaring into my ears. I tried to conjure a train whistle in my head. Nothing. After several attempts, I screamed curses at the gods that had taken me from my time and refused to show me the way back.

Wet snow lashed my face as I drove my paddle against the wind and current to Claude's cabin. My back ached. I shivered in the spray from waves breaking over the prow. This would be my last trip in the canoe until next spring. I'd have to start making the trip on foot. *Why bother? Nothing ever happens.* My inner voice taunted me. *But what if one time . . . ?*

Father and son were coming out of the barn as I climbed the rise to the house. Jean-Pierre ran to me, a small wooden box clutched to his chest. "*Maman, regarde.* A mouse."

I sank to the grass, my face in my hands, heart thudding in my ears.

Then Claude was beside me, his hand under my elbow. "Catherine, it's just a mouse. It's harmless."

"It's not the mouse."

"Then what?"

"No one's ever called me maman." I raised my tear-soaked eyes to his. "I left before my daughter could speak."

Claude's face closed momentarily as he glanced down at J.P.

I swiped at my tears.

J.P. put his arm around my neck.

"It's all right, Catherine." Claude brushed a strand of hair from my face, and gentleness returned to his features. "Come. Supper is almost ready." He pulled me up off the grass and guided me back to the house. Jean-Pierre held my hand.

After our meal, Claude tucked Jean-Pierre into bed, and we settled in the living room with our tea. His legs were stretched out to the fire. "You have a daughter?" Smoke from his pipe curled over his head.

I nodded. "Amelia." Under his penetrating gaze, I added, "She's a year old now."

He sat up straight. "You left your infant daughter behind to find your grandmother in the wilderness? In winter? I thought you lived with your mother in Toronto. You never said anything about a husband."

"I don't have a husband." I gave him a steady stare.

Claude dropped his gaze to contemplate the flames. Without looking at me, he asked, "So your mother is caring for your baby?"

"No, Amelia is with my grandmo—" I stopped too late.

His head jerked up. "The grandmother you've been looking for?"

I shrank under his narrowed eyes.

A bubble pressed up from my stomach and into my chest. I needed to tell him the truth. Did I trust him? I took a deep breath. "Let me start again. Amelia and I lived right here with my grandmother," I pointed to the floor, "when I got lost."

Claude lowered his cup. "No one has lived here but me. I built this house."

"You live here now, but . . . Oh God, you're going to think I'm crazy—" I put my hands over my face.

He reached across the space and gently pulled my hands to my lap. "Catherine, tell me."

"My grandparents married in 1934. My grandfather, Jacques Dumont had inherited his parents' home . . . this house." I paused. "When the house was destroyed by a tree in 1955, they built a bungalow on the same spot. That's where my grandmother still lives."

"19 . . . ? What tree?" Claude was leaning forward, eyes dark with confusion.

"The maple beside the house was hit by lightning and crashed through the roof."

"Impossible! It's a sapling." He guffawed and sat back.

"It is now."

His brow creased.

"I was born in 1957." I emphasized the year.

His eyes locked on mine.

"In January 1981, while I was snowshoeing by the far bend in the river, I blacked out. When I woke up, it was 1881."

His voice dropped to a whisper. "Impossible."

"I know. But here I am. I've gone back to the clearing to try to return to my own time, but nothing happens."

"That's where you go in the canoe?"

I nodded, my eyes on the sparks spiralling up the chimney. I rubbed my sweaty palms across my skirt.

He stared deep into the fire as though he was searching for something that wasn't there.

"Maman, papa, pee pee."

I lifted my head.

Claude raked his fingers through his hair. "Can you . . . ?" He gestured in Jean-Pierre's direction, grabbed his coat and left.

"Maman!" Jean-Pierre's urgent cry startled me to my feet. I moved automatically, pulling the chamber pot from under the bed and setting Jean-Pierre up to pee. What was I thinking? Claude could throw me out. He could have me committed for lunacy.

With Jean-Pierre settled for the night, I turned to my own bed and curled into a foetal position. My mind churned with possible scenarios all night. Should I slip out before dawn and go to Nelsonville? Or maybe to Elisabeth in Webbwood? Perhaps I could build a shelter and stay at the jump site until I could make it work.

When Claude hadn't returned by morning, I began our usual routine with breakfast for Jean-Pierre.

"Where's papa?" Confusion wrinkled his young forehead.

"He's working."

Jean-Pierre went back to spooning porridge into his mouth, maple syrup dribbling down his chin. It was normal for his father to work long hours.

My feet found excuses to take me past the window every few minutes. When the rhythmic pounding of the engine from the saw shed started, I sighed with relief. At least he hadn't gone to Nelsonville to get the authorities.

Fear and confusion had turned to anger as the day passed with no sign of Claude. How could he just walk away after I'd poured my soul out to him?

While Jean-Pierre and I baked molasses cookies, and potatoes, carrots, and rabbit roasted over the fire for supper, silence returned to the outdoors. I watched Claude come up the rise, and then I quickly turned back to the work top before he came through the door.

We ate in silence. I'd leave in the morning. Claude could find another woman to look after his kid, I fumed.

As I cleared the table, Claude moved to his chair by the fire. I gathered Jean-Pierre into my arms and nuzzled his neck. Pine and musty leaves with a hint of smoke. We sang all six verses of Chevalier de la Table Ronde before his eyes finally drooped.

"Good night, *mon gars*," I whispered, kissing him on the forehead.

"Catherine, please sit." I couldn't read the expression on Claude's face. "I'm sorry I reacted so badly."

I pushed away my angry retort and stared at the fire.

"I don't know what to say. I want to believe you, but . . ."

I raised my head. His eyes seemed lighter as they met mine. Was that because of the firelight? "You don't have to say anything. I'll leave in the morning. All I ask is that you keep my secret." My lips felt stiff around the words.

"You said you were afraid I'd think you're crazy." He leaned toward me, elbows on his knees, hands reaching. "Catherine, I think you are the sanest, kindest, most intelligent woman I have ever known."

I chewed my inner lip to hold on as my anger slid down my legs and out my toes.

"We both carry pain from the past, but the past is dead. The future doesn't exist until we reach for it." He stared into my eyes.

I stared back. Where was he going with this?

"I want us to live in the present. To do that we both have to let go." Claude slid to his knees in front of me, the warmth of his hands soothing mine. "I'm ready to start a new life." He swallowed hard. "I want it to be with you."

I felt my heart drop. Then it was racing in my throat. I couldn't exhale. My eyes darted around the cabin. "I need to think." I stepped around him, pulled on my coat, and ran to the barn.

Étoile and Beau nickered a soft greeting as I slipped through the door. Moonlight pooled on the floor from the high window. The cow swished her tail in anticipation, only to stop and turn her head

Rhubarb, Strawberries, and Willows

away when she saw it wasn't Claude. "Sorry, Crème. It's just me." She'd never forgiven me for my clumsy attempts at milking.

I burrowed into the pile of fresh straw in the corner. The sweet smell tickled my nose. I adjusted my position to flatten the sharp stalks pricking into my legs through my skirt, but nothing could distract me from the turmoil churning my mind into a frenzy. Claude made me laugh. I felt safe to be myself around him. I looked forward to our times together over meals and in front of the fire. I caught myself watching his lips and remembering their moist warmth. When my hand brushed against his, electric flashes flicked through me. Did I love him? Tekakwitha had seen something between us. But how could I abandon Amelia?

Elisabeth's words rang through my head, "God places us where we are for a reason. Figure out why He has placed you here. Otherwise, you will always be visiting, not living."

Is this my place now? Is that why I can't make the jump happen?

The barn door creaked open. "Catherine?"

"Over here."

His feet scratched across the open space. His silhouette loomed above me.

I held my breath.

He hung the lantern he was carrying and dropped to his knees. "I'm sorry. It was too much, too fast."

I saw forever as our eyes met in the dim light.

I put my fingers to his lips and pulled him down beside me in the straw.

Strawberries

STRAWBERRIES

Chapter Nine

The slight breeze wafting up the hill from the river moved the fire smoke past the house and barn but did little to dissipate the heat rising from the iron kettle. My eyes burned and strands of hair clumped on my sweaty brow as I worked the scraps of fat and tallow into the boiling lye ash with a wooden paddle. Overcome by the acrid fumes, I turned my back on the bubbling solution, leaving it to thicken.

Breathing in the fresh spring air, I took a moment to survey my domain. Reflections of the three ten-foot high weeping willows in our pasture rippled on the tea-coloured surface of the river. Early June sunlight coaxed the plants in the kitchen garden to poke their hopeful heads from the fertile soil. My mouth watered at the thought of corn on the cob roasted in the fire, the juice of sun-warmed tomatoes running down my chin, and the satisfying crunch of raw carrots pulled directly from the ground and rinsed under the pump.

An entire family of rabbits could shelter under the dark green rhubarb plants taking over one side of the garden. *I'll take some cuttings to the Strawberry Social in a few weeks for the new settlers.* The adjacent strawberry patch shone more white than green, the blossoms boding a plentiful berry harvest.

I'd had those plants ever since the spring seven years ago when we'd travelled by steamer across Georgian Bay from the town of

Spanish to the port of Midland. Claude needed to register his license to operate a scow across the river for the Spanish River Lumber Company. Fighting nausea, I'd been stranded on the steamer's deck for the entire fifteen-hour trip, Claude at my side, while three-and-a-half-year-old Jean-Pierre slept below in our cabin.

Once Claude had concluded his business and I'd completed my shopping, we'd explored the town of Midland

"Are you throwing away those plants?" I'd called to the widow culling her strawberry and rhubarb plants, her black dress flapping in the breeze.

The woman stood upright, hand supporting her lower back. "You want them?" An errant lock of grey hair tickled her face.

"Oh, yes, please. We can pay you."

She dismissed my offer with the wave of her hand. "You're not from around here." Her faded eyes narrowed.

"No, we're from Nelsonville."

In response to the tilt of her head, I added, "North of Lake Huron."

"You can't grow these up there," the widow declared, "but you're welcome to them. You can use that old wagon." She pointed to the corner of the fence.

Jean-Pierre helped Claude load the plants I'd selected. While the woman and I took cuttings from her weeping willow, she whispered, "It's a girl."

"What did you say?" I turned in time to catch a glimpse of a black hem disappearing around the side of the house.

Laughing together at Claude's efforts to control the laden toy wagon with one wobbly wheel and a handle that barely reached his knees soon distracted me from my confusion at the woman's comment. I only understood when my nausea continued once we were home.

"Maman! Maman!" I was pulled back to the present by my six-year-old daughter, Sophie, scampering out from the stand of birches flanking the garden. She clutched a bouquet of blue and white bell flowers in her hand. Stopping mid-stride, she cocked her head toward the high-pitched whistle of the late-morning train. The hypnotic clickity-clack of the iron wheels over the tracks held us both like granite statues until the train's third hoot faded south. Sophie ran up the hill to present me with her bouquet.

"Can you put these in my hair this afternoon, maman? I almost caught a baby rabbit. He dove behind a tree root this big." Sophie extended her arms as wide as she could. "And there was a secret cave behind the root."

"Just like Alice."

"Who?"

"Alice in Wonderland. Maybe we'll buy the book next fall when we go to Sainte-Anne-des-Pins."

Sophie's nose twitched. "Eww! What's that smell?" She pinched her nose.

"That's lye. I'm making soap. Now, go put the flowers in the yellow vase with plenty of water."

"Okay." Sophie skipped along the porch and disappeared inside. The original log cabin now crouched behind a taller addition with living space, kitchen, and a sleeping loft for the children. Windows on three walls provided cooling cross breezes in summer. We'd turned the old cabin into our bedroom sanctuary.

Strong arms embraced me from behind, accompanied by a whisper of "*Je t'aime*" in my ear. "I thought you were going to wear those britches—*jeans*, you call them—when you make soap?"

I leaned into him. "Didn't want to draw attention with all those supply wagons crossing on the scow this morning."

Claude nodded. "Maybe you can draw my attention with them tonight." He waggled his eyebrows.

I playfully pushed his hand from my ass. "I need to pour this soap."

Claude removed the kettle from the fire. "There's been a lot of hammering coming from the barn this morning. Think I'll check on J.P.'s progress with the doghouse."

As he crossed the courtyard, my eyes admired how his broad back tapered to narrow hips. Once he disappeared into the barn, I returned to the soap, ladling the goop into jars. Tekakwitha's voice whispered in my mind. *Don't hold the jar when you're filling. If you get hot lye on your hands, douse it with cold water right away, and rub bear fat salve into the wound.*

Swatting at the blackflies circling my head now that I was clear of the fire, I went inside in search of my daughter.

"*Regarde,* maman." Sophie guided me through the house she'd laid out on the floor in front of the hearth, delineating walls with Jean-Pierre's wooden building blocks. "Here is *le salon* where the *papa* is sitting by the fire while the maman is making the food in *la cuisine.*"

"What are the children doing at the table?"

"The girl is making a picture, but the brother is doing his *mathématiques.*"

"*Très bon,* Sophie. This looks just like us." Sophie's paper dolls reflected our individual colouring—dark hair and eyes for her and her father and blond and blue for Jean-Pierre and me. "Want to help me make the cinnamon crisps for us to take to the Gagnon's this afternoon?"

Sophie gathered flour and oil from the cupboard and filled a cup with water. We fried thin unleavened pancakes in the cast-iron pan. I brushed them with melted butter, and Sophie followed, sprinkling each warm pancake with a cinnamon and sugar mixture before we baked them in our outdoor oven. Once cooled, they'd be a crispy bliss on the tongue.

"Sophie, what are you humming?" I sliced the cold venison and cheese while Sophie set the table for lunch.

"The song you always hum when you work." Sophie hummed through the verse and then sang the words to the chorus.

> *Loggers may have jammed her*
> *Miners they have dammed her*
> *But the Spanish keeps rollin' along*
> *Her tea waters mirror*
> *Birches, pines and poplars*

"*And the Spanish . . .*" She faltered.

I realized my wide eyes had alarmed her. Forcing a smile, I joined in. "Okay, now big finish . . . *keeps rollin' along*," we sang together. I hugged my daughter, burying my face in her silky, chestnut curls. No harm. As long as we stayed away from the last verse.

"*Je t'aime,* maman."

"I love you, too, *ma petite.*"

Outside, a series of bumps finishing with a long squeak of wood dragging on wood. "Maman, come see," Jean-Pierre called from the porch.

I followed Sophie out, wiping my hands on my apron. Claude was leaning against the porch pillar, grinning broadly, one hand stroking his short beard.

"This is so cool, J.P.!" Sophie's voice was muffled as her head and shoulders disappeared through the rounded opening.

Jean-Pierre stood beside the lopsided wooden doghouse, blue eyes brimming with pride.

"Great job, J.P. Your puppy's going to love it."

"I had some trouble with the roof, *maman*, but *papa* said we could put it here so the porch roof can keep it dry," Jean-Pierre explained. "This wall leans a bit because I didn't make it . . . um . . . square?" Jean-Pierre looked to his father who nodded confirmation of the correct concept. "From here, the puppy can see the yard, the barn, and our door to protect us."

Bony bare wrists and ankles poked from his clothes as he leaned over the house. How had he gotten so big?

"*Bon.* Wash your hands, you three. Lunch is ready."

* * *

"Sophie, Jean-Pierre! Come on!" Claude was waiting at the scow, ready to ferry us across the river to our neighbours'.

The children raced down the hill and across the pasture as I walked behind, carrying the plate of cinnamon crisps and a jug of sumac lemonade. The morning breeze had picked up, worrying the river's surface with choppy wavelets.

At the edge of the scow, Jean-Pierre was quick to offer me his hand. "*Merci mon gars.*" His smile took over his entire face.

"*Regarde-moi,* papa!" Sophie twirled to show off her new boots and her lacy ruffled skirt. I'd woven the wildflowers into her curls, and she clasped a bouquet of the remaining flowers for Adeline in her fist.

"I see Sophie is not the only one who has dressed for *la visite.*"

My heart skipped at Claude's admiring look. I twirled, like Sophie, so he could appreciate my new, sky-blue skirt.

With Sophie and I firmly clasping the iron rail, Claude cast off the line. Jean-Pierre moved sure-footed across the rocking pine-planked floor of the scow to ring the bell, signalling Maurice we were ready. With a jolt, the harness engaged. The cable attached to the scow front twanged. Maurice's horse walked in a circle, winding the cable around a large spool to pull the scow across the river. Water slapped against the side of the scow's platform. Claude and Maurice had seen a hundredfold increase in crossing revenues from travellers and roving pedlars in the past year. Within minutes, we juddered against the eastern riverbank where Maurice connected the scow's ramp to the landing.

Three years before, Maurice and Adeline Gagnon had moved from Trois-Rivières. Claude had shown Maurice how to job-log his property in winter and reforest it in spring. Now Maurice supplied logs for Claude's railway tie operation, and the two men worked their fields with shared farm equipment.

"*Bonjour, Bienvenue!*" Maurice's voice rumbled from his barrel chest. Looking like a younger, dark-haired Santa Claus including the twinkling eyes, he assisted the children onto the landing.

"I understand we have business to conduct, *petit Monsieur Dumont.*" Maurice addressed Jean-Pierre. "Perhaps you and your papa will come with me to the barn to examine our puppies?" He winked. "I believe we also have a surprise for you, mam'selle Sophie."

Jean-Pierre glanced at his father, who nodded his permission. The two children raced toward the barn. "The puppies are with their maman in one of the stalls," Maurice called after them. "You may look, but wait for us before going in."

Maurice addressed me. "Adeline is preparing refreshments."

"I'll go up to help her. How is she feeling these days?"

"We think things are going well, but it is our first . . . She isn't suffering in the mornings anymore, *merci bon Dieu*, and has more of her usual energy." Maurice's brow creased. "Sometimes she seems so touchy . . . so . . ."

"That sounds normal." Claude laughed.

I playfully punched his arm. "See you later." I left the two men making their way to the barn, already deep in conversation.

The brilliant mob of blossoms bordering the pathway waved a greeting as I climbed the small rise to the log cabin nestled against a stand of poplars and spruce.

"*Bonjour, Catherine.*" Adeline called. The firm bulge of her pregnancy pressed against my abdomen as we embraced. "*Regarde* my beautiful porch. Maurice built it this week."

"It's perfect. I foresee many happy hours with little ones playing out here." I offered my plate and jug. "Here's some sumac lemonade. And Sophie and I made these cinnamon crisps this morning."

"*Bon, merci.*" Adeline added my plate to her mini venison *tourtières,* dried blueberry scones, and maple baked beans, covering everything with a cloth to protect it from deer flies.

"Your walkway is gorgeous. I recognize the black-eyed Susans, but what are the others?"

"They're all from here." Her lustrous auburn hair bobbed in curls around her face as she gestured animatedly. "The tall scarlet ones are bee balm, the purple ones are asters, and those bright yellow ground huggers at the edge are cinquefoil."

"What are those long boxes for along the front?"

"I want to grow herbs to make the medicines Tekakwitha told us about when she visited last fall. Have you seen her yet this spring?"

Over the years, Tekakwitha had visited Claude and me each spring and autumn. She shared stories of the difficulties of acceptance she and Ma'iingan had faced when they first arrived in their village, and the gradual successes Ma'iingan was achieving in bringing his people back to their culture. We even met Tekakwitha's husband once. Shortly after the arrival of the Gagnons, Tekakwitha had accompanied me on one of my visits. Her comments about Adeline's gardens had ignited a spark between the two women.

We settled in twig chairs on the porch. "Actually, she visited us this winter. She has a baby daughter Waawaatesti."

"How wonderful!" Adeline's voice trailed off as our eyes met. "Is there something wrong with her?"

"Dewe'igan, her husband, was killed while hunting last fall." Kind, gentle Dewe'igan, master drummer for his village, had adored Tekakwitha and their children.

"Oh, no. I'm so sorry."

"He was shot through the heart with the arrow of the man that always tries to stir up trouble against Ma'iingan. It was declared an accident."

Adeline gasped.

I swallowed heavily. "She came to us because that man was suddenly appearing at her door in the middle of the night. Ma'iigan was working for the Hudson's Bay Company for the winter, so Tekakwitha felt it would be safer for her to leave the village."

"Where did she go?"

"After a few days' rest, she asked Claude to take her and the children to Nelsonville. She takes care of the Edwards children while Mrs. Edwards bakes for John Hall's General Store."

"I'm glad she's safe. I'll remember her in my prayers."

The mourning doves cooed. We each took a moment of reflection while the bees buzzed through the blooms.

It was evident from her rosy complexion that Adeline and the baby were doing well. When I asked her if she'd seen the midwife in Nelsonville yet, Adeline began fidgeting with her apron. "Maurice wants me to see a doctor. My sister almost died in childbirth. He's afraid. But . . ."

"What's the matter?" I reached out to take her hand, remembering how alone I'd felt out here when I was pregnant with Sophie. Adeline was barely twenty years old.

"I've never been to a doctor here. What if I can't speak English well enough. What if he finds there is something wrong and I won't understand?" Her soft hazel eyes welled up with tears.

"Oh, Adeline, everything'll be fine." I patted her arm. "Your English is excellent, but I could come with you if you'd like. We could go to Webbwood by train and make a day of it, see the doctor, and do some shopping? What do you think?"

"*Oui! Merci!*" Adeline threw her arms around my neck.

"Let's plan our day trip for sometime next week. *Ca va?*"

Her eyes danced. "*Oui, ça va.*"

Our moment was interrupted by the arrival of the men and children. Jean-Pierre had selected a male puppy, white with a few black patches and two black paws. "I named him Snoopy," he said.

"Snoopy?" Adeline asked.

"Never heard that name," Maurice said.

Claude looked at me through narrowed eyes, mouth pulled tight. Keep smiling, I told myself, holding my breath.

"Snoopy is Charlie Brown's dog," Jean-Pierre explained. "Charlie Brown is in love with the little red-headed girl. Lucy is his friend. She's very smart. Maman tells us stories about them."

"Must be an English children's story," Adeline mused.

Sophie announced, "*Mon oncle* had a surprise for me too, maman!"

I released my breath. "You better tell us. You've waited patiently for your turn."

"*Mon oncle* showed me the kittens. He said I could have one. Pleeease."

"What did papa say?" I asked.

"He said we have to talk about it. But, in case you say it's okay, I've already picked one out, and I'm going to name her Lucy." Jean-Pierre whispered in her ear. Sophie positioned herself beside the table. "The cat can catch mice in the barn and house, and she can sleep in the barn or maybe with me?" Her brother smiled encouragingly. "She'll eat bugs and moths in the house, and it'd be *ben* cool," she whispered, scrambling back up on her seat.

Adeline clapped her hands. In the end, each of our children would have a new pet within the week.

* * *

Once the children were settled in their beds, Claude climbed the ladder to their loft to kiss them goodnight, while I cleaned the kitchen below them. I heard Jean-Pierre ask his father for a bedtime story. Claude protested, saying their mother was the better storyteller, but finally relented in the face of their pleading.

"*Il était une fois un petit garçon,*" Claude began. "His name was Claude. He lived with his maman and papa on a farm outside of a town called Compton in Lower Canada. It was a dairy farm with green pastures rolling like waves as far as the eye could see. The boy had two older brothers, Clément and François; two younger sisters, Hélène and Micheline; and one younger brother, Robert."

"Did he have a dog?" asked Jean-Pierre.

"Several dogs worked with the family on the farm to manage the cows. Every morning, Claude and his brothers woke while it was still dark, milked the cows, and then walked to school. Claude loved school, especially *mathématiques* and *sciences.*"

"Like me," said Jean-Pierre.

"Clément loved farming and hated school," Claude resumed. "He understood how to grow hay and how to care for the cows. Whenever he went into the barn, all the cows would moo and follow him with their gentle brown eyes. He stopped going to school when he was twelve and spent his days working on the farm. Their papa always said Clément had 'cow magic' and he'd own the farm someday."

"What about the other brothers, papa?" Sophie asked.

"François hated farming, and he didn't like school much, either. He was always getting into fights. When he turned sixteen, his papa sent François to the army to become a soldier."

"I don't think I'd want to be a soldier," Jean-Pierre commented.

Chores done, I moved to sit on the bottom rung of the ladder where I could hear better.

"François didn't want to be one, either, but he was afraid of his father, so he did as he was told and went to the army."

"What about Claude, papa?" whispered Sophie. "What did he do?"

"When Claude was sixteen, his *maman* wanted him to go to the city school to become a priest. However, Claude didn't hear the call from God, so instead, he studied at the university in Montreal and became an engineer."

"What's an engineer?" asked Sophie.

"A person who designs machines, roads, bridges. He can even invent new things to solve problems."

"Like you, papa," Jean-Pierre said.

"*Oui, mon gars*, I suppose."

"What did Claude do when he finished university?" asked Jean-Pierre.

"Claude stayed in Montreal to work for a railroad company. Now, *mes petits*, it's time for you to sleep."

"Papa, did Claude get married and have children? Did he live happily ever after?" demanded Sophie.

"I'll tell you more of the story another day. Good night."

I busied myself at the new wood stove so Claude wouldn't know I'd been eavesdropping. Once I heard his foot hit the floor, I remarked, "It took a while to settle them."

Claude put his finger to his lips and beckoned me to him. We stood together at the bottom of the ladder like two conspirators.

"Sophie, you know the boy *papa* told us about is him, right?"

"But how can that be? Papa began with '*Once upon a time...*'"

"Sometimes adults try to fool us. Let's ask him to tell us more next time, and you'll see."

"Okay..."

The children grew quiet, likely drifting off into dreams of their new pets.

This was our time. We settled on the porch, cups of tea in our hands. I leaned into the warmth of Claude's arm around my shoulders, feeling a peace I'd believed I'd never find. The days were long now as we approached the summer solstice. We watched the light show playing on the trees as the water reflected the fading sunlight, creating an endless kaleidoscope of patterns. I imagined Gran and

Amelia were looking at the same trees. The thought comforted me. Claude relaxed beside me, and I laid my head against his neck.

"Now, who is this Charlie Brown?" Claude's voice carried a forced lightness.

"I grew up reading the stories and singing the songs about him and his friends."

His hand tightened on my shoulder. "Catherine, we agreed you need to hide your past. You saw the Gagnons' reaction."

"I'm sure other mothers make up stories for their children." I shifted position so I could look into his eyes. "The children know all the fairy tales like *Le Petit Chaperon Rouge* and *Snow White*. I also tell them stories about a girl named Laura who lives on a farm on the prairies with her settler family." I pressed on as the lines around his eyes relaxed. "What harm can there be in hearing stories about children like themselves?"

He sighed, pulled me back to his side, and tightened his arm around me, so I snuggled in to reassure him. Claude kissed the top of my head. "The blackflies are getting bad. Let's go in."

We beat a quick retreat into the house. Under the quilt I'd made for our bed, Claude pulled me close. I breathed in his scent of outdoor breezes, machine oil, and sunshine as my hands caressed the hard muscles of his abdomen. Feeling his heart beat against my cheek, I let my hands wander, my fingers playing around his groin. He inhaled sharply. I crossed my leg over his thigh. His callused hands stroked my face; his fingers combed through my hair; his soft lips covered my breasts with kisses. Soon, we were moving together, slowly at first, then with greater urgency until I felt him explode inside me. Waves of ecstasy rippled through my own body. Our passion spent, we rolled into each other's arms. I'd never dreamed a man could make me feel so alive.

Claude murmured, "*Je t'aime, cherie*. My life is nothing without you."

"*Je t'adore*," I whispered and slid into sleep.

STRAWBERRIES

Chapter Ten

Sophie spent the thirty-minute train trip with her face pressed up against the window, searching the passing glacier-scored granite rock cuts and evergreen forests for animals. Adeline and I sat on wooden benches across from each other, planning our day.

"*Regarde,* maman, a bear. He's watching us." The engineer let out three sharp toots of the train's whistle. The black bear dropped his head, turned and charged into the shelter of the forest.

The locomotive chugged into the station in a cloud of smoky steam. The train's whistle announced our arrival in Webbwood.

"You look so much more relaxed now," remarked Adeline. "Are you nervous on trains?"

"Oh, no, I'm fine." I forced the frown from my brow. Claude had driven us by wagon, west, to Stanley Station to catch the train that morning. Not only was it shorter than backtracking east to Nelsonville, but it meant we would avoid crossing the bridge at my jump site. Given the mesmerizing effect the train whistles had on Sophie and me at home, Claude and I felt it prudent to avoid the bridge.

The train jolted to a stop. Standing in the narrow aisle, I smoothed the gathered skirt of my light-weight cotton dress. I still found long skirts and high collars restricting, but the natural fibres breathed in a way my 1980s synthetic clothing never could.

"What a vibrant shade of blue plaid. Is that a new dress?" Adeline asked.

"*Merci*. Claude bought it for my birthday. Feel." I leaned closer.

Adeline fingered the edge of the flounce that draped my shoulder. "So soft. Maybe I can find something like this to make a maternity dress. I don't fit into my regular dresses anymore." She smiled ruefully as she showed how her waistband rode up under her breasts.

Collecting our baskets and umbrellas, Adeline and I each gripped one of Sophie's hands and descended onto the wooden platform and into the red station house. Sophie sneezed at the smell of freshly-cut wood. The chubby-cheeked station master squinted through the round, wire-framed magnifiers perched on his nose as he processed our request to reserve a storage crib adjacent to the track.

"Just tell the shopkeepers crib number fourteen. We'll stow your purchases until your return trip."

Sophie giggled. I nudged her. "Thank you, sir."

"Pleasure to be of assistance, ladies. Now, right through that door, you'll find our main street." He pointed to a double door on the wall opposite the platform.

"Could you direct us to the doctor's office, please?"

"Certainly, take the first left past the Wild Horse, the second right, and halfway down on the right, you'll find a big yellow house. There's a sign on the fence."

The clouds were so low we could practically taste the raindrops waiting to fall on our shoulders. Webbwood's main street ran straight out in front of us.

I turned to Sophie. "What was all that giggling about?"

"His Santa Claus glasses bounced up and down on his nose when he talked."

"I was waiting for them to fall," Adeline confided. My two companions dissolved into laughter.

Then Sophie joined me at the porch rail. "*Maman*, look at that pretty white building."

"That's a church, Sophie. See the tall tower with the bell and cross?" The building's back butted up against the rock face that marked the end of the street, some two hundred feet ahead. Four oaks, branches reaching as high as the church roof, flanked the walkway. And diffused light from the interior haloed the person sweeping the stoop in front of the open wooden door.

"It's so big. Not like the little house in Nelsonville. Can we go see it?"

"Maybe later, Sophie."

Built tightly against each other, six wooden buildings ran up each side of the packed-dirt road. The new reds, blues, greens, and yellows of their fronts screamed prosperity.

"Mary's Bakery and Café, Gamache Smithy & Stables, Sadowski's Dry Goods," Sophie read the painted signs aloud. "Maman, what's a apo . . . apothe . . ."

"Apothecary," I helped. "It's a place where you buy medicines."

Three young mothers gathered in front of Goodman's General Store, bouncing babies on their hips, while two toddlers chased each other around their skirts. The taller of the group pulled one companion into her story with animated hand and head movements. The other, poorly dressed, appearing malnourished rather than petite, held herself back from the conversation. Across the street, in front of the London and Canada Bank, a skinny older woman embraced her friend, back hunched to avoid contact with the shorter woman's enormous bosom. Nudging each other with their elbows, their eyes followed an attractive woman in her mid-forties walking past. She held her shoulders erect as she nodded her head to the gossips. I smiled. Some things are the same in every era. A few wagons rolled up the street.

"*Bon,* Let's go," I took Sophie's hand and we descended the steps to the wooden sidewalk on the left side. It was barely ten o'clock.

"Maman, look at that lady! She's only wearing her corset and petticoat." Sophie pointed to a second-storey balcony across the street at Belle's Hotel. "That man is taking her inside. He must be her brother."

The tinkling of a piano and the arguments of rough male voices assailed us as we passed the Wild Horse Hotel and Saloon. Two men staggered through the swinging doors, across our path, and into the street.

"Maman, those men look hurt."

I'd heard the stories of gambling, drinking, and prostitution brought to communities by lumberjacks with time on their hands in the offseason.

"They're fine, Sophie. Let's go." She had to trot to keep up as I pulled her along, Adeline hurrying behind us. Our left turn immediately past the saloon took us off the sidewalk and onto the narrow residential road network snaking its way around rock outcroppings and swamps. Pastel blue, yellow, and white clapboard houses bordered both sides, most with large red or green drive sheds in the back. Trees shaded verandas and front yards. Not a leaf moved in the sultry air. We found the doctor's house right where the stationmaster had said we would.

Approaching the yellow two-storey home, I felt Adeline's steps falter. "What's wrong, *ma tante*?" Sophie asked.

"I'm fine, just a little nervous," replied Adeline, pushing her hair from her damp brow.

Linking my arm through Adeline's, I said, "Lead on, Sophie. Let's see this doctor so we can get on with our shopping." Sophie skipped up the stone path to the door and was already speaking to the smiling woman behind the table in the reception area by the time Adeline and I walked into the office. Mrs. Laura Jones, Dr. George Jones's wife, and a trained nurse, was explaining to Sophie that the doctor was currently with a patient, but he would be ready to see us in a few minutes.

Recognition sparked in Mrs. Jones's hazel eyes. "It's Catherine Dumont, isn't it?" She emerged from behind the table to take my hand. "You're looking very well. Don't tell me—this young lady is the baby Sophie we delivered? My goodness, you're a beauty," she gushed as she lightly pinched Sophie's cheek.

I introduced Adeline. Laura Jones smiled in welcome. "Now, Madame Gagnon, let's get a few measurements before you see the doctor."

Dr. Jones understood French, but Adeline managed fine with her English. He found that the baby was developing well, that Adeline was in good health, and confirmed that she could expect her child to be born toward the middle of October.

Sophie was declared to be in excellent health and very bright and precocious. We all laughed in wholehearted agreement with the diagnosis.

We were preparing to leave when Dr. Jones suggested I also should undergo a routine examination. This hadn't been my intent, but I could hardly disagree under the scrutiny of my daughter and my friend. Laura assured me she and Adeline would keep Sophie occupied.

"So how are you feeling these days, Catherine?" Dr. Jones's blue gaze met mine over his frameless half spectacles. His hair was completely grey, and his cheeks sagged more than when I'd seen him five years before, but he still had that grandfatherly expression that made you feel you might tell him anything.

"I'm doing very well. Thank you, doctor." I put on my most convincing smile. "The children are growing like weeds. We have a comfortable home, and Claude's businesses are thriving. We are truly blessed."

"Have there been further miscarriages?"

I shook my head no, keeping my gaze on my lap to avoid his eyes.

"Catherine, you do understand the danger you and the child would be in if you became pregnant?" He tilted his head to catch my eye. "We almost lost you the last time. You're taking the precautions I suggested?"

"I did have a miscarriage last year," I admitted. "I was barely two months along, just a little bleeding. It only took me a couple of days to recover." I raised my eyes to meet his. "I do understand the ramifications, Dr. Jones, but there's a part of me that sometimes longs for another baby." I could never share with Dr. Jones or his wife the feeling I had that having another child might help fill the hole in my soul named Amelia.

Dr. Jones leaned across his desk. "I won't pretend to understand the yearning, but if it's any consolation, you're not alone. After our third child, Laura dearly wanted a fourth." The doctor removed his glasses. "Unfortunately, we were unsuccessful in conceiving. It weighed on her for some time. Perhaps it would help you to speak with her, you know, woman to woman."

"Yes, thank you, doctor." *That could never happen.* But his warning about further pregnancies did leave me shaken.

I rejoined Adeline and Laura who were laughing as Sophie regaled them with tales of her kitten, Lucy.

We said our goodbyes.

Accustomed to the limitations of John Hall's General Store in Nelsonville, we were anxious to uncover the riches of our first shopping trip in Webbwood. Our first stop was Goodman's General Store. In addition to purchasing the usual flour, sugar, and oats, I indulged in small amounts of spices, tea, coffee, and cheese. Sophie spent the majority of her time viewing the brightly coloured sweets in the penny candy jars.

Having arranged for the delivery of the food purchases to our storage crib, we explored the other shops. Sophie wandered along behind us, clutching her small paper sack of candy, sucking on a red-and-white peppermint stick and gawking through the open shop doors.

"Maman, why are those ladies all wearing the same dark blue dresses and black aprons? Their caps look cool." Sophie gestured to a group of women hurrying across the street.

"Shh. Sophie. If you have a question, come and ask me quietly." I brought her close. "Those ladies are Mennonites."

"What are Mennonites?"

"They're a group of people who all follow the same religion. They live according to their beliefs in their own communities."

Sophie tilted her head in a moment of thought.

I waited for the next question.

"Okay," she said. "Can we look for the Alice book?"

I almost snorted out loud. Adeline chuckled beside me.

"Thanks for reminding me. Let's look in Sadowski's Dry Goods."

"I'd like to visit the tailor, first," Adeline said, gesturing to the store beside us. "Maybe I can find a shirt for Maurice." Happily, we found affordable ready-made shirts and pants for Claude, Jean-Pierre, and Maurice at Favreau's Men's Wear.

Stepping into Sadowski's was like entering a treasure chest. Everything—fabric, kitchen needs, hardware, and more—crowded the floor-to-ceiling shelves behind the U-shaped wooden counter. Sophie pressed palm prints into the glass fronts of the counter, admiring the jewelry displays while in search of her book. The tedium of hand sewing clothes was not my favourite way to pass precious free time, but women's ready-made clothes were too expensive. I bought wool cloth to make winter skirts for Sophie and me. Adeline selected enough tiny floral print in the light cotton material I wore for two maternity dresses.

Sophie appeared at my side, pulling on my arm. When I leaned down, she whispered, "I found the Alice book, maman."

"Excellent. Help me select wool for sweaters for us all, and then we'll ask the lady to bring out the book." Knitting was something I did enjoy, especially on those snowy days when we were stuck indoors. We also selected wool for the coming Gagnon baby. I intended to pass my baby clothes on to Adeline, but a new knitted sweater would make a nice Christmas gift. I arranged for our purchases to be delivered to the storage crib though Sophie was adamant that she'd carry her book. Finally, it was Adeline who convinced her to give it up, pointing to the rain wetting the shop's windows.

With our shopping completed, we purchased lemonade at Mary's Café and settled ourselves on a bench in the churchyard, munching our picnic lunch of bread and cheese. The tree over our bench offered sufficient shelter from the slow rain.

"Kate? Kate!" I recognized the German-accented voice. A short, rotund, woman was gesturing at us from across the street. "Oh my goodness, it *is* you!"

My heart rate accelerated like a racehorse in mid-gallop. I couldn't deny knowing the woman without creating a scene, but she was the only other person who knew my secret. Could I trust her to keep mum? "Sophie, stay here with Adeline. I'll be right back." I ran across the street. The wagons passing behind me blocked us momentarily from view.

"Elisabeth. How wonderful to see you! I go by Catherine now," I blurted.

The smile on Elisabeth's face froze briefly, head tilted to one side. As the wagons moved on, she came to life, linked her arm in mine, and we crossed the street.

"This is my dear friend Elisabeth Schroeder. She and I knew each other when I first arrived in Nelsonville. This is my friend Adeline and—"

"And your daughter. She may not have your colouring, but she has your spirit shining from her eyes. I would know her as yours anywhere." Elisabeth shook Sophie's hand. "What's your name?"

"My name is Sophie. Why did you call my *maman*, Kate?"

"*Ach*, when I knew your maman many years ago, I called her Kate as a nickname. She reminded me of a fairy princess I knew," Elisabeth explained with a twinkle in her clear blue eyes. "Do you have a nickname?" As Sophie shook her head, Elisabeth continued, "Looks like it will rain all day. Would you like to come to my home for *Kaffee und Kuchen*—that's coffee and cake? My farm is on the edge of town, five minutes from here. Yes?"

At the mention of cake, Sophie dispelled any confusion about names from her mind. "Can we, maman? I don't drink *Kaffee,* but I like *Kuchen.*"

My panic bubble popped. I could count on Elisabeth to follow my lead in the conversations. "Well, we do have some time before our train . . . What do you think, Adeline?"

"Oh, I do not want to intrude on your reunion. I can stay here or in the church."

"Nonsense. A friend of Ka— Catherine's is always welcome in my home. Besides, it looks like the baby will be coming in a few months?" Elisabeth nodded to Adeline's abdomen. "I have some teas and ointments to make you more comfortable. Come, come."

Our oiled silk umbrellas protected us from the heavy drizzle as we marched along behind Elisabeth.

"This is the house my husband built for us when we first settled here." The Schroeder home was one room, made of logs. "Paul, my son . . . you remember him, don't you, Catherine? Of course, you do. Well, a few years ago, Paul and I added the summer kitchen in the back. Last winter, we bought a wood stove, so much easier for cooking and baking than the fireplace." The white-washed gate creaked. Elisabeth led us up the stone pathway toward the bright red door. "I will live here until I die, with the spirit of my husband wrapped around me in every log."

Beyond the red barn and several smaller sheds, an acre of land burgeoned with green plants standing in disciplined, well-weeded rows guarding the vegetable treasures they nurtured.

"Come in. Sit." She gestured to the round table under the front window. "I will make coffee."

While Elisabeth stirred up the coals and set the kettle on the stove against the back wall, Adeline and I settled around the table. Sophie wandered through the sleeping area clustered opposite the kitchen, trailing her hand over the multi-coloured knitted blanket covering the bed, passing the pine wardrobe, and admiring the photo in a carved wood frame on the dresser.

"Where is your husband?"

"Sophie, we don't ask that. I'm sorry, Elisabeth."

"*Ach,* it is the way of children. Sophie, my husband was killed many years ago while working the spring river drive."

"Your gardens are beautiful. There are so many flowers I don't recognize and others I haven't seen since I left home," remarked Adeline, admiring the view of the front flower gardens through the lace-curtained window above the table.

"Thank you. Many of those are herbs and flowers for my medicines. I have collected them from many places and interesting people over the years." Elisabeth's ample cheeks pinked with the joy of having found a gardening kindred spirit.

Happy to let Adeline and Elisabeth continue their conversation, I kept a watchful eye on Sophie, who was now testing the comfort of the brown horsehair settee, rocker, and wingback chair clustered around a window opposite our table. Crocheted ivory antimacassars adorned the backs of the furniture, and an oval braided rag rug graced the plank floor.

Sophie resumed her exploration, attracted by the display of hand-painted porcelain cups and saucers and floral serving plates in the flat-to-the-wall pine cabinet. I was about to warn her not to touch the china when Elisabeth arrived at her side, inviting her to select a cup and saucer for each of us, and explaining how she and her husband had brought these dishes all the way from her home country across the ocean. Then, the two of them moved back to the kitchen, where Elisabeth engaged Sophie in arranging the cake pieces and cookies on the plate. The two heads, one blond with pronounced greying streaks, and one a lustrous chestnut brown, almost touched as they bent over their task.

"So are you still working in the camps?" I asked Elisabeth, as we enjoyed our coffee and apple-cinnamon pound cake.

"About four years ago, I stopped. Since the railway came in 1883, there is so much lumbering going on, too many men crowded into small bunkhouses. So many fights. I did not want that life for my Paul." Elisabeth went on to explain how she and Paul had created a six-bed bunkhouse for lumberjacks in the loft of their barn. They employed them to clear and work their land during the summers.

"Now, I act as the agent for a cooperative of farm wives. We sell fruit and berries, vegetables, meats, baking, cheese and knitted socks to the camps."

I grinned at Elisabeth. She'd realized her plan just as she'd described it to Mr. Campbell.

We learned Paul, now nineteen, was to be married in September to a Mennonite girl named Anna.

"Does Anna wear a dark blue dress and black apron?" Sophie asked.

Elisabeth looked confused. "She does but her apron is white."

"We saw a group of Mennonite women in town," Adeline explained.

"Do you think she'd give me one of her cool caps?" Sophie asked.

"Sophie," I exclaimed. "That isn't nice. Besides, you can't wear one. You're not Mennonite."

Elisabeth offered Sophie an oatmeal cookie and resumed her story. "Paul has built a two-room house at the other end of the property for him and his bride. They will be near, but I'll keep my own house." Elisabeth's eyes glistened with pride. "Paul is the town clerk, and he helps work the farm with me."

My heart swelled to hear of their success, feeling I may have played a small part in assisting them, just as they had saved my life almost a decade ago.

In response to her questions, I told Elisabeth a little about Claude and our life together until the time came for us to return to the station and catch our train. "Do we have to go, maman?" wailed Sophie. "It's so cozy here."

We all felt the sense of sanctuary Elisabeth's simple little home wrapped around us like a mother's arms.

"Yes, but I'm sure Elisabeth will invite us back."

"Of course, my home is always open to you. Before you go, come with me." Elisabeth led us into the summer kitchen where she selected jars from a wall of shelves, stacking them on the wooden worktable in the centre of the room. She began opening each container and wafting it under Adeline's nose before measuring portions into envelopes and small jars. "I am giving you a tea of chamomile and a little rosemary to help with digestion as the baby gets larger. Here is an alfalfa and bear grease ointment for back pain, which will help now and during labour, and this sage and beaver fat cream you must use after the baby is born."

Adeline nodded, catching each direction as it dropped like a penny from the older woman's wisdom. "Rub the cream on your abdomen each day, and it will help tighten the skin again. It is also good to help soothe your lower parts after the baby is born, and you can even use it on the baby's bum."

"*Merci*, you are so kind. Maybe one day we can spend some time in your garden?"

"*Ach*, of course. It would be my pleasure. Now, Sophie, please take Adeline to the worktable. You will find two packages of *Kuchen*, one for you and your family and one for Adeline to take home. I need to speak to your maman for a moment, and then we will walk to the station."

Once the two had left the room, Elisabeth turned to me. "Kate, you have made a good life. I was worried when you left me that spring." As I opened my mouth to speak, Elisabeth placed her hand on my arm and interjected, "No, no. Don't be afraid. Your past is safe with me. I am so happy that we might see each other when you come to Webbwood—right?"

As she turned to join the others, I touched her shoulder. "We'll definitely visit. I'm excited to have you in our life." I choked, eyes glistening with tears. Dr. Jones's warning still troubled me. "I do have one request though. Do you have any of that tea that prevents pregnancy?" I gestured at the wall of jars.

"Of course I do." I watched Elisabeth reach for several jars and prepare small linen sachets, thinking what a remarkable person this woman was, her heart as big as the land around us. "This is a mild mixture of blue cohosh which will stimulate the uterus. It is good to drink during your fertile periods to discourage pregnancy. If you are concerned you may have become pregnant, then, use this one—Queen Anne's Lace—the morning after." She held up each packet in turn. "Finally, here is some smartweed. This stops bleeding, and I thought it might be good for you to have it for Adeline in case she has a problem after birth. I didn't want to scare her." I gave Elisabeth a big hug, and then we turned and joined Sophie and Adeline. Fortunately, the rain had stopped, and the sun was already drying the high ground.

At the station, I supervised the loading of our goods from the storage crib onto the train while Sophie, Adeline, and Elisabeth chatted on the platform. When it was time to leave, Sophie wrapped her arms around Elisabeth's ample waist, gave her a big kiss, and promised to visit again soon.

Moments after the train departed the station, Sophie dropped off to sleep with her head in my lap. Adeline and I talked quietly for a few minutes before each of us retreated into our own thoughts. My mind chugged along to the rhythm of the train's wheels over the tracks. How was Claude going to react to our encounter with Elisabeth today? Sooner than I expected, my musings were interrupted by the conductor announcing our arrival at Stanley Station.

STRAWBERRIES

Chapter Eleven

The screech of a blue jay jolted me from sleep. Rolling onto my back, I felt the coldness of the empty space beside me. Claude's work clothes were gone from their hook. Ever since my excursion to Webbwood, he'd broken our morning routine. We'd usually lie in the warmth and love of each other's arms before rising together. It had been four days now without him, and I'd had enough.

If only Sophie hadn't gone into such detail upon our return from Webbwood. Jean-Pierre's eyes had grown wide at his sister's descriptions of the riches in the stores and the sounds of the crowded street.

"How was the train ride?" Claude asked her.

"The scenery moved so fast, but it got boring. Just rocks, trees, water. And we passed a bear. The whistle was so loud it hurt my teeth."

Claude mouthed "nothing" at me, eyebrows raised.

I shook my head.

Claude's shoulders relaxed.

But Sophie had saved the best part of her story for last. "This is *Kuchen* from Oma Elisabeth." With an air of drama, she'd placed the package in the centre of our table after supper.

The smile froze on my face. For a moment, the world stopped turning. As Sophie explained the meaning of *Kuchen* and who *Oma* Elisabeth was, Claude's back became rigid. The dawning realization we'd stumbled on a piece of my past etched deep creases across his brow.

Apparently, while waiting at the station for the train, Sophie had confided to Elisabeth she didn't have a grandmother and had asked if Elisabeth would be interested in the role. Elisabeth responded she would be honoured and suggested they use the term *Oma* from her native German.

"She can be your *Oma* too, J.P. She has a son, Paul, who's getting married soon. Can we go to the wedding, maman?" Sophie unwrapped the package. "Here, J.P., try this." She cut a ragged corner and passed it to her brother.

"Elisabeth?' Claude hissed.

I put my finger to my lips. "You remember, the cook at the lumber camp." I whispered.

"You took our daughter to her house?" He gave me the one-eyebrow-raised look. "What were you thinking?"

"Claude, it's okay. We can trust her. She won't say anything about where I'm from." I smiled to disarm him.

"You mean, she knows all of it?" His upper lip curled.

I nodded slowly, hands up in a placating gesture.

His fist hit the table.

The children jumped.

I glared him into silence. "Bedtime," I announced. "Up you go." Both children pecked their father on the cheek and climbed the ladder to the loft. Neither asked for a bedtime story.

By the time they were settled, Claude was already in bed, eyes closed, back to me. I crawled in beside him, relieved we could put off discussion until morning. Since then, he had been working from early morning until late at night. This morning, I decided, we would talk.

The horses whinnied as I strode past the weeping willows in the pasture, early morning dew dampening the hem of my skirt. The rough planked shed on the riverbank reverberated with the laboured buzz of the saw. In the gentle breeze, smoke billowed into the air and floated over the river. I peered inside. Powdered sawdust shone in the shaft of sunlight from the single window, illuminating my lover's silhouette. He muscled a log into position like the next offering to the saw god.

He sensed my presence and turned off the machine.

"Claude, we need to talk," I said to his back.

"I don't know what there is to talk about." He turned to look at me. "Have you thought about what would happen to us if people knew where you come from?"

"I can't control random events like running into Elisabeth on the street."

"And to hear of this latest incident from my daughter?"

"When was there an opportunity for me to tell you? Claude, be reasonable."

"*Maudit*, Catherine! I thought it was reasonable to want to protect the ones you love, but how do I protect you from this?" The blood mounted above his shirt collar, visible through his tan.

I threw my arms in the air. "You knew from the beginning who I was and where I came from."

"*Écoute*, Catherine. You don't understand the people here. Remember the Lalondes? People in Nelsonville thought Manon's habit of decorating her porch with raven feathers and strings of fish-eyes was harmless until Eleanor Fensom said she'd seen her dancing nude on her porch in the full moon."

"Come on, Claude. No one believed that."

"John Hall told me whenever Manon came into his store, the other women all left. Mothers didn't let their children play with the Lalonde children. The next summer, they were gone."

"All right, but we're out here in the middle of nowhere."

"Enough!" His eyes darkened. He turned his back and slammed his fist into the log sitting on the saw.

"Claude, what's going on?"

He hunched over. I touched his back.

After a long moment, he raised his head. New stress lines marred his brow, and his cheeks seemed suddenly to have shrunken. "*Chérie*, I'm sorry. There's something I should've told you long ago."

He took a deep breath, but I placed my index finger across his lips and tilted my head toward the door. Two heads were peering around the jamb.

"First one to the house gets to decide how the eggs will be cooked," I said.

The two children ran ahead.

"I should never have kept this secret, *chérie*." Claude followed the children, turning back at the door. "I promise I'll tell you everything tonight."

* * *

The pines turned to flat black as the sun sank behind them. Spring peepers launched into their nightly mating ritual, their high-pitched seduction song jingling like bells of hope. Claude mounted the ladder to tuck our children in for the night, and I pictured the evening ritual—Lucy, the striped tabby kitten nestled into her little basket beside Sophie's bed, Snoopy settled down in his wooden box on the opposite wall. Jean-Pierre had been persuasive concerning this arrangement, pointing out the pets were still babies. Neither Claude nor I found it in our hearts to ban the two little animals to the outdoors.

"Papa, we need a bedtime story. Pleeeeeease," Sophie begged.

Jean-Pierre piped up, "Tell us more about Claude."

A moment's silence. Then, "Where did I leave off?"

I positioned myself on the bottom rung of the ladder.

Jean-Pierre jumped in. "Claude went to the city and became an engineer. Papa was that when you married my maman?"

"Who says this story is about me?"

"Well, papa, your name is Claude," Jean-Pierre pointed out, "and you're an engineer."

Claude cleared his throat. "You're right. I knew your maman from the time we were children. We married and moved to Montreal. That's where you were born."

"Where is my real maman?"

"J.P., you remember I told you, your maman became very ill after you were born."

"Do you miss her, papa?"

"I did for a very long time, *mon fils*."

"Is that why we moved here?"

"*Oui*, Jean-Pierre."

"And that's when you found my new maman?"

"And me, J.P.," Sophie piped up. "Without maman you wouldn't have me as your sister."

"That's right, *mes enfants*. Your maman and I found each other. Now, under the covers."

"Papa, was my real maman as nice as maman?"

"Yes, my son."

My cheeks were wet.

"Okay, you two. Sweet dreams."

Claude descended the ladder, took my hand, and led me out to our porch bench. We watched the stars appear as the light faded, fingers entwined. The soothing soughing of the wind through the pines enveloped us.

"*Chérie*, I told you Gisèle died in childbirth." He paused. "That's not true. There's something I've never told anyone since I left home."

My stomach clenched, but I kept my expression neutral as I nodded. How did she die? I kept my silence.

"Gisèle and I married as soon as I completed my studies. We moved into a two-room apartment in Montreal, and before long, Gisèle was with child."

It was difficult to hear the joy in Claude's voice, but I reminded myself, the important thing was we were together now.

Claude continued, "I insisted Gisèle live at home with her parents for the final few months. All went well with the birth, but imagine our surprise when we became the parents of twins—a boy and a girl."

I stared at him. Had I heard right?

"Jean-Pierre and a girl, Janine. Gisèle was eager to have our family together, so when Janine and Jean-Pierre were a month old, she returned to Montreal. I surprised her with a larger apartment."

Claude paused for such a long time I began to wonder if he was emotionally overcome. "I'm sorry. I know it must be hard for you."

"I need to hear it." I gripped the edge of the swing, resisting the urge to reach out and touch him.

He took a breath and went on. "A few months into our new life, influenza hit the city. Before long, some of the children in our building became ill. Gisèle and I agreed she and the babies should return to Compton. She was to take the train the next morning."

It was completely dark outside now. Claude's voice was raspy from talking. I suggested we move inside to our bedroom.

We settled in our chairs across from each other. The lantern on the mantle dissipated the shadows from Claude's face. "That night, Janine came down with the fever. We tried everything to cool her. I took Jean-Pierre to our neighbours' apartment. It was horrible watching my baby daughter, lying in her cradle, struggling for breath."

Claude was crying now. "Janine died the next day. Gisèle was inconsolable. I scrubbed everything in the apartment, hoping J.P.'s return would bring her out of her despair." He took a shuddering breath. "Days turned into weeks. Gisèle continued to sit in front of the fire, rocking while she clutched Janine's blanket."

Claude turned to me, reaching for my hands. "It was terrible. She wouldn't care for herself. She ignored J.P. I couldn't reach her." He bent forward, his head in his hands, and I stroked his hair.

He looked up. "I can't lose you, Catherine."

"I'm not going anywhere," I murmured. "How did Gisèle die?"

He took a deep breath. "She didn't."

My eyes grew wide.

"She's still alive."

I clenched the arms of the chair. Claude's mouth was moving, but I couldn't hear him above the drumming in my ears. He squeezed my hands, stroked my face, smoothed my hair. Finally, his voice broke through. "Catherine, Gisèle's in a hospital for lunatics in Montreal."

I stared into the black fireplace. "You deserted her?" My voice cracked.

"I send money each year. The doctors told me there was nothing they could do. J.P. and I needed a fresh start."

I saw the pleading in his eyes. "You let J.P. think his mother was dead?"

"Catherine, he was a baby. You're the only mother he's ever known."

"Doesn't he deserve to know the truth? Do you want your son to live a lie?" My voice was rising with each word.

Claude's head remained in his hands for a long time. "Aren't we all living a lie right now?" His voice was barely audible through his fingers.

"We let people assume we're married to protect our children." I retorted. "Now I know why you never mentioned marriage." I stood and began pacing in front of the fireplace, reaching to touch him, pulling back, wrapping my hands across my stomach. "I'm such a fool!" I dropped onto the edge of the bed.

Claude turned to face me. "We have a good life together. What would be gained from revealing the details of our pasts?"

I was tempted to go to him. Could he be right?

"Catherine, please. She was gone. J.P. would have been a pariah. Nothing needs to change." He leaned into me.

I wanted to reassure him. But was it really possible to just move forward? "What if Gisèle is well and wants you back? What if someone from your past finds us?"

Claude jumped to his feet. "I'll never leave you." He grabbed me by the shoulders. "What about you? Should I live in fear you'll one day leave me to return to your old life?"

"Maman!" Sophie cried out from the loft. "*Les monstres,* maman!"

I rushed from our room and climbed up the ladder. I gathered Sophie in my arms, rocking her. Soft snores from the other bed told me Jean-Pierre hadn't been disturbed. As soon as Sophie was breathing evenly, I stretched out beside her, unwilling to return to my own bed.

STRAWBERRIES

Chapter Twelve

I lay in the dark, my daughter's even breathing tickling my neck. I hadn't attempted to return to my old life for years, but Amelia and Gran travelled with me daily. Watching Sophie, I'd catch myself wondering whether Amelia was doing the same things. Each night, I sent a prayer of thanks to Gran.

As the first light of dawn painted the sky, I disengaged Sophie's limbs from around my body, and slipped down the ladder. Claude lay sprawled face down across our bed, fully clothed, cheek mashed by the pillow. My fingers longed to push back the auburn locks falling across his brow.

After scribbling a short note asking him to feed the children when they awoke, I made my way down the hill to the river. He'd know where I was going. Claude's respect for how I processed inner turmoil was one more reason I loved him so much.

I dragged our cedar strip canoe into the water and kneeled just back from the centre, my skirt folded under my knees. A few strong paddle strokes propelled me into the reflection of rosy dawn on the water. The current under the smooth surface pulled southwest toward Lake Huron.

To my right, sandhill cranes instructed their youngsters how to forage along the shore. The young birds appeared ready to topple from the height of their spindly legs as they pecked at the plants along the water's edge. Their parents, barely discernible within the foliage, kept vigil. A beaver head popped to the surface, swimming about ten feet off my left gunwale, keeping pace with me. We continued our side-by-side journey for nearly a mile until he peeled left toward a finger bay. With several slaps of his broad, flat tail, he dove beneath the surface toward the pile of sticks and mud on the far bank.

Towering pines leaned out over the water, their root base eroded by winter damage. Around the next sweeping bend, the iron railway bridge spanned the narrow part of the river, precisely as William Van Horne had planned. Water eddied around the two stone pier supports. Amazing. From treacherous wilderness to a booming chain of towns in less than a decade thanks to a railroad, and I'd had a front-row seat through it all.

I tied both ends of the canoe against a clump of bushes on the right shore and clambered up the rock face, slipping on lichen, shimmering grey-green in the morning light.

I walked the ties for twenty feet along the track away from the bridge to where a faint path of flattened grass veered left. A few steps off the mound of the track bed, I slipped through a shoulder-width parting in the birches. The clearing opened out before me. Earthy aromas rose from the springy moss underfoot. Midges and pollen danced in the shafts of sunlight piercing through gaps in the leafy canopy. This place had been the root of my terror. Over the years, I'd avoided it despite my earlier unsuccessful attempts to return to my own time. Today it was the only place I could think of to go. Settling on a log with my back against a solitary boulder, I started to reason my way through the chaos in my head.

"Okay, so, a man travelling with a baby would stir up questions. A wife lost in childbirth was a plausible explanation. But why didn't he tell *me* the truth?"

I began pacing around the clearing. I'd trusted him, told him everything. What if Gisèle had recovered and came looking for him? She had a legitimate claim on him. What else hadn't he told me?

Head flung back, arms wide, I shouted, "Fuuuck!"

Birds fled to the sky.

I slumped back onto my log, folding forward like a deflated balloon. Gran's voice insinuated itself into my head. *Got that out of your system?* I nodded to the empty clearing, scrubbed my palms across my wet cheeks. *Good. Now that you know what you know, what are you going to do with it?*

I sat silent, gathering my thoughts. A doe and its fawn stepped tentatively into the clearing. The mother pulled down a cedar branch, holding it for her baby to nibble.

Claude would do anything for his children. I saw his love for me in his eyes, felt it in his hands. He was a gentle lover, hard worker, didn't drink, or gamble—a good man. I thought we'd built a beautiful life together . . . until yesterday.

I hugged my arms around my middle. Gisèle could unravel it all. Maybe I should go now before I was pushed out.

A rabbit, brown summer sweater pushing into its winter white trousers, hopped into the edge of the clearing. The doe stared, unmoving. The fawn dropped its head toward the rabbit, and then they all melted into the trees.

I picked up dead leaves at my feet, shredded them, then threw them onto the moss carpet. I could go to Sainte-Anne-des-Pins or even Toronto. But, what about Sophie? She was mine . . . but she was also his. Could I support us without him?

Standing to stretch my legs, I circled the clearing, the fingers of my outstretched hand rifling through the ragged edges of the birch bark fringes. I loved him. I loved our children. So . . . stay?

I kicked a crumbling pine log. Hundreds of black ants abandoned their home.

Claude hadn't seen Gisèle in a decade. I'd tell him he needed to go see her.

Finally feeling a sense of control, I dropped onto my log, leaned back, and closed my eyes. The wavering five-tone whistle of the white-throated sparrows calling to each other lulled me to sleep.

* * *

The earth trembled. A sharp whistle. Loud roaring battered my ears. Letting out a cry, I leaped to my feet, and a gust of wind hit me in the chest. "No, no, no!" I screamed. I lost my breath and fell to my knees, pressing my forehead into the moss, hands over my ears.

It seemed like forever before the ground stopped moving. I felt rough hands pulling mine from my face. Arms encircled my body. Familiar scent. Hoarse murmuring, "Catherine, it's me. Shh, *mon amour.*"

I relaxed into Claude's chest, his heartbeat strong and steady in my ear. "It was the train." My voice quavered. "My God, I was terrified I'd gone back."

He held me tighter. His lips sought mine. His caresses became insistent.

"Stop." I pushed him away.

He dropped his arms. His eyes wounded.

"You call me your wife, your lover, so why didn't you tell me the truth?" My arms came out from my sides, palms up.

He knelt in the moss at my feet. "*Chèrie*, I wanted to. I almost did the day you told me your story. But . . . time went on . . . Sophie came . . . We're so happy." His palm warmed a spot on my outstretched leg. "I was scared you'd leave me." His eyes held mine. "I'm sorry. What can I do?"

"I need to know there are no other secrets."

"None." His eyes didn't waver.

I met his gaze. "Gisèle might have recovered and be looking for you . . ."

Claude maintained a profound stillness. His struggle whipped his facial features like the wind raising waves on the river. "I haven't seen her since I left with J.P. The reports that used to come from the institution each year started coming through my brother, François, three years ago." His face calmed. He stood, put his hands on my shoulders, and looked deeply into my eyes. "After the harvest, I'll take the train to Montreal."

"Thank you."

He held my hand as we walked out of the clearing.

"Where are the children?"

"J.P. is helping Maurice with the addition, and Sophie is decorating the crib with Adeline." He stopped and turned me to him. "When I read your note, I knew where I'd find you." His face clouded. "When I heard your screams, I ran like a madman behind the train."

"I thought the jump was happening."

"And you didn't want it to?"

I looked out at the river. "No, I didn't." Amelia is in my thoughts every day, but I trust Gran will make sure she's always loved. Turning back to Claude, I put my hand on his arm. "I belong here with you and our children, but secrets have a way of clawing their way to the surface. I can't be at peace until we know Gisèle's state."

He held me, whispering into my hair, "I promise I'll find out in the fall."

STRAWBERRIES

Chapter Thirteen

Alouette, gentille alouette
Alouette, je te plumerai.

Je te plumerai la queue
Je te plumerai la queue
Et la queue, et la queue
Alouette, Alouette
A—a—a—ah

Maurice's baritone led us through the folk song, telling the story of how we plucked the lark in retribution for having woken us. The pines had echoed with our singing off and on for two hours. Sunlight dappled the auburn flanks of the two horses pulling our wagon along the road to Nelsonville. Maurice and Claude took turns on the reins from the raised front seat, while Adeline and I chatted on the benches in the back. The children spent their time searching the passing forest for signs of animal life.

"Sophie, J.P., *regarde*! A moose." Claude put his finger to his lips as he pointed into the swamp at the curve of the river. Maurice brought the horses to a halt. We stared through the trees as the moose raised its antlered head, chewing pensively on water plants and assessing our presence. Maurice's soft tongue clicked, sending the horses forward.

Sophie broke into song, her sweet, clear voice rising on the warm air, filling the open space above us.

> *Land of the silver birch*
> *Home of the beaver*
> *Where still the mighty moose*
> *Wanders at will*

At the end of her song, she took a bow to our applause.

"Why does the community hold a Strawberry Social on July first each year?" Adeline asked the children.

After a moment of thought, Jean-Pierre responded, "It's the day Canada became a country."

"This is like Canada's birthday," Sophie added.

I joined in. "What year was Canada born as a country?"

"1867," Jean-Pierre said. "Sooooo . . . Canada is twenty-one years old today."

"*Bravo, les enfants!*" Adeline praised.

"Are we there yet?" Sophie moved back and forth between the benches. "It's taking all day!"

"Don't be a baby, Sophie," Jean-Pierre teased her. "It's only been a couple hours, right, papa?"

"*Oui.*" Claude turned around. "And here we are. Over the track and into Nelsonville." More than a dozen new houses had sprouted next to the original seven I'd seen on my first visit nine years ago. The new railway station with its raw plank platform was identical to the one in Webbwood. A two-storey addition on one side accommodated the stationmaster, Joseph Edwards, his wife Margaret, and their six children.

"Why does it say Nelson Station and not Nelsonville?" Jean-Pierre asked, pointing at the black-and-white sign mounted on the station wall.

Rhubarb, Strawberries, and Willows

"The government named it Nelson Station." Claude's smile tightened. "We didn't argue. We were just happy to get a stop."

Maurice brought the wagon to a halt. "Everybody out."

Claude jumped down to help us disembark.

Maurice manoeuvred our wagon into a spot among at least twenty other buckboards, the mini-vans of 1888, crammed into the gravel area in front of the station. Claude and Maurice each led a horse to the pasture beyond the Spanish River Lumber Company's stable, then joined the men gathered along the pasture's split-cedar-rail fence, one foot resting on the bottom rail.

"Sophieeee!" A petite girl of Sophie's age ran toward us. Her mother, Estelle Beaudry waved in greeting from under the trees. She and two other women were spreading white cloths on a long table where the strawberry desserts would be displayed.

"Mariiiiie!" Sophie responded.

Jean-Pierre cringed. "Oh, no."

"Now, J.P., be nice."

"But, maman, she's such a pest, with that squeaky voice and her black curly hair flying everywhere. Can I go find Joey Jr.?"

"Remember to find us when the lunch box auction begins."

The two girls collided in a hug as Jean-Pierre hurried away in the opposite direction.

"So many people . . ." Adeline stared wide-eyed. Vendors had set up their booths along the edge of the field.

"Fresh cool lemonade here, folks!"

"We've got licorice, peppermint, cherry candy!"

Travelling pedlars clanged pots with spoons, "Step right up!"

A sign reading Church Fund hung in front of a line of tables. Preserves and jams glowed red, orange, and purple in the sunlight. Knitted socks, hats, and mittens lay in close ranks. Hazel Jeffries waved and mouthed, Thank you, from behind the tables. I'd donated several jars of strawberry rhubarb jam and three pairs of socks to the cause.

While Jean-Pierre and Joey Jr. joined the baseball game in the distant corner, Sophie and Marie played Red Rover with the other girls. Groups of women good-naturedly shooed away children playing tag around their legs.

Adeline and I left our desserts with one of Estelle's helpers.

"Catherine, so nice to see you. That blue plaid really becomes you."

I turned to the middle-aged woman who had come up beside me. "Thank you. Clara Hall, this is my neighbour, Adeline Gagnon."

Clara took Adeline's hand in both of hers. "Welcome." New grey strands were showing in Clara's light brown hair. "My husband and I own the General Store." She nodded toward the wide wooden building with a full veranda across from the station, the pine so fresh it glowed golden in the sunshine.

"It's very grand," Adeline said. "Do you live upstairs?"

Clara shook her head. "No, that's our hotel. I've had to live with the store in my house for almost ten years." She pointed behind her to the house where the sign had hung in earlier times. "I'm finished with being surrounded by canned goods, farm tools, and rough men just to be able to enjoy a fire in the evening."

We were sharing a sympathetic laugh when Margaret Edwards and a few others joined us. Still statuesque after six children, Margaret had not a hair out of place and a smile so broad that it engulfed her whole face. "You must be about five months along, dear?" she asked, directing a nod at Adeline's abdomen. "Call on me if you need any help."

"Thank you. This is my first child. Catherine's been helping me prepare."

A snort from the hatchet-faced woman beside Margaret.

"I don't believe we've met." I held out my hand to the thin woman, standing stiffly erect. "My name is Catherine Dumont."

"Miss Ida MacGregor," she said in a clipped tone. Ignoring my hand, she turned to Anne MacLean, the woman at her other side. "So that's her? I've heard people say she's odd." Deep wrinkles

Rhubarb, Strawberries, and Willows

puckered around her faded grey eyes. Her tight lips disappeared into the severe lines around her mouth.

Margaret gasped.

Adeline's wide eyes met mine as she put her hand on my arm.

Clara Hall cleared her throat, her brows drawn in a disapproving frown.

Anne, who would never say anything bad about anyone, was red-faced as she led Ida to their picnic site.

The handbell began ringing. People broke out of their groups with hugs and waves. I shook off my discomfort and took Adeline by the elbow to stroll toward where the men had deposited our picnic baskets. Sophie and Marie ran across the field toward us, bonnets occasionally bouncing into view like small parachutes hanging down their backs.

Joseph Edwards mounted the raised platform, his voice booming from his broad chest, capturing everyone's attention as he began the box lunch auction. Each box lunch had been prepared and attractively packaged by one of the single young women giggling nervously at the side of the stage. The maker's identity was intended to remain secret until all the boxes had been auctioned off to the single men gathered in front of the auctioneer. The maker of the lunch and its purchaser would then share the lunch and get to know each other. An interesting take on the blind date, I thought. Inevitably as each box was held up, the girl who'd made it tended to broaden her smile. One young lady went so far as to stare hard at a young man, tilting her head repeatedly from him to the box in Mr. Edwards's hand. Finally, she yelled, "For goodness' sake, Fred, bid!"

Blushing, Fred mumbled, "A dollar!"

The field erupted in laughter.

After our picnic lunch, we joined the line with the other families, moving along the dessert table, plates and forks in hand. In response to each person's request, Clara, Margaret, and Estelle sliced and spooned golden-crusted pies, yellow cakes smothered with strawberries, and deep red crumbles.

Suddenly, a woman's scream broke the atmosphere. "Devil's food!" Ida MacGregor's outstretched arm pointed at me. "She's poisoning us."

My heart began pounding in my ears. Claude moved to one side of me, Maurice to the other. Adeline pulled both children to her.

Margaret's voice rang out, "Now, Ida."

Uneasy comments ran through the crowd.

"What does she mean, devil's food?"

"Who is that woman?"

"Johnny, spit that out right now!"

"Let's settle down everyone." Mr. Edwards's deep voice cut through the commotion. "Now, what seems to be the problem, Miss MacGregor?"

"We must rid our community of this woman." Ida shook a misshapen arthritic finger in my direction. Involuntarily, I stepped backward.

Another wave of mutterings.

"All right, everyone." Turning to his wife, Joseph asked, "Margaret, could you please enlighten us?"

"I'll try," she answered. "After I served Ida a piece of the pie she wanted, she tried to grab the whole thing. She said we needed to throw it away."

"Which pie?" Someone called.

Joseph put up his hands. Everyone hushed.

"It's my pie," said Anne. "When I ran short on strawberries, I remembered Catherine's strawberry rhubarb crumble from a few years ago, so I decided to add rhubarb to my pies this year."

Heads nodded. Margaret added, "Catherine has given many of us cuttings from her rhubarb plants."

"She is not one of us," Ida said. "She and her children have their own way of speaking."

I felt Claude's sharp intake of breath. I pressed up against his side. Ida's voice took on a strident tone. "Her son blasphemed. He said his dog was awesome. Only God is awesome." She thrust her fist into the air. "She must go!"

The crowd walked away, shaking their heads and exchanging comments about the mind of an old woman. Anne spoke in hushed tones to Ida as she led her across the field. Claude's shoulders relaxed next to me.

As Maurice and Adeline took the children and rejoined the line, people approached me, pressing my hand.

"We're sorry, Catherine," Joseph said. "Ida spent her life bringing the Lord's Word to the Indians after her parents and siblings died in a prairie fire. Three decades of deprivation seem to have affected her mind."

His wife added, "We knew Ida when we lived in the Red River Valley. She arrived here last week on the train, confused, exhausted."

Stout Richard Fensom had to tilt back his head to meet our eyes. "Catherine, Claude, you and your children are one of our leading families."

Clara touched my forearm. "Catherine, the women admire you."

I smiled my thanks as Claude and I turned to join our children.

"Claude, Catherine, could we talk for a moment?" Andrew Dever approached us. His earnest grey eyes were free of malice.

Claude and I exchanged a look of 'what now?' Still shaken by Ida's scene, I let Claude answer for us both. "Of course."

Andrew assembled Richard Fensom, Joseph Edwards, John and Clara Hall, and Hector and Anne MacLean to join us. He addressed Claude and I in front of the group. "Recently, we've been talking about the future of our community." The men nodded. Anne and Clara excused themselves from the group, and I started to do the same.

"Ladies, please stay," said Andrew.

A quick look of surprise passed among us as we rejoined the men.

Richard took over in his boyish voice. "Our area is booming. Lumber and rail companies want a stable workforce, men who settle with their families, but families need schools, churches, stores, doctors."

"Saint-Anne-des-Pins has been designated a hub on the transcontinental railroad." Joseph confirmed the rumours we'd been hearing. "It's been incorporated and renamed Sudbury."

Andrew cleared his throat. "There's a new road coming west from Sudbury. We need a bridge across the Spanish so the road will come to Nelsonville."

Emphatic murmurs of agreement.

"I've spoken with our Member of Parliament, James Glendinning." Hector leaned into the group from his six-foot-six height. "He counsels we present a proposal to the provincial government including a plan for the bridge and its benefits to our region."

Andrew asked, "Claude, would you consider working with the railway engineer to draw up the plan for the bridge?"

"If I may?" All eyes moved to Anne. "I think the proposal should include the benefits to the province as well as the region." Her cheeks pinked.

"Yes," said Clara. "After all, the railway has opened up lumbering to the benefit of the mills in the south."

Richard's eyebrows soared up his forehead. Hector and John smiled broadly at their wives.

Andrew turned to me. "Catherine, we'd like you to write the proposal." He smiled. "And it seems you have some able volunteers to assist you."

"We know this process will take considerable time," Hector said. "We need to begin soon, so Nelsonville is included." He turned to us. "Claude, Catherine, are you with us?"

Claude's head tilted slightly as his eyes met mine. "We're honoured to be asked," he said. "Perhaps you could give us some time to consider your request."

"Certainly," said Andrew.

After more encouraging comments and a round of handshakes, our group dispersed.

Claude put his arm around my shoulder as we walked toward our picnic site. "I suppose being asked to assist with the development of the community is a sign of acceptance."

"I don't think we can decline." I slipped my arm around his waist. "Besides, isn't this what we've wanted, a place to belong?"

He squeezed my shoulder. "I'll tell Andrew we'll participate. It'll be getting dark in a few hours. Let's gather our group and get on our way."

I nodded.

"Adeline and I can bring the baskets and meet you at the wagon."

Claude moved across the field with his easy stride, calling Jean-Pierre to him as he joined the group of men where Maurice was chatting.

The trip home was quiet. The wagon's rocking motion lulled Adeline and the children into sleep after a full day of sunshine. The men chatted quietly in the front before dropping into companionable silence. I was left to gaze at the passing fields and forests, alone with my reflections. Ida's reactions to the 1980s expressions made me realize that I might not be fitting into this century as well as I thought. Were her outbursts just the ramblings of an old woman or was there something more behind them? Either way, I resolved to keep my distance until she left. At least the community didn't seem to take her accusations seriously. It was nice to hear their support. And the invitation to contribute to the future of Nelsonville excited me. Based on my research, all the right players were in place. Hector was right—this would be a long process.

STRAWBERRIES

Chapter Fourteen

The creamy interior of the Meeting House glowed in the autumn sun streaming through the windows. It was a modest building without icons or paintings. The wedding would be part of the Sunday worship, no flowers, candles, or other adornments to mark the occasion.

"Maman, why are you smiling?" Sophie whispered. She craned her neck in all directions as groups settled into the honey-toned wooden pews, men and boys on the right and women and girls on the left.

"Just remembering supper last night," I whispered. We had taken the train from Stanley Station to Webbwood to attend Paul and Anna's wedding. At Elisabeth's urging, we were staying in her bunkhouse. The young couple had joined us for supper in Elisabeth's home. At first, Anna kept her eyes on her plate and only spoke when asked a question. Paul couldn't keep the sparkle out of his blue eyes when he looked at her. He'd filled out from the twelve-year-old beanpole I remembered, strong back and muscular limbs, but not much taller.

"Oma Elisabeth, this *Kuchen* is delicious," Sophie said, digging into her piece of almond pound cake.

"Mmm," Jean-Pierre agreed around a mouthful.

Elisabeth planted a kiss on the top of each child's head.

I caught Anna's grey eyes. "You two must be very excited about tomorrow," I said. "Was it hard convincing your parents to allow the marriage?"

Anna smiled. "A few months after Paul and I met, my mother started talking to me about marriage. I reminded her that our community didn't have any single men right now."

"We knew we were meant to be together." Paul ran his hand tenderly across Anna's fingers where they rested on the table.

Her face lit up. "I arranged for Paul to run into Mama and me in front of the café one afternoon."

"One cup of tea with me, and *Mutter* Ratzlaff knew I was the answer to her prayers," Paul grinned.

Anna laughed, strawberry-blond strands escaping her prayer cap. "That evening, Mama asked me how I felt about Paul. I told her I wanted to be his wife." Roses bloomed on her cheeks. "Soon, she had my father, my uncles, and my grandfather wanting to meet him."

Paul leaned forward conspiratorially. "I have to confess, that was an awkward meeting." He leaned back. "But I must have passed because the next thing I knew, the pastor was inviting me to be baptized."

Sophie's tug on my sleeve brought me back to the Meeting House. "Look, the women are wearing flowered dresses today."

I rested a hand on her knee. "Maybe the blue ones are work dresses, and these are for Sundays."

"Why do the men all have beards?"

"It's part of their religion." People were beginning to stare. "Now, shush, Sophie."

My eyes followed Claude and Jean-Pierre walking down the aisle, one mature and one new edition of the same tanned, slender frame. They slid into their places on the men's side of the room. We shared a smile as Claude's eyes met mine over his shoulder.

"Maman, it's starting." Sophie wiggled in excitement beside me.

The pastor moved to the front of the assembly where a dozen men and women formed a double semi-circle. The congregation rose as one. The assembled choir filled the space with their song in four-part harmony, and after the first line, the congregation joined in. Closing my eyes, I absorbed the layers of sound. Birds singing, water flowing over rocks, wind blowing in the leaves, all at the same time.

Sophie whispered, "I want to learn to sing like that."

I opened my eyes to the wonder shining on my daughter's face. I hugged her close.

In his sermon, the pastor spoke about the duties of husbands and wives. He called upon Anna and Paul to come forward. Paul was dressed in a brown wool suit and was accompanied by his close friend, Hans, Anna's older brother. Anna was accompanied by her brother's wife. Her modest, long-sleeved light blue dress followed the Mennonite style. The entire bodice was embroidered with tiny blue flowers, beautiful in their subtlety, Elisabeth's gift to her new daughter-in-law. The bride carried her bible in place of flowers.

The pastor directed the couple to hold hands and then led them through a version of the traditional Christian vows. After pronouncing them husband and wife, he invoked a blessing upon them. No kiss was given; no rings were exchanged.

Members of the congregation were invited to offer words of advice to the wedded pair. Several stepped forward.

"Do not let the love for your children become so all-consuming that you neglect the love for your husband," offered a young woman carrying a baby on her hip while twin toddlers stared from the pew.

A grey-haired man whose unlined, tanned face and easy movement made it impossible to guess his age, said, "Thank your wife for the meals she puts in front of you, for the loving, comfortable home she creates, for the clean clothes she provides."

"Take time together each day to connect with gentle words, a sharing of thoughts, and prayers of thanksgiving," shared a very old couple, bent over their canes.

The wedded pair and the witnesses remained at the front of the church during the singing of the final hymn.

"Maman, why are you crying?"

I brushed the tears from my cheek. "Tears of joy, Sophie," I whispered. Would Claude and I ever be free to marry? Would he want to after all this time?

Outside, the churchyard vibrated with sound and colour as people congratulated the couple. Children begged to be set free to play. Young men gathered around Paul, bursts of laughter and elbow nudging punctuating their comments. No one was in a rush.

Claude and Jean-Pierre joined us.

"Oma Elisabeth, here we are!" Sophie called. Elisabeth pulled both children under her arms like a mother hen protecting her chicks. All three chattered at once about the service, the singing, and what would be happening next.

"She truly is a remarkable woman," said Claude.

"Elisabeth was a rock when I was terrified. She's a good choice for a grandmother."

Claude's arm around me elicited some disapproving looks.

"You know I love your touch, but . . ." I nodded in the direction of the nearest group.

His abrupt disentanglement and reddening face drew a few smiles from the older women and giggles from the younger ones. As he withdrew to join the other men, more than one pair of female eyes followed his broad back and narrow hips across the yard.

When a group of older women called to Elisabeth to join them at the schoolhouse behind the Meeting Hall, Jean-Pierre and Sophie ran to play in the field with the other children.

"The women will be laying out the wedding lunch." An apple-cheeked Mennonite woman, about my age, but almost a head shorter than me, appeared at my side. I hadn't heard her approach.

"I'll go help."

"Oh, there's no need. The female elders of the community make the lunch and sweets as their gift to the newly married couple." She smiled shyly. "The younger women clean up."

I smiled and offered my hand. "My name is Catherine Dumont."

She took my hand. "I am Gertrude Patzwald. I know who you are."

My smile froze. Our eyes locked. She took a step back, dropped her head, and stammered an apology. A light breeze teased our skirts.

I softened my expression. "I don't think we've ever met."

"We haven't, but people talk about you." Gertrude leaned in closer and whispered, "You are joyful. They say you speak as freely to men as you do to women."

I gulped. "When they say this about me, are they angry, or fearful?"

"Some are uneasy, some curious." She glanced around. "I really shouldn't be seen talking with you."

"Gertrude, why did you approach me?"

"I have to go, but, you see that white house with the green door over there?"

Following her eyes, I nodded.

"There's someone who wants to meet you. I'll be at the back door in five minutes." She turned and left.

Still reeling, I made my way across the field toward the children.

"Maman, come meet our new friends." Sophie took my hand. Gertrude's green eyes and delicate features were reflected in six-year-old Ella. Ten-year-old Peter, must have inherited his brown eyes and husky build from his father.

As the children ran off to resume their game of tag, I strolled casually back toward the house. I didn't have to go. But I was curious.

Eyes darting in all directions, I slipped down the side of the house to the backyard. A pathway of flat stones separated the house from the garden's rows of carrots, beans, and potatoes. The path ended at a Dutch door, the top section thrown back to let in light and air.

Gertrude stood framed in the open space, balancing a baby on her hip, long curls peeking out from his blue cap.

"I'm so glad you're here. Come in." She unlatched the lower half of the door. "This is my grandmother's house."

Following her gesture, I sat on the chair at the pine table that dominated the neat, well-organized kitchen, complete with wooden work surfaces, several floor-to-ceiling pine cabinets filled with plates and cups, and a wood cook stove.

Seeing my gaze rest on the hand pump over the basin, Gertrude said, "My grandmother struggles to walk, so my parents were permitted to install an indoor pump for her."

I needed to talk to Claude about installing one of those.

I was about to ask why she had invited me here when we heard the shush of slippers dragging across wooden floors. "Ah, here comes Grandmother."

A diminutive grey-haired woman shuffled into the kitchen.

I stood.

Our eyes met.

"It is as I thought. Please sit."

Why did she look like she recognized me?

After popping the baby into his wooden high chair, Gertrude assisted her grandmother into a seat. Then, she busied herself with tea preparation while her grandmother fixed me with her inscrutable gaze. "So, how is Evangeline?"

I gasped. "Evangeline?" I attempted to knit together the frazzled strings of my composure.

"Humph." The old woman's faded blue eyes didn't waver from my face.

As Gertrude placed a cup of tea on the worn surface in front of each of us, the grandmother went on as if reciting a passage from memory, "Evangeline was born in 1914. She was engaged to Jacques Dumont in 1932. Jacques had two sisters, Rita and Cécile.

His family lived on the river in the home you and your husband have built."

Panic bubbled up my throat. How could she know all of this?

The grandmother smiled, revealing two teeth on the top and three on the bottom. "You're her spitting image. I would recognize those eyes anywhere."

Gertrude pulled out a chair.

"Before you sit, dear, please fetch the wooden box from the table beside my bed."

Gertrude disappeared down the hall to do her grandmother's bidding.

"Ma'am, what you claim is impossible. This is 1888."

"Now, child, you have nothing to fear from us. Drink some tea." She gazed at me. "It was the winter of 1832. My family was ministering to the Indians in this area. Evangeline was ill when the Indians brought her to us. They'd found her wandering in the woods. My sister and I nursed her back to health."

Gertrude returned carrying a six-inch-square, worn pine box.

"*Danke*. Join us." The old woman gestured to her granddaughter. "At first, we thought there was something wrong with Evangeline because she was like a small child having to learn how to do the simplest things. Yet she knew how to read and write."

The woman sipped her tea, raising her cup toward me to do the same. I did.

"Then, one summer day, while Evangeline and I were working in the garden, she confessed she came from a hundred years in the future."

Her eyes measured me.

I kept my expression neutral.

"At first, I thought it was just her mind rambling, but she seemed to know so much."

145

The woman placed her thumbs on the bronze catch of the box. The lid sprang open. She removed a white handkerchief bearing a stylish letter *E* embroidered in Gran's favourite colour—purple.

I inhaled sharply.

She nodded. "I made her two for Christmas. She left this one behind." The grandmother pulled on a white corner peeking from her sleeve and shook out her own handkerchief, the letter *A* embroidered in emerald green. "And she made two for me."

She sat for some time with her eyes closed. Gertrude refilled our cups. I focussed on breathing.

"Evangeline was with us for nearly a year." Her voice rasped. "My older brother, Johann, loved her joy of life, her sweet abandon, so unlike the control our young women are taught. And she loved him back."

She cleared her throat. "They were to be married in February 1833. Then, January twenty-first, Evangeline disappeared." The green *A* swayed as she dabbed her eyes. "It was bitterly cold that day, but she insisted on going out to gather evergreen boughs to adorn the exterior of the Meeting House for the wedding." The woman looked down at her hands as if noticing their wrinkled state for the first time. "When Evangeline hadn't returned by afternoon, the men mounted a search."

A small sniff escaped the old woman. "Evangeline's tracks in the snow ended in a clearing at the edge of the river. Everyone believed she'd become lost and slipped into the water."

She took a deep breath. "Johann never recovered from the loss of Evangeline. Our parents encouraged him to find another, but eventually they relented, realizing it'd be an injustice to foist his sad soul upon any woman."

Her eyes took on a faraway look as she gazed through the door. "I always wondered if maybe she did come from a different time and that she'd gone back there." Sharp focus returned as her gaze fixed on me. "Now, I can see it is all true. Does she still live? Has she had a good life?"

"I don't want to be rude." I rose from my chair. "But I believe you have me confused with someone else."

Gertrude touched my forearm. "Your secret is safe with us."

Turning to go, I said, "Ma'am, it was a pleasure to meet you. I must go and collect my children."

"When you see your grandmother," replied the old woman, "tell her Amelia has never forgotten her."

I froze. The old woman's words fragmented my brain like a grenade. When Gran and I had prepared the nursery, I'd found Amelia's Room carved on the plank under the window of the spare room. Gran had claimed she didn't know anything about it.

Outside, the clang of the school bell crashed me back into action.

"The lunch is ready," Gertrude said. "Perhaps we'll see you at the meal."

Nodding to the two women, I exited and retraced my steps along the pathway. I took a deep breath. *Focus on the upcoming meal, Catherine. There'll be time later to unravel what Amelia told you.*

STRAWBERRIES

Chapter Fifteen

We were all still at the breakfast table. Claude was taking longer than usual to finish his coffee.

"Maurice and I are working in the woodlot downriver all day."

"Sunny day for it." I rose to clear the table and prepare it for our home school morning of reading, writing, and arithmetic classes.

"I'll need two lunches."

"Doesn't Maurice usually bring his own?"

"Need one for our new helper." The corners of his mouth twitched.

"You have a helper, papa?" Jean-Pierre had been asking all winter to work with his father.

"That depends, J.P. Can you miss school classes today? We need someone good with the horses."

Jean-Pierre let out a whoop.

"Maurice and I will trim the trees. Think you can hook the logs to Beau's harness and drag them to the riverbank?"

Jean-Pierre flung his arms around his father's neck. "*Oui,* papa. *Merci,* papa!"

"That's not fair. I want to miss school, too!" wailed Sophie.

"*Mais*, Sophie, Adeline has requested your help with *bébé* Celestine today." Claude winked at me. "Only if maman doesn't mind."

Celestine had burst into this world exactly as planned in mid-October. What a thrill to support my friend through the birth.

Luckily, Dr. and Mrs. Jones had prepared me should the baby come early—they'd arrived just in time to watch me catch the baby girl.

"Okay, go." I waved them off. "I can't wait to read all about it in your journals tomorrow."

Once they were ready, I sent the children outside.

"Claude, when are you going to Montreal?"

He stopped with his hand on the door latch.

"Look, I know you didn't go in the fall because of Paul and Anna's wedding. And then there were the meetings with our member of Parliament regarding the bridge"—I took a ragged breath—"but it's January . . ."

He turned to face me. "We're in the middle of logging."

"Okay, but when?"

Silence.

"Papa, come on!"

He hunched his shoulders. "I'll go after the spring drive." Yanking open the door, he paused on the threshold, but then closed it softly behind him without looking back.

The muffled silence of a winter morning engulfed the house. I regretted upsetting Claude, but I needed him to keep his promise. I couldn't keep dragging around the late-night images of Claude's arm around Gisèle in the sunlight while I walked away alone into the shadows.

I swung my arms, shook out my wrists, and did some toe touches. Crunching sounds vibrated in my inner ear as head circles released the tension in my neck and shoulders. Both animals were curled up on their braided rag beds, enjoying a morning nap by the fire. I sighed. This evening, I'd thank Claude for giving me the gift of this day to myself, and together we'd come up with a plan for his trip.

I intended to take advantage of the day's quietude to finalize the proposal for the road bridge across the Spanish River. Claude had completed the design. The Nelsonville Bridge committee, led by Mr. Dever, along with the lumber and railway companies, had all approved his plans. I usually worked at the desk in our bedroom, but with the children away, I decided to spread the drawings and my notes on the kitchen table.

I was in the bedroom gathering materials when I heard heavy footsteps on the porch. Dropping my armload of documents on the table, I walked toward the door. Knocking, accompanied by more foot stomping, elicited a low growl from Snoopy at my side.

"Who is it?" I called, resting my hand on Snoopy's head.

"*C'est la maison de Claude Dumont?*" questioned a deep male voice. "*François Dumont ici.*"

I cracked open the door. Lighter complexioned, same bony nose, tall and lanky like something engineered to bend with the breeze, the man was clearly Claude's brother.

"François, so nice to meet you. I'm Catherine, Claude's wife." I opened the door wide. "*Entrez.*"

"*Merci* Madame." He removed his hat, greasy shoulder-length curls tumbling forward. "It's freezing, and I've travelled a long way." The hardness around his hazel eyes as his gaze met mine sent a frisson down my spine.

I heated coffee while he removed his outer clothing. "Claude didn't mention you were coming."

He rubbed his hands together in front of the fire.

"I trust the family is well?" I gestured for him to sit at the table.

"*Oui,* everyone is well, but there is little work for me on the farm"—a Gallic shrug—"and with only military training, there is nothing for me in Montreal."

I made a sympathetic sound as I placed coffee and scones in front of him.

"There's much talk of opportunity in the west," François continued. "I remembered Claude had come to this area, so when the train stopped in Sudbury, I asked if anyone knew him." He slurped his coffee. "Come, sit with me."

I hesitated and then perched on a chair across from him.

"The wife of the stationmaster there," he shook his head. "she made me coffee, too, and told me she'd heard my brother had settled on a plot of land near the Spanish River." His tone seemed friendly enough. "She didn't say anything about a wife."

I moved my hands down to my lap.

"I thought I'd ask for him at each stop." He paused. "Mrs. Edwards told me all about Claude and Catherine Dumont and their two children."

I pressed my palms against my thighs. "I'm sure Claude will be thrilled to see you. He shouldn't be too long."

"Really, Madame?" His smile didn't reach his eyes. "I could swear I saw him and Jean-Pierre—he's getting to be a big boy—accompanied by your neighbour, heading into the woods on the south bank of the river."

Had he been spying on us? I balled my hands into fists to stop their shaking.

A smile of feigned innocence. "Perhaps I am mistaken . . . ?"

"I'm sorry, I need to pick up my daughter." I stood. He didn't move. "You're free to wait for Claude in the barn." He flipped from beguiling to belligerent in the flap of a hummingbird's wings, wrenching me back into my seat by my arm.

My first impulse was to fight him, but he was at least five inches taller than me and well muscled. I concentrated on my breathing. "Would you like some more coffee?"

"That's better." He leaned back in his chair.

How had I ever seen anything of Claude in him?

"Another scone. And something stronger in the coffee."

I added whiskey to his cup.

"*Merci*, Catherine." He accepted the cup and scone. "Ahh!" He smacked his lips. "You know how to warm a man."

My skin crawled, but I maintained my smile.

He leaned forward, palms pressed on the table top. "Has my brother told you he left his grieving wife to suffer in the filth of a lunatic asylum?"

My fingers gripped the wooden seat. "Gisèle is ill. He sends money for her care."

François sneered. "So that's the way Claude told you the story. He always was the one with the words." He sat back, holding out his cup. "Not so much coffee this time, eh?"

He moved his fingers to brush mine before he released the cup. I met his stare. Turning, I stalked to the kitchen despite the quaking of my knees.

"Stupid Clément," he sneered. "He thinks the best thing in life is standing in cow shit up to his knees."

I placed the cup in front of him.

Greedy gulps replaced his earlier slurps.

"Go to the army, François, they said." He spat. "You can make something of yourself. Women love a man in uniform."

I made a mild sound of agreement. "I heard your parents bought you a commission."

"A life of 'Do this, do that' . . ." He flung an arm in each direction. "Hah! *Non, merci.*"

He slammed down his empty cup. "Bring me the bottle!"

I did.

As the level of liquor in the bottle lowered, his words slurred. "Gisèle was so full of *joie de vivre.*" He began snuffling. "I loved her. She was supposed to be mine; then Claude came back."

He dropped his head onto his forearms folded on the table in front of him. Quietly, I eased forward in my chair, but he snorted and jerked awake, sat up, hazel eyes piercing into mine.

"We'll see how charming he is when I take something he loves." He lunged across the table. "Come here, woman!"

I pushed backward, knocking my chair to the floor. My eyes darted toward the door. I'd never make it. I needed to keep him calm until the whiskey could do its work.

I forced a friendly tone. "Why don't I fry you up some breakfast?"

Not waiting for his answer, I walked to the kitchen and pulled eggs and pork slices from the indoor cooler and the loaf of bread from the cupboard. "This won't take long." I stirred up the fire, moving the iron skillet from its usual resting place at the back of the stove to the front, over the direct heat.

Suddenly, he grabbed me from behind. His sour breath of whiskey and rotting gums filled my nose as he kissed my neck.

I elbowed him in the chest. "Get off!"

He pulled my right arm up my back. "Breakfast can wait," he growled, trapping me between the counter and his body.

I tried to kick him as his hand slid up under my skirt, but his knee pinned my leg against the cupboard. I freed my left hand and grasped for the bread knife, my fingers just having closed on it when he slammed my forehead into the wooden counter. Stars exploded across my vision. His hand squeezed mine until the knife dropped. Two fingers snapped. I screamed.

Snarling.

A yowl from François. "*Maudit chien!*"

A high-pitched whine, a sliding sound across the floor. A thump. *Snoopy.*

François pushed my legs apart, his hand slapping rhythmically against my thigh as he masturbated his penis to an erection. He thrust into me. I whimpered. Before long, his pumping became frenzied. I focussed on the pain in my hip banging against the counter edge. A grunt of triumph.

"Now I have my brother's whore!" François gave my hand a final squeeze. I screamed again and then vomited. With a slap to my ass, he barked, "Now make me breakfast, bitch."

My eye fell on the skillet, smoking on the cooktop. François was behind me. I spun and swung the skillet like a baseball bat at his head. He slid to the floor. Panting, I stood over his unconscious body, poised to deliver a second blow.

When François didn't move, I lowered my arm. The skillet slipped from my grasp and rattled against the floor. I shuffled to the table and took a bracing swallow from the whiskey bottle. A two-inch cut above François's eyebrow oozed blood, and a lump was rising on his forehead.

"That's going to hurt," I said aloud with bitter satisfaction. Pinpoints of blood from Snoopy's bite spread through his beige woollen trouser leg below the knee. The dog pressed to my side. He whimpered softly as I stroked him. "Thanks, boy."

Another swallow of whiskey and I was ready to move. What I wanted most was a hot bath to remove his fluids that ran down my legs, but first I needed to make sure my family would be safe.

I trussed François up like a Christmas turkey where he lay, wrapping lengths of curtain cords around his body to pin his arms. After damping down the fire, I stepped out into the courtyard. The cool air helped to revive me as I squatted in the snow and rubbed the rough crystals against my skin handfuls at a time.

I knew where the men were working, and there'd be plenty of evidence of their trail in the snow.

I rushed out to the barn for my snowshoes and snow pants, careful not to use my left hand. Claude would not be happy when he saw my gear, but it was the only way I could move quickly through the snow. Once I related the events of this morning to the two men, my snowshoes and pants would completely escape notice.

Soon, I was striding over the snow, my throbbing left hand cradled across my chest. A few wispy white clouds were combed like an infant's silken strands across the blue sky. The crisp air cleansed the stink of François's foul breath from my nostrils. The caress of the winter sun on my face melted the loathing caused by his touch.

The tracks of small animals and the pine trees dressed in their snowy gowns replaced the images of his leering smile and threatening gaze. Soon I would be in my husband's arms. Claude would deal with his brother and keep us safe.

At the railway bridge, the men's trail veered to the left, away from the tracks. I heard them calling to each other through the forest, their shouts punctuated by the faint whistle of the approaching train.

"Claude! Jean-Pierre!" The locomotive steamed around the curve, belching black smoke, throwing snow to both sides of the track. The pounding of the wheels obliterated my calls.

My head filled with roaring. Terror throttled me. I was helpless, frozen. A punch of wind knocked me off my feet. Everything went black.

STRAWBERRIES

Chapter Sixteen

I lay spread eagle on my back, face wet with snowflakes. Dull grey replaced the blue sky. In the distance, I heard the sound of rubber tires sloshing over slushy pavement. I rolled onto my knees, and a sharp pain seared up my arm.

Tucking my injured hand against my chest, I stood and looked around. Evergreens wore their snowy gowns. Crumbled stone bridge piers split the river—no bridge, no track. All those fruitless treks, and now here I was, back. And my family was lost. I pictured Claude sitting on our settee in front of the fire, hugging Sophie and J.P. against him as tears coursed down their cheeks. I dropped my face into my hands and sobbed.

Once my crying jag subsided, I swiped the tears away. This was all François's fault. What would Claude think when he opened the door to find his brother tied up on the floor? What lies would François tell?

"Asshole!" I yelled. The ice chunks bobbed unbothered in the black river.

The snow was falling faster. My only hope now was to get to Gran and find out what she knew about how I could get back. I turned and followed the old track route. As I crossed the highway bridge, I imagined Gran's arms around me and mine around Amelia, her head against my chest. Around the S-bend, the grey bungalow appeared out of the gloom, snow overhanging the roof. I followed the shoveled pathway to the back porch, past the silver mini-van parked in the driveway. Children's laughter inside. I took a deep breath, mounted the steps and knocked.

"Can I help you?" A woman my age, straight brown hair brushing her shoulders, looked at me with direct brown eyes.

"Julia?" My best friend from university. Last time I saw her was when she'd stayed with us to do her practice teaching sessions in Espanola. Was she back for the next session? Had time stood still here? Her body was a little fuller than I remembered. Those tiny lines around her eyes were new.

Her hand flew to her mouth. "Kate?"

Diamond ring and wedding band.

"Oh, my God! Kate!" She stepped out and closed the door.

Her eyes raked over me. "It's really you." She pulled me into her arms.

I nodded, my head over her shoulder.

Three pairs of eyes, two brown and one blue, stared through the door's sidelight.

"Stay here. I'll be right back." Julia disappeared inside.

"Who's that lady, Mom?"

"Come on, kids. Daddy's taking you to Tim Horton's," Julia called. "Get your stuff. You can dress at the front door."

A man's face, familiar but with more experience lines, grey highlights in the brown hair falling over his ears, waved uncertainly through the window.

I sank into a lawn chair. Time had definitely passed while I was away. There'd been a special current between Julia and our doctor, David Jones, when they met at Gran's for Thanksgiving and again at our *Réveillon de Noël* those months before I jumped. A tingle of warmth touched my heart.

The blue eyes were back at the window.

The door opened, and a girl that could only be my Amelia stuck her head out, waves of honey-toned hair falling over her shoulders. "Are you okay?"

My heart pounded in my ears. "Hi." I gulped air. "I'm . . . okay." I white-knuckled the edge of the chair to restrain my impulse to reach out to her.

"Amelia," Julia called from inside the house.

My heart exploded.

"Coming, Mom." She closed the door. I stared at the spot where my beautiful daughter had stood. My fingers twitched, remembering the silkiness of her baby hair, the velvet feel of her cheek. I'd always thought I'd come back and Gran and I would tell Amelia who I was. Where was Gran? Why was my daughter calling Julia *Mom*?

Children's laughter and the sound of car doors slamming brought me back to the porch. Silence.

"Everybody's gone." Julia appeared at my side, taking my elbow as she guided me into the house. She stripped off my outer clothing and sat me in Gran's rocking chair in front of the wood stove. My gaze wandered. Same orange, yellow, and lime-green throw cushions crowded for space on the sectional couch. Same pine harvest table and chairs.

Julia reached to fold my hands around a cup of tea. I cried out as her fingers touched my broken ones.

"Oh, my God. I'm sorry." She grasped my wrist and laid my hand into her open palm. The index and middle fingers were bent sideways at the middle knuckle. "What happened?"

I shook my head. "Do you have ice and maybe some aspirin?"

Julia wrapped my injured hand in a towel, and I rested it on a bag of ice. The aspirin kicked in quickly. Much faster than willow bark, I mused, as the throbbing subsided.

Julia pulled up a chair beside me.

We stared into the fire.

"So, um . . . I'm not sure what to say." Her brow wrinkled as I caught her eyes.

"Gran?"

"Sure." Julia covered my good hand with hers where it rested on the arm of my chair. "Gran is fine. She's in a nursing home . . ."

I gasped.

"It's temporary," Julia reassured me. "Just while she recovers from breast cancer treatment. But she won't be coming back here." Julia drew a breath. "She's moving to the retirement home. Her heart's failing because of the chemo."

My eyes welled with tears.

"She kept telling us you'd come back." Julia stared into the fire. "When David and I insisted on calling the police, she told us 'how it is with the Dumont women.'" Julia crooked her fingers into the air like quotation marks. "We thought she was losing her mind." She turned and looked directly into my eyes. "You really did that?"

"Travel into the past?" I met her gaze. "I did. But I didn't know Gran did."

"She sent us to the Webbwood museum where we found a journal entry beside a hanky embroidered with a purple letter *E*." Julia gave a nervous laugh. "The entry had been written in 1832 by a young Mennonite woman named Amelia. She wrote that Evangeline Robitaille had appeared one January day and had been lost in a snowstorm a year later."

I stood. "I need a minute." I walked on shaky legs down the hallway to the bathroom. I struggled to pull down my jeans mostly one-handed. It burned to pee, and I dabbed gingerly at the swelling with a wad of white toilet paper. I'd forgotten the wonder of having hot water flow from the taps. With another ball of paper moistened under the tap, I wiped my thighs again. It was a far cry from the snow bath I'd had that morning in another century altogether. Why was I back now I asked myself, staring at puffy, red-rimmed eyes in the mirror.

When I returned, Julia had refilled my cup, and a plate of homemade chocolate chip cookies sat on the coffee table.

"After our experience in Webbwood, we agreed to give Gran the benefit of the doubt, and she agreed to call the police."

I remained still.

"The police found snowshoe tracks and searched the banks up and down the river." Julia's voice quieted. "Eventually, they assumed you'd drowned and closed the case."

I raised my injured hand against my chest. "And Amelia lives with you?"

"Yes." Julia nodded. Her eyes darkened. "Gran and I wouldn't have survived without David's support when you disappeared. We started dating that spring." She took a breath. "After graduating in June, I was hired to teach French and Spanish at Espanola High, and ten months later, David and I married." Her features relaxed. "When Gran couldn't keep up with Amelia, she asked us to consider taking her. We've had her since she was three."

I frowned. "What does she know?"

"She knows we aren't her real parents. She believes her mother drowned." Julia wrapped her arm around my shoulder. "We love her like our own." Her face clouded over as she pulled back. "But, of course . . . as her mother . . ."

I took her hand. "I have to get back to my husband and children."

She stared at me. "You have children?"

I nodded.

"But, after all the complications with Amelia, I thought . . ."

"Jean-Pierre is my husband's son. His mother died in childbirth." My good hand shook as I tucked my hair behind my ear. "Sophie is ours. It was bad, but we made it."

She pressed her hands in her lap. "What about Amelia?" Hope and desperation took turns playing across her face.

I stared blankly at her for a moment. I wasn't ready for this, but she deserved an answer. It would be devastating for Amelia if

I told her I was her mother and then left her again. Could I take her with me? Away from everything and everyone she knew, into a world fraught with danger? And what about Julia and David? I took a deep breath. "For years I tried to figure out how to get back." I dropped my eyes. "Then, without warning, here I am. I missed Amelia so much, but eventually I realized that I needed to live in my new reality." I raised my eyes to Julia's. "I hope you and David will keep loving her as your daughter."

"Absolutely." Her brow folded. "And if you can't get back?" Jane whispered.

"I'm going back." My conviction was all that I had to cling to right now.

Julia nodded. We cried in each other's arms.

Julia was the first to sit back into her chair. "David's taken the kids home to Espanola." She straightened her sweater. "We only use the Riverhouse as a retreat on weekends when David isn't on call. He'll come back to pick us up tomorrow morning."

"Tell me about them."

"Jennifer Joan—Joan after my mother—is eight, and Robert is six." Julia grinned. "They love their big sister. All three keep us busy."

Over the next few hours, Julia and I peeled back the layers, introducing each other to the last nine years of our lives. I learned my daughter tended to march to her own drummer. She'd inherited an artistic flair from her Great Gran, whom she called GG, enjoying painting, singing, dancing, and writing. Julia and David had made a good life and were well respected in their small town.

At some point, we switched from coffee to wine, and Julia brought out some cold slices of day-old pepperoni pizza. It tasted like heaven.

"What was it like?" Julia's eyes grew bigger as I shared the details of my life in the past. I faltered as I told her about the rape and how it caused me to be at the jump site today. She held me as I broke down and sobbed.

Julia drew me a full bath with Epsom salts to ease the pain. Soaking in the full spacious tub I cried on and off in a confusion of devastation and shock.

It was well after midnight by the time we fell into bed. My mind was consumed with worry for Claude. I couldn't see his eyes, couldn't talk to him. I couldn't pull him to me and tell him I was his and always would be. I could only lie still long enough to drop into the pocket of quiet I'd cultivated inside myself over the years. It was always there. It would take practice and conviction to reach it over the coming year.

STRAWBERRIES

Chapter Seventeen

"Are you sure I look okay?" I asked Julia for at least the tenth time. The mirror had shown me the new wrinkles from the strain of the last few days.

"You look great. Relax." Julia gave me a shove to the door. "She's waiting for you." The squeak of her rubber-soled shoes faded down the corridor.

I traced EVANGELINE ROBITAILLE with my finger on the nameplate. Would she ever forgive me for leaving her? For not being there when she needed me most?

"Hello?" Gran's voice was thready. "Is that you, Kate?"

My resolve to maintain calm dissolved as I pushed open the door. Gran's frame barely disturbed the covers of the bed in the softly lit room. The salmon-coloured walls, bright window coverings, and pastoral landscapes were pleasant; but it wasn't home.

"Katie!" Gran's voice was her own.

In three bounds, I was across the room and on the bed. The arms that encircled me were thinner than I remembered.

"You're back. You're actually back."

I propped myself on my elbows, catching her happy grin. She spotted my bandaged hand. "What happened?"

"It's nothing. Just a couple of broken fingers. David set them for me." I slipped off the bed and onto the chair beside it. "Gran, I missed you so much. I tried over and over to get back."

"I know, dear. I know." She patted my arm.

"Julia said you knew where I went."

She nodded.

"You were the Evangeline Robitaille that Amelia told me about." Eyebrows raised, Gran nodded again.

"Why didn't you tell me?" My eyes searched hers.

Her face crumpled. "That question has haunted me since you left." She reached for my hand. "All those nights walking the floor with the baby, knowing what you were facing, praying you were safe. Amelia's fingers wrapped around my pinkie kept me from succumbing to the dark."

I stared at her hand on mine.

"That I could have hurt the person I loved most because I held back my story almost defeated me. Baby Amelia kept me going." She squeezed my hand. "Can you forgive me?"

I wrapped my arms around her. "It's not your fault. I probably would've tried to figure it out if I'd known."

We both sat back, taking a moment to compose ourselves.

"So, you met Amelia?" Gran's voice brightened.

I laughed. "She asked me to tell you she's never forgotten you."

"I want to hear more later." There it was, Gran's take-charge expression. "What have you and Julia decided about your return?"

"We're leaving Kate Walker in the river. I'm Catherine Dumont, your cousin's granddaughter who has come to visit."

Gran looked skeptical.

"I'll keep a low profile. If anyone asks, I'll say I've been doing mission work abroad."

"I suppose." Gran looked thoughtful. "You have changed, and there aren't a lot of people around who knew you back then." She paused. "And what about our Amelia?"

I took a shaky breath. "Nothing will change for her." I forced a smile.

"So you aren't staying."

"No, Gran, I'm not." I held her gaze. "I have to figure out how to get back. It's where I belong."

Gran's eyes drooped.

"Will you help me?"

"We'll figure it out." Gran yawned. "So will I see you tomorrow?" She lay her head back on the pillow and closed her eyes.

"You bet, Gran," I whispered as I kissed her cheek. She was already asleep.

* * *

I strolled along snowy residential streets from the nursing home to Julia and David's house. Modern ranch and split-level homes standing behind their large front yards gave way to front porches of early 1900s storey-and-a-half clapboard houses crowding the sidewalk. Downtown, the Victorian manors evoked the era of prosperity created by the pulp and paper industry.

The ten-minute walk gave me time to absorb the state of Gran's health. Maybe I could rent an apartment or house while Gran and I figured out how the jump worked. Gran could live with me once she was strong enough to leave the home.

Walking up the narrow driveway that ran the full length of Julia and David's three-storey Queen Anne, I almost collided with the snow-covered car. That wasn't there this morning. I stepped to the side. Wait, is this . . . ? Brushing snow off the hood, I laughed as the red paint emerged through the mantle of snow. My enthusiasm changed to embarrassment in the face of giggles from Julia, Amelia, Jennifer Joan, and Robert, spying on me from the broad-pillared veranda.

"David's mechanic gave it a once over," Julia called. "We figured Kate would approve of you using it while you're here."

"Thank you." I grinned, blinking back tears. "Hey, kids, wanna go for a ride?"

"Can we, Mom? Please?" the kids chorused.

"Okay, but just a short one. Dinner will be ready in half an hour."

"No problem. Come on, *mes petits*. Pile in." The children slipped and slid down the driveway. Jennifer Joan pushed the front seat forward for Robert. When he was bent over, she gave him a firm shove on his bottom, so he tumbled headfirst into the back seat. Then, she joined him in a giggling pile of arms and legs.

"Amelia, why don't you sit up front?" I suggested.

"Thanks." She smiled shyly at me.

I turned the key and the car leaped forward, then stalled. *What the . . . oh, yeah, the clutch. This isn't like driving horses.* Two pairs of wide eyes looked at me in the rear-view mirror. Beside me, Amelia's hands were braced against the dash. "Sorry kids. I'm a little out of practice." I chuckled, then depressed the clutch. The engine sprang to life at the turn of the key. With the car in reverse, I leaned over the back of the seat and slowly released the clutch. We jolted, almost stalled, and then jerked our way down the driveway. *This was going to take some getting used to.*

* * *

After supper, dishes, baths, and homework, the three children were settled in their beds, and peace descended on the house. Julia and I sat at her kitchen table, drinking tea. David was doing paperwork in his study.

"I love your house." I said. "It has so much character with the old mouldings and the high ceilings."

"Thanks." Julia smiled. "It's big, but with five people, we were feeling pretty crowded before David moved his practice out of the first floor and over to the medical building a few years ago."

"Back in my time, we saw Doctor George Jones in Webbwood." I paused. "Any relation?"

"Glad David's not around." Julia grinned, looking over her shoulder to make sure he hadn't come in. "You'd be here for the next two hours." She poured more tea. "Short version, David's grandfather was George's grandson, Daniel."

I held up a hand while I figured out the generations. "Okay."

Julia continued. "Back in 1906, the Spanish River Lumber Company set up their mill here. Daniel was hired as the company doctor. He married Sophie Dumont, the daughter . . ." Her hand flew to her mouth. "Oh my God! Your Sophie?"

I jolted upright. Sophie was David's grandmother? I searched David's image in my mind for a likeness. With a shaky breath, I said, "That means I'm related to your husband—we're family!"

Julia grinned. "The Joneses passed the practice down through the generations."

We both sipped our tea and stared off into space for a moment.

"You in touch with any of our group from University?"

Julia's smile faded. "You know how it is, career, distance, family . . ."

"Sure." I sat back in my chair. "At least you can pick up the phone occasionally." There were many times in the early days when I'd longed to be able to reach out to one of my friends.

"And we get together the third weekend of October every year at Laura's cottage in Bala."

"No kids?"

Julia nodded. "And lots of wine." She covered her mouth, trying to hide a yawn. "Sorry. It's getting late." She stretched her eyes open. "Can you handle one more night on the pullout in the living room? Tomorrow we'll rearrange the attic so you can have the full third floor."

I carried our cups to the sink. "Thanks, but I think I'd rather find a place on my own."

She looked puzzled.

"All of you together as a family . . . well . . . it's just . . ."

"Of course. What was I thinking?"

"Since I have wheels now," I said, grinning and leaning back against the counter, "I thought I'd ask Gran to talk to *tante* Rita. Maybe I can use her place."

"Or maybe the Riverhouse?"

My eyes widened. "Really?"

"You'd help us a lot." Julia sighed. "Gran wants us to use it, but with three kids and David's hours working Emergency at the hospital, it's hard to find the time, especially in the winter."

"I'd love to. The place holds so many memories, and I think I'd feel closer to home there." I stretched. "But I'm prepared to brave one more night on your couch."

"No problem." Julia emptied the teapot into the sink. "There is something you should know." She turned to me, and her eyes teared up. "The cardiologists say Gran only has a few months."

My lower lip quivered. "Thanks for telling me." I took several shaky breaths. "I'll talk to her doctor about what I can do to support her. Maybe she'll even be able to come to the Riverhouse."

"She'd love that." Julia smiled. "Now, I really have to head up to bed. I have classes in the morning."

We hugged.

"Goodnight. And . . . thanks."

* * *

Rhubarb, Strawberries, and Willows

January 25, 1989

Dear Diary,

Things are weird around here. We were at the Riverhouse on Saturday when this lady knocked on our door. My mom went out and talked to her. Then, Dad took us for hot chocolate and donuts at Tim's. He had a funny look on his face, but when I asked him, he said he didn't know the lady.

Her name is Catherine. My mom said she was looking for my GG because she's some kind of cousin or something. Mom knows her too, but she hasn't seen her in nine years. Why didn't Mom know she was coming? And why didn't Catherine know GG doesn't live there anymore?

She was wearing a long skirt, like in pioneer times. Her hair reaches to her waist, and I can't help but smile back every time she smiles. Two of her fingers were broken. She screamed when Dad straightened them. She had a purple bump on her head too.

She says I can call her tante Catherine. Today she took us for a ride in a red punch buggy Dad had fixed up for her. It used to be my real mom's. I got to sit in the front seat and pick the radio station. JJ and Robert had to sit in the back. We drove all over town before supper because tante Catherine said she needed to practice the gears. She bought us coke and chips. But we weren't allowed to tell Mom.

I think I'm going to like tante Catherine. I hope she stays for a while.

Amelia

STRAWBERRIES

Chapter Eighteen

Traffic was light, and my little bug hugged the slushy pavement. My eyes darted from side to side, and I slowed to slightly below the speed limit around long curves and on the crests of hills, where I knew police liked to hide. My driver's licence was long expired, and it was in the name of a dead woman. I'd decided to drive without a licence rather than risk discovery by applying for a new one, but I'd never planned on driving down here. As I left the snow-covered rock cuts, swamps, and bush of Highway 69 behind me and joined Highway 400 southbound into Toronto, Gran's voice rang in my head. "You need to see your mother." Even singing along with Carole King on the tape deck didn't release that anxiety.

The last time I'd seen my mother was on the Christmas Day before my jump. *Tante* Cécile and *tante* Rita had joined Gran and me for our *Réveillon de Noël* after midnight mass on Christmas Eve. Seeing the two of them together, I was reminded of how sisters could look so opposite. Rita remained thin and wiry like my grandfather Jacques, while Cécile's five-foot frame carried an additional twenty pounds from the birth of each of her five children. *Tante* Rita brought her twin, fourteen-year-old granddaughters, Chloe and Carmen, who were living with her while their parents worked in Africa. The girls were polite and eager to help, not surprising after almost a year under tante Rita's roof. David was on-call so unable to join

173

his sister in Barrie, and Julia only had distant relatives in Vermont. Our little Riverhouse managed to expand and absorb everyone. We had feasted on *tourtière,* turkey, roasted potatoes, mashed turnips, carrots, and freshly baked bread. Amelia was passed from person to person, kicking her chubby legs and waving her arms when the girls wiggled her teddy bear in front of her.

Sated after our meal, we lounged in the living room, sipping coffee and tea and savouring pieces of tante Cécile's famous *tartes aux pommes* and *tartes au sucre*. Out of the corner of my eye, I caught Gran's slight head tilt at *tante* Rita. Then, she tapped *tante* Cécile's shoulder as she walked past her and settled at the upright piano. Flexing her arthritic fingers, Rita tuned her fiddle. Cécile moved the coffee table to the side of the room. First, we sang traditional Christmas carols in both languages, then, French folk songs. The aunts convinced David to try step-dancing. He ended up in a tangle of limbs on the living room floor, the aunts' feet flicking the air as they danced around him, Rita's fiddle never missing a note. The walls reverberated with sound until the early morning hours.

My mother arrived from Toronto mid-afternoon on Christmas Day. She looked like she'd stepped out of a fashion magazine as she came through the door. Her tall, slim frame was draped in a cashmere camel coat flaring to mid-calf, and knee-high leather boots hugged her long legs.

I got up to meet her. "Hi, Mom."

She curled her lip as she took in the room. Breakfast dishes overflowed the kitchen sink and counter. The twins were playing on their new Intellivision game on the TV. The rest of us sprawled on the couches, dozing or reading. Most of us still wore pajamas.

"Suzanne, you made it." Gran smiled.

My mother winced. "Susan, Mother."

Gran's smile tightened. "Come. Sit." She patted the chair beside her, but my mother didn't move.

"Amelia's sleeping if you want to see her." I moved to the hallway.

"No, don't wake her." She stayed by the door. "I have presents in the car."

"Let me bring them in." David pulled on his coat and boots. *Tante* Rita motioned to the twins, and they followed David out.

"Amelia will be up soon. Maybe you want to feed her?"

"I won't be staying, Kate."

Tante Rita gasped. Tante Cécile tsked.

"Oh, okay . . ." I looked down, steadying myself. "Maybe another time . . ."

Julia broke in to introduce herself. My mother shook hands with her, pecked both aunts on the cheek, and gave Gran a quick hug.

The twins burst into the room, laden with gifts, followed by David, his knees bending under the weight of a large box.

"There's more," called the twins as they disappeared back outside.

My mother moved through the room, distributing her brightly wrapped boxes, smiling as each person expressed wonder at her generosity.

The girls danced around the room, squealing in unison, "A Walkman!"

Tante Rita and tante Cécile fingered their cashmere shawls, marvelling at the softness, shaking their heads. There were cashmere scarves for David and Julia.

Gran leaned over and whispered to me, "She called and asked who would be here today."

Of course she would.

"Mother, does it fit?" My mother called to Gran from across the room.

Gran sat stiffly, her gift sitting on the floor beside her. "I'm sure it does, dear."

"Try it on."

Gran pulled on the royal blue Jessie G Parka. The contoured seams were fitted perfectly along her frame.

"That's wolf fur around the hood, so the ice won't clump from your breath. It's filled with real down, not that polyfilla stuff."

"Thank you. It's very nice." Gran gently folded the parka back into the box. A single mom in town was going to be getting a nice jacket.

"I assumed you'd have a crib"—my mother caught me in her sites—"so I got a stroller and high chair. I'm sure David will help you assemble them."

I looked at her. "I can handle it, thanks, Mom."

She shrugged and dropped three boxes in my lap. "And a few little outfits, mostly size one and two for her to grow into."

I unwrapped each box, holding up silk and cotton dresses, designer jeans, and woollen sweaters with matching hats, all from Melijoe. Every outfit would have cost more than I spent on clothes in a year for myself. "This is really too much."

"Nonsense. Enjoy, everyone. I have a long drive home." Hand kisses to the air, a wave, and she was out the door. She hadn't even taken off her coat.

How would she greet me now? The doorman called up to announce my arrival. My mother waited in the hallway as I stepped out of the elevator. A few grey strands glittered in her chin-length blond hair. In my best black pants, white shirt, and red cardigan, I felt frumpy beside her slim, brown suede skirt, yellow crew-neck sweater, and artistically arranged multi-coloured scarf. Her face was smooth under the light foundation cream.

I searched her grey eyes.

"Oh, Katie!" She pulled me into her arms.

I relaxed into her embrace.

My mother stepped back first. Holding me by my shoulders, she sized me up from head to toe. By the time her eyes met mine again, I was braced for the assessment that defined our reunions. My hair was too shaggy . . . I would look healthier with some blush . . . A fitted shirt would bring out my figure . . .

"Katie, I'm so relieved you're okay!" She led me in. "I'll make coffee, or I have herbal tea if you'd prefer."

"Uh, coffee's fine." I perched on the edge of the leather sofa while she boiled water in the kitchen. The white walls and black furniture of the living room were as I remembered from those two months I'd spent here after university before my flight to Gran's. Her 'Austerity Chic' design, as she'd called it, now vibrated with new accent cushions and throws of gold-threaded brocades in deep blues and burgundies. Merlot-hued tulips the size of watermelons bloomed on the wallpaper separating the dining room from the kitchen.

I turned to the sound of tinkling china behind me. "Your place . . . it's so different."

"The colours make me happy." She pushed the plunger on the French press. "The years after we lost your dad were not my best."

I reached across to touch her hand.

We shared a look. Maybe this wasn't going to be such a terrible visit after all.

While she poured coffee in the china cups, I gazed out through the floor-to-ceiling windows. White wicker settees and rockers on the balcony sported canary-yellow cushions against the leaden backdrop of Lake Ontario.

"I can't get enough of that view of Toronto Island." She took a deep breath. "We spend a lot of time out there no matter the weather." The colour rose in her face when I looked at her. "I met someone a few years ago." Her eyes sparkled the way I imagined mine did when I thought of Claude. "I don't feel lost anymore."

"I'm happy for you, Mom."

"Now, tell me what happened." She turned her body toward me. "Your Gran insisted on some silly story . . ."

My expression stopped her in mid-sentence.

She gasped at my slow nod.

"So, it's true?"

"Yes, Mom, it's true. I travelled back a hundred years."

For the next hour, her eyes never wavered from mine. When our cups were empty, she didn't move to refill them.

She grasped my hand when I told her about Abe and the lumber camp.

When I shared the encounter with William, she commented, "So that's who Van Horne Avenue in Sudbury is named after."

She smiled hearing about Claude, Elisabeth, and the Gagnons, and laughed at the antics of Jean-Pierre and Sophie.

François's face flashed across my vision. I faltered.

My mother frowned. "What's wrong?' She must have seen the memory darken my face.

I shook my head and forced a smile. "Nothing." I paused. "Do you believe me?" I held my breath through the long silence. Had I misunderstood our new-found ease?

Then, she nodded.

I exhaled. "Did you ever feel it? You can't move. The only thing you hear is the clickety-clack and—"

"The damn whistle. It burns into your mind." My mother moved to the window, arms hugging across her chest.

"What the hell, Mom?" I threw up my arms. "You knew what could happen and you didn't warn me? Protect me?" I struggled to slow my breathing. "Unbelievable." I shook my head.

She leaned into me. "When I was growing up, the French were looked down on by the English. They had big families, were usually labourers, and spoke a confusing mix of French and English." She tilted an eyebrow. "Being French *and* freezing every time you heard a train, that would have been social suicide."

"But Gran and *papère* spoke both languages perfectly. And you only had one brother."

My mother turned to face me. "That didn't matter."

"So, what did you do?"

"I decided to make myself English. I attended Lively District High instead of Collège Notre-Dame, and found myself a good

Anglo boy." Her expression hardened. "And got the hell away from the Riverhouse as soon as I could." Her eyes bored into mine. "And now you tell me you've been wasting your university education living with a Frenchman, raising his son and your illegitimate daughter."

"Claude's an engineer." I sounded defensive even to my own ear.

"Don't tell me you intend to go back?"

I stood up, fists at my side. "I belong with my husband and children."

"And what about the daughter you left behind? You going to desert her again?"

"That's unfair." I swiped at my tears. "I didn't leave her by choice. I tried hundreds of times to get back, but I couldn't make it work."

She straightened her skirt. "Well, I have no interest in raising another child."

I dug my nails into my palms.

"I've transferred your trust fund into Amelia's name under David's guardianship." She returned to sit on the couch.

"I know." I dropped down beside her.

"Kate, I feel like I've spent half my life floating." She rested her hand on my knee. "When Jeff was killed in the car crash on the way home from his prom, your Gran and *papère* were so absorbed in their own pain, they didn't see mine."

She'd never talked about her brother. Gran was the one who'd brought him to life for me.

"Then, when your father died, it took me a long time to figure out how to face the world alone."

I held her gaze.

"When you disappeared, I had to grieve over the loss of my only child." Her expression softened. "Katie, I was so relieved to hear you'd returned from the dead."

I smiled. "So, when do I get to meet your new man?"

Her eyes darkened. "Never, if you choose to pursue your plan to go back. My life is simple and happy, and I'm not about to complicate it with my daughter's stories of time travel."

For the past hour, I'd felt I'd glimpsed Suzanne Dumont. But in the length of a breath, the Susan Walker mask was fitted into place, and I was staring into the face of the mother whose expectations I never seemed to meet.

She stood.

I stared at her for a moment before rising. I wanted to tell her how angry I was because she never supported me. I wanted her to know that she'd made feel as if I didn't measure up. "I forgive you, Mom." I couldn't believe I'd said it.

Her hands covered her face.

I stood frozen.

"I know I wasn't the mother you wanted, but I only wanted the best for you," she sobbed.

I put my arms around her. "I know. We just don't want the same things, Mom."

"I hope you find what you're looking for," she murmured against my shoulder.

With one final squeeze, we separated, and I found myself in the hallway.

The drive home was like navigating through a fog of doubt. What if François had poisoned Claude against me? What if Gisèle was alive and well? What kind of mother was I, contemplating leaving Amelia again?

Five hours later, as I turned through the S-curve, instead of the Riverhouse, my mind superimposed the house Claude and I had built on the reality in front of me. Jean-Pierre and Sophie's laughter rang in my ears. The warmth of Claude's arms engulfed me. I knew where I needed to be.

* * *

February 3, 1989

Dear Diary,

Tante Catherine has moved to the Riverhouse. She comes for dinner every Wednesday and Sunday. Sometimes she takes us for a drive and treats.

I stayed home from school today because I was sick. TC stayed with me because Mom and Dad had to go to work. It was the best day. I read her my story about a girl who lives with her grandmother by a river. She finds a magic spot under a maple tree in the middle of the bush. When TC asked me why the spot was magic, I told her I didn't know. We made a list of the things that could happen under that tree.

I even showed her my painting of the girl sitting in the magic spot. She said she loved it and I should use it for the cover of my book when it's done. I feel like I'm a real person, not just a kid, when we talk. I hope she stays for a long time.

Amelia

STRAWBERRIES

Chapter Nineteen

It was almost suppertime, and I was on my way to visit Gran. Strong winds drove the densely falling snowflakes of the late March storm into a frenzied dance until I couldn't see where the road ended and the snowbanks began.

Gran's health had improved sufficiently to allow her to live independently in an apartment connected to the seniors' complex. A nurse dropped in daily with an IV bag of drugs designed to maintain her quality of life over the months remaining to her. She wasn't strong enough yet to spend more than a few hours at the Riverhouse. Perhaps by the spring.

Each morning, I stared out the window at the black ribbon of river and wrote my letters to the adult Amelia would become, telling her about her 1880s family, my life, and the jump.

In the afternoons, I spruced up the interior of the Riverhouse, my gift for when she came of age. I gave each room a fresh coat of paint, refinished the pine floors, and organized the clutter in the basement.

Evenings, I visited with Gran. Her stories bridged the gap for me between the baby Amelia I'd left behind and the girl I was getting to know. In turn, I breathed life into Claude, Jean-Pierre, and Sophie. We talked about the challenges of survival in a world without twentieth-century amenities, both agreeing there was much to be said for underwear, indoor plumbing, and toilet paper. Joy suffused her expression when I told her of the full life her friend Amelia had lived, but her shoulders slumped when she learned Johann had never married.

Twice a week, we joined the Joneses for supper, and most weekends, the children spent at least a day with me at the Riverhouse. "Don't get too attached. Be careful what you say—she's a smart girl," the voice in my head cautioned. I chose to kick it to the back corner. Their presence helped the ache in my arms of wanting to envelope my other children.

Some nights, I awoke to the sound of my own voice murmuring soothing words into the pillow, my mind believing I'd heard Sophie calling out in her nightmares. Other nights, I'd fall into the same restless dream. Claude's hand running through my hair, his lips on mine, his scent of sunshine and sweat engulfing me. My hands remembered every detail of his body. His voice in my ear said my name with a blend of tenderness and urgency as no one had ever said it before and as no one ever would. I'd awake to emptiness, pull the blanket over my head, and pray for sleep.

I pulled into the parking lot of the Espanola Retirement facility. As I stepped out of the bug, the wind buffeted the stack of Tupperware containers I balanced in my arms. I'd taken to cooking lasagna, spaghetti sauce, and shepherd's pie for Gran and I to reheat. Today, over lasagna, we intended to assemble all we knew about the jump in search of the key to controlling it.

I was almost at the door of Gran's building when a high-pitched ringing filled my head. My feet flew out from under me. Food containers floated through the white-speckled sky. There was a crack as the back of my head hit the pavement. Then, blackness.

* * *

Voices drifted in and out like sitting in the lunchroom at coffee break. The sharp smell of disinfectant inflamed my nostrils. Faces haloed by bright lights blurred and wavered until I had to squeeze my eyes shut to suppress nausea. When I tried to lift my head, a sharp pain shot from back to front. Firm hands pressed my shoulders flat, and a familiar voice admonished me to remain still.

"David?" I mumbled.

"You're okay, Catherine. Stay still. You took a nasty bump to your head."

"Gran . . . ?"

"We already told her. She's waiting to see you just as soon as we get you settled."

"What happened?"

David looked concerned. "We were hoping you'd be able to tell us."

"I remember getting out of the car and walking to the door of Gran's building." I sipped from the water the nurse offered. "Then, there was ringing in my ears, and I fell and hit my head."

"Has this ever happened before?"

"N-no." This wasn't the first time. I pushed the memory from my mind.

"Don't worry," David soothed. "I'm keeping you here for twenty-four hours for observation." He leaned and whispered, "Don't worry. No one knows who you are. I used the OHIP number of a lady who refused to be admitted earlier today. I'll erase it later." Then, he turned to the nurse and told her to set up an IV for fluids and order blood tests.

"I'll be back later tonight. In the meantime, you need to rest."

Once I was settled, Gran came through the door, arms wide. "Katie, you gave us such a scare." She gave me a hug and sat on the chair beside the bed, keeping hold of my hand. "How are you feeling, dear?" Concern clouded her eyes.

"I'm sorry." I frowned. "Just before I lost consciousness, I saw all these containers falling from the sky."

"Those were the meals you made, remember? You must have dropped them when you fell. My neighbour, Mr. Campbell, found you lying on your back in a puddle of red. Poor man thought you were bleeding." She chuckled. "He rushed across the parking lot into Emergency."

"Must have been quite a sight."

Gran grinned. "When David came on the scene, he saw pasta noodles on the ground around you and realized it was tomato sauce in your hair." She became serious again. "You could have been there for hours before someone found you."

"Do I really have to stay overnight? I'm feeling better."

"You may have a concussion." She tucked the blankets around me.

A weighty silence settled over us.

"Is it still snowing out there?" I attempted a chuckle. "Driving a car is a whole different experience from driving a horse and wagon."

Gran captured me in her direct gaze. "Katie, I'm not leaving until we talk about the real issue."

I knew she meant business when she used my old name. My eyes dropped to my hands folding and unfolding the blanket draped across my legs. "I'm not sure I understand what you mean." I kept my eyes glued to the bed.

"David has some concerns about you, not related to your head injury." Gran pressed her hand over mine, stopping its compulsive worrying of the blanket. "Look at me, Kate."

I felt I was trying to push words into water. "The tests might show I'm pregnant." Then, the words rushed out. "I kept hoping my body was just confused by the jump, that maybe, if I ignored it . . ."

"Hmmph," Gran said.

I dropped my gaze to the covers. "After Sophie was born, the doctor in Webbwood was adamant it was unsafe for me to have more children." Tears coursed down my cheeks. "Each time I've been pregnant, I've had fainting spells. I've had a few miscarriages."

Gran made a sympathetic sound.

"What am I going to do? If I have the baby, I can't leave it behind." I pushed my head back into the pillow as a wave of nausea hit. "But, I can't stay. I can't live without Claude and the children."

"I know, child." She rubbed my knee.

"Do you think a baby could survive the jump?" My eyes raked her face.

"Sweetheart, first things first. You need to share everything about your other pregnancies with David." She kissed my forehead. "Now, try to get some rest."

STRAWBERRIES

Chapter Twenty

Gran stood at the window of the Riverhouse when I came down the hallway. "Another generation of Canada geese are getting their feet wet." She sighed, looking out at the backyard now blooming with June flowers. "There's a timelessness along a river."

I touched her shoulder.

She turned to me. "All done?"

I nodded. "The crib's up from the basement. I just need to clean it." I pressed a hand to the small of my back.

"I'm sure Amelia will be more than happy to help."

"She'll be able to keep her room when she's here. The crib fits just fine with me in Robert and Jennifer's room." I twisted from side to side to ease my back. "I can't believe Julia and David kept that James Lumbers painting hanging in Amelia's room all these years."

"Julia knew how much that painting meant to you. She thought it would be a nice connecting thread for Amelia to the mother she never got to know." Gran paused. "Do you still see the ghosts like that?"

I nodded. "That's why I believe I can go back. Ouch!" I plopped down on the nearest chair and rubbed my palm over my abdomen. "That was a solid kick."

"Maybe you should rest," Gran said. "How about some tea on the porch? I've just made a fresh pot—Belgian chocolate."

I tsked. "You're supposed to rest and let me take care of you."

Gran flapped her hand at me. "Long as I'm still standing, I can boil water."

I helped her move to her porch rocker, tucked an afghan around her legs, and returned to the kitchen to carry the tea tray.

Chocolaty steam circled my head as I rocked gently on the porch swing. The resinous scent of pines bristling with new growth brought the laughter of my children echoing through the forests to my mind. Any minute, I expected to see Claude come striding across the yard, removing his straw hat to wave. His face would light with a smile as he saw me working in the garden, or hanging clothes on the line . . . The train whistle filled my head.

Gran brought me back with a touch on my knee.

"Gran, how did the words *Amelia's Room* end up carved under the window in the bedroom?"

"It's not much of a story." She stared at the river, a faraway look clouding her eyes. "Sometimes, I wonder why I wandered so far that day. I knew it was the anniversary of my jump when I went out." She came back to me, her faded blue eyes glinting. "I loved Johann and looked forward to our marriage, but I desperately missed Jacques."

Listening to her was like listening to the voice of my own heart.

She sipped her tea. " Oh, this *is* good."

I nodded.

"Mennonite men at the time were permitted to marry women outside the religion, but girls had to marry within the sect," she continued.

"They'd loosened that up by 1889," I said, remembering Anna and Paul.

"That's good." She smiled. "Amelia was terrified her family would marry her off to another community, so we made a pact. Wherever Johann and I lived, we would always have a room for her in our home." She sipped her tea.

"But, you never married Johann."

"I never forgot Amelia and my promise to her. When Jacques and I moved into the Riverhouse, he carved *Amelia's Room* under the window of the spare bedroom. And when we rebuilt, he saved the plank and installed it in the new house."

"You mean, you told pépère?"

"Of course I told him. Catherine, I was gone for a year."

"He believed you?" I tried to imagine my practical grandfather welcoming back his fiancée from the previous century.

"What mattered to Jacques was that I returned to him." Gran's face lit with a brilliant smile. "He loved me, and he knew I loved him. We moved forward with our lives together." Gran settled back into the chair, watching the geese. "When I saw the carving, I knew I was in the right place."

A woodpecker drummed on a hollow tree nearby.

"I miss Claude, J.P., and Sophie." I swallowed hard. "What if they're angry and don't want me back? What if he's found someone new?"

"Oh, Catherine."

"What if he doesn't want the baby when he finds out François raped me?"

"Do you believe Claude loves you?"

"Absolutely."

"How did he respond when you told him where you came from?"

"He was incredulous." I shook my head. "Despite his doubts, he accepted it." I stood to ease the tingling in my legs. "Maybe I don't need to tell him about the rape. Chances are it's his baby anyway." I blushed.

She looked at me. "What if François told Claude to hurt him? How will Claude react if you say nothing?"

I rubbed the bumps on my two mended fingers. "I couldn't stand it if he rejected me."

Gran held my hands, "You can't live a lie." Her eyes lightened. "Right now, focus on the opportunity to know Amelia, and enjoy the birth of this baby."

I nodded.

Suddenly, Gran pressed her lips tightly together.

"Gran, what's wrong? Are you sick?"

She waved her hand dismissively. Then, at my insistent glare, she said, "Have you thought about what you'll do if you can't get back? I won't be here to help you."

The lines on Gran's face seemed suddenly deeper, her eyes more sunken.

I went to her and wrapped my arms around her shoulders. She leaned into me, holding onto my arm with one shaking hand. We stayed that way for a few moments until the pain in my back forced me to straighten.

"Just before my jump, I heard the train on the track," Gran said, almost like she was talking to herself. "And the whistle."

"Me, too." I waved my hand, index finger pointing into the air between us. "Both my jumps happened after lunch."

Gran nodded. "Mine, too."

I snapped my fingers. "There's a train that crosses the bridge every day at one o'clock. That must be the one we hear."

"But, when I jumped, the railway in the past hadn't been built yet." Gran's brow furrowed.

"Right," I said. "Same for me, so how could we hear a train? In our heads?"

We let the silence grow between us.

"You said you tried to come back."

"Over and over again." I swallowed to settle the quiver in my voice. "And it never worked. Then, with Claude. . . and when Sophie came along . . . I just gave up."

Gran patted my hand. "Of course, child. You did the right thing, you started a new life. Maybe the jump is connected to the trains?"

Suddenly, it was like in the cartoons where a light bulb goes off above the head of one of the characters. "Gran, what date did you jump?"

"It was January 21. I'll never forget it."

"Me, too." My voice squeaked. "And the Spanish River Train Disaster happened in that spot on January 21, 1910 at one o-clock in the afternoon."

We solved it!" Gran crowed. The grin disappeared from her face as her brow furrowed. "But we each travelled back and returned once. What makes you think you can do it again?"

"Because I still feel the pull with every train." I lowered my voice. "It might not work, but I have to try. I have to believe I'm going to make it back."

"That's my girl." Her face relaxed. After a moment, Gran added, "I thought I'd find it hard calling you Catherine, but it hasn't been difficult at all."

"Do I really look that different?"

"It's not what I see on the outside, it's who I see shining from the inside."

"I love you."

"I love you, too, my sweet."

"I think I heard a car door slam."

Amelia came around the corner of the house, skipping along the path to the porch, ponytail bobbing. Julia followed, carrying a small suitcase.

"Good timing, ladies." Gran opened her arms as Amelia mounted the stairs. "We've been waiting for you to help make the crumble for tomorrow's Social."

"I've been counting on you to help me pick the strawberries," I added.

My girl looked at me and beamed.

* * *

"Amelia, come on sweetie," I called. "Breakfast's getting cold."

Amelia slid into her place at the table. "Sorry, I was writing."

"That's cool. Are you writing a story?"

"No, I was writing in my diary. You know, like your journals?"

I paused, working to maintain my smile. Had she inadvertently stumbled upon the letters I'd been writing? "How do you know about my journals, sweetie?"

"Gran told me. Wanna see my diary?" Amelia jumped up and raced to her bedroom.

Gran cast me an apologetic look. "She was looking for you one evening, and I mentioned that you were writing your journal."

Amelia burst into the room holding out a blue-and-cream linen-covered book. "You can read it if you want."

"It's beautiful," I said. "Diaries and journals are personal. They're a safe place to express our thoughts and dreams." I smiled. "I'm so glad you're writing one."

Amelia's grasp on the diary froze. We all remained still as the train's whistle penetrated our bones, coming back to life as the clickety-clack of the railway cars faded into the distance.

Gran caught my eye. "Well, ladies, I think it's time to get ourselves to the Social." Her voice shook.

Amelia cleared her dishes from the table and ran to her room.

"Did you see that?" I asked.

"That's a first. Maybe it was just a coincidence."

"But that's exactly what I've seen in Sophie since she was five years old."

"Let's enjoy the day. That's all I can handle—one day at a time."

"I'm sorry. You're right."

With the car loaded, we began our fifteen-minute drive down the highway to Nairn Centre. "Amelia," I asked. "Why do we celebrate a Strawberry Social on July first?"

"It's Canada Day," Amelia replied. "Dad says it's like Canada's birthday."

"That's right."

"Tante Catherine, can we listen to the radio?"

"Why don't we pretend we're settlers? They didn't have radios, so what do you think they did when they travelled?"

"They sang?"

"Right," said Gran.

I began to sing "The Ballad of the Spanish."

> *Home to beavers, geese and otters*
> *Ducks, bass, pike, and the bear*
> *Paddlers love her beauty*
> *You can hear the loon call there*
>
> **Chorus:** *Loggers may have jammed her*
> *Miners they have dammed her*
> *But the Spanish keeps rollin' along*
> *Her tea waters mirror*
> *Birches, pines, and poplars*
> *And the Spanish keeps rollin' along.*

When she joined in on the chorus, I was flooded with memories of another little girl whose voice was just as sweet and sure.

STRAWBERRIES

Chapter Twenty-One

The Jones family beckoned to us from the shade of a maple tree as we pulled into the parking area. What had started as an open field near the railway station a hundred years ago in Nelsonville was now the site of a baseball diamond, soccer pitch, and community centre. Nearly two hundred people were spread across the open spaces, examining vendor stalls, setting up picnic sites under the trees, and stopping to chat with friends and neighbours. For a brief moment, I closed my eyes and was transported back to a parking lot filled with horse-drawn wagons. My nose twitched with the imagined scent of hay.

Julia's touch on my arm brought me back. "You're looking wistful. Everything okay?"

"Yeah, I'm fine." My voice shook slightly. "Amelia sang all the way here. She sounds just like Sophie."

Her brow furrowed. "Maybe we should take Amelia home with us."

"No, please, don't. She needs this time to build her memories with her GG, and it's good for Gran to have her around." I sighed. "I get to build my memories, too."

With David's assistance, Gran was soon ensconced in her lounge chair. While I laid out the blankets and baskets, I heard one of Gran's friends greet her behind me. They chatted in French about Gran's health, how big Amelia was getting, and the challenges of dealing with an aging body. When a third voice joined them, I overheard Gran explain who I was.

The first woman said her goodbyes and sidled over to me. "I don't recall Marcel Robitaille having any daughters. He is your papa, *n'est-ce pas?*"

I caught my breath. This had to be a descendant of Estelle Beaudry, the same black curly hair, matronly build, and sparkling dark eyes.

"Micheline Beaudry." She smiled and extended her hand.

I shook it. "I'm not from here. My family lives in Penetanguishene. I'm staying with Gran until the baby is born . . ." I raised my left hand to expose the naked ring finger.

"Oh, I'm sorry. I didn't mean to pry." She patted me on the arm and ambled across the grass.

"Nicely played," chuckled Julia.

I exhaled sharply. "Yeah. She makes a good point, though. Guess I should have thought through my cover story a little more."

"It's fine. She seemed satisfied with your explanation." Julia pulled my arm. "Come on. Let's take our desserts over to the table."

A woman about my age with a firm, curvy figure turned to take our desserts.

"Hello. I'm Ida MacGregor." Her eyes danced. "These look delicious." Younger version of the same plain hatchet face as her namesake in the past. She had to be a direct descendent—but how was that possible, given that the old Ida was unmarried and well past child-bearing years when I met her?

A woman with lines so heavy her skin seemed to sag off her skull looked over her wire-rimmed glasses at Julia. "I'm disappointed in you, young lady," she said. "Respect for elders seems to be lost on you hippies."

"I'm sorry, Mrs. Fensom." Julia stepped back and gestured toward me. "I should have introduced you earlier. This is Catherine Dumont. She's visiting Evangeline Dumont, her mother's cousin."

"A visit that will likely end with the birth of that baby." She nodded at my abdomen. "And the father?" Her false teeth clacked.

I was about to ignore Julia's restraining fingers on my arm when Ida stepped between us. "Now, auntie, you're showing your age. Hippies went out of style two decades ago." Then, with a wink to me, Ida led the old lady away. "Oh, look. The opening ceremonies are about to begin . . ."

Families gathered in front of the makeshift stage. Amelia settled Jennifer Joan and Robert on the blanket near Gran as a portly man directed the counsellors and other dignitaries to seats on the platform. His pressed khakis barely broke a crease.

"That's Mayor Hall," Julia said in my ear. "Nice man, but tries too hard."

I took a sidelong glance at her. She seemed to glide through life, comfortable in her cocoon of convention, while I seemed to be forever surging with rebellion.

"What was that reaction to Ida MacGregor all about?" Julia's question broke into my thoughts. "You looked like you'd seen a ghost."

"I think I did. That Ida is a younger version of the Ida MacGregor I told you about, who accused me of devilry at the Nelsonville Social."

"Could be a coincidence," Julia said.

"Same close-set eyes, narrow head, and beaky nose? This Ida is definitely related to the other one." I grimaced.

"Mom, tante Catherine, the ceremony is starting," Amelia whispered.

Julia and I redirected our attention to the activities on the wooden platform. I gnawed on the puzzle of the two Idas while the speakers on stage regaled the gathering with tales of Nairn Centre's history. Things seemed to be coming to a close as the mayor began acknowledging members of the historical settler families who still lived in the town.

"The Dumonts have been in this area from the 1870s."

My attention was jolted back to reality. Everyone was looking at our family gathered beneath the tree.

"Evangeline, we are honoured to have you joining us again this year," said Mayor Hall.

Gran waved from her seat.

Then, he turned his attention to the crowd. "How many here have rhubarb growing in their gardens?"

Most families raised their hands.

"Almost all of us do." The Mayor smiled broadly. "As the story goes, a young Mrs. Catherine Dumont brought rhubarb back to her garden on the Spanish River from Midland in the early 1880s."

My face must have registered my shock. In response to Gran's slight head motion, I rearranged my expression to mirror her bland one.

Julia leaned into me. "Please tell me that wasn't you?" She gasped in response to my shrug.

"Rhubarb is the devil's food! That Dumont woman brought the devil to this community!" screamed Mrs. Fensom. Tense laughter rippled through the audience, but my stomach clenched. Ida appeared instantly at the old woman's side, calming her as she led her away from the gathering.

Mayor Hall removed his straw hat and mopped a sheen of sweat from his forehead with his handkerchief. "Sorry 'bout that, folks." He gave a nervous chuckle. "I'm sure she's fine. Maybe a little too much sun." His voice resumed its deep boom. "Now, please join our school choir in the singing of our national anthem. Happy Canada Day!"

Across the field, under the spread of ancient maples and oaks, families unpacked their lunches. Julia kept throwing me looks ranging from incredulity to respect as we laid out the fried chicken, potato salad, pickles, and raw vegetables. I poured lemonade.

The mayor made his rounds through the families. When he arrived at our site, he asked after Gran's health and complimented her on her appearance. His bushy eyebrows flicked briefly when Gran introduced me as her distant cousin, Catherine Dumont.

"I'm sorry about Mrs. Fensom. I believe she suffers from dementia."

I acknowledged his apology with a nod.

He cleared his throat. "I've been reading the old settler journals. My ancestor, Clara Hall, was one of those scribblers. She had a great deal to say about Catherine Dumont."

"Interesting," I said.

"Yes, Clara and John held Catherine and Claude Dumont in high esteem." Then, with a tip of his hat, he added, "Enjoy your day."

Julia, Gran, and I exhaled audibly.

"Kids," David said, "why don't you go join the line-up at the strawberry table? We'll be right behind you."

The three children ran to join the crowd waiting to select from the strawberry desserts displayed on the trestle tables under the trees.

"I confess," David said, "I had my doubts about your story." He squeezed my shoulder. "I'm beginning to question those doubts."

"Thanks. I know this must be crazy for you." I smiled. "But hearing I'm in Clara Hall's journals means the jump . . ."

"Okay, okay, enough with the chatter," Gran broke in. "There are three kids over there almost at the front of the line. I'd enjoy sampling some of those strawberry desserts."

"I'm on it, Gran!" David sprinted to join the children. Julia and I followed, arms linked.

After dessert, Gran dozed in the lounge chair. While the others explored the activities and enjoyed the musical groups on the field, I packed up our baskets and carried them to the car.

"It's Catherine, right?"

I bashed the back of my head against the open trunk lid.

"Ida, I didn't hear you come up." I rubbed the sore spot. "Is there something I can do for you?"

"I wanted to apologize for my aunt's outburst earlier."

"No problem."

"My aunt and a few of her friends have been reading the journals they found when they were clearing out the old Methodist church."

"Mmm hmm." I turned back to packing the trunk, my heart beating in my ears.

"Both journals mentioned Catherine Dumont. What really caught my aunt's attention was the scene Clara described between you and Ida MacGregor at the Strawberry Social of 1888."

I froze. "You mean my Gran's ancestor and yours?" I forced slow breaths.

"Of course, how silly of me," Ida's mouth twitched into a half smile. "In my aunt's confused mind, she was probably reliving the journal entry."

"Poor dear." I turned to face her. "So there was an Ida MacGregor in Nelsonville a hundred years ago? An ancestor of yours?"

I caught a flitting sideways eye movement. "Yes, both journals refer to an elder Ida MacGregor who stayed briefly in Nelsonville. Her mind seemed to have been deranged by a life of loss."

My mouth twitched into a weak smile.

"Well, I didn't mean to delay you. I imagine you want to get your *gran* home." She started to walk away. Then, she stopped and turned. "Family relationships can get muddy over generations, can't they?"

* * *

July 1, 1989

Dear Diary,

Today was the best Strawberry Social ever. I didn't want to go at first because my pioneer skirt was too short, but tante Catherine fixed it, and all the girls were jealous when they saw the ruffle. She said that's what pioneer moms did so they didn't have to make new skirts when their kids grew.

Mom says I can stay with GG and tante Catherine for as long as they'll let me this summer, but I'm in charge of making sure we all go home for supper every Wednesday and Sunday.

This is going to be the best summer ever!

Amelia

STRAWBERRIES

Chapter Twenty-Two

Sept. 2, 1989

Dear Diary,

It's hard to believe GG is gone. Dad says it's okay to feel sad. He says if we talk about our memories of her, it'll help us feel happy that she was part of our life. Like when she used to put her hand over mine to show me new brush strokes. I can't think about that. It hurts too much.

Mom says GG will never be totally gone because a part of her is in me. She says I have her strong spirit and love of life and that by living my life with joy and courage I'll honour her. That sounds scary. I don't want to disappoint GG.

Tante Catherine says she misses GG too. But she has her baby now. Maybe she won't want me around anymore. Maybe she'll go back home. I hate this!

Amelia

* * *

I sat beside Lois on the porch swing, mutely staring at the same river scene Gran and I had admired countless times. She'd say how lucky we were to have the beauty of creation flowing right outside our door. Bands of yellow poplar and red maple leaves threaded through the deep green pines under a leaden sky.

"I don't think I can do this," I said.

Lois put her arm around my shoulders. "It's hard, but you're strong. Give it time."

"I feel weak without her."

"What would Gran say to you right now?"

"She'd tell me to get off the pity pot." I gave a half-smile. "She'd tell me to be happy because her pain is gone, and she'd want us to celebrate her life, not wail about her death."

"Try that." Lois gave me a final squeeze. "I think I hear the baby."

I slid forward to push myself to my feet.

"Stay." She touched my arm. "I'll bring her out. Auntie Lois is coming, Evie-Jayne."

I caught my breath as my gaze fell on Gran's empty rocker. This afternoon was Gran's funeral. Tomorrow, Evangeline Jayne Dumont and I would begin preparing for our return to the past.

"Here you go, baby girl." She placed Evie-Jayne in my arms. "There's your mommy." She turned to re-enter the house.

"Can you sit for a bit?"

"Sure." Lois sat on the settee.

"Thanks for being here."

Lois, who had first entered our lives after our chance encounter at the library all those years ago, had re-entered our lives several weeks ago, suddenly appearing at the Riverhouse. Gran had been sitting out on the porch when Lois came around the corner. Just then, I'd emerged from the kitchen carrying a tray laden with our mugs, the teapot, and a plate of oatmeal raisin cookies.

Lois had stopped halfway up the porch stairs. "Oh." Her hand flew to her mouth as our eyes met.

I froze in the doorway, holding my breath.

Gran's gaze moved from Lois to me. "Well, come on, ladies." She laughed. "We have a lot to catch up on." Lois had spent almost every day with us since.

Lois's hand on my knee brought me back to the present. Her face looked about to crumple as she told me she'd been selected for a lead part in an Australian TV series. "They need me on set in Perth in ten days," she grimaced. "I have to leave in a week."

"That's wonderful."

"But I hate to desert you, especially with the baby and Gran . . ." Her eyes filled with worry.

"I'll be fine." I waved my hand. "It sounds like cars have pulled in next door?"

She gave my knee a quick squeeze. "Maybe Rita and Cécile. I'll check." Lois disappeared down the side of the house.

"We want to meet Evangeline's cousin's granddaughter before the funeral." Tante Rita's scratchy voice floated to me while she was still out of sight. "We heard she's pregnant. Is it true there's no papa in the picture?"

"That's right," Lois said.

"*Mon Dieu*, that poor girl."

"Shush Rita, she might hear you." Cécile's lower tones admonished her sister. "It's the way these days. Better than the 'shotgun marriages' in our time."

"Ah! Here she is!" As spry as ever, Rita was the first to round the corner. "*Bonjour,* Catherine!"

"*Bonjour,*" I replied. "So nice to meet you. Evangeline would be happy you're here." I kept my head down, avoiding their eyes as I held the baby up for them to admire. "Please come and meet Evangeline Jayne Dumont." Please don't recognize me, I prayed.

The aunts only had eyes for the baby as they leaned over Evie-Jayne. Rita stroked her sparse covering of light blond hair, and Cécile offered her finger for the baby to grasp. Since her birth four days ago,

I'd found myself searching her features. She was blond like François but so was I. Her eyes were slightly almond shaped like Claude's, François's were rounder. She was long, even though she'd come a month early, but all three of us were tall. I already loved her more than life itself regardless of who her father was, but would Claude?

Lois suggested the aunts settle on the porch while she got refreshments. We exchanged pleasantries about their trip, and they expressed their sadness at the loss of their sister-in-law while *tante* Rita rocked Evie-Jayne on her bony shoulder. I kept casting surreptitious glances at the two ladies, but no recognition seemed to register on their faces.

"Was Suzanne here when . . . ?" Cécile scrunched up her face.

I shook my head. "Suzanne? Oh, Susan. She phoned, but she couldn't make it up in time."

Rita sniffed into the air, and the two women exchanged meaningful glances.

"She'll be here for the funeral," I added.

"What about poor little Amelia?" Rita asked. "She's alone in the world, now."

I smiled. "Amelia is thriving in her adopted family. Gran has left the Riverhouse to her."

"*Formidable!*" Rita said.

"It will stay in the family." Cécile added her approval.

Tante Cécile cuddled Evie-Jayne to her ample bosom while I excused myself to shower and change for the funeral. No sooner had I left than they began quizzing Lois. I listened in on the conversation from the bathroom window, which overlooked the porch.

"Last week when Daniel cut the grass, he said Evangeline was here?" Rita said.

"Yes," Lois said. "She was able to move back because she had Catherine to help her. Then, on Tuesday morning, Catherine was unable to wake her. She was rushed to hospital by ambulance."

I shuddered. I'd found Gran that morning, her skin translucent like onion skin, blue veins standing out on her closed lids. When I squeezed her hand, her fingers were cold and waxy.

Lois continued, "Catherine's water broke, and she went into labour while she sat by Evangeline's bed in the hospital."

A small gasp.

"They had to do a C-section. The baby was fine, but we almost lost Catherine. Couldn't stop the bleeding."

"Too bad Evangeline never got to see the *bébé*," said *tante* Cécile.

"Actually, she did." I heard the smile in Lois's voice. "Evangeline regained consciousness for a brief time, so they wheeled Catherine and the baby into her room."

Two wheezing sighs.

"Evangeline died with the baby in her arms and Catherine holding both their hands."

The click of purses opening and closing, followed by tissues rustling. Tears streamed down my face.

Cécile recovered first. "*Voyons, donc,* since Evangeline was a Robitaille and Catherine is a Dumont, then . . . ?"

Rita interrupted. "Lots of Dumonts and Robitailles moved from Québec to homestead in Ontario. She must come from a LaFontaine Robitaille who married a Dumont down there."

Cécile murmured her agreement. "But Catherine looks familiar, eh, Rita?"

My mouth went dry.

"I've been told she bears a strong resemblance to Evangeline when she was her age," Lois offered.

"*Ben oui*, that's it!" Rita said. "Especially around the eyes, and she carries herself proud like Evangeline, *n'est-ce pas,* Cécile?"

I breathed a sigh of relief.

"We thought Evangeline felt she was better than us with her thick, shiny hair, slim figure and her high school education," Cécile said.

"Then, the first time Jacques brought her home for dinner, she jumped right in to help with the dishes." Rita grinned. "She even took the leftovers out to the pigs."

The aunts laughed.

Cécile said, "That's when we knew Evangeline was the right girl for our Jacques."

Evie-Jayne mewled. I heard the scrape of a chair. "I'll take her in," Lois said. "Thank you for dropping by. See you at the funeral."

Lois and I exchanged a smile watching through the kitchen window as the two women wended their way across the grass to the cottage next door, all the while talking and gesticulating.

* * *

The double doors of All Saints Anglican Church in Nairn Centre stood wide as community members streamed in. When every pew of the century-old, white clapboard church was filled, people leaned against the plastered cream walls around the perimeter. Two triple brass candelabra burned on the altar. A sunbeam from a crack in the heavy clouds outside sent red, green, and yellow flickers dancing across Gran's pine coffin through the stained glass window. The strains of "Fly Me to the Moon" drifted into the rafters as the organist played a medley of Gran's favourite songs.

My mother arrived just as the service was about to begin. Her black wool suit hugged her form, and not a hair was out of place. She acknowledged me with a nod and a quick handshake. Then, she glanced at Evie-Jayne and murmured, "Not another one."

I hugged the baby close, staring hard at my mother.

The minister led us through a short service including the singing of "Abide with Me." When he invited people to come forward to share stories about Gran, there was a line-up down the aisle. We heard how she'd organized the Ladies' Group Christmas Bazaar for forty years, how she'd helped convince the School Board to keep

Nairn Centre Public School open despite declining enrolments. We learned about her toy drives, a feral cat rescue program, and a young mothers support group she'd initiated. My heart swelled.

Amelia pulled on my arm. "I'm gonna be just like her," she whispered to me from behind her hand.

As soon as Gran's coffin was interred, my mother was in her car, heading south. She didn't even make an appearance at the reception in the community centre.

"How're you two doing?" Lois put an arm around Julia and me as we stared at Gran's grave. Evie-Jayne slept against my chest in her sling. We were the last mourners in the cemetery.

"I'm okay. It helps that so many came." I jiggled the baby.

Lois searched my eyes. "What about your mom?"

"It's better she didn't stay. She left us behind years ago."

Julia covered her face with her hands. Lois and I held her until her sobs subsided.

"I'm sorry . . . she was like a grandmother to me." She pressed her fingers to her eyes.

"I'm the one that's sorry." I kept my arm around Julia's shoulder. "I've been so wrapped up in myself, I never even thought about how hard this is for you."

We both gave a big sniff and smiled at each other.

Evie-Jayne fussed. "I better feed her before we go into the reception. I'll duck into the kitchen through the back door."

Lois turned toward the building. "I'll make sure everything's going okay."

"I need a minute." Julia pulled her fingers through her hair.

"Take your time." I squeezed her shoulder and then crossed the cemetery to the narrow, cracked concrete walkway around to the back of the community centre. The kitchen door stood open. A quick peek around the jamb revealed the gleaming stainless steel counters of an industrial grade kitchen. Other than a few trays of cheese and crackers and a bowl of potato chips, the place was empty.

I sat on the only chair, lifted my top, and cuddled Evie-Jayne against my bare breast. A few steady breaths calmed my jangling nerves. A slight pinch to my nipple gave Evie-Jayne a target, and she buried her chin in my breast, opened her mouth, and latched. She had this figured out already. I felt the rhythmic motion of her temple under my fingers as she sucked and swallowed.

"Oh, sorry, you're still here." Julia stopped in the doorway.

"No problem. She's almost done."

We were sharing a sad smile when Lois popped her head through the door. "Ready?"

I walked through the reception. People leaned in to offer their condolences and admire Evie-Jayne sleeping in my arms. My expression felt frozen between a smile and a grimace as I acknowledged their comments. All I wanted was to be at home alone with my baby where I could pull the blankets over my head until the crushing weight in my chest eased.

A group of very old mourners bent over their canes, clustered near the refreshment table. They were sharing their memories of Gran, inquiring after peers who were not present, and checking on the health of those who were as I joined them. I thanked them for coming and moved on.

I found tante Rita and tante Cécile by the windows, relating my connection to the southern Robitailles and Dumonts to a group of elderly Francophone couples, telling my story as if it were a truth they'd always known. Each one gave me a brief hug or squeezed my hand.

David appeared at my side, Amelia's arms wrapped around his waist. "Have you seen Julia?" He ran his fingers through his hair, leaving it sticking up in all directions.

"She's circulating. Amelia, come here, sweetheart." I stretched out an arm, and she slipped under it.

David tilted his head toward Amelia and raised his eyebrows. I nodded.

Amelia and I sat on the chairs set up around the perimeter of the room. "It's okay, baby." I let her cry in my lap, stroking her hair and murmuring soothingly until I felt her relax.

Eventually, she sat up, pushed her hair behind her ears, and scrubbed her tear-streaked face with her palms. "Why are people laughing like they don't even care that GG's gone?"

"Actually, Amelia . . ."

I jerked at the sound of Ida's voice at my other side.

"The people here are remembering all the great things about your GG." She held out two glasses. "Lemonade?"

"Thank you," I responded stiffly as Amelia took one of the glasses.

Ida pulled up a chair. "I've heard so many stories about your GG today. I'm sorry I didn't get a chance to spend time with her."

Amelia's mouth twitched as she tried to smile.

I caught sight of David beckoning from across the room. "Looks like your dad needs you." I kissed the top of her head.

"I love you, tante Catherine."

"Me too, honey." She hugged me. I whispered in her ear. Then, she pressed her lips to Evie-Jayne's cheek and ran to her father.

"Tough day," Ida said. "You and Evangeline seemed close for distant relatives."

I said nothing.

"I see some of Evangeline in Amelia." She paused. "There's something remarkable about the Dumont women. Or is it the Riverhouse women?" She frowned. "Somehow I get the feeling Kate was of the same mold."

I looked her straight in the eye. "I wouldn't know." I stood up, adjusting the baby in her sling. "People are leaving. I need to say goodbye." I walked into the main hall without a backward glance.

STRAWBERRIES

Chapter Twenty-Three

October 14, 1989

Dear Diary,

I still miss GG. When I get really sad I remember what tante Catherine whispered to me when that lady was talking to us at the funeral. Just before GG died she told tante Catherine:

I'll never be far, I'm as close as the wind.

When the wind blows I feel GG's hand on my face, and I feel better.

School's okay, but I don't have many friends. Mom says I have to try harder, but all the girls care about is who the cutest boy is in our class, clothes, painting their nails, and trying to look like Madonna.

I like going to the Riverhouse to help tante Catherine on the weekends. She says I'm like a big sister for Evie-Jayne when I play with her and rock her in her cradle. Sometimes I write my story while tante Catherine writes her play about a train crash that happened near here a long time ago, and then we read our work to each other. I feel like a real writer.

Amelia

* * *

Lois left the week after the funeral. We managed brave smiles as we wished each other well, knowing we'd never see one another again.

I didn't leave the Riverhouse for days at a time, dozing when Evie-Jayne slept. Nights, I found myself on the porch, wrapped in a blanket of memories. The touch of Claude's callused hands. Sophie's sweet singing. Jean-Pierre's lopsided grin. On top of it all, I missed Gran terribly. Sometimes, in the middle of a happy memory, a fist would close around my heart and squeeze tears from my eyes.

David or Julia checked on me daily by phone, and I resumed the twice-weekly visits for dinner to the Jones home. Occasionally, Amelia spent a weekend with Evie-Jayne and me. I cherished our moments together, me writing while she painted landscapes using the techniques Gran had shown her to capture the light on the river.

Evie-Jayne wriggled like a tiny seal whenever I wrapped her up in her sling. We walked my bush trails each day, stopping to check the beavers' progress in their preparations for winter in the nearby pond. Minutes into the walk, she'd drop into a contented sleep. With the arrival of snow in early November, I switched to snowshoes. The shadows of Claude and the children, alive but in another layer of time, were our constant companions. On the days when the ambiguities of my plan to return to my past life threatened to pin me to my bed, Evie-Jayne kept me moving forward.

Although he remained skeptical about my plan to return, David thoroughly examined Evie-Jayne and me, pronouncing us both at the peak of health. They'd performed a tubal ligation during the Caesarian to protect me from future pregnancies.

Memories of dental care in the late 1800s in Northern Ontario drove me to see a dentist before leaving.

Finally, January 21st arrived. My last night in this century. I'd been battered by a storm of doubt. The day before, Julia and I had sat with Amelia at the kitchen table and told her I'd be leaving the next day.

She'd scrunched up her face at the news. "Why do you want to go? Don't you like it here?"

"I do, but I need to go back to my own home." I bit my tongue to stop the tears gathering in my eyes.

"I can live with you, help you. Can't I, Mom?" She turned pleading eyes to her mother.

"But you need to go to school, sweetheart. And *tante* Catherine belongs with her family," Julia said.

Amelia turned wide eyes to me. "You said I'm like a big sister to Evie-Jayne." Her chin quivered. "And I can take the bus to school."

I reached out to touch her arm.

"No!" Her chair crashed to the floor as she stood. "You can't go. I won't let you!" She ran to her bedroom, and we heard her sobbing on the bed.

"I better go to her." Julia rose.

"No, let me." Her distress was like a punch to my gut. How would Amelia ever forgive me when she learned I was the mother who had left her behind, not once, but twice?

I found Amelia sprawled face down on her bed. I sat beside her, careful not to touch her until she was ready.

After a few moments, she rolled over. "First Gran, now you. How'm I ever gonna learn to be a Dumont woman?" Her pupils were huge.

I took her into my arms and rocked her. "Oh, baby, you already are one. It's in your blood."

She pushed away from me, nibbling on her bottom lip.

"Remember, every time you feel the wind . . ."

"It's like Gran touching my face," she finished.

"I love you, Amelia." I hugged her tightly, drinking in the feel of her one last time. "You need to go home, now. Your mom's waiting." I released her.

"I love you, tante Catherine. I'll never forget you."

I shook with silent sobs as I heard the back door close. "And I'll never forget you," I whispered.

It had taken until four in the morning before I finally reconciled that my place was in the last century with my family while Amelia belonged here with hers.

After our regular morning routine of breakfast and playtime, Evie-Jayne slipped into her nap while I wrapped my journals in a quilt I'd sewn for Amelia. I rubbed one of the patches of soft fleece adorned with giraffes against my cheek. Pieces of Amelia's baby blanket. I traced a large pink bloom with my index finger. An image of Gran wearing her flowing summer skirt to the Strawberry Social. My fingers stopped to enjoy the soft nap of worn denim from my old jeans. I smiled, remembering Amelia's observation that it was time for me to buy new jeans, since mine were worn thin. I hoped the familiar patches would bring back happy memories for her. Stowing the packed journals in Gran's old cedar trunk in the attic, I was momentarily overcome as I imagined Julia giving Amelia the journals, and Amelia reading them. In one of my versions, her face shone with joy as she learned the truth, in the other, she threw them to the floor in anger.

Evie-Jayne's gurgles from below restored my resolve, and I descended the ladder. "Okay, baby girl, time to go." It wasn't quite noon, but I was anxious to move. The watery sunlight of an hour ago had been replaced with gently falling snow, nothing that threatened to delay our progress, but I preferred to avoid having to rush with so much at stake.

Within minutes, I'd bundled Evie-Jayne into her snowsuit. After one long last look, I closed the door behind us.

The red bug handled the snowy road without hesitation. Stopping at the curve, I drank in the view of the house with the river meandering blackly against the pristine snow-covered banks. In a few hours, I hoped to be watching the same dark river cut its way through the winter banks a century back in time. The house and barn would be different, but the constancy this place held for me in both centuries kept me grounded as I turned the corner.

I parked my little bug in the snowplow turnaround of the old logging road. David and Julia planned to drive out in the evening to pick up the car and take it to Sudbury to be sold. Walking in my layers of winter clothing, pockets stuffed with underwear, and a baby slung to my chest was going to test my reserves. A two-kilometre walk would place us in the clearing with plenty of time to spare.

I pulled a sleepy Evie-Jayne from her seat and strapped her securely under my full-length woollen coat. The baby snuggled into the familiar position and was soon sound asleep. The snow-covered evergreens muffled us in a white world capped by a steel grey sky. Between the trees flanking the trail, I periodically glimpsed the river as I walked.

Singing "The Ballad of the Spanish" gave my feet rhythm through the steadily falling snow.

> *Loggers may have jammed her*
> *Miners they have dammed her*
> *But the Spanish keeps rollin' along*
> *Her tea waters mirror*
> *Birches, pines, and poplars*
> *And the Spanish keeps rollin' along.*

"Pretty song."

Startled, I lurched sideways, grasping a silver birch on the edge of the clearing for balance. "*Merde!*" My gaze locked on the familiar face. "What are you doing here?"

Ida stood at the other end of the clearing.

"Saw your car pull into this road . . ."

"You mean you *followed* me? How dare you!"

"Oh, come on, Catherine." She took a few steps toward me. I stepped backward. "I just thought, two women of similar age in a small village—maybe we can be friends?"

I glared. "Ida, friends call each other to invite them for tea or coffee. They don't follow them and appear out of nowhere." I stared hard at her.

"Those boots are convincing, but the snowshoes . . . ?" She grimaced.

"Please leave." My heart was racing twice as fast as the ticking of the clock in my head.

"Why don't we stop playing games, Catherine? I know why you're here." Her smile became sinister. "Your portal will open in a few minutes to carry you back."

I gaped.

"Did you think you were the only one?"

"What are you talking about?" I wrapped my arms around Evie-Jayne.

"There are portals like this and people like you all over the world. All I want to do is jump into yours with you."

I was so close. I wasn't going to let her jeopardize my plan. "You're crazy."

"I've seen the future."

"What?"

"The MacGregor women are travellers, too, but we don't have our own portal, so we piggyback on others."

The rising wind blew snow from the trees around us.

Ida tightened her scarf. "I thought I'd try going back to a simpler time."

"Back?"

"I was born in Montreal. There's a portal in Place Royale."

"How do you know where these supposed portals are?"

"Journals. The Idas in my family record every portal as we find it and pass the list through the generations. The old Ida you know wrote about your portal in 1832." She paused. "My mother told me about the one in Montreal. I'm going to look for one in Toronto."

Gran had travelled in 1932 . . .

Ida saw the revelation on my face. "Old Ida travelled with your Gran. She'd run away from home to avoid a forced marriage and was sleeping in this clearing when your Gran stumbled onto the site. Ida jumped in with her."

I heard the faint sound of a train whistle.

"You've told your story. Now, I want to be alone." I walked to the centre of the clearing.

Ida didn't move.

I tore my watch from my wrist. It beeped one o'clock as it hit the snow. "Get away!" I shouted.

The piercing whistle of the approaching train bored into my brain. I couldn't move. Evie-Jayne screamed. As I wrapped my arms tightly around the baby, the last thing I saw was Ida suddenly racing toward me. Something smashed into my side, and I lost consciousness.

STRAWBERRIES

Chapter Twenty-Four

A baby was crying. Sun warmed my face, and a brilliant blue sky glittered through my partially opened eyes. "Oh, God!" I sat up.

Evie-Jayne kicked her chubby legs against my chest. "It's okay, baby." I pressed my hands around her arms, her legs, and over her back. She'd come through unscathed. I pushed myself to my feet and glanced around. The snow-covered log rested to one side; a glint of the river sparkled between the pines, and the black railway track broke the white of the snow.

"We made it!" I fist-pumped the air. We were alone in the clearing. "Come on, baby girl. Let's get home."

Snowshoe prints preceded us out onto the tracks. Ida *had* hitch-hiked with us when she slammed into my side. I wondered why she hadn't waited to make sure we were all right, but then, what did it matter? We'd never see each other again. I pushed all thoughts of portals and travellers out of my mind and headed toward home.

A two-hour trek brought us to our homesite as the wintery sun hovered above the horizon. "Look, Evie-Jayne! A sundog!" I pointed to where ice crystals projected a second sun into the sky. "That's a good omen."

Long shadows crossed the snowy fields. Images of Claude at the table, helping the children complete arithmetic problems while the aroma of moose stew floated from a bubbling pot in the fireplace set my heart racing. What if there was a woman stirring the pot? My image crumbled as my mind filled with the fear that this woman was more than just someone Claude had hired to help with the children. I stopped, taking in the deep snowdrifts between the house and the barn. Claude had always insisted on keeping the courtyard clear as a safety measure. Now only a narrow path, flattened from single-file foot traffic, broke the white expanse. The welcome smell of wood smoke drifting from the chimney did nothing to relax the hair starting to rise on the back of my neck.

I mounted the porch as a male voice yelled from the interior, "Get me my whiskey, whore."

I knew that voice. But it couldn't be. I peered through the window. François was yanking a young woman by her long black hair as she placed a glass of whiskey on the table. She looked up. My eyes locked on Tekakwitha's. Recognition flitted across her face before she turned away.

What was that bastard doing here? Where were Claude, Jean-Pierre, and Sophie?

I retreated to the barn just as light from the house flooded the porch. Beau tossed his head in greeting, Étoile nickered. "Hello, my sweet." I rubbed her nose. Evie-Jayne still slept against my chest, covered by the folds of my coat.

I heard Tekakwitha call over her shoulder. "I need eggs for dinner." The shaft of light disappeared, and the door clicked closed. She tottered along the path toward me, her pregnant belly impeding her speed.

Stepping inside, she whispered, "Catherine?"

When I emerged from the shadows behind the door, she took hold of my hands. "Is Claude with you?"

"He's not here? Where are J.P. and Sophie?"

She dropped my hands. "It isn't safe here. You must go."

"But, why are you here? Is Ma'iingan with you?"

The last rays of daylight through the barn windows illuminated lines of exhaustion across her forehead and around her mouth. She shook her head. "He's up north again trapping for the Hudson's Bay Company." She began collecting eggs. "After Ma'iingan left, the men brought liquor back into the village. I left to keep my children safe. Claude said you were in Toronto and that I could stay with him until Ma'iingan returned."

"And François?"

"Claude left at the end of May. He took Sophie to someone named Oma, then took the train with J.P. He said I could stay in the house with my children as long as I needed to." Her brow creased. "François came after Claude left. He forces me to cook, clean, and lay with him." She hung her head. "And now, I am going to have his child." She looked at me, eyes wide with fear. "You must go."

"Did Claude say when he was coming back?"

She shook her head.

Outside, the house door banged against the wall. We both jumped.

"How long does it take to get eggs!"

"I must go." Tekakwitha waddled back to the house.

Evie-Jayne began to fuss. We settled into the straw in the back of the barn, and I put her to my breast. At least Sophie was safe. Where had Claude gone with J.P.?

Evie-Jayne finished and began to doze. My safest alternative was to take the train from Stanley Station to Webbwood in the morning. I'd be with Sophie, and perhaps Elisabeth would have more information. I could send the North-West Mounted Police back here to rescue Tekakwitha. The darkness of the barn enfolded me as I made a nest in the straw to keep us warm.

Suddenly, the barn door creaked. I roused, holding Evie-Jayne's head against my chest, heart thumping.

"Catherine?" Tekakwitha's whisper flooded me with relief.

"I'm back here."

She swung the lantern to light my corner. "I brought you some bread and cheese."

"Thank you." I took the food and began eating.

Evie-Jayne gurgled.

"You have a baby?"

I opened my coat. "This is Evangeline Jayne." I smiled. "She's four months old."

"She's beautiful." Tekakwitha cupped her belly thoughtfully for a moment and then held out a crumpled page in her hand. "Claude asked me to give this to you if you came back before he did."

I clutched the paper to my chest.

"*Câlisse!*" François shouted from the house. "What are you doing out there, you dirty . . . ?"

Her face contorted in fear as she turned and clumsily hurried back to the house. Peeping through the barn door, I caught a glimpse of François swaying on the porch, wearing nothing but filthy long johns. "Who's out there with you? Your drunken brother?" He grabbed Tekakwitha by the arm as she mounted the porch and flung her into the house, kicking her in the back as she fell forward.

Two little faces appeared at the window.

Tekakwitha let out a sharp scream.

I hid the still-sleeping Evie-Jayne back into the straw.

"I know you're out there, you good-for-nothin' . . ." François screamed through the open doorway. "I'll keep kicking her until you show yourself!" He lurched against the doorjamb, one leg raised.

Without further thought, I strapped on my snowshoes and charged into the courtyard. "Stop!"

"What the . . . ?" François craned his neck forward, peering into the darkness.

Behind him, Tekakwitha cried out, "Catherine, run . . ."

"Catherine?" François stepped to the edge of the porch. "*Mon Dieu!* My lucky day!"

"Still playing the big man, beating and raping women, I see." My fists clenched in my mittens.

"Get in here!" Droplets of spittle shot from his mouth, reflecting in the light from the house like beads of venom.

"You want me?" I stood my ground. "Come and get me."

"You little bitch!" He started pulling on his boots, tipping unsteadily from side to side.

I ran down the hill and along the riverbank, ducking as icy strings of willow branches slapped my head. A backward glance revealed his silhouette bent double, gasping for breath. The fool was still only clad in his long johns. "Can't keep up?"

He let out a growl and resumed plodding through the snow.

The black outline of the saw shed loomed ahead. I could slip through the nearest door, hide in the inky depths, and then slink out the side door to get back to the house and lock him out.

I tripped over a log wedged between the wall and the raised threshold. New plan. I groped along the interior until my fingers curled around the handle of the wooden mallet Claude used to knock the logs into place. I hefted the shaft with both hands, bent my knees slightly, and waited in the shadows beside the entry.

François's ragged breathing announced his arrival. "You're mine, now, bitch!"

He yelped as he pitched forward over the log. His forehead hit the edge of the conveyer, with a loud crack. I brought the mallet down between his shoulder blades. The air huffed out of his lungs, and he dropped to the floor.

I escaped back up the hill to the house, my legs finding new energy at the sound of Evie-Jayne's cries in the barn. I scooped up the baby, charged up the porch through the still-open door, and slammed it firmly shut behind us. Chest heaving, I laid Evie-Jayne on the settee and tore off my snowshoes.

"There's a locking bar," Tekakwitha panted from where she lay on the floor.

This is new, I thought. I dropped it into place and dragged the pine jam cupboard for extra insurance to barricade the door.

Water and blood were pooling around Tekakwitha's drawn-up thighs. She waved weakly toward the table where a boy of about four had his arm protectively wrapped around the shoulders of his younger sister. Their thin little bodies were rigid.

I searched my memory for his name. "Come, Wiisagi, and . . . ?"

"Tesi," he said.

"Your mama needs her rest." I urged them up the ladder.

Evie-Jayne began to cry.

"Time for bed, children," I called as their bottoms disappeared into the loft. Then, I turned to the baby, freeing her from her outdoor clothing, and settling her back on the settee, walled-in by pillows.

Tekakwitha was still on the floor, rocking back and forth and moaning. Her forehead was hot, her face and neck wet with perspiration, yet she shivered uncontrollably.

"The baby is coming," she whispered, her desperate gaze holding mine. "It's too soon."

"How early?"

"One moon." She arched her back and resumed her panting.

"It's all right. We'll do this together." I helped her stand and shuffle to the large armchair in front of the fire. "I'll put water on to boil." My eyes darted from the door to the bucket beside it. Going across the yard to the pump would be too risky. I could scoop snow from the veranda.

"Claude put in a pump." Tekakwitha pointed to the kitchen.

A brief smile played around the corners of my mouth as I remembered mentioning the indoor pump in Amelia's kitchen to him after Paul and Anna's wedding. I stoked the fire, filled two large pots, and set them to boil.

Now what? I needed to appear confident to keep Tekakwitha calm. I grabbed one of my nightgowns from the bedroom dresser and pulled some blankets and towels from the pine box at the foot of the bed. Images of Claude and I in the bed danced across my vision, but Tekakwitha's moans brought me back to reality.

I covered the windows with blankets. Nothing existed outside of our warm, candlelit cocoon. Time disappeared.

Throughout the night, I sponged Tekakwitha's face and neck with warm water and lavender and supported her when she felt the need to walk. At times, she dropped into a fitful sleep in the chair, throwing off the blankets, only to awaken shivering and bathed in sweat.

When François didn't reappear, I assumed he was still lying unconscious in the shed. Later, I imagined him sheltering in the barn, planning his attack. Eventually, I pushed away all thought of him, refusing to consider what could befall a barely-dressed drunk out cold in minus thirty degrees. Each time my thoughts wandered, Tekakwitha's wails pulled me back.

The children rose as daylight tiptoed around the edges of the blanketed windows. They approached their mother, mouths drawn down, eyes wide.

"Mama?" Tesi whispered.

Wiisagi caressed his mother's arm.

Tekakwitha opened her eyes and forced a smile as she suppressed a groan. She spread her arms, and both children snuggled against her. "It's all right." Her body tightened, and she exhaled sharply. "Go. Obey tante Catherine." And she squeezed her eyes shut.

I gave the children toasted bread and dried apples to munch on as they half-heartedly played with the dogs and cats fashioned out of rags and string in front of the fire.

"Do you remember a dog and cat living here?" I asked.

Wiisagi responded to my question, whispering so as not to disturb his mother. "Mama snuck Snoopy to *mon oncle* Maurice because that man kept kicking him," while Tesi disappeared into the back corner under the loft. I heard her rummaging through the crates.

The little girl emerged, clasping a mass of wriggling grey-striped fur tightly to her chest. "Luthy!" she announced, eyes sparkling.

I gave a relieved laugh as she handed me the cat.

"Catherine!" Tekakwitha called urgently.

"I'm here." I moved to her side and took her hand.

"It's close." Her eyes overflowed, the tears coursing down her hollow cheeks where bruises bloomed from François's latest attack. With my assistance, she positioned herself into a crouch against the edge of the chair.

"Would you be more comfortable in bed?"

"This is better for the baaaaa . . ." Her face contorted as she rode the wave of another contraction. Gasping in the aftermath, she prodded her abdomen. "The little one is pushing on my spine. I think he's facing the wrong way."

My chest tightened. "You mean he's breech?" In response to her puzzled expression, I clarified, "He's coming out feet first?"

She shook her head. "His head is down, but his back is against mine. We need to help him face the other way." She screwed her hand in the air to demonstrate.

"How do we do that?"

"I need to give him space to turn. Help me get on my knees."

I swallowed hard and tried to calm my breathing as I supported her onto all fours on the floor. "I helped with a birthing in our village where the baby had to be turned. When he comes out, pull the cord to the side."

"Okay. What else?"

"Keep warm cloths on my back."

I draped her lower back with cloths soaked in hot water. At the onset of each contraction, she dropped her shoulders and chest, raising her behind. Between the pains, I helped her move back to her knees. She sang softly to the baby while Wiisagi and Tesi sat on either side of her, stroking her belly in circular motions.

I laid out the two thin leather laces she'd prepared to tie off the umbilical cord, scrubbed the sharpest knife with lye soap, and laid it beside the laces. A large basin of warm water waited to bathe the newborn. Towels and baby blankets warmed on the drying rack in front of the fire.

The concentration of our preparations lulled us into a world focussed solely on the baby. Suddenly, Tesi squealed. She had felt pressure against her palm.

"Don't stop, Tesi," I said. "Keep rubbing." I joined her and felt movement under my hand. "There he goes. Come on, little one."

"Push him, Catherine." Tekakwitha took deep, slow breaths. "I can't stop . . . Oh, no, no . . . !" Her wail spiralled to a scream. The baby was crowning.

"Push!" I said and forced the cord to the side as the head cleared.

"One more," I yelled. Then, with a final whoosh, I was holding a tiny baby in my hands. "It's a girl!" I was laughing and crying at the same time.

Tekakwitha slumped backward against the chair, hair plastered to her forehead. Wiisagi stood at my elbow, holding a warm towel open. Placing the baby on her mother's abdomen, I grabbed each lace as Tesi handed it to me, tied it tightly around the umbilical cord, and cut the cord between the two laces.

"She's not crying." Tekakwitha's voice was filled with panic.

"Let me take her." I moved the baby onto my lap on the floor, massaging her chest and jiggling her tiny body. The baby's mouth gaped open and closed several times, the chest rose sporadically. Wiisagi stroked her feet while Tesi stood beside us, holding a fresh baby blanket. Both children began humming the song again. Within the eternity of another thirty seconds, we watched the little one's attempts to catch her breath.

"Come on." I turned her on her side and cleared her mouth with my little finger.

And then it came. A soft mewling accompanied by several ragged sighs. The baby's colour deepened from waxen to red as her cries became stronger. When her breathing was even, I placed her on her mother's chest.

"Come little one, you're safe." Tekakwitha guided the baby to her breast. "Thank you." She smiled at me. "Children, come see your little sister."

Tesi and Wiisagi pressed to their mother's side.

"I'm so proud of you. You helped bring your sister into the world."

Tesi jumped around in glee while Wiisagi stood by, grinning.

Tekakwitha turned her head to me. "Catherine, I'm so tired." Her eyes fluttered closed.

One look at the floor spurred me into action. "Children, give your mama a kiss and then up in the loft. You can play quietly!"

The children wordlessly followed my directions.

The sheets on the floor continued to absorb what seemed an enormous amount of blood. She had expelled the afterbirth, but blood continued to trickle steadily from between her legs. The signs were frighteningly familiar.

I pivoted her chair. Scooping up her legs, I rested her feet on the edge of the dining table. Next, I wadded a pillow of fresh sheets to elevate her hips.

Hydration, I remembered, was as essential as elevation, but with no IV . . . While the water boiled, I chased a pesky memory. Rummaging through the cupboard, my hand closed around the jar of smartweed—*for bleeding* Elisabeth had said.

I shook Tekakwitha by the shoulder. Her open eyes drifted unfocussed around the room, but her colour had not deteriorated further. The blood flow seemed to have stopped, though I had no way knowing if it was pooling in her uterus. I decided to hope for the best.

"Drink this." I held the cup to her lips. She swallowed.

I bathed and swaddled the baby and then snuggled her back into her mother's arms.

Next, Evie-Jayne began her hungry cry. After a few moments rest while Evie-Jayne suckled, the children poked their heads over the edge of the loft, asking for something to eat. I took eggs, pork strips, bread, and jam from the cupboard, and soon the children and I were seated at one end of the table while Tekakwitha's feet remained perched on the opposite end. She nibbled while we ate.

The light behind the blanketed window had faded to darkness. Revived by food and tea, we remained at the table, reliving the past twenty-four hours, each one contributing to the story of how we'd brought the sweet angel into the world.

"Mama, what is our sister's name?" Wiisagi asked.

"I have my son, Wiisagi-ma'iingan, strong as his uncle the wolf, yet clever like the coyote."

Wiisagi squared his shoulders and pushed out his bony chest. I applauded.

"My daughter, Waawaatesi, sparkles as she flits from place to place, bringing light wherever she goes like the firefly."

Tesi pressed against her mother's side, eyes shining. Her mother stroked her hair.

"And now, I have my butterfly, Memengwaa, who came to us on fragile wings. We shall call her Gwaa."

We all tested the name, nodding our approval.

"Now, it's time for bed," Tekakwitha said.

"But we aren't sleepy," protested Wiisagi.

"I have an idea." Within moments, I was dragging the oval wash tub out from the storage area under the loft. Setting it in front of the fire, I lined it with a sheet and filled it with warm water and a few drops of lavender. Tesi and Wiisagi hung back, doubt clouding their faces as I dipped Evie-Jayne into the tub. My daughter kicked her chubby legs and giggled as the warm water splashed over her head.

I beckoned to Tekakwitha's two little ones. "Want to help me?"

Tesi came forward first.

"Here." I handed her the cloth. "You can wash her while I hold her."

Tesi gingerly held the cloth at arm's length.

"That's it. Wipe it over her legs. Gently."

Soon, Tesi was running the dripping cloth over Evie-Jayne's body. The more the baby wiggled, the further Tesi leaned over the edge of the tub until she teeter-tottered head first into the water. Coming up sputtering, she looked ready to cry, until, in the face of our laughter, she broke into a smile and started bobbing. Flapping her arms on the water's surface, she called to her brother, "Look, Wiisagi, I'm swimming."

Within seconds, Wiisagi had peeled off his clothes and sunk into the tub beside his sister. I tossed in some soft soap to make bubbles, then dried and dressed Evie-Jayne for bed. Tekakwitha supervised the bath from her chair, while she drank more smartweed tea. With Evie-Jayne settled, I rekindled the bedroom fire, refreshed the bed, and then dried, and packed the two children off to bed in the loft.

Next, it was Tekakwitha's turn. A warm sponge bath relaxed her. I brushed her black hair, leaving it to flow freely in waves down her back. Gingerly we lowered her feet. The bleeding seemed to have slowed to a normal discharge. I helped her into a fresh nightgown and moved her and the baby to the bedroom where we could elevate her hips and legs, but where she could sleep in greater comfort.

Unsure of her tradition, I wrapped the afterbirth in a rag and stashed it in the cold storage cupboard.

Even breathing enveloped the house as I sat in front of the fire sipping tea, freshly bathed, and wearing one of my winter nightgowns. Evie-Jayne slept peacefully in my arms. Jeans, snow pants, and parka lay in a heap on the floor in the corner where I'd dropped them, like a moulting cricket. Tomorrow, I'd deal with their safe storage. A few faint rusty stains remained on the sheets and towels hanging over the drying rack by the fire, despite my vigorous scrubbing in the tub of bathwater.

Gazing at my baby, I let the tears come. Alone in the firelight, I felt a little emotionalism could be justified.

Rhubarb, Strawberries, and Willows

Tomorrow, I'd have to brave the barn. We needed milk and eggs as well as whatever else I could find in the root cellar. Tonight, though, I needed sleep.

As I settled into my bed of blankets and quilts on the floor in front of the fire, I heard the sound of crinkling paper under my hip. How could I have forgotten? I dug for the folded page. My heart fluttered as I gazed at Claude's familiar handwriting in the firelight.

Ma très chère Catherine,

If you are reading this letter, then you have returned to our home. I will be back. Please wait for me.

That terrible day when we returned to the house, it looked like there had been a fight. I pray the blood wasn't yours?

The children had clung to me. Swallowing my own panic, I set them to gathering the papers and placing the furniture upright while I went to milk the cows and check the barn. I found the trunk open and your other-time clothes missing. My heart sank.

Returning to the house, I told the children you'd gone to Webbwood to visit Oma Elisabeth. Then, because it was late, you were likely staying the night with her. I suggested someone must have tried to rob us when they saw the house unoccupied. Reassuring them all would be well, I managed to get them off to bed.

Then, lantern in hand, I followed your trail. When I came to the end of snowshoe prints in your clearing by the railway track, I knew.

Catherine, I thought you loved us too much to have run away.

When you didn't return I began telling everyone, including the children, that you'd taken ill and Dr. Jones in Webbwood had sent you to a special doctor in Toronto.

Day after day, I saw your reflection in the window, heard your voice on the wind through the pines, and breathed your scent in our bed. The house felt like someone had permanently blown out all the candles. One day I realized I couldn't remember the last time I'd heard my children laugh, or seen their sweet faces light up in joy. After months of waiting and hoping for your return, we needed to escape this place.

That's when I resolved to keep the promise I'd made to you. I have travelled to Montreal and Compton to visit my parents and siblings and to check on Gisèle. I've taken J.P. with me to meet his grandparents and the rest of the family. I will tell him about his mother and his twin sister on the way.

Sophie is living in Webbwood with Elisabeth where she can attend school. Elisabeth required no explanation, and I know whatever conclusions she has drawn will be kept close to her heart.

Tekakwitha may still be living in the house. I will let her tell her own story.

My dearest, darling Catherine, the dream of holding you again, kissing your face and hearing you tell me you love me is what keeps me moving forward. If all goes well, J.P. and I should be back home in September.

Je t'aime mon amour

May 15, 1889   Claude

September? But this was January. Why the delay?

I reread the letter just for the joy of hearing his voice in my head until I dropped into a deep, dreamless sleep, the letter pressed to my chest.

STRAWBERRIES

Chapter Twenty-Five

The muffled stomping of horses' hooves. Daylight was streaming in around the window covers. Voices outside startled me into full wakefulness.

" . . . feed bags . . . horses . . . sleigh." A man's voice was giving directions.

I sat up, my stomach contracting.

Heavy stamping resounded on the porch. Someone tried to open the door. The lock bar and the heavy cupboard held. I stood frozen in the middle of the room, hugging the shawl around my shoulders.

"Hello?" His voice was like a symphony to my ear. "Tekakwitha, it's Claude. Are you all right?"

Footsteps moved along the porch. I ran to the window and ripped down the blanket. Our eyes met. His hand pressed against mine on the glass.

I pushed the cupboard aside and clawed at the lock bar. Then, I was in his arms. His scent mingled with winter freshness filling my nostrils.

"Catherine, *ma chère, chère*, Catherine," he murmured, his lips against my hair, my face pressed tightly into his chest. He drew me in for a kiss. I gave myself over to the soft moistness of his lips on mine. Jean-Pierre wrapped his arms around our waists. "Maman, maman!"

Hungry baby squawks interrupted our reunion. Claude looked to where Tekakwitha stood in the bedroom doorway, holding Gwaa and grinning.

I broke from our embrace. "Tekakwitha gave birth to Gwaa last night." I motioned for her to sit.

"*Bonjour,* Monsieur Claude," Tekakwitha said.

Claude's brow wrinkled. "When did you get back?"

"Let's talk after breakfast." I squeezed his arm.

"Of course," Claude cleared his throat. "I'd best go pay John Hall's driver so he can be on his way back to Nelsonville." He backed through the doorway, motioning Jean-Pierre to remain inside.

"Jean-Pierre, can you please stir up the fire and set water to boil?" I called over my shoulder as I moved to Tekakwitha.

He nodded and began removing his outdoor clothing.

At Tekakwitha's side, she leaned into me and whispered, "Catherine, can you tell him?" She bit her lip. "It is hard for me to . . ."

I put my arm around her shoulder. "Of course, but you know what happened with François wasn't your fault. Claude will be angry, but not with you."

"Still . . . to speak of such things to a man . . ." She drew her mouth tight.

"Don't worry. I'll take care of it."

She gave me a grateful smile.

Wiisagi and Tesi scrambled down the ladder and ran to their mother. "Is Monsieur Claude here?" Wiisagi asked.

"Yes," I said, "and you need to get dressed. You don't want him to think you're sleepyheads."

The children giggled.

"J.P.!" Tesi screeched. Both children ran to hug him.

"J.P. can you help these two get dressed, please?" I gave him a hug and kissed the top of his head.

He squeezed my waist before letting go. "*Oui.*" He shepherded the two children up the ladder.

Tekakwitha moved to the bedroom. "I'll settle Gwaa and make breakfast." When Claude came in, she was kneading dough for biscuits while pork slices sizzled in the iron skillet, and I was making coffee.

"*Bonjour,* Monsieur Claude," Wiisagi and Tesi chanted as they climbed down the ladder.

Claude scooped them both into his arms, nuzzling their necks with his beard.

"Let go!" Tesi squealed.

"Arrr!" Claude growled. "Not until you tell me where you're going."

"The barn! J.P., wait."

Jean-Pierre was already at the door, pulling on his coat and boots.

"We have to get eggs and milk," Wiisagi explained.

Claude set them on their feet. "Off you go."

"*Viens*! But first, we pee." They followed Jean-Pierre to the outhouse.

Tekakwitha and I laughed. It felt good to feel lighter.

Evie-Jayne let out a hungry cry from the cradle.

Claude looked at me.

I felt the corners of my mouth twitch. "I need to feed her." I picked up Evie-Jayne and tilted my head toward the ladder. Following me up to the loft, his body moved as if it was a giant question mark. We sat opposite each other on the children's beds, knees touching across the narrow space. I introduced Evangeline Jayne to her father. His eyes filled with wonder as he held her. My heart quickened. Then, as I put her to my breast, he devoured her with his eyes, stroking her feet, her arms, trying to catch up on four months in the first few minutes.

Downstairs, the children burst through the door. "Here are the eggs, Mama. And J.P. showed me how to milk Crème." Wiisagi's voice rose into the rafters.

"Crème says moooo," Tesi said.

A few minutes later, Tekakwitha called, "Breakfast is ready."

We heard the scrape of chairs against the plank floor and the happy chatter as the children settled around the table. Claude went down, returning with two plates laden with eggs, pork, and buttery biscuits. He set them on the tiny table between the beds and sat down opposite me again.

"*Mon amour*, I never gave up hope, but to also bring this gift." He caressed my cheek.

I took a deep breath. "I didn't go back on purpose. I was searching for you when suddenly . . . the train . . ." My chin quivered. "I had to wait until January twenty-first to come back."

"January 21? The house . . . ?" He reached across the space to touch my leg. "Were you hurt?"

I bit my lower lip. I searched his face, my heart thudding in my ears. "He raped me."

"*Mon Dieu*, Catherine." He moved to sit beside me and held the baby and me in his arms. We rocked together until Evie-Jayne's protests brought us back. I laid her on the bed.

"It's all my fault." His voice was tight. "I should've put in that lock bar sooner."

"The bar wouldn't have made a difference." I swallowed hard. "I let him in."

He gasped. "You knew him?"

"It was François." I sucked in my lower lip.

His eyebrows rose. "My brother?"

"He saw you and J.P. leave that morning."

"He was watching our house?" His eyes narrowed and the pupils shrank to pinpricks.

"He said he was on his way out West and remembered you lived in this area, so he asked around, and when Mrs. Edwards told him where you lived, he decided to visit."

Claude looked like he was ready to say something. Then, he gave his head a gentle shake and waved with his hand for me to continue.

The words spilled out. "At first, he seemed friendly . . . then . . ." I watched his face. "I tried to fight him off, but . . ."

"*Câlisse de tabarnak!*" he exploded. "I'll kill him!" He bumped his head on the low ceiling as he tried to stand.

There was a sudden silence from below.

"It's okay," I called. "Monsieur Claude just bumped his head."

The sound of cutlery on plates and children's chatter returned.

Claude dropped down beside me, muttering further curses on his brother.

I looked at the sleeping baby and then back into Claude's brown eyes. "She might not be yours," I whispered, my heart in my throat.

He was silent for a long moment. Then, he reached for her. She opened her eyes and gave her father a bright smile. "Of course she's mine." He smiled back and gently bounced her in his arms.

The pressure in my chest melted away. I urged a biscuit on him, and we ate in silence, easing into being together again.

Claude's shoulders relaxed. "Last night, we stayed in John Hall's hotel. He told me François had arrived in Nelsonville a year ago." His brows drew down. "Staggered into town with a burn and a bump on his forehead and a bite on his calf. Claimed he'd been attacked by a bear." He let out a bitter laugh. "No one believed him, but because he claimed to be my brother, John took him in." Claude bit into a strip of pork.

"Snoopy bit him. And after he—" I swallowed. "I knocked him out with the hot frying pan and tied him up."

He shook his head. I saw the admiration in his eyes before he refocussed. "John said François started running card games in a hut behind the hotel." A nerve vibrated along his jaw. "His debts piled up. When he was caught cheating, he fled."

I rested my hand on his knee. "When I got back two days ago, I found François here with Tekakwitha. He'd been keeping her prisoner, raping and beating her for months."

"*Mon Dieu.*" He held his head in his hands. "Poor Tekakwitha."

"Gwaa is François's child."

He grasped my hand. I winced when his thumb pressed against the bumps on my fingers. Gently opening my hand, he asked, "What happened?"

I gulped. "They were broken when he—"

"Where is the bastard?" His voice was low with menace. "I'll tear him limb from limb."

"He was drunk when I got here, so I hid in the barn." I described how I'd lured him into the saw shed and hit him with the mallet. "I don't know where he is now."

Claude stared at the rafters behind my head. Then, his gaze dropped to Evie-Jayne. "I'll find him." He disappeared down the ladder with his baby daughter in his arms.

I took a few deep breaths, smoothed my hair, and followed him. The entire lower space had been cleaned up. "Thank you, Tekakwitha, for a lovely breakfast."

"J.P. was a big help."

Jean-Pierre grinned, basking in the recognition.

Tekakwitha looked drawn.

"Are you all right?" I asked. "The bleeding . . ."

"Everything is normal," she smiled. "I'm just tired." She moved to the bedroom. "Tesi, Wiisagi, play quietly by the fire, and don't bother *tante* Catherine."

"Yes, Mama." The children collected their straw and rag figures and settled on the rug.

Meanwhile, Claude had returned Evie-Jayne to her cradle. He was pulling on his boots and coat.

"Where are you going, *papa*?" Jean-Pierre asked.

Claude grabbed his tuque, and before heading out the door, he said, "I need to check the saw shed."

Jean-Pierre and I watched his father leave.

"Is papa angry because of what *mon oncle* François did in Nelsonville?"

I gave Jean-Pierre my full attention. "How do you know about that?"

"I heard *papa* and Mr. Hall talking. I know it's not nice to listen, but they were so close."

"It's okay, *mon gars*. Your papa will settle things with your uncle." I put my arm around his shoulders. "Let's sit by the fire. Would you like to hold your baby sister?"

We sat side by side on the settee, watching Wiisagi and Tesi playing with their rag animals. Lucy was curled next to Tesi on the rug. The little girl's hand drifted to the cat's head every now and then.

Jean-Pierre held Evie-Jayne on his lap. "Look, maman, I can make her smile." He wiggled his eyebrows, and she rewarded him with a grin. He turned his eyes to me. "Why did you go away?"

"I needed special care from a doctor in Toronto, so your sister could be born." The truth was not a viable alternative, at least not yet.

"But, maman, you didn't even say goodbye." His brow creased. "And the house was such a mess . . ."

"I know J.P., but I was very sick and had to leave right away." I smiled brightly. "I'm back now, and so are you, and tomorrow we'll get Sophie. Soon, our whole family will be together."

The corners of Jean-Pierre's mouth drooped. Even Evie-Jayne's efforts to touch her brother's face with her flailing arm failed to distract him.

"What's wrong, *mon gars*?" I put my hand on his shoulder.

"When we were with mamère and pépère, papa told me about my real mother and my twin sister."

"Oh, I see." I paused. "That must have been hard for you."

"We went to see them in the ground."

"In the—" It hit me. "Oh."

"Papa was sad." He exhaled loudly. "But I felt like it was a story in a book about other people—another boy in a family I didn't know." His blue eyes were filled with shadows.

I took Evie-Jayne from him and placed her in the cradle.

"After we saw my mother's grave, papa left me with mamère and pépère and went to Montreal to speak with the doctors. The whole time papa was away, they kept talking about how sad I must be to not have a mother or a sister. Then, one day, I told mamère and pépère I *do* have a mother and a sister." He tightened his lower lip.

I longed to pull him into my arms, but he needed to be free to talk.

"When papa came back, they told him we should stay with them and forget about you and Sophie."

"Oh, dear."

"That's when papa packed our things, and we moved to *ma tante* Hélène's house. Papa told mamère and pépère we'd be going home in few days. Mamère began to cry. Pépère yelled, and told him not to come back. Papa slammed the door when we left."

"Oh my." Things had clearly gone badly, yet they'd been away for over eight months. I held my tongue, sensing there was more to come.

Jean-Pierre stared at the fire, absently rocking the cradle with his foot. "I played pirates with my cousins in the barn. They showed me how to shoot an arrow, and we went hunting in the forest. It was fun at *ma tante's*." His hands fidgeted in his lap.

I laid my hand on his knee to stop the vigorous rocking of his foot, fearing he was about to tip Evie-Jayne out of her cradle.

"One day, the adults called us together and told us pépère got sick in the night. They said he had a stroke?"

I nodded.

"They said *le docteur* wasn't sure what would happen next."

"So you and papa stayed to help the family?"

"*Oui*. Papa helped *mon oncle* Clément with the farm chores, and he did all the paperwork *mamère* used to do, so she could take care of *pépère*."

"Did *pépère* get better?"

He shook his head. "All he could do was lie in bed and eat whatever *mamère* fed him. We all helped on the farm, and in September, I went to school with *mes cousins*."

"How did you like school?" I asked.

"You would have been so proud of me." Jean-Pierre grinned. "I could read and do maths better than *mes cousins*. The teacher helped me with writing. She told papa I was a good learner just like him."

I raised my eyebrows.

"The teacher went to school with *papa* when they were children. She seemed very happy to see him."

"I see." The piquance of jealousy spiced my curiosity. "Did the teacher have children?"

"No, maman," he laughed. "She didn't have a husband. But I heard her say to papa it would be her pleasure to help him take care of me." He paused, frowning. "When I asked papa what she meant, his face turned red, and he just shrugged and said he didn't know. But I think he did."

I smiled. "Let's leave that between your father and the teacher." The room had become quite dim.

"We've been talking for a long time." I pulled him into my arms. "*Je t'aime mon fils*. I missed you so much. I thought about you every day."

I felt him stiffen in my arms.

"Mamère and pépère said family is about blood, and you and Sophie aren't my family because we don't share blood."

I spoke slowly, swallowing my anger. "It's true, some family members share blood, and they share similarities, like how you are tall, thoughtful, and quiet like your papa. I'm sure your papa sees some of your birth mother in you, too."

"So Sophie and Evie-Jayne *are* my sisters because we all share papa's blood?"

I nodded.

"But what about us?" he asked.

I placed my hands on our two hearts. "J.P., you are in my heart where all our blood flows. You'll always be my son."

I was rewarded with an exuberant hug. "*Je t'aime,* maman."

"*Merci, mon gars.* Now, can you stir up the fires while I begin cooking supper? Your *papa* should be back soon."

"*Oui,* maman."

What was taking Claude so long? He'd left for the shed over two hours ago.

I was standing at the kitchen worktop when Tekakwitha emerged from the bedroom and sidled up to me. Gwaa rested in a sling against her chest. "Everything is well with J.P.?" she whispered.

"He's fine." I smiled. "Just needed to get some things off his chest."

"Monsieur Claude is still not back?"

I held her gaze. "He went looking for you know who . . ."

She squeezed my arm. "It will be all right."

I nodded. "Thought I'd start making supper."

"I'll help. There's moose in the cold cupboard, and I can make some bannock."

"Perfect." I sliced the slab of moose meat, cut up potatoes and carrots, and put it all to roast in the wood oven. Tekakwitha dumped flour, baking powder, and sugar in a bowl, adding milk as she mixed. Once the bannock dough was kneaded, we broke off fist-sized pieces and flattened them under our palms.

Tekakwitha was frying the hockey puck-sized buns to a golden brown in the iron skillet, and I was preparing tea when we heard stomping on the porch. Her eyes flew to mine. We both exhaled when Claude stepped in alone, brushing snow off his jacket.

He straightened his shoulders. The lines around his mouth seemed tighter.

Tekakwitha and I stood, frozen while he kept his head down and removed his outdoor clothing.

"Did you find him? Is he . . .?" My voice croaked into silence as his eyes met mine. He gave his head a slight shake, nodded toward the children, and mouthed, later. What the hell did that head shake mean? Was François gone? Was he dead?

"Mmm! Smells delicious." He forced a cheery tone, then joined the children in front of the fire, playing a bowling pin game with the boys while Tesi looked on until we called them all to the table.

Supper was filled with children's laughter. Claude made animal noises for Tesi and Wiisagi to identify, and Jean-Pierre joined in, contorting his facial expressions to mimic the animals when they were stumped.

With the sweet warmth of apple crisp in their tummies, the children were soon ready to sleep. Jean-Pierre slept in his own bed; Wiisagi occupied Sophie's, and Tekakwitha took Tesi and Gwaa with her into our bedroom. Evie-Jayne slumbered in her cradle beside Claude and I in front of the fire. I was pouring our second cups of tea when Claude broke the silence.

"I found François."

At last. I stopped in mid-pour. The tea pot rattled as I set it on the table and fixed my eyes on his face.

The orange firelight flickered in his deep brown eyes. "Face down in the saw shed with a deep gash across his forehead."

My hand flew to my mouth.

"Frozen." He looked down, shook his head. "Stupid, drunken bastard." The words rumbled from his chest.

I inhaled shakily. My hands trembled. "What have I done?" I whispered. I dropped my eyes to the fire. François's face leered at me through the flames. "I killed your brother." My voice lay flat in the quiet room.

Claude moved to embrace me, but I pushed him away.

"Catherine . . ." His voice echoed down a long black tunnel, but I couldn't make out what he was saying over the sound of François in my mind, crowing that he'd won.

Then, Claude was beside me, pressing a glass of whisky against my lips, stroking my hair. "Drink."

The whisky burned down my throat. "I lured him out there." I couldn't look at him. "I thought he'd wake up." I clutched the glass. My eyes watched the firelight dance red and yellow through the amber liquid.

Claude was calm. "You did nothing wrong. His stupidity and arrogance killed him." He took my chin into his hands, forcing my gaze to meet his. "*Je t'aime.*" He drew me down onto our bed in front of the fire and held me close, my head on his chest.

"What do we do now?"

"I made him a pine box. He'll keep in the shed 'til spring."

I pushed back and sat up. "I meant you and me . . . What do *we* do now?"

Claude's brown eyes flickered golden. "After you disappeared, I began to feel like I was disappearing too, because I didn't have anyone around me who really knew me. I couldn't even find myself in the mirror. These last years you were there with me when life grew stormy. You always found me when I felt lost. That's when I realized I needed to keep my promise and face my family and Gisèle. I should have done it long ago." He took a deep breath. "Gisèle died three years ago. She never regained her self."

"I know. J.P. told me."

His brows raised.

"That's for tomorrow," I said. "So what do we do now?"

He smiled. "Now, we live without shadows." And he kissed me deeply. I forced the shadow of François's leering face into a back corner of my mind. Locking it away would require more time and energy than I could summon right now.

Gwaa's cries came from the bedroom.

I pulled back from our embrace and pushed myself to my feet. "I need to tell Tekakwitha."

"Now?"

"She shouldn't have to spend another minute in fear." I pulled my shawl around my shoulders, and padded into our bedroom.

STRAWBERRIES

Chapter Twenty-Six

"Good morning, my love." I kissed Claude and placed a cup of coffee beside him on the floor. Then, plucking Evie-Jayne from her cradle, I plopped her down beside him. "Here you go, sweetie. Cuddle with *papa*."

The aroma of freshly cooked porridge laced with maple syrup drew Wiisagi and Jean-Pierre down from the loft.

"Everyone to the outhouse first. Hurry, your porridge is waiting," Tekakwitha said. Her eyes met mine over the children's heads as they ran out the door.

I turned to my husband. "Claude, Tekakwitha and I need to see François."

His eyebrows shot up. "But he's . . ." He grimaced. "Are you sure?"

"*Oui*, Monsieur Claude."

He looked from one to the other of us. "I'll get him . . . er . . . ready." With a quizzical backward glance, he headed out.

Tekakwitha and I sat with the children while they ate their breakfast though neither of us could swallow a bite.

"J.P., papa and I are going to get Sophie today. I need you to help Tekakwitha. Maybe take Tesi and Wiisagi outside to build a snowman or ride the sled down the hill?"

"*Oui,* maman."

253

"*Merci, mon gars.*" I tousled his blond locks. "And when I get back, we'll need to shorten this hair."

He smiled and then called the children to the door and began a dressing game with them, reciting the same ditties I'd used with him and Sophie. "First you put your legs in. Then you pull the pants up. Jump, jump, jump . . ."

Claude patted the little ones on the head as he came through the door. "He's in the barn. I'll put him back in the shed later."

"*Merci.*" I put my hand on his chest on our way out. "*Mon chèr*, keep an eye on the babies?" My voice quivered.

He put his hand on my shoulder, looked at the barn, and then back to me.

"He can't hurt us." I squeezed his hand, and he let it drop.

I felt his eyes on my back as I marched across the courtyard, catching up with Tekakwitha at the barn. He turned into the house as I pulled the barn door closed. I stood facing the door, fists clenched at my sides. I'd lain awake all night, planning what I was going to say, anticipating the release I would feel. Anger suppressed the ambivalence I felt about my role in his death.

I took a deep breath and turned, the musky smell of livestock bringing me no comfort today. Tekakwitha was backlit by a glowing cloud of dust moats drifting through the sunbeams that crisscrossed the barn. I moved to her side.

The pine box, sitting across two bales of hay, was barely discernible in the dim light under the loft. The lid leaned against the bales. I squeezed Tekakwitha's hand, and we walked up to it.

I gasped.

Tekakwitha took a step backward.

François's waxen face was frozen into an open-mouthed sneer, his lip curled to one side. Ice pearled along the lashes of his closed eyes. The split in his forehead glistened white, surrounded by blackened blood down both temples. His darkened fingers were claws frozen to the front opening of his long johns.

"You sick bastard," I muttered. The speech I'd prepared last night dissolved into a pool of sadness within me. "I'll never forget what you did, but I didn't intend for you to end this way." I glared at him. "At least you won't hurt anyone again." I turned on my heel.

Tekakwitha was staring past François, eyes glazed. I perched on a bale of hay on the other side of the open space. With a deep intake of breath, she took two steps forward. Her low voice resonated into every corner of the barn. "You made me feel weak, but my children gave me the strength to survive." Her shoulders squared. "Whenever you creep into my mind, I will squash you like a mosquito." She squeezed her thumb and index fingertip together in the space above his face. Then, she turned and joined me.

We sat without talking. The dust continued to dance in the sunlight. The horses nickered into the silence, Crème mooed. The chickens scoured the dirt at our feet, looking for lost seeds.

"I was going to scream at him, curse him." I stared into the sunbeams.

Tekakwitha put her hand on my leg. "I know, me too. But he gave me Gwaa."

"I want to hate him, but seeing him like that . . . How can I feel sorry for someone so evil?"

"When we were little, Nokomis told Ma'iingan and me tales about the trickster, Nanabush. He was greedy, selfish, and lazy." Tekakwitha smiled. "Whenever he did anything stupid or evil, he'd say to himself, 'There's another thing my human beings can do.'"

I tilted my head.

"Nanabush made humans and because he had weaknesses, Nokomis said, we all have weaknesses." Tekakwitha picked at the stray strands in the bale. "We have to forgive ourselves and others."

I took a deep breath. "Do you forgive him?" I nodded toward the box.

She shrugged and gave a small smile. "I feel like I dropped a heavy fur from my shoulders."

I nodded. "Me too. I guess that's a start."

We hugged.

"My gran told me once that when disaster strikes, sometimes the best thing is to find a new start," I whispered.

"Wise women, my Nokomis and your Gran."

Together, we picked up the lid and slid it into place, turned, and walked out of the barn and back to the house, hand in hand.

* * *

Tekakwitha remained with the children while Claude and I travelled by wagon to catch the train in Stanley Station. Evie-Jayne slept in her usual position under my coat. We sat together on the driving seat, a bear rug over our legs, the warmth of his thigh pressed against mine feeling like home. The sleigh's runners whispered through the snow.

I rested my mittened hand on his knee. "J.P. told me about your trip, your parents, everything."

He glanced over. "*Oh, mon Dieu*, Catherine. I'm sorry. I wanted to tell you but . . ."

"It's good you didn't. J.P. and I had a good talk about family, blood, love."

"I'm glad he had a chance to meet his family," Claude said.

"Maybe one day he'll visit them again."

Claude shrugged. "Perhaps. But it will be without me." His inner peace shone from his clear brown eyes.

The sun warmed our shoulders. Chickadees filled the woods with the constant repetition of their name. Flashes of cardinal red and jay blue brightened the dark green branches as we followed the snowy track.

When we arrived, smoke etched lines into the infinite blue sky from the chimneys of the dozen homes clustered around the Stanley Railway Station paddock.

"Why don't I buy the tickets while you settle the care for the horses?" I dropped from the wagon onto the platform. Claude drove the horses around to the back to meet the stable hand as I pushed open the door to the waiting room. The warmth from the pot-belly stove in the corner made my cold cheeks sting. An elderly man dozed on the wooden bench, his head resting sideways on his hand.

"Madame Dumont?" Mr. Strain called from behind me in his strong British accent.

I turned to the ticket wicket. "Hello, Mr. Strain."

"Nice to see you." He tucked his conductor's pocket watch back into his jacket pocket. "Off to Webbwood today? Train will be here in a few minutes."

I smiled, appreciating the proper English manners that curtailed prying comments like an observation that he hadn't seen me in a long while. "Two return tickets, please. And one child's ticket from Webbwood."

Mr. Strain made a quick calculation, and we completed our transaction just as the train rumbled into the station.

Claude and I found a compartment to ourselves. Once the train was underway, Claude turned to me, his eyes soft. "Gran?"

I smiled broadly as I recounted my brief time with Gran. He held me as tears flowed when I told him of her passing. But describing my reconnection with Julia and Lois restored me.

When I brought Amelia to life for him, his eyes sparkled. "She sounds like her mother's daughter."

Afterward, we sat in silence, holding hands. In my head, I wrapped my memories of Amelia and Gran in the quilt I'd sewn, placing the package carefully into the back of my mind. It might not often see the light of day, but like a cherished heirloom, its presence brought me peace. In Webbwood, we disembarked into brilliant sunlight, snow squeaking under our boots, and anticipation filling my heart as we walked to Elisabeth's door.

* * *

"*Ach! Mein Gott!*" Elisabeth's hands flew to cover her open mouth as she stood in her doorway. "*Kinder, kommt rein.*" Grasping us each by a hand, she pulled us inside. "Catherine, Claude, I can't believe it!"

Closing the door behind us, she stepped back so her crinkled blue eyes could take us in from head to toe. "And you are both well, yes?" She gathered us into her embrace. "*Gott sei Dank.*"

Evie-Jayne gurgled.

"What's that? A baby?"

Elisabeth released us, smoothing her hands over her hair.

I opened my coat. "This is Evangeline Jayne. Evie-Jayne, meet your Oma Elisabeth."

The baby smiled as Elisabeth ran a finger along her cheek. My friend's face threatened to crumple as our eyes met. "Come, take off your coats. I will make *Kaffee*." She turned toward the kitchen. "Sophie will be so excited." She clapped her hands. "But we still have time. She won't be home for about an hour." Her brow furrowed. "Or maybe you want to go to school now and get her?"

I took both Elisabeth's hands in mine. "We'll wait until she comes home." I smiled. "*Kaffee und Kuchen* sounds wonderful. Why don't you and I make it together?"

Claude cleared his throat, glancing toward the door. "I'll shovel off the porch, bring in some wood." He retreated out into the wintery day.

Elisabeth put the water on the stove to boil while I freed Evie-Jayne from her sling and laid her on the settee. Then, I rinsed the cloth filter and measured fresh grounds so Elisabeth could cuddle the baby.

"You went back, didn't you?"

I looked up sharply. "How did you know?"

"Claude said he thought you did. In our hearts, we both knew you would find your way home to us." She came into the kitchen, bouncing the baby on her shoulder. "*Ach*, Catherine, that man was broken without you."

Tears of gratitude slid down my cheeks. Elisabeth asked so little and understood so much. Gran's voice moved through my head. *Choose your path, Kate*, she'd said. *Once you've gone all the way around, and closed the circle, the purpose of your journey will become clear.* I'd taken Gran's reference to closing the circle as meaning the end of life, but now I saw how life continuously plants pathways before us.

"Catherine?" Elisabeth put her hand on my arm. "I should not have said anything. Please forgive an old woman . . ."

"No, Elisabeth, it's all right." I smiled. "I got to know my Amelia, and I brought back our new baby. Life is beautiful. And you're the most remarkable friend I could ever have." I clasped both her hands in mine. "Thank you."

While we sliced raisin pound cake and arranged almond cookies on a plate, I recounted my journey back to my time, my decision to return to my family, and my intention to remain here. Elisabeth listened without question, calm as if I were telling her about a trip to the general store.

Over coffee, Claude spoke of his own long absence. "I love my family, but"—he took a long breath—"the final decision to leave came when J.P. said he wanted to go home so we could laugh again."

Elisabeth made a sympathetic sound.

"That's when I realized life was waiting for me here." Turning to Elisabeth, he said, "Thank you for taking Sophie."

"That child, what a joy! So full of life." Elisabeth beamed. "We have managed well together, but she misses her family." She nodded to herself. "I will miss her."

I reached across the table and touched her arm.

As if on cue, the frozen porch planks squealed under light footsteps. Sophie burst through the door. "I'm home, Oma Elisabeth! I'm sorry I'm late, but—"

Her eyes locked on both of us sitting at the table. "*Papa, maman!*" Her screams shattered the peace. I passed Evie-Jayne to Elisabeth as Sophie launched herself into my arms. Claude hugged us both. I felt like I was going to melt with joy, holding my daughter in my arms.

"I thought I'd never see you again, maman. Papa, why were you and J.P. gone so long?"

I brushed her hair from her face. "Sophie, we'd never leave you."

Evie-Jayne squealed.

Sophie pushed herself back to her feet and turned wide eyes to her grandmother. "Oma, whose baby is that?"

I took Evie-Jayne back from Elisabeth. "This is your sister, Evangeline Jayne."

Sophie looked from me to Claude and then back to Evie-Jayne. She paused, brow creased. Then, her expression smoothed. "That's why you went to Toronto."

I nodded. That was the safest story, at least for now.

She leaned into the baby, smiling broadly. "Hello, Evangeline Jayne. I'm your big sister, Sophie."

The baby waved her chubby arms. Sophie laughed. "That's right. I have so much to teach you."

Evie-Jayne grasped a handful of her sister's hair and pulled.

STRAWBERRIES

Chapter Twenty-Seven

Maurice nuzzled his beard into Celestine's neck. She was still giggling as he handed her up into the wagon.

"What a big girl" I said as I took the twenty-month-old from her father and set her beside Sophie on the rear-facing bench. Celestine flung her chubby arms around Sophie's neck, still clutching her rag doll.

Maurice's hand lingered on his pregnant wife's back as she mounted the steps.

"Celestine, *dit bonjour à tante* Catherine," Adeline said as she settled herself beside me.

Celestine graced me with a smile and whispered, "*Bonjour, ma tante Catherine."* Her auburn curls had escaped her bonnet in unruly tangles. Returning her attention to Sophie, Celestine showed how she and her doll were clothed in identical outfits.

Jean-Pierre sat up front between his father and Maurice. Evie-Jayne was securely tied to me in her sling, her basket stowed at my feet.

"Everyone ready?" Claude asked.

"*Oui*, papa." Sophie pulled Celestine close.

"*Allons-y!*" called Maurice.

The wagon jolted forward. Fortunately, the logging companies had smoothed out the spring mud ruts on the road. Within minutes, we were swaying in time with the wagon's rhythm, settled into conversation to pass the two-hour trip to the Nelsonville Dominion Day Strawberry Social.

I turned to Adeline. "You look wonderful!"

She smiled. "Just like with her." She nodded her head toward Celestine. "I was so tired in the first three months, hated the smell of food. But now, I have energy again, and I can't stop eating." Her eyes sparkled in the sunlight. "I fear I won't fit through the door by the time the baby comes."

We laughed, and she put a hand on my arm. "It's so good to have you back. And Evie-Jayne, she's fine?"

"Yes, she's perfect." Claude and I had visited Maurice and Adeline within days of our return. We'd shared our stories, Claude recounting his visit to his family, omitting the matter of his first wife. My story included a dangerous pregnancy and admission into a Toronto hospital, resulting in a successful birth.

"Have you heard from Tekakwitha?"

I nodded. "She and her three children are back in her home village. Ma'iingan stopped drinking alcohol while he was away. When he returned from his trapping job up north, he banned alcohol from his village."

"I'm so happy for her. It was generous of Claude's brother to keep her on as his housekeeper."

I barely covered a snort.

"I took a pie to them once. François met me at the scow landing and wouldn't let me go to the house. That's the only time we saw him." She frowned. "Whatever happened to him?"

I flashed on the day when Claude had disappeared into the trillium-carpeted woods, hauling the pine box like a log behind the horse. He'd emerged from the trees after dark, shoulders bent. I'd wiped a smudge of dirt from his cheek and led him into the house.

I turned to stare at the passing bush. "He moved west when Claude returned." My fingernails bit into my palms. I forced down the bile rising over the lump in my throat. In Claude's arms, I'd overcome the pain, but the anger and guilt sometimes broke over me, even in the midst of the happiest moments.

"I missed our trips to Webbwood while you were away." Adeline broke into my thoughts.

I forced a smile. "Well, we can remedy that. Have you seen Dr. Jones yet?"

She shook her head. "I think I should see him soon." She nudged me with her elbow.

I grinned. "Let's plan a trip within the next few weeks. We'll take the girls. Perhaps stay overnight with Elisabeth."

Evie-Jayne began to fuss, and Celestine was wiggling to get off the bench. "Claude, let's take a break so the children can move around and I can feed the baby."

The men found a place with a private clearing where I could nurse beneath the green shade of several old maples. I sat on a cushion of moss under the trees. Behind me, the children's shrieks as their fathers chased them mingled with the birds' trills. The river flowed below my sanctuary, but I only had eyes for my daughter. I never got tired of watching Evie-Jayne's temple move in rhythm with her sucking.

"What a picture!" Claude chuckled. "I wish I were an artist."

"Mmm. It is beautiful in here, so many greens."

"I meant you, mother and child."

I felt my face grow warm.

He knelt beside me and brushed my cheek with his hand. "Looks like she's sleeping. We ready?"

I nodded. Claude pulled me to my feet and enveloped us both in his arms just as Sophie and Jean-Pierre burst into the clearing. Giggling at the sight of us embracing, they took Claude's open-arm invitation to complete our family hug.

* * *

An hour later, our wagon joined the melee of arrivals jostling for a spot to park in the designated area beside the red Nelsonville Railway Station.

"Sophie, J.P., before you run off to join your friends, please help carry the baskets to our picnic spot."

"But, maman," Sophie wailed. "I need to find Marie. I haven't seen her for so long. Can't *papa* and *mon oncle* Maurice do it?"

"They need to take care of the horses."

"It's okay, maman, I can make a few trips," said J.P.

Sophie threw her brother a grateful smile, jumping off the wagon to make her escape before I could overturn his offer.

"Sophie, stay in the field. When the box lunch auction begins, come to our spot. *M'entends tu?*"

"*Oui,* maman. *Merci,* maman. *Merci, J.P.*" She sprinted, pigtails flying, toward the gathering of girls in the far corner of the field.

Laden with Evie-Jayne, Celestine, and bags with their diapers and bottles, Adeline and I made our way toward the picnic areas. Jean-Pierre strode ahead, balancing two picnic baskets and blankets, bent on finding exactly the right spot.

He ran back to us within moments, arms empty. "Maman, I got to your favourite tree at the same time as Mr. Fensom. He let me have it for us." Jean-Pierre pointed to where I could see our old patchwork quilt and the Hudson's Bay blankets with their distinctive stripes. "*Ma tante*, would you like me to take Celestine?"

"I think she is ready to explore if you take her hand." Adeline lowered the little girl to her feet. She put her hand on her back as she straightened. "*Merci*, Jean-Pierre."

I watched my son steer the little girl over the uneven terrain toward the blankets, taking the time to point out the activity going on around them. Images of my last Strawberry Social with Gran and Amelia under that very tree floated superimposed on the current scene. It was like a Jim Lumbers painting, but with the modern period as the ghost.

When Celestine fussed to be picked up, he carried her back. "J.P., you've been an incredible help. Can you please take our desserts to Madame Beaudry over at the tables before you go to your friends?"

"I'll be happy to take those for you so the boy can play." I jumped at the familiar voice behind me. I turned. Our eyes met.

"Ida MacGregor." She stuck out her hand.

I stood frozen.

"I'm the other Ida MacGregor's niece," she said with a wry smile. "My father was working up on James Bay when he heard about the death of his parents. He always felt guilty that he never tried to find out what had happened to his sister Ida, so just before he passed he asked me to look for her. It's been quite a trip across the north and out west. And then, when I finally tracked her to here, I find out the poor lady passed away a week before I arrived." She momentarily dropped her eyes.

Jean-Pierre stepped forward. "Pleased to meet you, Mademoiselle MacGregor." He shook the proffered hand and turned to me. "Maman, is it okay?"

"*Oui* . . . Go play. Remember, come back—"

" . . . when the auction for the box lunches starts." He grinned and ran off across the field.

"Such a polite young man," Ida said. "And who is this gorgeous little one?" She stroked her finger across Evie-Jayne's cheek while her gaze returned to my face.

I broke our connection and shifted the baby to my other hip. "I'm Catherine Dumont, and this is Evie-Jayne." The baby smiled and waved her arm as if in greeting.

"I'm Catherine's neighbour, Adeline Gagnon, and this is my daughter," Adeline called from the other side of the tree where she was chasing Celestine. "*Dis bonjour à Mademoiselle, Celestine.*"

"*Bonjour*," Celestine said. Then, she was off in her wide-legged toddler run across the field, arms waving to evade her mother's grasp.

I looked around, leaned in, and hissed, "What are doing here, Ida?"

"Catherine, relax. When Mrs. MacLean heard about my long, fruitless journey, she persuaded me to stay awhile."

I raised my eyebrows.

"I'm off to Toronto tomorrow. I've got to find that portal. This era is too unrefined for my liking. I need hot baths, sweet smelling soaps, electricity."

Over Ida's shoulder, I caught sight of Anne MacLean, Clara Hall, and Mrs. Fensom converging on us from their various picnic sites. "Oh no."

"Catherine, so good to have you back!" Clara brushed her hand over my upper arm.

"My goodness, dear, you look positively radiant. And who is this little joy?" Anne leaned around me to catch Evie-Jayne's attention.

"Ida, I see you've already met Catherine," said Mrs. Fensom.

"So nice to see you all." I acknowledged each woman with a warm smile pasted on my face. Holding the baby forward, I introduced her.

Above the oohing and aahing over the baby, Anne MacLean commented, "We missed you at last year's social." Her head was pushed forward.

Mrs. Fensom fixed her eyes on my face. "We heard you'd left due to a medical emergency?" She raised an eyebrow. "But all seems to be well?"

"There were complications, but all is well now." I smiled.

She drew her mouth into a firm line. "My husband says Mr. Dumont took Jean-Pierre back home to Montreal and left Sophie with a woman in Webbwood."

Ida moved to position herself between Mrs. Fensom and me.

"That's right. Now, ladies . . ." I jounced the baby to my other arm.

Anne jumped in. "And where's your husband's brother, that François Dumont?" A corner of her mouth curled.

Clara glared at her.

I squared my shoulders. "As I understand it, Claude made restitution to your husbands for his brother's debts." I looked around, brows raised, until I received nods of acknowledgement. "Then, let that be the end to it. Now, I really must excuse myself." Turning my back, I placed Evie-Jayne on the blanket and began rummaging through the bag for a clean diaper and cloth.

I heard Anne's and Mrs. Fensom's muttering voices fade away as Clara shepherded them toward the dessert tables.

"Well done." Ida plopped herself down on the blanket. "Tough crowd, but you handled them like a pro."

"Thanks." I gave her a sideways glance as I continued to change Evie-Jayne.

"They're harmless." Ida sighed. "With no TV, I guess they need to make their own soap operas."

"Well, I'm not interested in being the subject of their gossip." Evie-Jayne whimpered as I tugged hard on her dress. "Sorry, baby." I picked her up and kissed her.

"Mrs. Fensom looked like she was catching flies with her mouth." Ida starting laughing.

I chuckled. "And Anne's head almost came off her neck, she had it pushed so far forward."

"Clara was ready to hit their two heads together, just like on *The Three Stooges*."

"Yeah, Clara's one of the nice ones." My internal main spring was almost back to its normal level when the box lunch auction was announced.

"Would you, um, like to join us for lunch?"

Ida's eyes widened, and a surprised silence fell between us. I smiled ruefully and gave a slight shrug.

"Thanks, but I succumbed to the pressure of the ladies and have submitted a box." She got to her feet.

"That- that's . . . ah . . . interesting," I stuttered.

"With a face like mine, you take advantage of any opportunity for a little male company." Ida picked up her mint-green skirts and jogged across the grassy field. When she arrived at the auction, she smoothed her skirts, tucked stray hanks of straight brown hair into her bun, and moved through the crowd to take her place among the other women. She was spunky—I had to give her that.

I stood, bouncing Evie-Jayne in my arms. Jean-Pierre and Joey Jr. waved as they parted. In the centre of a gaggle of girls, my eye picked out the sky blue of Sophie's bonnet.

"What are you watching, my love?" Claude had come up behind me.

"Sophie. Does she seem all right to you? She still has those nightmares."

Claude put his arm around me. "She had a hard time being left behind. I wonder sometimes if I shouldn't have taken her with me but, with my family . . ." He shrugged. "She's resilient, like her mother."

The girls dispersed, and Sophie headed toward us.

"Lunch is ready." Adeline had set the food out on the blankets. We sank to the ground, prayed our thanks for the bounty of our lunch, and began eating.

Maurice waved his fork at Claude in between bites of tourtière. "I'd like to discuss some designs with David Brosseau for the harnesses we use on the scow. With so many travellers these days, we need to find something more comfortable for the horses."

"Great idea!" Claude crunched into a piece of fried chicken. "Let's chat with him before we leave today."

"I met Lucille Latril, from one of the new French families." Adeline was passing Celestine pieces of bread and pickled vegetables. "She and her husband, Leo, are homesteading downriver from us. Maybe you and I can visit her sometime?"

"Absolutely," I said.

"*Celestine, fais attention!*" Adeline grabbed a cloth to catch the pickle juice dripping down her daughter's arm.

I let the chatter flow over me, my heart feeling as if it were wrapped in a warm glove. And then it hit me. The perpetual knot under my diaphragm was gone.

Claude leaned in and whispered, "Sweetheart, I don't know what you're thinking, but that look becomes you."

"It's this," I said, spreading my arms. "I'm where I belong."

We smiled.

"Maman, everyone's lining up for dessert." Jean-Pierre pointed to where the long tables were arranged under the trees.

"Okay, let's all go together, and then afterward, you can join your friends again." I picked up Evie-Jayne.

Sophie and Jean-Pierre ran ahead with Claude and Maurice not far behind. Adeline and I brought up the rear, Celestine walking between us.

Mr. Dever approached our group as we joined our husbands in the line. "So nice to have you back." His smile warmed his tanned face. "We're meeting in Hall's General Store after dessert, and we'd like you to join us." He looked from Claude to me. His brow cleared in response to our nods of agreement.

"What do you think that's about?" I asked as we watched Mr. Dever approach the MacLeans.

Claude gave his Gallic shrug. "Maybe a new approach for the bridge proposal?"

* * *

An hour later, we joined several other couples in Hall's General Store. Sacks of grains, rice, and flour slumped against each other under the windows of the front wall. Bolts of brightly patterned cloth ranged like a rainbow to the ceiling behind the counter on the left. Metal tools and hardware glinted in the natural light from pegs to the right. A *U*-shaped wooden counter guarded the goods from grasping customer hands and their children's sticky fingers. Several women were already seated in chairs arranged in the middle of the store. With Evie-Jayne asleep in her sling, I settled in the vacant chair next to Estelle Beaudry while Claude joined the men lounging against the counter.

Mr. Edwards cleared his throat. "Thank you everyone for coming. You may have heard our request for a bridge across the Spanish at the north end of town was denied. Seems we are too small to be recognized for investment by the provincial government."

Several people muttered.

Estelle said. "But six new French families moved into the area just this spring."

"And at least that number of English settlers," said Anne MacLean.

Clara Hall shook her head. "Without churches and a school, people aren't going to stay."

"Last winter, I lost over two hundred dollars in stock for my store because the scow was tipped by an ice flow." John Hall's brow wrinkled in frustration. "I need a reliable link to the Sudbury road to keep my store supplied. We need the bridge."

Mr. Edwards sighed. "The government says it will only build bridges and roads where there are towns."

"But without government funding . . ." Andrew Dever's mouth twisted downward.

"This is a circular argument." Everyone turned to the stranger at the back. "Robert Bell, Geological Survey of Canada." He smoothed down his beard.

"I invited Mr. Bell to join us today," Mr. Edwards explained.

The man pushed back his wavy black hair. "I've been hired by a group of mining companies to survey the river above High Falls for the installation of an electric power generating dam."

"We don't need electrical power," said Mrs. Fensom.

Mr. Bell's kindly eyes and soothing tenor spread like honey over the assembly. "Significant mineral deposits have been found. I'm sure you'll see mining activity soon."

"Are you suggesting the mining companies will build a bridge?" Richard Fensom's voice rose. A wave of murmurs rippled through the room.

Claude stood behind me. I pulled him down to whisper in his ear.

"Catherine, we don't stand on ceremony here." Mr. Edwards's voice stopped me in mid-word. "Please, if you have a suggestion . . ."

Claude nodded at me.

"I've heard that Webbwood is preparing a submission for incorporation as a town."

Hector MacLean's brows rose. "Are you suggesting we incorporate?"

"It might be worth considering." Mr. Bell's eyes were sizing me up.

Andrew Dever folded his arms across his chest. "Sounds like a waste of time. We still won't have a bridge."

"Governments think with their pocketbooks," I said. "So we have to show them that a town with a bridge here will be good for logging, mining, and commerce."

Claude squeezed my shoulder and then picked up my thought. "The government lives on the taxes from our natural resource industries. The industries need a reliable workforce."

John Hall's eyes lit up. "And our settler families are that workforce as long as we have services like transportation, schools, and churches to keep them here." Understanding dawned on the faces around the room.

Within minutes, we'd decided to divide our efforts into two task forces, one to prepare the submission for incorporation under Hector's leadership, and a second, led by Clara, to begin the process of opening a school funded by the school board. James and Flora Hammond donated a corner of their land on Smith Street for a church, and several women volunteered to approach the logging companies for donations of materials. Everyone would pitch in to construct the building. The church would be shared by all congregations.

"Attention, everyone." Mr. Edwards's voice rose above the discussions. "Thank you for your enthusiasm. But we are here to celebrate, and I'm sure our families are waiting for us."

Strolling arm in arm back to our blankets, Claude patted my hand in the crook of his arm. "I think a shopping trip into Nelsonville next week will give me a good chance to chat further with Hector." His expression became serious. "You know I believe it should be you, but . . ." His smile offered an apology.

"Claude Dumont, you are a man ahead of your time." I squeezed his arm.

"It's good to be back, isn't it?"

I nodded.

"Things looked friendly with the ladies."

I snorted. "Don't let appearances fool you. I'm astounded at the hypocrisy of women like Mrs. Fensom and Anne MacLean." I felt my lip curl. "They cloak themselves in Christian caring, but when their oblique attempts didn't elicit the information they sought, their cloaks cracked open, and the sanctimonious bitches attacked as if they would beat the details out of me."

Claude stopped to face me, eyebrows raised.

"We'd heard you'd left due to a medical emergency," I mimicked. "Why did your husband and J.P. leave? Why did Sophie remain in Webbwood? Where is François . . . ?"

"They brought up François?"

"They did, but I kept my cool. Stuck to our story and provided the merest of details." We began to walk again. "Of course that frustrated them more because there were no tantalizing morsels to spin."

Claude threw his head back, laughing. Evie-Jayne kicked her legs at the sound, eager to be freed from the sling.

STRAWBERRIES

Chapter Twenty-Eight

Our daily three-mile journeys to Stanley Station were punctuated with moments of conversation and song wedged between comfortable silences. I turned around to check on my children riding behind me in the wagon. Sophie was distracting three-year-old Evie-Jayne, using her mittens as puppets, while Jean-Pierre stared at the passing snow-covered trees. At thirteen, he was already up to his father's shoulders, and his voice was starting to crack. So was his commitment to school.

Driving freed my mind—the hum of the engine or creaking of horse harnesses, the drone of tires on the road or the shushing of runners through the snow. It's funny, I thought, how when we venture out into a new place, we dare to dance as if no one knows us. Some from my time would look derisively at teaching in a school of twenty children in a railway car in the middle of nowhere in 1892, but as far as I was concerned, I was living my dream.

"Maman, me going *l'école*." Evie-Jayne's muffled exclamation floated up to me through the scarf Sophie had tied across her mouth. All three were bundled so their only visible features were their eyes.

"*Oui, ma petite,* you are going to school, today."

Our morning had begun like any other until Claude announced he'd be travelling to Nelsonville today.

"What about Evie-Jayne?" I'd asked.

"Hector wants me to review the latest submission for incorporation. Can't you take her with you? You have a classroom full of babysitters."

I glared at him. "Can't *you* do your trip on Friday when we don't have school?"

"There's a government man coming. Hector wants everything reviewed before he meets with him."

"This is our third try in two and a half years. What more can they possibly want?"

"You tell me." He tilted his head to give me a sideways look. "Are we getting close?"

I stopped stacking the breakfast dishes and reviewed my memory of the little history booklet the Nairn Centre citizens had compiled as a centennial project in 1996. A quick calculation in my head. Still four years until the inaugural meeting in 1896. "Might be one more try after this." I sighed. "Sophie, J.P., please get Evie-Jayne dressed. She's coming with us today."

* * *

"There you are, Madame Dumont," Mr. Strain pronounced in his strong British accent. He tucked his trainman's pocket watch into his coat. "I see you have the littlest one with you."

"Me *va à l'école*."

"Yes, my sweet, you're at school." The kindly man with the rosy cheeks and stick-like bowed legs lifted her out of the sleigh. "Now, children, hurry inside the station house. Mrs. Strain has some tea and biscuits waiting." He took Evie-Jayne and Sophie each by the hand. Jean-Pierre rushed ahead to open the door. "I lit the fires in the schoolcar, but it'll still take some time to warm up," Mr. Strain called over his shoulder.

The smell of fresh biscuits wafted on currents of warm air from the open house door. "*Bonjour mes enfants!* Sit at the table." Mrs. Strain greeted my children. "There's butter and jam for those biscuits."

The door closed on the scene just as Evie-Jayne announced, "*Bonjour*, Mrs. Strain. *Moi à l'école* today!"

The kindly couple had "never been blessed with children" as Mrs. Strain expressed it, which in her words, "kept them free to share in the joy of everyone else's." Mr. Strain met us each school morning to unhitch and stable the horse, and at the end of the day, the wagon or sleigh always stood ready for our journey home. The entire school often enjoyed cookies or slices of cake, compliments of the station-master's wife.

I grabbed my worn leather satchel from the sleigh. Turning, two people waiting on the platform caught my eye. The young woman was nearly my height. Her features were muffled under her heavy woollen coat and bright red scarf, but her moss green eyes took my breath away. I'd seen those eyes before.

The familiar baritone voice confirmed the impossible. "Kate? *Mademoiselle* Kate Dumont Walker?"

"Abraham?" I squeaked.

He grasped the young woman's hand and pulled her toward me along the platform. "It is you!" He swallowed me into his embrace. Then, stepping back, he drew his daughter forward. "Louise, this is the woman I told you about, the one I rescued."

I bristled at the word, but had to admit he had indeed "rescued" me. "*Enchantée, Mademoiselle Louise.*"

She took the hand I offered and pulled down her scarf. "*Bonjour, Madame.*" Her broad smile revealed white even teeth and a fine aquiline nose.

"Did you find your grandmaman?" Abe asked.

I shook my head. "Sadly not. Since you are here, I assume the second rebellion did not go as hoped?"

"*Malheureusement, non.* But me, my two sons, and my two daughters have made a good life on our land above the gorge south of here. Louise is named after our great leader."

"And your wife . . . ?"

Abe dropped his head. "She passed a few years ago." His eyes glittered with unshed tears, but his face brightened with pride as he added, "My Louise, she works for Sadowski's Dry Goods in Webbwood." He wrapped his arm around her shoulder and drew her to him until I feared she'd completely disappear into his huge bulk. "She is learning the business."

"That's very admirable, Louise. Do you plan to open your own store?"

Louise's eyes sparkled. "I am engaged and will marry this summer, but papa feels I should have a skill to support myself, should the need arise."

"A wise man, your father."

"And what about you, Kate? How is your life? You did not return to your mother in Toronto?"

"No. You may remember Claude Dumont?"

Abe nodded. "The engineer on the river."

"Yes. I am Catherine Dumont now, and we have two children. And I also teach school here." I nodded toward the railcar on the siding. "Now, I'm sorry, but I must prepare the school before the children arrive."

"*Bien sûr.* Perhaps we will see each other again. I bring Louise to the train to Webbwood each Monday morning and collect her on Friday afternoon."

"Abe, I'm sure our paths will cross. Claude will be so excited to hear that you have returned. *Au revoir.*"

I tramped along the freshly shovelled path across two sets of tracks to what appeared to be a typical train car. The three metal stairs to the landing at the back of the car had been scraped clear of ice, ready to receive the twenty pairs of feet that would soon be entering. I smiled, thinking about Abe and our brief reunion. Claude would be happy to see him again. Perhaps we could invite him and his family for dinner one Sunday.

Wood fire currents warmed the air against my cheek as I stepped through the door. I hung my coat in the cloakroom and dropped my boots on the rack in front of the first of the two wood stoves. Headings painted on the slate board for the date, the weather, and the temperature waited for one of the younger children to complete after our opening exercises.

My fingers drifted over the scarred pine surfaces of the double desks as I walked down the central aisle to my table. The second classroom space was furnished like the first, but with taller desks to accommodate the children aged eleven to sixteen. A second wood stove at the far end ensured good heat distribution throughout.

I took a moment from my vantage point to admire what we'd accomplished in under a year. Settlers around Stanley Station had felt stranded when it came to schooling for their children. The school in Webbwood was too far for daily horse travel, and too expensive by train. The lumber company declined to provide building materials for a new school building at Stanley Station, citing their recent commitment to Nelsonville for their school. Then, one day, Mr. Strain had come to the rescue—an old passenger coach permanently parked on an unused siding at the station. The rail company was on board and made the donation. When the parent group had approached me to take on the teaching duties, Claude and I agreed. I was already spending hours each day teaching our own children. We found a rhythm to our daily lives to provide the same opportunity to those around us.

I felt alive designing the space, supervising the fathers who constructed and installed the fixtures and furniture and working with the mothers who helped me establish our school calendar, hours, and payment strategies for the purchase of books and supplies. I wondered if this school was my purpose for being transported back in time. Was the next political leader, lumber company president, Florence Nightingale, or mining engineer in my class? Who knew? What I did know, was that I was making a difference in the lives of the children and their families, and that was enough.

At nine o'clock, I stepped onto the platform, rang the hand bell, and greeted each child coming through the door. Sophie moved past me.

"Sophie, where's Evie-Jayne?"

"Mrs. Strain said to tell you that she can keep her until after lunch."

Jean-Pierre walked past. "She says she's sorry she can't keep her all day, but she has quilting this afternoon."

I smiled and sent up a small blessing for the kind woman. After a morning with Mrs. Strain, Evie-Jayne would likely nap most of the afternoon.

Once coats were hung and boots were lined up around the stoves, each child grabbed a small braided rag mat from the stack against the sidewall. Everyone gathered in the central space to sing "God Save the Queen" and recite the Lord's Prayer. Then, they sat on their mats while two children presented show and tell items.

A light tap on the door interrupted our review of the daily plan.

"Excuse me, Madame Dumont. I'm sorry to interrupt."

"Oh, that's all right. What can I do for you, Mr. Strain?"

"I've just received exciting news." His eyes were shining." Mr. William Cornelius Van Horne is coming to visit us today. Or, that is, he's not coming just to visit us . . . I mean . . . Oh, dear." He began wringing his hands. "Let me start again. By the way, do you know who Mr. William Cornelius Van Horne is?"

The walls pulsed with the rapid beating of my heart as I squeaked out my response. "If I recall correctly, Mr. Van Horne is the engineer employed by Prime Minister Macdonald to survey the transcontinental train route."

"Yes. Mr. Van Horne has been conducting a west to east inspection of the entire route and tributaries now that they are complete." He turned to the children. "He's the president of the Canadian Pacific Railway. His private train will be stopping here in Stanley Station to pick up a new load of wood. He won't be here long. His train must be parked on the spur east of the Spanish River Bridge by one o'clock to clear the track for the afternoon westbound train out of Nelsonville." He turned back to me. "But if there's time, I could introduce him to the children." His voice rose in question. "It would be a wonderful history lesson . . ."

The voice in my head screamed, Refuse, but what kind of teacher turns down an opportunity for her students to meet a man who has changed the face of their country? I forced a smile. "I'm sure the children would enjoy meeting him if he's inclined to speak to them. Now, we must resume our lessons."

I sent the older children back to their seats for their usual writing period. Sophie and her friend were soon working on their journals. Others continued with their stories. Jean-Pierre and his friend, Jacques, bent their heads over a joint project describing tree management.

This was my time with the six-to-ten-year-olds. We all read the date: Thursday, January 21, 1892; *jeudi le 21 janvier, 1892*. My expression froze on six-year-old Tom, in his role as weather monitor for the week, drawing a sun and a blue thermometer showing minus twenty-five degrees in the appropriate square on the calendar. *Jump Day! What was I doing around trains today?* My gaze swept the room. Sophie and Jean-Pierre continued to work with their partners. So innocent. *Relax*, my inner voice admonished. *You're nowhere near the bridge.*

I surveyed the younger children copying and solving addition questions as I walked up the aisle. Sitting at my desk, my thoughts moved to the hurricane of memories evoked by the Van Horne name.

What if William recognized me? He probably didn't even remember who I was. I'd keep the focus on the students.

We were settling in after recess when a sharp train whistle announced Mr. Van Horne's imminent arrival.

Moments later, the schoolcar rocked gently as the private train chugged past it and into the station. The children had become inured to the routine train arrivals and departures four times a day. However, the idea of a private train for one passenger had captured their imaginations. The locomotive designed to pull much longer strings of railway cars through steep mountain terrain gleamed blackly in the bright winter sunlight. Mr. Van Horne's private car stopped adjacent to our school. The royal purple exterior was soon overshadowed by glimpses of the opulent interior, visible through our windows into his. Red velvet curtains were tied back with gold-tasseled ropes, revealing leather and velvet settees and overstuffed chairs. The students gasped at the sight of the oval dining table sparkling with silver candelabra and a golden coffee service set on a crisp white tablecloth. Most of my students lived in one-room cabins, eating with wooden spoons from tin plates, and sitting on thinly cushioned wooden chairs.

Tom let out a yell as the curtains in the back end of the private car opened. "That bed is as wide as the whole car!"

A sharp rap at the door startled the children back to their seats.

"It must be him!"

"Can you see him?"

They craned their necks.

In strode Mr. Strain, drawn up to his full five-foot, four-inch height with his head held high and his chest puffed out. "Madame Dumont, children, I present, Mr. William Cornelius Van Horne." He gave a slight bow and then stretched his arm to the side like a magician's assistant.

The students leapt to their feet, wide eyes fixed on the man who filled the doorway. More grey was speckled through his beard than I remembered. Somewhat over six feet tall, Van Horne's bearing conveyed an impression of suppleness and endurance.

"Ohh! He's soooo big!" Tom whispered into the silence.

"So I've been told." William's stern expression melted into a bright smile and a sparkle lit his eye. "But one day, my young friend, I wager someone will say the same about you."

At a nod from me, Jean-Pierre left his seat and offered an official welcome to our visitor. William solemnly shook his hand. Then, he walked down the aisle, asking each child's name. Little fingers disappeared in the shake of his large hand. Once he was settled on the chair in the central meeting space, the students all gathered on their mats at his feet.

"Mr. Van Horne, may I present our teacher, Madame Dumont." Mr. Strain drew me forward. "She has been the inspiration and the driving force in the success of our little school."

"Pleasure to meet you, Madame." Our eyes met. Was that a flicker? "My congratulations on your success and my admiration for your dedication to shaping these young minds."

He turned back to the children. "So, children, tell me, what do you learn here?"

"Reading, writing, arithmetic."

"*Écriture, lecture, mathématiques.*"

William leaned toward Jacques. "*Tu parles français?*"

Jacques nodded.

William raised his brows at me.

"I teach reading, writing, and mathematics in both English and French according to family choice."

"We learn about the world."

"And stuff that happened in the past."

"Ah." William nodded. "Geography and history."

"And science," added Jean-Pierre.

"Impressive." William looked at me for a long moment before turning his attention back to the children. For the next hour, he captivated them with his humorous and harrowing anecdotes about the building of the railway. Not one mention of the hundreds of Chinese workers who lost their lives under deplorable conditions in the construction of the western section. Did the man not have a conscience? Across Northern Ontario the railway largely employed lumberjacks looking for summer work and newly arrived Irish immigrants. Our communities flourished as these workers settled in the area instead of moving west with the track.

Railcars jostled and screeched on the siding beside us. When the sunlight returned on one side of our school, William rose.

"Children, I have thoroughly enjoyed myself with you today, but it's time for me to leave if I'm to be clear of the Spanish River Bridge." He paused. Then, stroking his beard thoughtfully, he sat back down. "That bridge puts me in mind of a story. When my team and I were surveying the best crossing point for the Spanish River, we found a youth sleeping on the bank right where the bridge is now. Although he seemed to understand us, he remained silent and my men concluded he was mute. I insisted the young man travel with us at least as far as Webbwood for his own safety. What do you suppose I discovered about that youth after a few days with us?"

The children began to call out suggestions:

"He wasn't really lost."

"He didn't speak English."

"He was an escaped prisoner."

William laughed. "Actually, I found out that 'he' was really a smart young woman who could read, write, and speak English and French."

"Just like you, Madame Dumont," said Jacques.

"Why did she disguise herself as a boy?" Sophie asked.

"It started with a case of mistaken identity by my men, which I suppose she felt safer to maintain."

Was his glance directed at me?

"In the end, she was most ungrateful and ill-mannered. Instead of letting me get her to safety, she tricked my men and ran off." William threw me a wink.

Bright sunshine poured through our windows. William stood. "Now, children, I really must leave."

He shook my hand. "Madame Dumont, thank you for letting me visit." His penetrating stare sent prickles down my spine.

Shutting the door, I leaned my back against it, breathing deeply. He was gone, and I wouldn't be seeing him again.

STRAWBERRIES

Chapter Twenty-Nine

I looked up from my reverie to find twenty pairs of eyes on me. "Okay, let's get out our journals. Write down at least three things that you learned today from Mr. Van Horne."

A sharp forward jerk.

"Madame, we're moving!"

Accelerated clacking of wheels.

The children pressed their faces to the windows. I raced to the door, tugged it open, and stepped into the frigid air. Instead of open space, my gaze was filled with snow-encrusted purple. Jumping the gap, I pounded my fists against the car's door. "Stop the train!" The icy wind threw my words behind me and tore at my clothes.

William yanked open the door, pulled me in, and slammed it behind me.

"You have to stop this train now!"

"I knew it was you!" Triumph sparked from his eyes.

I grabbed his lapels, pulling his face down to mine. "Stop the damn train, *now*!"

His hands folded around my forearms. "Can't. We need to clear the bridge."

"Don't touch me." I jerked myself free.

His gaze softened. "What's the harm in a little thrill for the children? My locomotive will reverse us back to Stanley Station once the other train has passed."

I ran through the car, grasping the forward door just as William's manservant came through.

"Tell the engineer to stop the train now."

The man remained in the doorway, eyebrows raised to his employer.

I tried to push past him, but he held his wide-legged stance.

"My baby is back at the station." I screamed into his face and kicked him in the shin.

He winced and stepped back to wedge his arm across the door frame.

I turned to William. "I'll tell the authorities you kidnapped an entire school of children!"

William's expression remained unmoved.

I swung my arm. The manservant ducked so my fist grazed the doorjamb.

I shook the pain from my hand. "What will Lucy say when she hears?" I hurled over my shoulder.

William's eyes narrowed, his shoulders dropped, and he nodded. The manservant limped out the door leaving William and I locked in a glare, my chest heaving. Within seconds, the train slowed and came to a stop. I felt a lurch, and then a backward movement. Without a word, I stalked past William.

The children's wide-eyed faces greeted me as I burst into the schoolcar.

They all started talking at once:

"Where are we going?"

"Why did we stop?"

"I thought we were going to tip over."

I raised my hand for silence and pasted on a bright smile. "We've been attached to Mr. Van Horne's train by mistake."

"We're going backwards," said Tom.

I took a steadying breath. "They're taking us back to our siding in Stanley Station. Now, boys and girls, let's get out our lunches and enjoy the trip."

My stomach churned. I focussed on Sophie and her friends tracing patterns with their fingers on the steamy window as snow floated up from the track. I pressed my fingers to my temples. The possibilities of what might have happened gripped me like a vice. Whenever I'd experienced the jump, I'd been outside. Would the car have shielded us from the effects of the portal? Could the entire car have hitchhiked with us like Ida did with me? I shuddered.

Within minutes, the train slowed, and Mr. Strain came into sight, rocking from foot to foot on the Stanley Station platform. As soon as we slid to a stop, I stepped out onto the car's landing.

"Madame Dumont, you are all safe?"

"Yes, quite safe, Mr. Strain."

"The terror." He wrung his hands. "Seeing our little schoolcar disappear down the track."

I clung to the car's handrail, feeling as if I'd just run a marathon.

"My apologies." William's voice floated over my head behind me. "All a silly misunderstanding. Now, perhaps you can direct my engineer in moving the schoolcar back to its siding?"

"Of course, sir." Mr. Strain drew himself together and marched to the locomotive.

"Maman." I turned to see Sophie standing in the schoolcar doorway.

Tom peered around her skirt. "I have to pee!" He was holding himself while crossing and recrossing his legs.

I turned to William. "The children use the Station's facilities, but they can't be outside while the cars are moving. I need to get back to them."

"Come, son." William grasped Tom by the hands and guided him across the gap. "In you go." The manservant's hand appeared and took Tom through.

The cars jolted.

William cleared his throat. "Kate, er, Madame Dumont, I'm sure others have the same need as Tom." His blue eyes twinkled as he raised his eyebrows. "We have facilities. There are refreshments, and you and I could catch up . . . ?"

He was right. We were stuck until the cars were rearranged.

I stepped into the schoolcar and clapped my hands. "Children, Mr. Van Horne has invited us to visit his car."

Shouts of glee.

"Form a line at the door. Jean-Pierre, Jacques, help the children cross one at time to Mr. Van Horne." William waited on the platform of his car to assist with the exodus into the purple railcar. His manservant showed them to the facilities and encouraged them to serve themselves from the dining table which he'd quickly laden with biscuits, muffins, dried fruit, nuts, and three kinds of jam glistening in white ceramic pots. I remained at the door where I could keep a watchful eye on my troop, my white-hot rage cooling to a simmer.

When all were transferred, William approached me, hands extended, palms up. "Kate, I am truly sorry. Can we talk?" He pointed to two forest-green wingback chairs in the corner. "Here? You can still watch them. They have a lot to explore." He chuckled. "And some surfaces have yet to be touched by sticky fingers."

At that moment, Mrs. Strain knocked on the door, Evie-Jayne dozing in her arms. "Madame Dumont, is everyone all right?" She leaned to peek past my shoulder. "Oh, my!"

"Yes, everyone is fine." I pulled Evie-Jayne against my chest and buried my face in the tender spot between shoulder and head. Her familiar scent calmed my racing heart. "Thank you for your help this morning."

Mrs. Strain flapped her hand. "Oh, she's a good little one. Very busy, mind, and she is becoming quite a talker." She continued drinking in the scene behind us.

"Thanks again. I suppose you need to get to your quilting group?"

"Oh . . . yes." She tilted her head back and extended her hand. "So nice to meet you, Mr. Van Horne." Then, after one more glance, she turned and descended the stairs.

By now, Evie-Jayne was fully awake and craning to see the commotion behind me. "*Maman, des biscuits.*" She squirmed to get down.

I set her on the floor just as Sophie came over. "I can take her." She took Evie-Jayne's hand and led her away.

"Don't let her have too much jam," I called.

"Shall we?" William gestured toward the chairs.

The train lurched. The children cheered. I staggered, and William caught me by the arm. "There's going to be a lot of that."

I pulled my arm free.

Once we were settled, I couldn't hold back. "What were you thinking? Do you have any idea the danger you put us in?" I spoke in a low hiss.

William was leaning back in his chair. His fingers began to twitch where they rested on his knees.

"Our schoolcar hasn't moved for so long . . . I can't imagine what could have happened."

William leaned forward, resting his head in his hands.

I scanned the room. My eyes landed on three children examining the pen and ink pots on William's desk. "Move away from the desk, boys." Then, I turned back to him. "Why are you even here? The transcontinental route is north. We're just a side route connecting the ports."

He raised his head. "Remember when you suggested a different crossing for the bridge?"

I nodded.

"You seemed to know more than you let on. Your urgency was like a pebble in my shoe, irritating my thoughts off and on over the years." He took a deep breath. "I decided to see for myself how the bridge was holding up." He looked at me from lowered eyes. "Part of me hoped our paths might cross."

My mouth gaped.

"No, not in that way." He rubbed his hand over the spot where his hairline used to be. "You're articulate, clearly well educated. I just wanted to spend time talking with you." He exhaled loudly. "Lucy frequently reminds me that I act without thinking." A smile quivered around the corners of his mouth. His gaze took on a faraway look. "There was the caricature of my principal that ended my school career at fourteen." He shook his head. "And when I was in my early twenties, I hooked up a metal plate in the railway freight yard where I worked. It was a harmless prank until the foreman stepped on it. He wasn't amused by the electric shock. Lost my job." He chuckled and leaned back, tenting his fingers against his chest. "Tell me about your life."

I talked about Claude and our life together. He asked questions about the school, our hours, our fee of one cent per child for each day he or she attended to be used for the purchase of learning materials.

"What if a family can't pay?"

I leaned back into the chair. "They contribute their labour, clearing snow, cutting brush back from the play area, providing firewood, and building furniture."

"And who pays you?"

"I don't take pay." The way I saw it, I'd be schooling my children at home anyway, so why not give Sophie and J.P. opportunities to have friends. "I do go home regularly though with a fresh-baked pie, pot of moose stew, or loaf of bread donated by the mothers."

The car rocked as the one o'clock westbound train pulled into the station. Ten minutes later, the wheels screeched as the locomotive took up its journey westward, leading its four passenger cars and the tiny red caboose.

Alphonse came over to where William and I sat. "The track is clear. The engineer says we must leave immediately after the children are back in their car if we are to make Sudbury by evening."

"Alphonse, I'm sorry for my earlier behaviour." I held out my hand.

He shook it.

"Thank you for taking care of the children."

The man's weathered face lit with a smile. "My pleasure, Madame." He gave a slight bow of his head and returned to his duties.

I stood to call the children to order when William placed his hand on my arm. "You were frantic when we pulled out of the station. Evie-Jayne was safe with Mrs. Strain, so what were you really scared of?"

This could be my opening. If I could convince him to relocate the bridge, I'd save lives in the future. But revealing my knowledge would expose me too much. I couldn't risk it. Throwing him a faked grimace, I said, "We need to get into our school, and you need to get on your way."

He held my eyes for a moment and then let his smile meet mine. "I'll find out one day. Is there anything I can do to repair what I've done today?"

I thought for a moment. "Nelsonville is petitioning the provincial government to be granted incorporation. It would mean a lot to have your support."

He ran his fingers through his beard. "A letter from the president of CPR in favour of incorporation. Done." He winked.

"Thank you."

"Friends?" William asked, holding out his hand to mine.

"Friends," I responded.

"Please contact me if I can ever be of assistance." He pressed a slip of paper into my hand.

291

Jean-Pierre appeared at my side. "Everyone's in the school, maman." He extended his hand to William. "*Merci*, Mr. Van Horne. Goodbye."

William shook his hand. "My pleasure." He turned to me as Jean-Pierre walked away. "You're raising a remarkable young man, Kate."

No sooner had my feet landed on the platform than the purple car jolted forward and Mr. Van Horne's train accelerated eastward out of Stanley Station.

Mr. Strain pressed two envelopes into my hand. "From Mr. Van Horne," he said. He shrugged his shoulders in response to my raised eyebrows. I recognized William's scrawl on the outside. One was addressed to the Parent Group in care of Madame C. Dumont. I opened the one addressed to me.

> *Dear Kate,*
>
> *The enclosed funds are from the Canadian Pacific Railway and represent your annual salary as teacher of the Stanley Station Schoolcar. You will continue to receive a stipend of $100 each January via the Stanley Station Master in recognition of your contribution to the expansion of our young minds.*

I peered into the envelope and pulled out ten ten-dollar notes. Mr. Strain gasped beside me.

> *I ask that you pass the second envelope to the Parent Group. The Canadian Pacific Railway will cover the cost of learning materials for the children in the amount of $100 annually, also via the Stanley Station Master each January. I will also send a directive to affix brakes to the Stanley Station Schoolcar in order to avert any unscheduled movement of the car in future.*

I shared this information with Mr. Strain.

Please accept my sincere apology for my reckless behaviour today. I was quite overcome by the joy of seeing you again. Perhaps one day, when we meet again, you will trust me with your real story.

WC Van Horne

The man truly was an enigma. And my secret remained safe as I couldn't think of any reason we'd ever meet again.

The remainder of our day was dedicated to capturing our adventure. Some students drew pictures, a few wrote poems, and several made a three dimensional model of the purple car. I mused on how I would explain the day's events to Claude.

* * *

We arrived home to the mouth-watering aromas of a venison stew and biscuits. Claude greeted us at the door and helped Jean-Pierre put the horse and sleigh away while Sophie set the table and I put a sleepy Evie-Jayne to bed.

". . . purple on the outside."

"And this was Mr. Van Horne's private car?"

Claude and Jean-Pierre came through the door.

"His private *train*, papa. His locomotive looked like a dragon." They peeled off their winter clothing.

"Supper's on the table," I said.

"Maman, that's not fair," Sophie wailed. "J.P. is telling papa about Mr. Van Horne. I wanted to tell him about it, too."

"I just told him about Mr. Van Horne's train." Jean-Pierre slid into his spot.

Sophie joined her brother at the table. "Papa, you should have seen the inside of his car." Sophie launched into a description of sparkling glass, gleaming silver, and soft velvet.

"You saw all of this from the window?"

"And when he invited us in for refreshments after our ride."

Claude's eyebrows shot up.

Jean-Pierre picked up the tale. "Mr. Van Horne came and talked to us about the transcontinental railway. He told some funny stories, especially one about a young man who was really a woman he found wandering in the bush. She ran away from him."

Claude looked hard at me.

Sophie was swinging her legs under her chair. "Then, our car was connected to Mr. Van Horne's train . . ."

Claude dropped his spoon into his bowl, his back jammed against the chair. His eyes darted from me to each child.

"But it all turned out fine, papa." Jean-Pierre smiled at his father. "Maman ran to Mr. Van Horne's car and told him to stop the train. Then, we backed up until we were back at Stanley Station."

"It was a great adventure, papa." Sophie wrapped her arms around herself. "I think Mr. Van Horne felt bad about the mistake, so he invited us all into his car. There were biscuits, nuts, muffins, and three kinds of jam." She pushed her plate away. "Maman, I'm not hungry. Can I go to bed and read?"

"Me too?" Jean-Pierre asked.

"Sure."

"I've lost my appetite, too." Claude rose and walked to the bedroom.

I wanted to run after him, explain, reassure, but I decided it might be best to give him time to process what he'd just heard. I cleared the table and put away the leftover food, leaving the dishes for morning. Then, I climbed to the loft and tucked both children in for the night.

Claude was staring into the fire when I went into our bedroom. He turned to me, red wires threading through the whites of his eyes. "Van Horne. Wasn't that the man you were escaping from the day you came to me?"

I nodded. "That was a long time ago. I never expected to see him again."

"But he recognized you?" Claude kept his voice even as he looked back into the fire.

"Yes."

"Did you talk privately in his car?" He turned to me. "Does he know . . .?"

"He thinks there's more to me than I've told him, but he knows nothing."

I took my place in the chair beside him and let the silence engulf us for as long as he needed.

"When you left it was as if everything had been wrenched out of me." Claude shrank from my touch on his hunched shoulders.

I pulled back my hand. "The first time I jumped, it felt like a part of my soul was torn away. Then, I found you." I paused a moment to look at his bowed head. "The second time, after François . . . I felt the universe had crumbled. The birth of Evie-Jayne and my conviction that Gran and I had solved the portal gave me hope and direction." Tears coursed down my cheeks and dripped off my chin onto my hands in my lap.

"So how could you jeopardize everything I cherish in this world? You must have known what day it was."

"Of course I knew what day it was, but as long as I stay away from the bridge—"

"But you almost didn't!"

I jolted at his sudden, loud exclamation. I swallowed the anger of feeling unjustly accused and kept my voice calm. "There was no way I could have foreseen the events of today."

There was a long pause, but Claude's eyes softened as he met mine. "I'm sorry, *ma chère*. You must have been terrified." He opened his arms.

I flung myself across the space between our chairs. Holding me close to his chest, his heartbeat slowed under my ear. When he rose to stir up the fire, I returned to my own chair. My fingertips tingled in anticipation of soon caressing his lean frame, currently silhouetted in the fire's glow.

I smiled. "Something good did come from today. William promised to send a letter supporting Nelsonville's petition for incorporation." I paused, and then I pulled the envelope with its ten ten-dollar bills from my pocket and passed it to him. As I waited for him to finish reading the letter, my shoulders began to cave. By the time he looked back up at me, the smile had died on my face. "Today could have been a terrible disaster."

Claude let out his breath in a loud swoosh. "What if on January twenty-first each year, we spend the entire day doing things together as a family right here on our property, even once our children are grown and we have grandchildren?"

"I love it." I smiled. "Call it Dumont Family Day." A jaw-cracking yawn escaped me. "I'm exhausted. I'm going to bed, or I'll fall asleep right here."

As I stood, Claude swooped me up into his arms and deposited me on the bed. I fell asleep as he removed my shoes. My last thought was, "I love this man. Thank goodness there's no school tomorrow."

Willows

WILLOWS

Chapter Thirty

I scanned Nelsonville's rapidly filling schoolhouse from my bench behind a student desk near the back of the room. Mothers were seated around me, balancing babies and toddlers on their laps. Older children stood in the centre aisle while the men curled their backs to fit around the log walls. A constant low murmur played background to the winter chorus of coughs and sniffs. The indoor odour of damp wool clothing draped the assembly. Among the throng, I picked out the eager faces of the early settlers who would see the realization of their vision come to fruition today. The more recent arrivals wore their doubts and reservations on their brows.

"Maman, where are the books? And they don't have notebooks, just these little slates in the desks. I don't think I'd like to go to this school. It's not as good as our schoolcar."

"Shush Evie-Jayne. Schools can be different from each other. It doesn't mean that one is better." I had to agree with my six-year-old, though. Our schoolcar, festooned with student artwork, stories, and projects hanging on pegs around the room did seem more conducive to learning.

Seated on the other side of Evie-Jayne, Sophie traced letters and numbers with her finger on the little girl's leg to distract her.

I caught sight of the back of Claude's head in the front row. We'd both been invited to sit there in recognition of our contributions, but I chose to maintain a low profile and sit with our daughters. The gossiping crows who smiled to my face while pecking apart my every word and deed weren't going to get any grains to grind in their gossip mill.

Sophie's tap on my shoulder brought me back to the real purpose of my search of the room. "He's over there, third row, standing against the wall." She spoke softly. I grinned my thanks. I didn't know whether to be worried or happy that my daughter could read me so well.

Following her direction, I picked out Jean-Pierre's golden head poking above the sea of woollen tuques surrounding him. At almost eighteen, he was slightly taller than his father, and his shoulders carried the promise of future broadness and strength. I'd been skeptical two years ago when he and Claude convinced me school no longer had anything to offer Jean-Pierre. He was eager to learn by working side by side with his father, and Claude was overjoyed to have him. My reluctance to see him leave formal education was partially fuelled by the twentieth-century values I'd grown up with, but I had to admit it was also fed by the heart of a mother reluctant to see her little boy grow up.

Continuing my surveillance of the room, it was apparent I wasn't the only female appreciating Jean-Pierre Dumont. Several young women were primping, smiling, and even staring in hopes he would look their way. He remained oblivious to it all. Instead, he kept dipping his head and leaning sideways toward someone sitting at the end of the row where he stood.

"Maman, you're staring." Evie-Jayne's whisper drew my attention from my son.

"No. I was looking for your brother."

The sharp strike of the gavel brought the meeting to order.

"Ladies and gentlemen, quiet please!" Mr. Edwards raised his hands from where he stood beside the teacher's desk at the front of the room. "Thank you for coming today. I am pleased to present Mr. A. Dever, our duly elected reeve."

Polite applause.

Mr. Dever stepped to the podium. His voiced cracked and squeaked as he welcomed everyone. Then, clearing his throat, his voice took on a stronger tone as he read the proclamation certifying that the Townships of Nairn, Lorne, and Hyman were duly organized. He announced Richard Fensom, R.G. Lee, John Hall, and William Hunt as councillors. Each man joined Mr. Dever on the platform when his name was called. "Let the record show that today, Saturday, the seventh of March, 1896, at the hour of two o'clock in the afternoon at the schoolhouse in the village of Nelsonville, the first meeting of said council came to order."

The proclamation was greeted with applause and a few cheers.

The council members each swore an oath of office. They appointed Hector MacLean, a highly respected businessman well versed in the management of financial enterprises, as town clerk. A set of bylaws governing the operation of the council and its responsibilities to the people it represented was presented and accepted. Finally, the sixth bylaw was passed, stipulating that future meetings would take place on the first Monday of each month at the Forester's Hall at eight o'clock in the evening. With a strike of the gavel, the meeting came to an end.

Hector MacLean, proprietor of the Klondike Hotel, invited everyone to celebrate this historic event at his hotel in the town that from today forward would be known as Nairn.

Claude joined the girls and me as the crowd filed out. He exhaled loudly, cheeks puffed. "We made it."

I gave his hand a squeeze, and we turned toward the exit.

Knots of men were gathering around Mr. Dever and Mr. Fensom. "What is this going to mean for our families?" Asked a tall, blue-eyed Swede with two young boys hanging on his sleeve.

Mr. Fensom's reassuring tones wafted to us. "We'll be presenting a plan at our next meeting, but it means we'll have a government-funded school, new roads, and bridges, maybe even a doctor."

"We'll attract more jobs, which will bring families. We'll see shops and services right here in our town," Andrew Dever added.

"At what cost?" a man at the back of the group called.

"We don't have money for taxes," said another, his frayed shirt cuffs peeking out of his jacket.

I caught a few phrases about no education fees, working off taxes through labour, and caps on increases as Claude swept us toward the door.

"The committee wanted me to tell you how much they appreciated your work on the proposal and your suggestions on how to make their case. They never would have succeeded without your help." Claude smiled and gave my shoulder a squeeze.

"That's nice to hear, but they would have made it there anyway. After all, history tells us they did, right?"

"Ah, but would they? History only happens once, and you were here when it happened, so did it happen because of you?" He grinned as I tilted my head in thought. "Come, girls, let's get some refreshments."

Evie-Jayne grasped her father's hand and danced along beside him, sharing her views on how much better our schoolcar was than the schoolhouse where we'd just made history.

I sidled up to Sophie as we walked through the snow. "Who was J.P. talking to in there?"

Her wide-eyed innocence flipped to doe-soft pleading as she realized there was no way to escape my interrogation. "Maman, please don't tell J.P. I told you."

"It never came from you. Now, come on, give." I teasingly maintained a light tone.

"He was talking to Hannah, you know, the girl who came last year? She lives with the McDonalds."

I raised my eyebrows. "I always thought Marie was J.P.'s love interest."

"Everyone expected J.P. and Marie would end up together. They've known each other forever. Marie certainly wanted that. J.P. likes Marie, and he feels safe with her." She giggled. "But last summer at the Social, J.P. mistakenly bid on Hannah's box instead of Marie's."

"Oh, dear."

"And since then, he's been visiting Hannah every chance he gets to come into town. She really likes him, too. J.P.'s afraid you and *papa* won't approve because no one knows anything about her, but she's a really nice girl, maman."

"So, he plans to introduce us to her soon?"

"Yes, today. Please, give him a chance."

"If she truly is everything you say, then I can't see any reason for them not to continue being friends."

"I think J.P. has something more in mind. He's afraid you'll say they're too young."

"Too young for what?"

Sophie gave me a look loaded with innuendo, but before we could finish our conversation, we were waylaid by several of her friends. She threw me an apologetic smile and allowed herself to be towed along by the gaggle of teenage girls all speaking at once.

Was Sophie suggesting there was more to their relationship? *If so, they're right. They are too young.*

My mind was still in a whirl as I stepped into the Klondike Hotel. The lobby and assembly hall reverberated with excitement, joy, uncertainty, and skepticism wrapped in the scent of fresh baking and savoury meats. Claude signalled with his head that he was joining the men at the bar, and then he directed our youngest daughter toward me. Evie-Jayne spied Celestine Gagnon sitting at the child-size table in the portion of the dining room arranged for the children. She was watching her two-year-old brother rolling a wooden wagon back

303

and forth on the tabletop. The girls wrapped their arms around each other and bounced up and down in delight. Even as a two-year old toddler, Celestine had instantly become baby Evie-Jayne's protector. The relationship developed as they grew, until now, at ages six and eight, the two girls were best friends.

"Celestine, where is your maman?" I asked.

"Outside, she needed to get some air. I'm taking care of Jean-Marc."

"You girls can play. I'll watch Jean-Marc until your maman comes back."

Settling myself on one of the wooden adult chairs arranged around the room's perimeter, I exchanged smiles of greeting with several young mothers.

"Look at those silly girls over there," said a woman in her mid-twenties, hair pulled back into a severe bun. "All they talk about are boys and all they do is primp for their attention. Some of them have even coloured their cheeks. Next they'll be wearing those French fashions like in the mail-order catalogues."

We turned our attention to the giggling, head turning, and elbow-nudging group of teenaged girls gathered in the corner. Sophie was among them.

"I just don't know what this generation is coming to."

"Oh, come now, Charlotte. We were just like them at that age, trying to attract a boy, but terrified when one actually noticed us." Her blue-eyed friend laughed.

Nods of agreement all around. An attractive plump woman with naturally rosy cheeks heaved a wistful sigh. "I remember how uncomplicated life was back then. Now, it's all washing, cooking, cleaning, babies, and diapers."

"Life could be less work, Marianne, if you and Arthur exercised more restraint. Honestly, a baby every year?"

Marianne threw her friend a broad grin.

I picked out Jean-Pierre in the lobby, deep in conversation with a slim girl. She tucked her tight black curls behind her ears. His head bent to hers while she stood on tiptoe to speak into his ear. The intimacy of their position, the smiles they exchanged, the laughter they shared, told me more about this relationship than words ever could. How far had they gone? J.P. wouldn't . . . would he?

"*Bonjour*, Catherine! So good to see you!" Adeline's voice distracted me from my musings. My friend's thin shoulders hunched into our embrace. Stepping back, I took in her greyish pallor, white lips, and slightly moist forehead.

"Adeline, come and sit down." I pressed her into a chair. "Morning sickness still?"

Adeline nodded. "Yes, and not just in the mornings. It's past three months. After what happened with Josephine . . ." Adeline's brown eyes clouded.

I put my arm around her shoulders. "Let's take the train to Webbwood to see Dr. Jones on Friday. Just you and me. Sophie can take care of the girls and Jean-Marc for the day. We can have a nice visit with Elisabeth afterward."

"*Merci*, Catherine. I just get so scared, you know after . . ." Adeline's chin quivered.

"I know." I pressed my friend's clammy hand. "Now, you rest here. I'll get tea."

Six years before, Adeline had endured a difficult pregnancy resulting in the premature birth of a baby girl who didn't have the strength to grab hold of life. It had all happened while I was "away" having Evie-Jayne. My joyful return with a healthy baby just weeks after Josephine had died had made for a poignant reunion. Adeline's inner light had been restored after the successful birth of Jean-Marc, but we each would forever carry a small shadow within our hearts—hers was named Josephine, mine Amelia.

Part of me hoped to run into Jean-Pierre and Hannah as I threaded my way through the crowd, but the young couple had deserted their previous location and were nowhere to be seen.

Carrying tea for us, and a few tidbits for the children, I made my way back to the dining room. Adeline was looking more herself with colour returning to her cheeks. J.P. had folded himself into one of the tiny chairs, positioning it so he and Adeline could comfortably talk. He looked like a half-grown puppy with his knees up around his ears. I held back to take in the scene of J.P.'s head bent low, his blue eyes flitting up to Adeline's brown ones from time to time. Adeline kept her gaze even, nodding her head, letting him talk without interruption.

Evie-Jayne's joyous exclamation of "maman!" from across the room forced me to move. Jean-Pierre stood abruptly, tipping the little chair over backward. His face reddened to the tips of his ears. Everything about his stance screamed the desire to flee, but he squared his shoulders and kept his head up. Seconds later, Celestine and Evie-Jayne dragged a howling Jean-Marc across the room. Jean-Pierre scooped the solid toddler into his arms and began tossing him in the air, turning his howls into the most wondrous belly laughter.

The girls spied the scones and strawberry jam I'd brought and prepared morsels for themselves and Jean-Marc. Adeline sipped her tea.

With Jean-Marc now happily engaged in consuming the sweet strawberry treat, Jean-Pierre turned to me. "Maman, I need to talk to you about something. Papa found a quiet spot for us."

"Of course, J.P." This had to be it.

"I'll keep an eye on Evie-Jayne. You go, Catherine," Adeline said with a smile.

I followed Jean-Pierre through the crowds to a small service room near the kitchen. Claude was already there, wearing the parental expression of impending doom. I shot him a quizzical look. He shrugged. Before we had the opportunity to speak, Jean-Pierre entered the tiny space, leading Hannah by the hand.

"Maman, papa, this is Hannah. Hannah, these are my parents, Catherine and Claude Dumont."

The poor child was shaking like a leaf as he drew her forward.

"Very pleased to meet you, Hannah," I responded, grasping her sweaty palm and smiling.

"I'll get some chairs." Jean-Pierre disappeared through the door. Hannah looked longingly at the exit and his retreating back. Then, swallowing hard and with a deep inhalation, she turned her focus back to us, a nervous smile teasing the edges of her mouth. She wasn't what one would call a pretty girl, I noted. There was more depth to her than mere prettiness, more a serene beauty that radiated from within. As our eyes met, I caught a glimpse of something else, a haunted hollow that revealed itself briefly before she lowered the lids over her green eyes.

"It's very nice to meet you both." Hannah's voice was melodious even through her anxiety. "J.P. has told me so much about you." She fidgeted with her hands. "You both have university degrees. I'd like to go someday, but I don't think I'm smart enough, and I don't have any money." She glanced over her shoulder. "J.P. is taking a long time . . ." Her gaze flicked toward the door. "I'm sorry. I'm really nervous and a little scared and . . . oh dear." Hannah dropped her eyes to where her hands had been alternately folding and smoothing the gathers of her skirt at its narrow waist. Her thin shoulders slumped forward as she pushed black curls behind her ears.

"It's all right, child. You don't have to be afraid." Claude spoke as if to reassure a nervous stray cat.

The door opened, flooding our little space with the noise of the crowd.

"Here's J.P. with the chairs," Hannah said. Then, she whispered, "Thank goodness," as she positioned herself on the chair next to Jean-Pierre.

Once settled, Jean-Pierre cleared his throat and began an address that he'd clearly rehearsed. "Maman, papa, thank you for meeting like this. I'm sorry we have to do this so urgently but circumstances have created . . . What I mean to say is . . . We were planning to do this more slowly with you but . . ."

"What Jean-Pierre means to say is we have something to ask you, and because of recent events in my life, we need to speak to you now instead of doing things in a more proper way." Hannah shot an inquiring look at Jean-Pierre, who sent her a relieved smile and nodded for her to continue.

"Perhaps it's best if we start from the beginning?"

Claude and I both nodded.

"I imagine you've heard my story about how Mr. and Mrs. McDonald kindly took me in last year. All I remember from the past is the name Hannah written in icing on a cake with fifteen candles." Hannah paused to collect herself.

Jean-Pierre patted her hand where it lay in her lap as he took up the tale. "The McDonalds decided to give Hannah a home. She attends school and also helps Mrs. Hall in the schoolhouse."

The colour rose in Hannah's cheeks under Jean-Pierre's praise.

"J.P., you seem to know a great deal about Hannah. When did you two meet?" asked Claude.

Hannah's light laugh tickled the air in the small space. "It was quite by accident! You see, at last year's Strawberry Social, I contributed a box lunch. Jean-Pierre bid on it, mistaking it for another girl's."

"Yes, I thought it was Marie's, based on the description, but instead I ended up eating lunch with Hannah." His eyes never left her face as he spoke.

"It seems you've become quite good friends since then?" I recalled Sophie's earlier disclosure.

"Yes, J.P. and I meet when he comes to town. It's always proper, with other people around, and in public places like Mrs. Edwards's café."

"The two of you seem to have developed quite a . . . friendship over these past months, right under my nose. I never saw any sign of these assignations when J.P. accompanied me to town." Claude's stern manner brought the two young people up, backs pressed ramrod straight into their chairs.

I leaned forward. "So, what is this urgent matter you wanted to discuss?"

Jean-Pierre took a deep breath. "Mrs. McDonald is very ill, so the McDonalds are moving to Toronto to live with one of their daughters."

"And Hannah's not welcome?" I asked.

"Their daughter feels I've taken enough charity from her parents." Hannah's eyes teared up. "It was never my intention to take advantage of anyone. I'm grateful to the McDonalds for taking me in and have done everything I could to repay their generosity."

"She really has, maman. These last months, Hannah has cared for Mrs. McDonald, managed all the household and meal duties for the three of them, and she still found time to help at the school and continue her own studies." Jean-Pierre's fingers tightened around Hannah's hand. "We love each other."

My heart dropped.

"If circumstances were different, we'd have a proper engagement, but the McDonalds are leaving next week, and Hannah has nowhere to go. Will you give us your blessing so we can be married?"

The room lost all its air. I felt Claude's body tense beside me. Jean-Pierre stared at his father and I, brow creased as if he were waiting for the guillotine to fall. The silence enveloping our private space seemed all the more oppressive in contrast to the raucous laughter of the crowd seeping through the cracks around the wooden door.

I gave Claude a quick look before turning to the young couple. "J.P., Hannah, this has all come as a shock. You're asking for a very big decision. You scarcely know each other. Marriage is a very big step."

"I love Hannah, and nothing's ever going to change that," Jean-Pierre declared.

"Madame Dumont, I know you might think I'm looking for someone to care for me." Hannah leaned toward us, her green eyes intensely focussed on our faces. "There are times when I feel terrified for my future. However, I've taken every opportunity offered to me. I can teach. I can become a housekeeper, a maid, a nanny. There are rich people who are looking to employ someone like me, so if you say no, I do have other alternatives. But I love your son, and he is and always will be my first choice."

"Thank you, Hannah, for your frankness." I couldn't in good conscience agree to these two marrying, yet I also couldn't abide the thought of abandoning Hannah. I looked to Claude and continued. "We need some time to think about your request. Why don't you both rejoin the activities, and we'll find you when we have an answer."

"*Oui*, maman. Papa, please," Jean-Pierre made one final plea as Hannah preceded him out.

The door was barely closed behind the couple when Claude let out a whooshing sigh. "Married? They want to get married?" He stood and started pacing in the tiny space. "It's out of the question." His arms flew into the air.

"It is a big step," I said.

"It's a monumental leap. How well does he even know her? And where did she come from?" He stopped in front of me, brown eyes narrowed as he scanned my face.

"She seems pleasant and level-headed. And she's very responsible."

He shook his head. "So let her pursue one of the alternatives she suggested."

I sat silent.

"Don't tell me you think this is a good idea? Catherine, you know they're not ready for marriage."

I took his hand. "No, sweetheart, I don't think they should marry." I pulled him down to sit. "But she's only sixteen." I fixed my eyes on his face. "I remember how terrified I felt, alone, confused, when you rescued me, and I was much older." I squeezed his hand.

The tension evaporated from Claude's face, and his shoulders slumped. He nodded.

In the end, we decided that Hannah would live with us. She'd join Sophie and Evie-Jayne in the loft while Jean-Pierre moved into the barn. Hannah would continue her studies and assist Sophie and I with the school. She would be treated like a member of our family, with the same rules, expectations, and advantages of our own children. If Jean-Pierre and Hannah felt the same about each other a year later, then they'd receive our blessing to marry.

I turned to Claude that night in our bed as he pulled me close. "And so our family grows again. We did a good thing today, Mr. Dumont, for your son and for a lovely young woman."

Claude returned the hug, and I heard the sleepy smile in his voice as he answered, "I can think of worse things to be doing than building a house for the newlyweds next summer."

WILLOWS

Chapter Thirty-One

I sat on Elisabeth's back porch and revelled in the early morning solitude, a multi-coloured, granny-square afghan draped across my shoulders. Webbwood's white church spire flashed magically into brief moments of clarity as the rays of the October morning sun penetrated the rising mist. Elisabeth's funeral the day before had been just like Gran's, a beautiful celebration of a warm, generous woman.

Memories of the events since the Nairn Incorporation the previous March drifted from my mind into the steam rising from the cup of fresh coffee in my hands. The tail of the memory of Adeline's and my visit to Dr. Jones in early April stuck in my head. After seeing the doctor, we'd spent the afternoon with Elisabeth, drinking tea and munching on breads, cheeses, fruits, and sweets. The conversation had turned to the arrival of Hannah into our family. Elisabeth's comments still rang in my ears.

"*Ach*! Young love. It flashes hot," Elisabeth said. "You remember?" We'd both smiled.

"So, how did you know whether it was infatuation or the ember of true love?" Elisabeth arched her brows.

Adeline looked off into the distance. "He was sent to help on his grandfather's farm in another community. When he came back two months later, we were changed."

I nodded. "Same for me."

"So, how will J.P. and Hannah test their first love when they're living side by side?" Elisabeth asked. "And are they strong enough to step away if, in the end, the infatuation dies?"

Leaving me unsettled to absorb her questions, Elisabeth moved her attention to Adeline. "So, my dear, you are still having nausea, and the doctor has told you to rest in bed and eat many small meals. *Ne?*"

Adeline looked surprised. "How did you know?" Her mouth turned down, eyes welled with tears. "How will I take care of my children and Maurice?"

Elisabeth's eyes moved from me to Adeline and back. "Catherine, you have a pair of young lovers who would benefit from some separation, and Adeline, you need help with the children and the household." She gave us both a hard look. "Well?" She raised her hands, palms up.

Adeline and I stared at Elisabeth and then at each other. Suddenly, we broke into broad smiles. By the time we'd left, we'd decided to propose to Hannah that she move in with Adeline and Maurice until Adeline could manage on her own again. The young couple would be able to see each other easily but would have some distance to keep perspective.

"You're all alone out here?" Claude's question startled me as he looked around the porch. "You know you were laughing just now?"

"*Bonjour mon cher.*" I tilted my face up to receive his morning kiss.

"That coffee smells great. Is there more?"

"Yes, there's some on the stove. Maybe you could top me up and put on a fresh pot?" I held my empty cup over my head." I'm sure Sophie, Hannah, and J.P. will want some when they get up."

With the coffee-making symphony playing as background music, my thoughts took me to the previous few weeks. After Adeline gave birth to a robust baby boy they named Jean-Guy, Hannah moved back in with us. She continued to be a hard worker, always ready to help, but she'd become more reserved, almost sombre at times.

Rhubarb, Strawberries, and Willows

Claude's hand on my shoulder interrupted my thoughts as he passed me a fresh, hot cup. "Claude, do you believe it was luck that put Hannah into our lives? Don't you think things happen for a reason?"

"What would be the reason for Hannah to suddenly arrive in our lives?"

"I don't know. I just have this feeling. I mean, look at how enthusiastically she embraced her role with the Gagnons. Wouldn't she have wanted to stay with us to be near J.P.?"

"Perhaps, or maybe living with us or moving to the Gagnon's were both better options than the alternative of having to fend for herself at such a young age," Claude pointed out. "I believe she demonstrated resourcefulness, kindness, and depth of spirit to accept what was offered."

"Okay." I drew out the word. "But then, look at how willingly Hannah moved in to help Elisabeth two weeks ago, putting her even farther away from the man she loves."

My eyes clouded with sadness. Elisabeth had been busy over the summers, tending her gardens, working with her co-op members, and negotiating food supply contracts for the coming logging season. But she'd never been too busy for a visit until this year. On more than one occasion, I'd felt she was avoiding me. So, the first time I'd seen her since April was when I dropped in unexpectedly a few weeks ago. I barely covered my gasp when she'd greeted me. Her shrunken frame felt like twigs in my embrace. Deep purple shadows under her eyes and a tremble to her hand betrayed her struggle. She told me she was dying of a tumour in her ovaries. Anna and Paul were stopping in each day, but they had their hands full with two toddlers and a newborn. Elisabeth needed someone with her twenty-four hours a day. When I recounted my worry to my family that evening, Hannah had immediately volunteered to move in and care for Elisabeth in her own home. Jean-Pierre had been crestfallen.

I looked at Claude. "I can't conceive of life without Elisabeth." Warm tears tracked down my cheeks.

He moved his chair close to mine and wrapped his arm around my shoulder. We watched the sun burn off the final wisps of mist.

Claude cleared his throat. "When Hannah agreed to move to Webbwood, the thought had occurred to me that maybe she was trying to avoid something between her and J.P."

"Exactly. I've been carrying a niggling doubt concerning Hannah's future as a Dumont. It always felt like there was something more to her, like a puzzle with a piece hidden." During the year long wait to return to Claude and the children, I'd read a great deal about the history of Nairn for my play. But I'd deliberately avoided seeking any information about the Dumont family. I wanted to live life as it came.

"Your doubts weren't wrong, maman." Jean-Pierre stood in the doorway. "She's gone. Hannah's gone." His back slid down the doorframe until his bum hit the floor. His forehead dropped into his palms, supported by his elbows on his knees.

"She's likely just out for a walk," I said, "or maybe she's gone to the shops."

"She's not at the shops, and she's not on a walk." Jean-Pierre's voice had a hard edge. "Hannah left at first light this morning. She woke me to apologize and say goodbye."

Claude and I exchanged wide-eyed looks. Neither of us moved, nor did we speak. Jean-Pierre took a shaky breath, squared his shoulders, and rubbed his palms into his eyes just like when he was a little boy. Then, he pushed himself back into a standing position.

"Come and sit." I got up and patted my chair. "Let me get you some coffee." I grabbed the empty cups and disappeared.

In the kitchen, Sophie was toasting buns, savagely spreading them with butter and strawberry jam. Evie-Jayne was arranging slices of cheese, hard boiled eggs, and apple wedges on a platter. I wrapped my arms around both girls and held them tightly to me, inhaling the lilac scent from their freshly washed hair, my fingers lost in the silky blond and chestnut curls tumbling down their backs.

"So, J.P. told you," Sophie's voice cracked.

I took in the red-rimmed puffiness of her eyes. "You know?"

Sophie nodded. "Yes, she woke us up to say goodbye, but I knew it was going to happen sooner or later." She began moving around the room. "Why did she have to leave the day after Oma Elisabeth's funeral?" Cutlery rattled as she dropped it onto a tray. "I thought she was my friend. I thought she loved Oma Elisabeth." The plates clattered dangerously close to cracking as they joined the cutlery. "How could she just go and leave me alone? She was going to be my sister, and now I'll never see her again." Sophie spun from the worktop to the table, the platter of buns in her hand. I lunged to catch several buns propelled into space by her momentum.

"Let's get the food out to the porch." She grabbed a tray. "Too many memories in here."

Our family ate breakfast in silence, relishing the jam made by Elisabeth's own hands from the strawberries in her garden, the apples grown in her small orchard, the cheeses, buns and butter made by Hannah under Elisabeth's watchful eye. Each flavour evoked memories of Oma Elisabeth that played across the faces of my family.

"Is Hannah coming back?" Evie-Jayne's question broke into our musings.

Jean-Pierre reacted first, kneeling in front of his little sister, grasping both her hands in his. "No, *ma petite soeur*, I don't think we'll see Hannah again. But she'll always be in our hearts and in our memories."

He returned to his seat, gazing out over Elisabeth's tilled gardens prepared for their long winter slumber. "After that first box lunch social, I couldn't get Hannah out of my mind. It was like I'd been hit with a bolt of lightning. All I wanted to do was look at her, listen to her voice, breathe in her scent."

"Oh, I know that feeling, my son," Claude said. "It was the same for me with your maman. When I lost her, I was sure I would never love again, yet here we are." He spread his arms to include us all. "I've found a depth of love I never dreamed existed." The gold flecks in his eyes glittered as they met mine.

Jean-Pierre received his father's declaration with silence. Claude's vulnerable disclosure would only be fully appreciated years in the future. Right now, our son believed no one understood his pain.

"She remembered more than she let on, you know," he said.

"I know," Sophie responded. "And no wonder she kept her memories secret. Did she tell you about the children in that first family?"

"She never told me," interjected Evie-Jayne. "What first family?"

"Hannah is a time traveller," Sophie said.

I felt as if I'd been gut-punched. My mind galloped while my body froze.

Claude's eyebrows shot up his forehead. His brown eyes fired a hard, quizzical look at me. His knuckles whitened where he gripped the arm of the chair.

Evie-Jayne gasped and put her hand over her mouth, but Jean-Pierre's expression remained bland. What had Hannah told him?

I forced a neutral expression, pulling the corners of my mouth into a reassuring smile. "Time travel? Where did you get such an idea?"

"Hannah remembers playing in a park with her *papa* when she was about six years old," Sophie said. "It was a park on a very high hill that she called Royal. It had a large cross on it. Her maman was dead."

"Montreal," Claude whispered.

"That's where she said she's going to find her father," said Jean-Pierre.

"Hannah thinks she had many aunts and uncles because every Friday night the whole family would gather for a special meal. The women would light candles, cover their faces with their hands, and say a prayer at sundown." Sophie's eyes engulfed her face. "On Saturdays, after a service in a place she said felt like a church but without a cross, everyone would go to the park. One Saturday, when her father wasn't looking, she slipped behind a big boulder. Suddenly her ears were filled with a roaring sound, everything started to spin, and then there was black."

"Sounds like she fainted." I spoke calmly despite the hammering of my heart in my ears. "Everyone remembers events from their past, ma chère. It doesn't mean they've travelled through time."

Jean-Pierre took up the story. "Hannah woke up in bed. A lady she didn't know was putting a cool cloth on her forehead. The lady was kind, but the children in the family teased her, pushed her, pinched her. So, the woman took Hannah on a long train ride to live with a couple who didn't have children. They lived in a tiny cottage on the Spanish, just outside of Nairn."

"This still doesn't sound like time travel," I said.

Sophie jumped in. "She said there was a machine that would make a ringing sound. When you put it to your ear, you could talk to a person that was in another house far away." Sophie moved to the edge of her seat. "She said there were wagons that moved without horses, and when you flicked a switch on a wall," she snapped her fingers, "a lamp would come on in the room."

Evie-Jayne's eyes sparkled.

Claude's eyes narrowed.

I was breathless. Telephones. Cars. Electricity.

Jean-Pierre's voice was barely audible. "At school, they did the date just like you do with our school, maman." He paused. "It was January 1986."

Claude pushed back into his chair.

"She lived with the couple for nine years." Sophie said. "Then, one day, a year ago in January, Hannah was walking along the river when she heard a roaring like a train in her ears. The next thing she knew—boom—she was lying in the snow at the railway bridge.

Prospectors found her and brought her to Nairn. That's when she went to live with the McDonalds."

No one spoke. The thin whistle of a white-throated sparrow calling Oh-sweet-Canada-Canada filtered through the trees.

Sophie mouthed the word "Go" at Jean-Pierre, while motioning with her hand. He turned to me and took a deep breath. "Hannah thinks you're a time traveller, too." The air left him with a whooshing sound. I'd never seen his eyes such a deep blue. They remained fixed on mine. I knew this day would come, but not yet. I wasn't ready.

Claude stared at me, his face flushed as if he were about to explode. My eyes pleaded with him to stay calm.

"Where would she come up with such an idea?" I scoffed.

Jean-Pierre's voice was tight. "We say 'okay', 'awesome,' and 'cool,' just like the people she lived with in the 1980s. She read the same stories about Charlie Brown at her school as the ones you told us."

Claude was shaking his head slowly at me, his mouth drawn into a severe line.

"Do you believe Hannah's story?" *What was I going to say if they said yes?*

Sophie's hands pleated the soft wool of her navy skirt, and she crossed and uncrossed her feet under her chair. Jean-Pierre studied the floor boards. I bit my lip to stop myself from breaking the silence.

When Sophie raised her head, her brown eyes glowed with conviction. "I believe her."

Jean-Pierre gave a slow nod.

"She never told me her story, but I believe it, too," Evie-Jayne said. She scooched to the edge of her chair. "*Are* you a time traveller, maman?"

Claude stood abruptly, grabbed my hand, and pulled me into the house. The children gaped, rooted to their seats.

Once in the living room, he stopped and whirled to face me. "Catherine, what are you doing? You can't tell them."

"They need to know the truth."

"Why? So they live in fear of revealing the secret?" He put his hands on my shoulders. "I adore you, but you can't tell them. It will tear their lives apart. A mother who claims she comes from the future?" He raised his arms. "They'll be the children of a lunatic." He turned away.

I hung back. "Is it better to leave them wondering? What if they decide to go to the railway bridge to test Hannah's story? What if . . ." I shuddered at the thought of my daughters repeating my experience. "You heard Hannah's terrible story. Do you want your daughters to go through that?"

Claude turned back. A nerve was twitching along his jawline.

"I have to tell them. It's the only way to keep them safe."

He pulled me against him so hard, it was as if he was trying to merge my body into his. "We'll move away. I will not lose you."

I gently pushed backward. "You'll never lose me. But, just like J.P. needed to know the truth about his mother, the girls need to understand what it means to be a Dumont woman." My eyes searched his until I saw the flash of gold flecks. I took his hand. "They're waiting."

When we returned to the porch, Jean-Pierre was holding Evie-Jayne on his lap while Sophie was talking to her.

" . . . but I don't think you change how old you are."

Claude and I resumed our seats. Evie-Jayne moved to her father's lap. I reached for Sophie's and Jean-Pierre's hands.

"Remember what happened to Alice in Wonderland?" I asked.

It was Sophie's favourite book. "She fell down a rabbit hole."

"She met those strange animals that talked," Jean-Pierre said. "It was like she was in a different world."

I took a deep breath. "At the railway bridge over the Spanish, there's a portal just like the rabbit hole."

Jean-Pierre gave a disbelieving chuckle. "Maman, how can there be a *porte* on the bridge?"

I smiled. "Not a door, it's an invisible portal, *mon gars*. And the Dumont women can go through it."

"I'm a Dumont girl. Will it work for me?" Sophie's eyes shone.
"Does it go to another world like the rabbit hole?"

"*Oui, ma petite.* It'll work for you and Evie-Jayne."

"How do you know?"

"Because you freeze when you hear the train pass near us on its way to the bridge." I paused to settle my breathing. "It goes from now to a hundred years into the future and back, but it only opens at one o'clock on January twenty-first each year."

"Have you gone through it, maman?" Jean-Pierre's eyes clouded.

"Yes, I have."

The children stared at me.

"Were you scared?" Sophie asked.

"How many times?" Jean-Pierre asked.

"I was terrified. I've gone through three times, twice by accident and once on purpose."

Sophie tilted her head sideways. "How can you go through a door by accident sometimes and on purpose other times?"

"The first time, I didn't know there was a portal. I was snowshoeing along a trail by the railway bridge, enjoying a sunny winter day, when all of a sudden there was the loud sound of a train's whistle in my ears, and I heard people screaming. Then, there was a hard thump in my chest, and I awoke, lying in the snow."

"Where did you go?" Evie-Jayne asked.

"I didn't go anywhere. I landed in exactly the same place, just a hundred years back in time."

Sophie asked, "Did you go on purpose the next time?"

"The next time was nine years later, and I hadn't thought about the portal for a long time. I was snowshoeing quickly, trying to find your father when, all of a sudden, there was the noise and the chest thump."

"Did you go a hundred years backward again?" Jean-Pierre asked.

I gave their hands a small squeeze. "No. I went a hundred years into the future." I tightened my grip on my children's hands. We were into this now, best to bring out the full truth. "When I was away for a year, I wasn't in Toronto, *mes enfants.*"

Claude let out a gentle groan.

"I was in the future."

Jean-Pierre's eyes narrowed. "So, Evie-Jayne was born in the future?"

I nodded.

Evie-Jayne's face lit up. "Wow! I'm a time traveller."

"The third time, I knew exactly what I was doing and used the portal on purpose to bring me here to you."

"Can I come with you the next time, maman?" I felt Sophie's knee dance against our hands.

"I won't be going through again, *ma chère.*" I pressed my hand firmly on her leg. "And you must promise that you will never try to use it."

Sophie's face fell. "But, maman. . ."

"It's too dangerous." I held her hand tightly. "Promise me!"

"*Oui*, maman, I promise." Her words seemed to be pulled from her like *la tire Sainte-Catherine,* the maple taffy we spread on the snow to cool on St. Catherine's day each year.

"I promise too, maman," whispered Evie-Jayne, eyes solemn.

Claude pressed his lips to her neck. "*Merci, ma petite.*"

"Did you know about the portal, papa?" Jean-Pierre's shoulders were pulled up to his ears.

"Your maman told me about it." Claude settled his hand on his son's shoulder.

"That brings me to my second promise." I made sure I had their eyes connected with mine. "You must never tell anyone about the portal. Others won't understand, and they could hurt you."

"You mean like when people shunned the Lalondes because Madame Lalonde danced naked in the moonlight and had those animal bones hanging on her porch?" Sophie asked.

"Yes." I quelled the smile dancing around the corners of my mouth. Incredible the things children absorbed. "Promise?"

"Don't worry. I don't ever want to talk about it." Jean-Pierre shook his head.

"Maman, can I talk about it with Marie? She's my best friend."

"No, Sophie, not with anyone." I squeezed her hand. "Understand?"

"*Oui, maman, je comprends.*" She drew her mouth into a pout. "But can I talk about it with you at home sometimes if we're alone . . . ?" Her voice rose at the end.

"Of course, *ma chère.* We can talk about it whenever you want." She nestled into my lap, and I took a steadying breath to settle the churning in my stomach.

The muscles in Claude's shoulders and neck relaxed, but his brow was still furrowed. "J.P., did you consider going with Hannah?"

"Hannah was a gift." Jean-Pierre blushed. "She smelled like a fresh spring rain." His eyes darkened to navy blue. "At first I really wanted to, but I realized that no matter how much we loved each other, I could never replace what she'd lost. I hope she finds her *papa.*"

Evie-Jayne slid from her father's lap to wrap her arm around Jean-Pierre's shoulder as I'd seen him do for her when she was troubled. He leaned into her embrace. "Maybe she'll come back once she finds what she's looking for."

"No, Evie-Jayne, we parted knowing we'd never see each other again. If I truly loved her, how could I have let her go by herself?" His brow was pulled down so tightly his eyes became slits. "I'm weak." He hit his fist on his thigh.

Claude pulled his son to his feet, gripping him firmly about the shoulders, and walked him back into the cabin. Moments later, we heard the front door close. Claude knew all about the pain of watching someone you love disappear into a darkness where you couldn't follow.

While the girls and I cleared the breakfast remains, I couldn't suppress the rancour I felt toward my own blindness. "I'm sorry, girls.

I should have told you sooner." I knew this day would come, but in the end, they heard it first from a stranger. "I didn't keep you safe."

"But you did." Sophie gave my shoulder a squeeze as she walked by me. "You and papa invented Dumont Day to keep us close."

Evie-Jayne wrapped her arms around us. "I love you, maman." The new glow in her eyes made my spine prickle with unease. I was going to have to watch her.

WILLOWS

Chapter Thirty-Two

"Make sure you get return tickets. And check the dates on them before you pay."

"Maman, I'm seventeen, not seven." Evie-Jayne shook her head as she went into the Nairn Railway Station.

I stood on the wooden platform, sheltered from the early morning freezing rain by the station's overhanging roof. Claude was seeing to the loading of our suitcases.

"Everything all right, Madame Dumont?"

My shoulders jerked.

"I'm sorry, I didn't mean to startle you." Joey Jr.'s forehead wrinkled with concern.

My mouth twitched into a weak smile. "I'm fine, thank you, Joey." I couldn't bring myself to add Junior to the young man towering over me. Joey, like Jean-Pierre, was turning thirty this year. The men had remained close friends since their childhood. Joey had taken over as stationmaster five years ago when his father retired. "How are your parents?"

"Mother is enjoying life in the big city. She helps my sister with the five little ones, especially since the twins were born. Dad, though, likes to come back here for extended visits. He says Toronto is so noisy you can't even hear the birds."

"Well, give them my best."

327

Joey Jr. nodded. "Eastbound train should be right on time. Looks like you're going a long way." He motioned with his chin at our luggage waiting on the platform.

"Evie-Jayne and I are off to Montreal for a few days."

"Have a nice trip, ma'am." Joey dipped his head and then continued down the platform to his office door.

I resumed staring at the dense evergreens on the other side of the tracks and picked up the train of thought that had been interrupted by Joey. Last March, six freight cars on a westbound train had plunged down a twenty-five-foot gulley at a steep curve just east of Nairn. Mrs. Hall's hands had trembled and tears had streamed down her cheeks as she'd recounted the grinding and crashing. She'd told of how the town's residents rushed to the site, slid down the snow embankment, and carried two injured men back to the Klondike Hotel. One man had died. I'd forgotten all about this accident, probably because it wasn't at the bridge. But who could I have warned if I had remembered? How do you tell someone in this century that you know the future?

I took a shaky breath. On January 21, 1910, just a few months short of three years from now, a doomed westbound train would depart this station at twelve forty in the afternoon and, twenty minutes later, it would jump the track at the bridge. The echoes of shrieking passengers had begun jolting me out of sleep most nights. My heart ached knowing lives would be lost. There had to be something I could do.

"Ça va, chérie?" Claude stood beside me, his hand on my arm. "You look pale."

"I'm fine." I covered his hand with mine. "Maybe a little nervous."

"You don't have to do this." Claude looked at me through hooded eyes.

"I have to try. Lives are at stake."

"How do you plan to convince Mr. Van Horne? You don't know if he can even do anything."

Rhubarb, Strawberries, and Willows

I turned to face him. "William designed this stretch of track. He's the only one I can turn to. Besides, his response to my letter was positive." I smiled.

"He invited you to visit while you were in Montreal under your ruse of exploring universities for Evie-Jayne, not because you want to talk about an impending railway disaster three years from now." He held me by my shoulders.

It was becoming impossible to maintain a conversation over the locomotive's hiss and the workers' yells as they loaded the baggage car.

Evie-Jayne appeared at our side. "Maman, they're calling for us to board." She kissed her father. "Don't worry, papa. I'll take care of her."

He hugged Evie-Jayne and sent her ahead with directions to get settled in our compartment. His eyes brimmed with love as he turned to me. "I love you so much, *ma chère*. Are you sure I shouldn't come with you?"

My lips lingered on his. "I love you, too. We'll be fine. You and J.P. have too much to do before spring breakup." I buried my face in his neck to drink in his woodsy outdoor scent. "I'll send a telegram when we get there."

"All aboard!"

Turning one last time on the car platform to drink in every inch of him, I smiled and waved, and then I joined Evie-Jayne in our compartment. We pressed our faces against the window, watching Claude grow smaller until he dropped out of sight around the curve.

"Maman, there's a dining car." Evie-Jayne waved a page in my face. "I know we brought our own food, but wouldn't it be romantic eating dinner from china plates and silver cutlery? Imagine, a white linen table cloth under a softly shaded light, dark forests streaking through the night." Her voice was wistful and her eyes focussed heavenward. "Can't you just see it?"

The glow of her cheeks and the sparkle in her eyes helped suppress my worries of the real purpose of our trip. "Yes, put that way, how can I possibly not see it? Of course, we'll take our supper in the dining car though I'm not sure how romantic it'll be sitting with your mother. And how is it that these romantic ideas are even in your mind, young lady?" I teased.

"Jane Eyre was only a year older than me when she met Mr. Rochester, and Elizabeth Bennett was just twenty. Hannah and J.P. were my age when they fell in love." Her voice petered out. "Maybe on Saturday we can visit the park at Mont Royal?"

"Sweetie, you know she may not even be . . . here."

Her shoulders drooped.

"But, a visit to the park would be nice," I said.

"*Merci*, maman!" Evie-Jayne flung her arms around my neck, and I hugged her back.

"Now, let's see about this romantic dinner, shall we?" I needed a distraction from the misgivings crowding my head.

* * *

"*Excusez-moi. Vous êtes Madame Dumont de Nairn?*" The pimply faced young man wearing a dark blue chauffeur's uniform approached us, nervously passing his cap from hand to hand. We'd just collected our suitcases and stood on the platform in Westmount Station, almost twenty-four hours after our departure from Nairn.

"*Oui, c'est moi.*"

"Excellent. I am Mr. Van Horne's chauffeur. Please follow me." He picked up our bags and proceeded along the platform to the exit. Evie-Jayne and I exchanged confused looks before hurrying to catch up to our disappearing bags. I was vaguely aware of the long red-brick building with its soaring pavilion-style roof before our guide exited through one of the large arched openings. As we emerged onto the street, he declared, "This is a new station, just completed last month." He put down a suitcase to gesture behind us. "You will notice the one-and-a-half-storey turrets at each end, framing this facade of arches. From here, you can catch a train to anywhere in North America." His chest puffed out proudly as if he'd been the one to build the station.

Evie-Jayne extended her hand. "My name is Evie-Jayne Dumont. You know a lot about this station."

"*Enchanté, Mademoiselle.*" The youth took her hand. "I am Étienne Legrand, future architect."

Their eyes met briefly over their handshake.

"So, you're studying architecture?" Evie-Jayne asked.

He shook his head. "For now, I must support my mother and my three sisters, so I'm Mr. Van Horne's chauffeur. But one day . . ."

Evie-Jayne's expression softened. "Is your *papa* ill?"

"My *papa* is in jail." The youth's eyes danced. "My *papa* believes we should keep Québec for the French. He and his comrades demonstrated their disagreement a little too forcefully when they tried to blow up Nelson's Column." He picked up the suitcases. "The street is clear. *Allons-y.*" And off we were again, hurrying to keep up with the receding back of our determined guide.

With our cases stowed and both of us seated in the rear of the bright red Star Automobile, Étienne Legrand warned us to hold on tightly. He deftly joined the flow of horse-drawn carriages, bicycles, and a few cars on la rue Sainte-Catherine. Evie-Jayne's eyes were popping out of her head. Her nails dug into my forearm as the vehicle gained speed, bouncing over the mixed road surface of cobblestones and hard-packed gravel. The narrow streets around the station perpendicular to Sainte-Catherine were lined with lazy buildings like old women who'd let themselves go. They seemed cantankerous with their cracked and peeling paint and broken porches.

"Please excuse my driving," Étienne said. "Mr. Van Horne brought this vehicle from England last month. I'm still improving my skills."

"M. Legrand, where are you taking us?" I asked.

"I've been instructed to deliver you to the mansion where Mr. Van Horne will be present to greet you."

"There must be some mistake. We have a reservation at a bed and breakfast on Sherbrooke, just in the shadow of Mont Royal."

"I'm sorry, Madame, but I must follow my instructions. You don't want me to lose my job, do you?" He cast a pleading look over his shoulder.

Evie-Jayne jumped in. "Maman, we can't let him lose his job."

"Perhaps Madame can take the matter up with Mr. Van Horne upon her arrival?" Étienne's eyes opened wide.

I nodded my assent.

With a dramatic exhalation of breath, our chauffeur continued brightly, "Now, please, sit back and enjoy the view. Montreal is a magnificent city with a rich history."

For the next thirty minutes, we wove around slower-moving traffic and up and down narrow streets. Étienne offered a running commentary of the passing brick and stone buildings that looked like one long, luminous oil painting from the vehicle window. Soon, he had Evie-Jayne fully engaged in the architectural significance and characteristics that situated each building within its particular period of development. I vacillated between marvelling at her easy manner with this young man and worrying over what was awaiting us at the Van Horne Mansion.

Étienne slowed to even less than ten miles per hour as we entered an area of majestic mansions with grand entrances rising directly from the sidewalks. He managed his smoothest stop of the trip in front of a three-storey greystone that dominated the corner of Sherbrooke and Stanley.

"*Voilà, Madame et Mademoiselle.* The Van Horne Mansion," Étienne announced. "Built in 1869 for Mr. John Hamilton and purchased in 1889 by Mr. Van Horne. You will see the characteristic soaring ceilings of architect Edward Colonna from the remodel Mr. Van Horne commissioned a few years ago."

"Legrand, are you going to leave our weary guests to freeze in that ridiculous carriage all day?" A petite young woman shivered in her black-and-white maid's uniform on the front step. "Monsieur Boudreau is on his way."

Étienne sprang out of the vehicle and opened our door, extending his hand to assist us.

I emerged from the vehicle to be met by the steely blue eyes of a middle-aged clean-shaven man, dressed in a black suit, hands clasped behind his back. "*Bienvenue, Madame Dumont, Mademoiselle Dumont,* to Van Horne Mansion. I am Antoine Boudreau, of the line of Boudreau butlers who have served the best and wealthiest families in our city for generations. You may simply refer to me as Boudreau." He dropped his head in a brief nod, revealing his white scalp peeking between the closely cut thinning grey hair on the top of his head. "Monsieur is waiting for you in the *bibliothèque* where tea and light refreshments have been laid out. Legrand, see to their luggage. Ladies, please follow me."

The young maid relieved us of our coats and bonnets at the door. To the left of the grand staircase, we followed Boudreau into a lamplit hallway. The mahogany panelling on walls and ceiling was reminiscent of Van Horne's railway car.

Evie-Jayne stopped to peer at a sepia-coloured photograph, one of the twenty or more on display on both sides of the passage. Each featured a stretch of track through a particular piece of Canadian landscape.

"Maman, this one shows our bridge."

"That's nice. Keep up, *ma petite.*"

Boudreau opened the double doors at the end of the hall and announced, "Madame Dumont and Mademoiselle Dumont." Evie-Jayne rushed to my side, and we stepped into the room together. A large wooden desk anchored the red Turkish carpet. Stuffed bookshelves covered the walls from floor to ceiling with a sliding ladder to provide access to the upper reaches. Beside the single window, several forest-green wingback chairs clustered in front of the fireplace.

"Catherine! So wonderful to see you again." William took my hands in both of his. His hair and beard were completely grey, and his face carried deeply etched lines of the outdoors, but his smile still danced in his eyes. William dropped one of my hands to take Evie-Jayne's. "And this must be Evie-Jayne. Why the last time I saw you, you were a toddler. Look at you, as beautiful as your maman."

She curtsied slightly and looked him in the eye. "It's very nice to meet you Mr. Van Horne. You have a lovely home."

I smiled.

"*Merci, Mademoiselle.*" William chuckled. "Come sit by the fire. My housekeeper, Madame Boudreau, has prepared tea and scones." Once we settled, William turned to me. "Will you pour, please, Catherine?" Then, he engaged Evie-Jayne in conversation about her educational and career aspirations.

I set a china cup rimmed with gold filigree in front of each of us. "Thank you for this wonderful welcome, William. Will we meet your wife, Lucy?"

William's mouth drooped.

Oh, no. Has something happened to her? Have I opened a wound?

"Lucy prefers the seaside even in this frigid weather. She's at Covenhoven, nearer to our son and grandchildren." He sighed. "My business keeps me in the city."

"What's Covenhoven?" Evie-Jayne asked.

I shook my head at her question.

"No need to reprimand the girl, Catherine. Covenhoven is our home by the sea near St. Andrew's in New Brunswick. Now, tell me about your holding. How are Claude, Jean-Pierre, and Sophie?"

Over refreshments, William regaled us with tales of when he and several partners established the Trans-Cuban Railway. When Evie-Jayne seemed bored with the conversation of railways and lumber,

William invited her to freely wander through the ground floor rooms to view the art.

He and I were engaged in the kind of conversation old friends have when they haven't seen each other for a while. I'd just steered the topic to the railway bridge across the Spanish when Evie-Jayne burst into the room. "Maman, you must come see the galleries. Each one is larger than our whole house. The fireplaces are carved and tiled like works of art. There are hundreds of paintings in golden frames, just like the ones we see in the library books in Toronto. Are the paintings yours, Mr. Van Horne?"

"They are for now. They'll go to the city's gallery when I pass."

"You must be very rich."

"Evie-Jayne. Manners. I'm sorry, William."

"No need to apologize." He turned to Evie-Jayne. "Thank you, for reminding me of how fortunate I am. I'm afraid I take things for granted. But you're the rich one. I rarely see my family, while you live in the bosom of yours." He smiled. "Now, I'm sure you'd both enjoy a brief rest before supper?" William pulled a green velvet rope near his chair, and we heard the faint tinkle of a bell somewhere in the house. I stood and signalled Evie-Jayne to do the same. Within moments, the maid appeared at the door. "*Oui, Monsieur.*"

"Yvette please take Madame and Mademoiselle to their rooms where they can rest and freshen up. Supper is served at seven. Yvette will collect you from your rooms and bring you to the dining hall at that time."

"William, I'm afraid we have a misunderstanding. We have accommodations arranged in a pleasant bed and breakfast further along Sherbrooke Street. Perhaps you could arrange for someone to take us there?" I gave him a firm smile. "As to dinner, we'd be pleased to return perhaps tomorrow evening if that is convenient? We've taken enough of your time."

I watched the affable old man with whom I'd just spent the last hour in pleasant conversation transform into the stubborn one I'd

335

escaped from while in Northern Ontario. "Catherine, I'm sorry, but it seems you're the one labouring under a misunderstanding. I invited you to my home; all is prepared for you." A smile played around his mouth, but his eyes were hard.

Our eyes locked. My mind raced. I didn't believe William had any dishonourable intentions, but it would also not be in my best interests to alienate his goodwill. I weighed my options while the silence stretched between us. Then, I dropped my eyes. "Thank you, William. Evie-Jayne and I will be pleased to be your guests."

"Perfect! I'll see you both at seven. Yvette, please." The warmth returned. He drew himself to his full height and squared his shoulders with a little more effort than I remembered.

We climbed the broad oak staircase.

"Here are your rooms." Yvette preceded us into a spacious mint-green room with a large canopied bed, a sitting area complete with settee, and a window seat overlooking the garden. "Mademoiselle's room is right next door, accessible from the hallway but also through this shared dressing room where we have hung your clothes. Monsieur felt you would prefer the view over the garden as it is quieter than on the street even though the rooms on this side are smaller."

"These are lovely, Yvette, *merci*."

"The *boîte à baignoire* for this level is at the end of the hall. Please ring if you require anything else." She gestured at the velvet rope. "I will return a few minutes before seven o'clock as Monsieur detests tardiness."

Yvette had barely closed the door behind her when Evie-Jayne came bursting through the dressing room. "Maman, have you ever seen such a big room? Mine is exactly like yours, but in periwinkle. And the bed." She sat on the edge and dropped backward onto the mattress. "I've never lain on anything so soft. It smells of fresh spring flowers." Flinging her arms around me, she began to dance around the room. "This is going to be the best adventure ever!"

"I don't see a pitcher and basin anywhere in here, so let's go check out this *boîte à baignoire*."

Walking ahead of me down the hall, Evie-Jayne's squeals confirmed my hope. It was a bathroom, complete with indoor plumbing. I watched from the doorway as Evie Jayne ran her hand over the flocked royal blue and gold wallpaper.

"Have you ever seen anything so elegant?"

In place of a response, I walked to the claw-footed tub and turned the golden knobs of the faucet. A drawn-out "Ahhhhhh" escaped me as I felt the hot water run over my hand and begin to fill the tub.

Evie-Jayne continued to exclaim over the fixtures, lifting the lid on the toilet, and twisting the knobs on the sink.

"Fetch the towel and dressing gown from your room, Evie-Jayne. We can each take a quick bath before dressing for dinner. Wear the best dress you have. Tomorrow we'll do some shopping to fit into this house."

"Maman, I found two large bags in the dressing room, one addressed to me and one to you. I peeked in mine. It's the most beautiful dress I've ever seen. Green like the fresh new shoots of corn in spring with ruffles of lighter shades. Come look!" She pulled me back to our rooms where we found a dress for each of us, complete with jewelry and shoes to match. By the time Yvette came to fetch us, we were more than properly attired for the evening.

Descending the stairs with our gored skirts draped smoothly over our hips and falling flatteringly in a widening flow to the floor, I felt like a queen accompanied by my darling princess daughter on our way to the ball. I wished Claude were the man waiting at the bottom of the stairs.

"Ladies, what visions of loveliness you are. Evie-Jayne, the greens are perfect with your youthful complexion while the cut gives you just the right air of sophistication. And Catherine, that blue with your eyes and hair, like radiant sunlight on a sparkling sea. I trust that everything is to your liking?"

"William, the rooms are marvellous and these dresses . . . How can I ever repay you?"

He stroked his beard thoughtfully, a mischievous glint in his eye. "I detest entertaining. Lucy is the one who ensures that we keep up our social obligations, but in her absence, you would do me a great honour if you would both assist me in hosting a small dinner party here tomorrow evening. Just a few close friends and a visit to the theatre afterward?"

Evie-Jayne gave a small gasp beside me.

I paused. This visit was becoming much more complicated than I'd anticipated, but I hadn't been to a theatre in years . . . "Yes, of course, William."

Evie-Jayne squeezed my arm.

William grinned. "Good. Now, let's enjoy our supper, and plan to retire early tonight. Tomorrow, Legrand will be at your disposal to take you wherever you would like—a tour of the city, a tour of the universities, some shopping."

True to his word, we were back in our rooms before nine o'clock and sound asleep by ten. Evie-Jayne ended up sleeping with me, as she had never slept in a room alone before. The next morning, William had already breakfasted and gone before we descended. Étienne provided us with an interesting driving tour of the city, let us off for some lunch and shopping, and then dropped us at the Université de Montréal campus. We needed to keep up appearances until I'd had a chance to speak with William about the real reason for our visit. And what was the harm in enjoying the city while we had the chance?

The small dinner party ended up being twenty guests, including several young men. They swarmed around Evie-Jayne like bees to the fresh green lily that her attire and manner evoked.

"She truly is her own mistress," William leaned in to whisper to me as I remained a vigilant bystander. "You will have nothing to worry about while she's attending university here. Which one is she considering by the way?"

"About that . . ."

"Never mind. Perhaps tomorrow you can tell me the real reason for your visit?" William pinned me with his knowing gaze.

Damn, this man always managed to rattle me. I felt a rock growing heavy in my stomach. "Perhaps you can introduce me to your friends before we go in to dinner." Slipping my hand through his elbow, I let him steer me toward the first small grouping.

The remainder of the evening went off without a hitch. I'm not sure what gave me more pleasure, the actors on stage performing George Bernard Shaw's "Candida" or watching Evie-Jayne's expression as she took in the soaring ceilings, towering columns, and sumptuous surroundings of the newly opened Bennett's Theatre. Our sides ached with laughter at the antics of the youthful poet Eugene Marchbanks as he tried to win the affections of clergyman, James Morell's wife Candida.

WILLOWS

Chapter Thirty-Three

"Maman, isn't this decadent?" Evie-Jayne heaped her plate with scrambled eggs, bacon, toast, and fruit from the platters arranged on the sideboard. Sunlight streamed through the open curtains of the floor-to-ceiling windows, throwing fireflies of light around the mahogany panelled walls of the dining room.

"It certainly is, but don't get used to it, *ma petite*."

"Ah, good morning, ladies. I hope this meets with your approval," William said as he entered the dining room.

"*Oui*, Monsieur Van Horne, everything is perfect," said Evie-Jayne. "And thank you again for last night. The dinner, the play, it was all like a magical dream. I'll carry the memory with me for a long time."

The corners of William's eyes crinkled with his smile. "It is I who must thank you. I've never had two more charming hostesses. You will be the talk of the Montreal English society for months. Now, what do you have planned for today?"

Before I could respond, Evie-Jayne said, "I'd like to explore McGill University this morning. If Étienne isn't able to drive us, we can take the tram." She turned to me. "Since it's Saturday, maybe we can go to the park at Mont Royal afterward?" Her raised eyebrows carried her insinuation.

"Of course we'll go to the park, but I didn't know you wanted to visit McGill." I looked at her sideways. "I doubt it'll be open today." "Monsieur's lecturer friend, Madame Charlebois, told me all about the university during dinner. She teaches there in the English Department and has offered to provide us with a tour. Isn't that fortuitous?"

"Yes, *ma chère*, very fortuitous." I directed my sardonic tone at William, who was looking like the cat who had just swallowed the canary. What was he up to?

After breakfast, Étienne pulled the car to the front of the mansion, brimming with enthusiasm at the opportunity to tour us through another part of his city.

An attractive older woman, a red wool coat hugging her petite frame, stamped her black leather ankle boots to maintain circulation in her feet as she greeted us with a smile in front of McGill's main entrance.

"Bonjour, Madame." Evie-Jayne held out her hand. "This is my mother, Catherine Dumont. Maman, this is Madame Charlebois."

The woman's dark eyes sparkled. "*Enchantée*, Madame. Now, if you'd like to come this way . . ."

I followed behind Evie-Jayne and the teacher, enjoying their easy conversation. When Evie-Jayne's questions became more specific concerning courses and resources, it dawned on me that, while Claude and I had hatched the pretence of university selection for Evie-Jayne, our daughter was embracing the possibility that university in Montreal might be more attractive than following in her sister's footsteps at the University of Toronto. I had mixed feelings about that, but Claude might be pleased for his daughter to attend his alma mater.

Shortly after noon, Evie-Jayne and I took our leave of Madame Charlebois. We caught the tram to the Avenue du Parc entrance of *le parc du Mont-Royal*.

"Madame says there are accommodations on campus, and it's easy to get around the city on the tram from there," Evie-Jayne said.

"That's nice. The streetcars in Toronto will do the same."

She made a face at me.

We armed ourselves with sandwiches and ginger beer purchased from a nearby street vendor and settled on a bench in a large clearing where several footpaths intersected. The area was teeming with clusters of immigrants who'd fled Europe seeking a safer, better life through employment in our country's burgeoning factories and foundries. All enjoyed the early spring sunshine. Each group gravitated to a particular location that they'd likely lain claim to. The air was filled with shouts in French, Italian, German, English, Polish, Russian—different languages with a single message to the children, "Stay close. Don't wander." The adults on the perimeter of each group subtly defined their border with a turn of their backs, faces toward their centre. I smiled at the children dancing and running together between the adults and around the trees, oblivious to the divisions their parents maintained.

An hour on the bench, sated by our lunch, I sensed that Evie-Jayne was beginning to despair.

"Times change," I said, resting my hand on her knee. "It's been over twenty years since Hannah came here as a little girl, assuming that it was in this time period. Maybe the Jewish families don't come here anymore."

Evie-Jayne sighed heavily. "I just thought . . . She was pretty sure her first jump, the one forward, was a hundred years . . ."

"But she was very young, and maybe this portal is more inconsistent than ours. A few years more or less means she could be ahead or behind us now."

Evie-Jayne's face fell. "I know, but I had to try."

Both our heads turned toward the sound of a new language floating above a group of people approaching from the avenue. First came the children, dark skirts or trousers peeking below their navy blue winter jackets, skipping and chasing each other up the pathway and between the trees. Then came the adults, men wearing skull caps or broad-brimmed black hats, some with blue-and-white prayer shawls draped over their black woollen suits. The women followed, in modest plain dresses and shawls reminiscent of the Mennonite style, some with headscarves, many with babies in their arms or toddlers within their firm grasp. The Jewish families gathered under the trees in the one space that had remained vacant, as if awaiting their arrival.

Our searching eyes scoured the Jewish women's faces, coming up empty each time. No one even remotely resembled Hannah.

Then, Evie-Jayne snatched my hand and nodded toward the child standing off to the side. "There, *maman*. See the little girl, about six?"

The long black, frizzy hair, the blue-green eyes, it was like looking into Hannah's face as we remembered it. "But it can't be. The time-lines don't fit. Hannah came to our time when she was fifteen in 1895, she can't be a little girl now in 1907."

"Sophie Esther Cohen! Come here this instant."

The little girl ran to the tall man who looked to be in his early thirties. "How many times have I told you not to wander near that boulder. Now, stay where I can see you." The man's voice seemed to have an edge of panic.

"*Oui*, papa."

Evie-Jayne blew out the breath that she'd been holding. "That's not Hannah. But she looks so much like her."

"Evie-Jayne, look." I nodded toward the shadow of a large tree opposite us. We both stared at the desiccated figure draped in an ill-fitting, food-stained coat. The figure emerged to stand in the bright sunshine, squinting toward the little girl and her father with one good eye, the other covered by an ugly black leather patch. "He seemed ready to approach the girl before her father called her to him," I said.

While we watched, father and daughter took their leave of the gathering and strolled hand in hand back down the walkway toward the tram stop. The strange figure turned abruptly and moved in the opposite direction. There was a familiarity about the person.

"Maman, look at the hair! That's not a man—it's a woman." Evie-Jayne had spied kinky black curls peeking out over the figure's drawn up collar.

"Man or woman, just leave the poor soul alone, Evie-Jayne."

"No, maman, look at her shoes."

The black boots with buttons running up the side gripped the woman's slender ankles.

"Why was she watching that little girl? I think it's Hannah."

Possibility fought with disbelief as I grasped my daughter's hand and pulled her along. "Come on." We followed the mysterious figure disappearing toward the street. When the figure slipped into a clump of bushes, we dropped to a nearby bench. Moments later, Hannah emerged, clothed in a modern coat of good quality, and carrying a large basket over her arm. She glanced around the park, her gaze paused on us before she dropped the basket and ran. Evie-Jayne chased after her while I collected the basket. Within moments, the girls returned to me, breathless, Evie-Jayne with a firm grip on Hannah's arm. Hannah wore the expression of a frightened rabbit.

"We aren't going to hurt you, Hannah. Tell her, maman."

Tight lines puckered her brow. "I told you, I'm not Hannah." She tried to jerk her arm free. "Let me go."

"It's okay. I'm J.P.'s little sister, Evie-Jayne."

Recognition settled in Hannah's eyes as they looked into mine. "Madame Dumont?"

"Don't be afraid."

Hannah pulled impatiently at the frizzy black hair that the wind blew across her cheek. Her chest moved in and out in quick breaths.

"Why were you watching that little girl named Sophie? She looks just like you." Evie-Jayne asked.

Hannah's shoulders tightened, and her eyes darted in search of escape.

"Is she yours?" I asked.

A storm of doubt passed across Hannah's face. Sadness chased the fear from her green eyes. She nodded. Her shoulders slumped.

"Come. Let's find a cafe where we can talk." I took her hand while keeping her basket over my other arm. She followed like a lost child.

Settled at a round table in the dark corner of *Chez Lucille*, we sipped coffee and let the buttery *petits pains au chocolat* melt in our mouths. Hannah stared at the table. Whenever Evie-Jayne seemed ready to break the silence, I shook my head gently at her. We were on our second cup of coffee when Hannah began in a low voice.

"How's J.P.?" She looked up. "I'm sorry I hurt him. I'm sorry I hurt you all."

"J.P. struggled after you left," I said.

Evie-Jayne jumped in. "He married Marie, remember, Sophie's friend, five years ago? They have two daughters, Rita, who'll be three soon, and Cécile is almost a year old."

Hannah's smile didn't erase the sadness in her eyes.

"You don't live with your daughter," I stated.

Hannah's eyes dropped to watch her fingers trace the grooves on the pine table. When she looked up, the green in her eyes had hardened to blue. "After I left you, I found my father. He was still living in the same apartment where we'd lived when I . . . umm . . . disappeared." The lines around her mouth softened. "He'd become a lonely old man, but within days of our reunion, he stood taller and walked more briskly."

"What did you tell him about your disappearance?" Evie-Jayne stared at Hannah.

"I told him I'd travelled to another time."

Evie-Jayne gasped. "Did he believe you?"

Hannah shook her head. "He dismissed it as the fantasies of a little child. When I argued, he became impatient, so I finally told him I'd been kidnapped and that it had taken me ten years to escape. That seemed to satisfy him." She sighed. "Eventually, *papa* asked me if I liked Nathaniel Cohen, a banker a few years older than me. Nate had expressed his desire to court me. I agreed."

"And you fell in love?" Evie-Jayne was leaning across the table.

Hannah's face lit up. "Yes. I felt safe and happy with him. Sophie Esther was born a year after we were married." Her mouth turned down. "Then, one day, Nate asked me what had happened during my time away. I told him the truth."

Evie-Jayne's eyes almost popped out of her head.

"Turned out, my father had asked Nate to ask the question as a test. When he learned I told Nate about travelling through time, they confined me to a lunacy asylum. They said it was to protect Sophie, and that I could return once the doctors cured me."

Evie-Jayne gave a choked cough.

"You poor child. I'm so sorry." I moved my chair closer to her and put my arm around her shoulders.

Tears threatened to drown Hannah's eyes. "I wasn't there long. I escaped to the street, hid with friends until I was able to secure a job as a nanny in another part of the city. But my heart aches for Sophie. My fingers burn to to touch her silky skin and tug her curls and watch them spring back into place."

I wanted to grab Hannah's hand and tell her I understood the pain of losing a daughter. I wanted to tell her I would help her clear her name so she could hold her daughter again. William might be able to help . . .

"You can't visit her?" Evie-Jayne asked.

Hannah shook her head. "They'll take me back to the asylum if they catch me. So every Saturday, I disguise myself and come to the park to catch a glimpse of her."

I worried this could happen to my girls. Maybe if I stopped the crash, the portal would close and they'd be safe forever. But to stop the crash and to help Hannah, I'd have to tell William my story.

What if they locked me up? Was I ready to risk my freedom to save lives? Could I even change history?

"You named your daughter after my sister, didn't you?"

"Sophie was a good friend at a difficult time in my life." Hannah gathered her basket. "I have to go. Please give my love to Sophie, J.P., and Monsieur Dumont."

Tears coursed down Evie-Jayne's cheeks.

Suddenly, a large male silhouette blocked the light coming through the cafe door. Hannah gasped.

Evie-Jayne followed Hannah's gaze. "Who's that?"

"That's Constable Dubois from the North-West Mounted Police. He keeps tracking me to take me back."

I grabbed Hannah's disguising coat from the basket and tossed it to Evie-Jayne. "Here, put this on. Cover your head with the scarf."

Evie-Jayne followed my directions.

I turned to Hannah. "Go through there," I nodded at the swinging door to the kitchen. "Find the way out and run."

Leaning into Evie-Jayne, I whispered, "When the Constable moves out of the doorway, run out the front. Let him catch you in the park. I'll come to you."

As Hannah disappeared through the kitchen door, I strolled to the front of the cafe. "Good afternoon, sir."

"Madame." He doffed his hat.

Evie-Jayne breezed by us.

The Constable whirled around. "You. Stop!" He took up the chase. Evie-Jayne dodged through the trees until she'd led him into the middle of the park. I trotted behind them, catching up just as the Constable caught my daughter by the arm.

"Gottcha," he panted. "Hannah Cohen, you are under arrest for unlawfully leaving court mandated confinement."

Evie-Jayne pulled the scarf from her head.

The Constable's eyes widened.

I came up behind them. "Kindly unhand my daughter, sir."

He glared at us. "I should arrest you both for impeding an arrest. That young lady is a danger to herself and needs to be returned to a safe place where she can be treated." He pulled a notebook and the stub of a pencil from his pocket. "Now, where is she hiding?"

"We don't know," said Evie-Jayne. "And we wouldn't tell you if we did."

"What my daughter means is that we are visitors to your city and unfamiliar with its sectors." I grabbed Evie-Jayne's hand. "We'll be on our way, sir. Our host is expecting us."

We were walking away when Evie-Jayne threw a final comment over her shoulder. "Mr. Van Horne hates tardiness. He would not be happy to hear you detained us."

I groaned.

WILLOWS

Chapter Thirty-Four

When Evie-Jayne and I returned to the Van Horne Mansion later that afternoon, Yvette informed us Mr. Van Horne had been called to a meeting and would be away all evening. We elected to have dinner in our rooms and get to bed early since we were catching the train at ten o'clock the next morning.

Within minutes of her head hitting the pillow, Evie-Jayne dropped into a sound sleep. Her chest rose and fell with her regular breathing. When had my baby become this young woman? Her left eye tilted slightly up in the outside corner like Claude's. She had my aquiline nose and high cheekbones. Any doubt of her true parentage had been erased as irrelevant from my mind many years before.

My body craved sleep, but each time I drifted, I was jolted awake by the echoes of the crunching metal of train cars, roaring fire, and screaming people. Eventually, I gave up and curled up on the settee, a woollen shawl wrapped around me.

After the train accident east of Nairn Centre last March, I'd plummeted into despondency and guilt. Over the years, I'd succumbed to the lure of my own reinvention, the mortar of love and belonging cementing me into this time. I'd pushed my knowledge of the future into my subconscious, and a man had lost his life.

I resolved to find time to speak with William in the morning. In my mind, I began to try out ways of broaching the topic. "Remember when I suggested a different crossing point for the bridge across the Spanish? You need to reroute the track outside of Nairn Centre and build that new bridge." Too direct. Maybe just ask him to send an advisory that all trains must slow to ten miles per hour when approaching the Spanish River Bridge. What would I say when he asked why? That the train is going to derail at the current bridge on January 21, 1910? And when he asked how I knew that, I couldn't even imagine the expression on his face when I responded, "I'm a time traveller," or "I come from the future."

Hannah's tortured expression as she related her story in the café floated in front of my eyes. I gave my head a shake. I couldn't take the risk, even with someone as intelligent as William.

"You can't change history, Katie. Remember when you are before you act."

I jolted upright. My head swivelled around the dark room. "Gran?" I whispered. I hadn't heard her voice in my head for more than a decade. She was right, but I couldn't let people die. I had heard their screams.

I still didn't have a plan when Yvette rapped softly on our door, announcing that breakfast would be served in thirty minutes.

William was already at the table when Evie-Jayne and I arrived in the dining room. After a quick bite, I sent her to pack while I spoke with William.

"I haven't forgotten how we left our last meeting." His eyes bored into me. "Am I finally going to learn who the real Catherine Dumont is?"

"There is something I wanted to talk to you about." I met his gaze.

William sat back in his chair, and raised his coffee cup to his lips.

"After the train accident just east of Nairn Centre last year . . ."

His eyebrows climbed his forehead. He leaned toward me across the table. "What accident?"

With a few quick sentences, I filled him in on what had happened.

"When did you say this happened?"

"March 1906."

He narrowed his eyes. "I was in Cuba, building a railway." He began pacing the room, and then he beckoned me to follow him. In his study, he pulled out the surveys for the track west from Sudbury to Webbwood and spread them across his desk.

"That curve is too gentle to derail the train," he muttered to himself. He turned to me, mouth drawn into a tight line. "What did the investigators determine the cause to be?"

"The maintenance crew reported difficulty with the track spreading when they plowed it. The final report stated the cause was muskeg softening during a thaw causing the rails to spread at the end of the curve when the ground refroze."

"Hmm." William stroked his beard as his finger traced the track west out of Nairn Centre, resting on the curve leading to the bridge.

"That curve before the bridge is on muskeg, too," I said. "Maybe the track should be rerouted to cross the Spanish here." I placed my index finger on the spot where I knew a new bridge would eventually be constructed.

William unrolled a second survey. Peering over his shoulder, I recognized it as the option I'd suggested the day I'd escaped from his men.

His eyes moved from one drawing to the other. "What do you know?"

I opened my mouth. This was the time to tell him. Hannah's agonized expression as she told her story superimposed itself on my daughters' faces. I closed my mouth.

William humphed. "By chance, did a time traveller warn you something would happen there in the future?" He kept his expression open.

My jaw dropped. I forgot to breathe.

"After my meeting yesterday, my friend, Superintendent Morris of the North-West Mounted Police told me of your little escapade in the park."

I choked on the rush of air as I inhaled deeply.

"He was concerned for your safety, involving yourself with an unstable young woman." The smile melted from his face. He leaned toward me. "So, tell me about this time travel."

My gaze flicked over the drawings and landed on William's face. Eyes wide. Mouth pursed. No sign of malice. Could I trust him? "William . . ."

Suddenly, Evie-Jayne burst into the room. "There you are. The bags are in the car. Étienne says we should go."

I looked apologetically at William. "I'm sorry. Maybe next time."

William shook his head, then broke into a wry smile as he escorted us to the door. "You are the master of leaving me unsettled." He shook my hand, holding it as he said, "I think I have what I need. I'll look into it."

What did he mean by that?

Evie-Jayne stood on tiptoe to give William a quick peck on his cheek. "Thank you for everything, Mr. Van Horne." Then, grabbing my hand, she pulled me through the door and into the waiting vehicle.

* * *

"Papa, papa!" Evie-Jayne was on the platform and in her father's arms before the train had fully come to a stop. "I missed you. I love Montreal. We went to the theatre, toured the universities, and we saw Hannah!"

"Whoa, slow down, *ma petite*! Where is your maman?"

"Maman! Papa's here." Evie-Jayne broke from Claude's embrace and ran down the platform to assist me with the bags.

The next moment, I was swept into Claude's arms. He was kissing my face and my hair, murmuring in my ear, "*Ma chère, ma chère*. I'm so glad you're home." Then, he hastily stepped back, red to his ears. After a quick glance around the platform, he picked up our suitcases and headed toward the wagon. Evie-Jayne fell into step beside her father and continued her animated recitation of our activities in Montreal. I grinned when she threw in tidbits about the city's history and architecture she'd learned from Étienne.

We started for home with Evie-Jayne wedged between Claude and I on the driving bench. A Hudson's Bay blanket covered our legs from the chill in the air under the spring sunshine. I filled Claude in on how we ended up staying in William's mansion rather than the bed and breakfast. His tightly-drawn mouth relaxed as Evie-Jayne regaled him with her lively descriptions.

"Papa, there was a real *boîte à baignoire* with a deep bathtub, a sink, and a toilet, not just a smelly cabinet like in the bed and breakfast in Toronto. And when you turned the knobs, hot and cold water came out of the spout. There was electricity, so when you flipped a switch on the wall, the room was flooded with light, like that." She snapped her fingers.

"I hope all this luxury hasn't spoiled you now you're back home," he laughed.

"Baths in front of the fireplace can be very romantic, especially by candlelight." Evie-Jayne giggled as she planted a kiss on her father's cheek.

"What's this about finding Hannah?" He asked.

Evie-Jayne's eyes sparkled as she related our reunion with the young woman. Tears flowed when she explained the hopelessness of Hannah's situation. Claude pulled her to him and we rode in silence for a while, enjoying the chick-a-dee-dee-dee as the little birds flitted through the bare birch branches. A repeated chirr rising in volume helped us locate a pair of robins carrying twigs in their beaks as they disappeared into a thick pine.

"I'm going to the back," said Evie-Jayne. Disengaging from her father's embrace, she climbed into the back seats and snuggled under the bear rug.

Claude shifted to put his arm around me. "How did William react to your revelations concerning the . . . you know . . . ?"

"After hearing Hannah's story, I decided it was too risky for me to tell him about the coming crash."

Claude's forehead smoothed.

"I did bring up last year's crash. He was out of the country when it happened and didn't know anything about it." I paused. "When I told him a man died, he became very agitated, almost like he felt responsible."

"Hmph," said Claude.

"He asked for the results of the investigation and then pulled out the surveys for the area. I reminded him of the muskeg under the curve by the bridge."

Claude spoke in a low voice. "So do you think Mr. Van Horne will take some action?"

"He promised he'd look into it. William's single-mindedness won't let him back away, and he's accustomed to pressing others to bend to his thinking. I'm hopeful he'll convince the government in time to save lives."

Claude grimaced.

"What?"

He inhaled slowly. "If those people don't die, the whole world changes."

I held my breath and then released it in a rush. "If I don't do something, then have I killed them?" My eyes searched his.

"Didn't you say the first news article reported about eighty died, but in the end it was forty-eight. Maybe that's where you make a difference?" He placed his hand on my thigh. "You did your best, *ma chère*. Maybe it's best not to contact William again."

I nodded.

Evie-Jayne's voice piped up from behind us. "Mr. Van Horne likes to use his power to get his own way. Because he's rich, the people around him give in to him. But he respects maman because she is a strong woman who knows her own mind. It's a game, and he likes the challenge, but he'd never hurt maman."

"Thank you for that reassurance, *ma petite*," Claude said. He swallowed the smile out of his voice.

"Now, since I have both of you here, can we talk about my university choice? I want to attend McGill in September."

Claude's eyes widened. "Really?"

I turned backward. "I thought we'd agreed on University of Toronto where you could board with the same family that Sophie lived with during her studies."

"Yes, but"—Evie-Jayne looked off into the distance—"imagine home is like strawberries, the sweetness of sun-ripened fruit heightening all five senses with comfortable familiarity. Toronto is like enjoying a vanilla ice cream on a warm day, a gentle refreshment in your mouth. But Montreal! Montreal is like the flavour of dark chocolate, lighting up your brain, jangling through every nerve until you want to dance, leap, and wave your arms for sheer joy. It'll be difficult to give up the strawberries, especially if all you are getting to replace it is vanilla ice cream. But to exchange strawberries for chocolate . . . That would be worth it. That's what I want! I want Montreal!"

"Wow, my sweet. Since you put it that way . . ." said Claude.

"Isn't the teaching program better in Toronto than at McGill?" I asked.

"Madame Charlebois says McGill's teaching program is highly reputable, but it has a strong writing program. I want to study to become a writer!" Evie-Jayne was glowing with exuberance.

The breath caught in my chest. "How will you earn a living? Writers don't make much money." How twentieth century of me.

Claude's hand returned to my knee.

"Madame Charlebois suggested that I could study English literature and writing so I could become a teaching assistant and eventually maybe even a lecturer like her." Evie-Jayne's voice took on a pleading note. "Maman, you know I like children, but I love reading and writing so much more, and Madame said she feels I have a flair in the way I express my thoughts and ideas."

"You can't argue with that," Claude muttered under his breath.

I glared at him. This was all his fault, suggesting university visits as a reason for our trip to Montreal. "And where will you live while you're studying?"

"I could stay in the residence or"—she paused—"I could board in Mr. Van Horne's mansion."

"That sounds like a safe alternative," said Claude. He was smiling.

"What?" I mouthed at him. He was supporting this crazy idea. "This is ridiculous," I said. "You are going to University of Toronto. I will not have my daughter living so far away in a strange city."

Evie-Jayne braced every muscle in her body, ready to stand toe to toe with me to get her own way.

Claude's even tone intervened. "We don't have to make any final decisions for a few months, so let's just give it some time. Your mother and I will consider your suggestion. Agreed?" He met our fiercely determined gazes.

I gave a curt nod, but I already knew I'd lost.

"Agreed," said Evie-Jayne with a broad smile. She knew her father could never say no to his youngest child.

"Now, let's enjoy this beautiful start to spring," said Claude.

"I love the way the fields look like a big quilt," said Evie-Jayne.

I smiled. The warmth of the bright spring sun always made my fingers itch at the anticipation of soon being plunged into the dark loamy earth.

Maybe it wouldn't be so bad for Evie-Jayne to attend university in Montreal. It wasn't that much farther away than Toronto. And under William and Lucy's watchful eye . . . I leaned into Claude and enjoyed the quiet as we made our way home.

WILLOWS

Chapter Thirty-Five

I stood on the veranda, arms crossed against the cold, watching the sleigh materialize through the falling twilight and glide into our snowy courtyard.

"Maman, maman!" Evie-Jayne charged into my embrace before the sleigh came to a complete stop. "I missed you so much!"

The scent of fresh snow and lavender filled my head. "*Bébée*, I missed you too! Let me look at you." I pushed her back. "As beautiful as ever."

She grinned at me through tears. "I should have come home at Christmas."

"You had research to complete, sweetheart." I brushed stray strands of her blond hair back from her face. "You're here now."

She sniffed loudly. "I'd never miss Dumont Day."

I took her hand and pulled her through the door. The warmth of the wood fire flushed our cheeks. "Are you eating properly? You feel a little thin."

"Oh, maman, you always say that." She laughed. "Of course I'm eating well. I live in Montreal. When I'm not munching on croissants, baguettes, or soups at the university café, I'm well-fed by Monsieur Van Horne's chef." Her eyes softened. "Monsieur sends his love and hopes that you and *papa* are well. Wait, he also asked me to give you this."

I continued appraising my daughter as she dug in her coat pocket. "That coat's a very interesting style, *ma petite*."

She handed me a slightly crumpled letter, familiar red wax seal of a train locomotive across the lip. Then, she twirled so I could appreciate the deep brown wool coat that draped elegantly to mid-calf. "I picked it up in a tiny shop in the Jewish quarter. This is such a cool story." Her eyes shone. "Last October, I'd ducked into the shop to keep warm while I was waiting for Hannah, when I heard this snooty English woman arguing with the tailor. She'd commissioned the coat for her daughter, and apparently, she didn't like the beaver fur trim here on the cuffs and collar." She thrust her arm toward me. "Feel. Isn't it luxurious?"

I ran my hand over the silky cuff. "Yes, very. Did you say you were waiting for Hannah?" I felt my forehead crinkle.

"It's okay, *maman*." She put her hand on my arm. "We get together every Wednesday afternoon. I'll tell you more about her after, but back to the coat . . ." She turned to take it off while she kept talking. "The rude woman felt he should have used fox fur. In the end, she stomped out of the store, not even asking for a refund. Imagine!"

"Incredible."

She nodded vigorously. "I tried to slip out of the store without the tailor seeing me to spare the poor man any embarrassment. But he called to me, asking if I needed help." She took a quick breath. "When I told him how sorry I was, he just shrugged. Are you listening, maman?"

Evie-Jayne had fully warmed to her tale, and I knew there would be no stopping her until she reached the end. Pushing all thoughts of Hannah to the side, I said, "You have my undivided attention, *ma fille*, but we will need to come back to Hannah."

"*Bien sûr,* maman. Now, where was I?" She began pulling off her knee-length boots, the leather so supple it pleated over the sole. "Oh yes, then, the tailor asked if I'd like to try it on. Despite my protests,

I found myself standing in front of the mirror wearing the coat. It looked like it had been made just for me. He kept saying, 'It is perfect for you. You take it. Take it.'"

My eyes widened.

"Then, he said some things in Yiddish that I didn't understand. That's when Hannah arrived. She explained that he was offering me the coat for free because the woman had already paid for it." She chuckled. "Seems the rude woman is one of his regular customers, and she does that quite often. Hannah said she'd benefitted from just such a situation, so I took the coat, and we left."

Our conversation was brought to an abrupt end as Sophie burst through the door. "*Papa* said you were here." My heart bloomed with love as my two daughters embraced, Evie-Jayne folding her long, lithe body to accommodate her older sister's prominent pregnancy belly. Our reunion tableau froze at the sharp clarity of the train whistle piercing the log walls, heads swivelling toward the sound of train wheels clicking and clacking along snow-choked tracks in the distance.

"Geneviève was getting cold outsi—Oh . . . I'm sorry . . ." Daniel stood in the doorway, wide eyes glittering in the interior lantern light. His eighteen-month-old daughter squirmed in his arms.

I was the first to refocus. "Daniel, come in." I rushed to the doorway. "Come to grandmaman, *ma chère.*" Geneviève thrust herself forward, arms wide, with a broad smile that struck me in the heart. Daniel's blue eyes, wide mouth, and tall frame marked him as Dr. George Jones's grandson.

"Daniel!" Evie-Jayne moved from her sister to embrace her brother-in-law. "How's my favourite doctor?" She stepped back. "Sorry if we scared you."

"No, it's okay. Sophie has explained it, but I, ah, can't say as I've ever actually seen it happen before." His brow furrowed. "Funny, Geneviève was very still in my arms just at that same moment. I wonder . . ."

"I'm sure it was just coincidence, sweetheart," Sophie jumped in. "She's been so up and down lately."

"How are your grandparents?" I asked Daniel.

His shoulders relaxed. "Grandpa George still likes to help my dad in the Webbwood practice. He means well, but I confess, I'm glad I'm in Espanola. It's just a little too far for him to drop in unexpectedly." He grinned and pointed over his shoulder. "I'm going to join the men outside, help with the unloading." He backed out the door.

"Now, let me look at you, my darling sister." Sophie's eyes raked Evie-Jayne from head to toe. "You look just like one of those Gibson Girls I see in *Vogue* or *Ladies' Home Journal.*" She fingered the flecked grey wool skirt that skimmed Evie-Jayne's slim hips before flaring into a mid-calf valance brushing the floor.

"Thanks sis, but I really can't wait to get back into my normal clothes, starting with this hair roll." Evie-Jayne began pulling pins from her head. In moments, her hair was springing loosely down her back. "Ah, that's better." She shook out her curly mane. "Before you think I'm spending all my money on clothes, maman, this travelling suit is from the same tailor I told you about, and it's the only fashionable thing I have." She continued to unbutton the fitted jacket that came to a *V*, emphasizing her waist. Lace from the high-necked puffy white blouse peeked through the front. "My clothes are still in the cupboard in the loft, right?" She was already making her way to the ladder.

"Of course, *ma chére*. Everything's just as you left it."

As her sister disappeared above us, Sophie asked, "Maman, who's that man helping papa? He looks too young to be one of J.P.'s friends."

"What young man?" I reached past her to move the curtain aside. It was too dark to make out any details. Geneviève wriggled in my arms, so I moved to the settee to unwrap her.

"He's French, but speaks English well, sounds educated. He's been moving the trunks from the wagon to the verandah while papa beds down the horses."

The bubble of Evie-Jayne's giggle floated down to us. Then, her old scuffed leather ankle boots appeared on the top rung of the ladder. "That's Étienne Legrand. You remember him, maman? Mr. Van Horne's chauffeur."

"The budding architect?"

"Yes. He finishes his studies this June." Her face glowed like the first blush of a new rose. "He didn't think it was wise for me to travel alone on the train, even though I told him I'd already done the trip several times over the past three years." The blush deepened and travelled down her neck. Her eyes slid from my raised eyebrows to her sister's abdomen. "You're positively glowing, sis. But it must be really uncomfortable carrying such a load all the time . . ." Evie-Jayne grabbed Sophie's hand and pulled her to the settee. Then, she reached for Geneviève. "Come to tante Evie-Jayne, *ma petite*."

I prepared tea and scones in the kitchen while the girls reignited their sisterly connection. Motherly love suffused my body as I watched the blond and chestnut heads almost touching. Nothing was more precious to me than this dance of fluid movement and murmured conversation punctuated by leaps of laughter, tippy-toe squeals, and breathy twirling gasps. Nothing gave me greater joy than looking into the eyes of my children, hearing their voices, feeling their embrace. They salved the wound in my heart called *Amelia*.

"Maman, are you all right?" Sophie's inquiry snapped me out of my reverie.

"*Oui*. Why?"

"Well the kettle is howling, and you're staring into the distance, looking as sad as if the world were coming to an end."

I forced a bright smile. "My world couldn't be fuller and brighter than it is right this minute. Now, Evie-Jayne, you really must tell us all about Hannah. Is she well? Is she safe?" I carried the tea tray to the small table in front of the fireplace.

"You've seen Hannah?" Sophie's eyes danced.

Evie-Jayne settled back into her father's chair, wet her lips, and began her tale. "I spent two years going to *le parc du Mont-Royal* on Saturdays whenever I could. I kept hoping I'd find Hannah again."

Sophie nodded. "But you said you never saw her."

"Right. Then, a few months ago, I caught a glimpse of the mysterious figure. Our eyes met before she turned and disappeared."

I sipped my sweet blueberry tea.

"The next week, she nodded her head at me and pointed her index finger down toward the bench where I was sitting. My hand brushed against a slip of paper wedged between the slats."

Sophie's eyes grew big. "What did the note say?"

"Lucille's café."

"That's it?" Sophie asked.

Evie-Jayne nodded. "When I looked up, Hannah had disappeared, so I went to the café, and there she was, sitting at the back corner table." Evie-Jayne recounted how Hannah had gone back into hiding after our encounter with the constable. She'd fled to another position as governess across the city and stayed away.

"So why did she come back?" I asked.

Evie-Jayne stared into the fire. "She said that the hole in her heart was so big that she couldn't fill it anymore. She wanted to return to her family before the hole swallowed her forever."

My stomach dropped. I inhaled loudly.

Sophie and Evie-Jayne stared at me, eyes raw with fear.

"I'm okay." I wanted to take their hands, but they would have felt my trembling. I took a shaky breath. "Hannah's been through so much."

Evie-Jayne nodded. "But she's strong."

"Did she go back to her family?" Sophie asked.

"She did, with Mr. Van Horne's help." Evie-Jayne relaxed into her story. "He asked a psychiatrist friend to examine Hannah. The man pronounced her physically and mentally sound, and he agreed to continue to be her physician. Hannah agreed to regular examinations. Then, one of Mr. V's barrister friends successfully petitioned a judge to lift the committal and release Hannah into her husband's care, provided he was willing to take her back."

"And he did?" Sophie's mouth remained open, eyes wide.

"He did. He still loved her and felt guilty for having committed her in the first place. So Hannah's been back home since the summer, little Sophie has her mama back, and Hannah is already pregnant." Evie-Jayne's eyes sparkled. We all wiped away tears of joy.

"What about her father?" I asked.

"He begged Hannah to forgive him, and she did. His health is failing, so he now lives with her family."

Loud stomping on the verandah. The three men burst through the door, slamming it quickly behind them to cut off the sharp draft of cold air. Daniel and Étienne continued their conversation while they removed their outdoor clothing. Claude remained quiet behind them. He raised his eyebrows at me, tilting his head toward Étienne.

I shrugged, as I moved to the kitchen. "You must be hungry. Sophie, please put the roasted potatoes in a serving bowl and mash the turnips while I carve the venison roast."

Evie-Jayne rose. "I'll set the table and put out bread, butter, and cheese." Her cheeks bloomed pink as she caught Étienne's eye.

"I'll help," said Étienne and followed her to the cupboard.

Evie-Jayne's colour deepened as she met her father's quizzical gaze. During our meal, Sophie quizzed Étienne about his family, and his studies.

"So, did you and Evie-Jayne meet at the university?" Daniel asked.

Étienne's eyes rested softly on Evie-Jayne. "I had the good fortune several years ago of touring *Madame* Dumont and Evie-Jayne through Montreal in my capacity as chauffeur when they visited Mr. Van Horne." His mouth curled into a wide smile.

Claude gave me a hard look.

Evie-Jayne giggled. "Yes, he talked non-stop about his beloved Montreal. A few months later, we both started at McGill, and since Étienne also continued his job, Mr. V. lets us use the automobile to get to and from the university most days."

Sophie nudged me under the table, nodding her head toward her father. Claude's eyes were fixed on his plate.

After supper, Daniel and Étienne took over the kitchen and washed the dishes. I smiled to myself. Daniel was following the example that Claude and I had set, where the cook did not clean up after a meal, but to see Étienne join in, confirmed my conviction that he was a perfect fit for our family. Sophie put Geneviève down for the night in the crib in our bedroom. Claude, Evie-Jayne, and I sat in silence by the fire.

"Did you know Legrand was coming?" he whispered, leaning into me.

I shook my head. "Evie-Jayne says he didn't want her travelling alone."

"Hmph." Claude sat back and crossed his arms.

Evie-Jayne moved her chair close to her father. "*Papa*, please give Étienne a chance. He's hardworking, intelligent, and kind."

"He's a chauffeur."

"But in six months, he'll be an architect. He already has an internship with a prestigious firm." Evie-Jayne's voice was rising.

Étienne appeared behind Evie-Jayne and put his hands on her shoulders. "Monsieur Dumont, I understand your concerns, but I have worked to support my mother and siblings since I was fourteen. Hard work doesn't scare me." He took a deep breath. "But not having Evie-Jayne in my life, that terrifies me." He moved to stand in front of Claude.

Rhubarb, Strawberries, and Willows

Daniel stopped washing the dishes. Sophie stopped in the bedroom doorway.

"Monsieur Dumont, I love your daughter." Étienne's eyes rested on Evie-Jayne's. "It would be my greatest honour if you would allow me to marry her." The young man bowed his head as if waiting for the guillotine to fall.

Evie-Jayne's fingers fidgeted in her lap. Her eyes were fixed on her father. Claude's mouth was drawn tight as he looked past the young man and stared into the fire.

The clock struck nine. A log in the fire dropped, sending a shower of sparks up the chimney.

Sophie perched herself on the edge of the settee. "Geneviève should sleep all night." She yawned. "And I'm ready for bed."

I smiled at her. "Well, if she does wake up, I'll take care of her. Do you think you can make it up the ladder?"

She nodded.

"Then, you and Evie-Jayne can sleep in the loft, and Daniel and Étienne can settle here in front of the fire."

"Certainly," said Daniel.

"Merci, Madame," said Étienne.

"You'll find everything you need in there," I pointed at the pine box against the wall.

Claude rose and went to our bedroom without a word. Étienne followed his back with his eyes. Evie-Jayne opened her mouth to speak.

I shook my head at her. "Don't worry. Everything will work out," I whispered and stood. "Good night everyone." I gave each a warm smile.

As I closed the door behind us, Claude rasped in a sharp whisper to avoid waking the baby, "Did you know about this?" His eyes drilled into me. He paced from the fireplace to the bed. "He's nothing but a chauffeur."

"You know he's more than that." I kept my voice even. "Evie-Jayne loves him, and he clearly cares for her. William thinks highly of him."

"Then, let him marry William's daughter." He shook his head. "She's too young."

"She'll be twenty-one this year. Sophie was twenty when she married Daniel."

"But Daniel was older and had started in his father's practice. Legrand and Evie-Jayne are the same age, and his prospects are tentative at best." Claude dropped into his chair and stared at the embers in the fireplace.

I sat in my chair. "You knew this was going to happen sometime."

He turned tortured eyes to me. "But it's too soon. And if she marries him, we'll lose her forever."

I rose to put my arms around his shoulders, and he pulled me onto his lap. I kissed his forehead. "Evie-Jayne was never going to come back here to live. Our darling intellectual has found her place in Montreal." I felt the tension leave his body.

"I suppose she'll have Clément, Robert, and my sisters nearby."

"You know they're going to marry whether you approve it or not."

He nodded. A slow smile softened his features. "Let's make them wait until morning."

I pushed his shoulder playfully. His arms circled my body, and his lips found mine. We sank into each other.

WILLOWS

Chapter Thirty-Six

The house whispered with the steady breathing of my family. Sleep evaded me. I looked out the kitchen window to where a red fox marched across the moonlit snow with a proprietary air under a storybook sky full of stars. We worked this land during the day, but he ruled the night. I pulled the knitted shawl tightly around my shoulders against the chill. The clock struck once. January 21, 1910. In twelve hours . . .

Turning, my hand brushed the letter from William that I'd dropped on the kitchen work top earlier in the evening. I held it to my chest and tiptoed back to our bedroom. Claude remained asleep. When had the grey threads in his brown hair widened to thick veins? *Time. Like the river current, it carries you inexorably forward. It passes quickly when you want to savour a moment, and then slows almost to a stop, frustrating anticipation. It even turns back on itself, creating whirlpools to compress the world into folds that you can slip through like a needle.*

I added a couple of logs to the fire and settled into my chair. For all his innovative thinking, William still clung to the traditional way of sealing letters. I cracked the image of a locomotive and unfolded the page. I already knew what it said, but scanned his distinctive scrawl anyway.

> *Dear Catherine*
>
> *I trust you and your family continue to thrive.*
>
> *Regrettably, over the past three years, my efforts have resulted in failure, and I have exhausted all options. In the absence of any incidents post the 1906 event, the government and its experts do not accept the danger of derailment due to muskeg under the track. Perhaps one day you will explain to me your insistence for moving the bridge.*
>
> *Evie-Jayne continues to be a most dedicated student and engaging house guest. Lucy rests easy at Covenhoven, knowing I am under Evie-Jayne's caring supervision.*
>
> *Yours*
>
> *William*

A thin blanket of relief from knowing this would be the last night I'd spend turning through options like a hamster in its wheel, buffered my anxiety. Should I remain silent? If I did, people would die. If I prevented it, havoc would circle each unexpected survivor like ripples from a stone dropped into a pool of water. Some survivors might be a pebble in a puddle, while others a boulder in a lake, but the rippling impact on generations couldn't be ignored. My mind replayed the scene as I had imagined it for months, if I decided to take action.

Me: You have to stop the westbound train from Nairn Centre today.

CPR agent: Why, Mrs. Dumont?

Me: Because if you don't, it will crash into the Spanish River at the bridge, and people will die.

CPR agent: And how do you know this?

I pictured his mouth twitching, wanting to laugh, but trying to remain polite.

Me: That's not important. People are in danger. You must stop that train.

That's when the agent speaks in a reassuring tone, asking me to sit while he contacts his superior in Sudbury. I pace the waiting room while he is gone. The agent returns with the doctor. If I'm lucky, it will be written off as a fit of hysterics common in women of a certain age going through "that time of life."

A log snapped. Claude rolled over. "Catherine?" His bleary eyes met mine. Then, he was on his feet and across the room to enfold me in his arms. "The crash?"

I nodded against his chest. "I have to do something."

His arms tightened. "We've talked about this. You can't take the chance. Think of the children."

"I know." During our months of conversations in the blackness of night, we'd concluded that if I tried to warn anyone, then, when the crash happened, I might be accused of sabotage, and Claude could be implicated. If I admitted coming from the future, I'd have signed my commitment to a lunatic asylum.

Claude sat in his chair and pulled me onto his lap. His hands smoothing my hair slowed my racing thoughts. It had been almost three decades since I'd first read those news articles in the Espanola library, but the events had been carved into my mind. The locomotive, baggage car, and one other car would make it over the bridge; two cars would submerge in the river and slip under the ice; the dining car would split and remain on the bank, and the second-class car would hit the bridge girder and bursts into flames. Three men working in the area heard the screams. Two joined in the rescue while the third man ran five miles back to Nairn Centre for help . . . Three men not on the train . . .

I pushed out of Claude's embrace. "That's it! Three men."

He looked at me with narrow eyes. "You'll have to give me more."

"The article said that there were three men working in the area. Two assisted with the rescue while the third ran back along the track to Nairn Centre for help."

"Okay . . ."

"Don't you see? You, J.P., and Maurice. You three can work the woodlot in that area today."

His eyes brightened with understanding, and his brows dropped. "But, Catherine, you can't change history."

I leaned over him and grasped his shoulders. "I'm not asking you to stop the crash. We're not changing history, we're only making sure it happens."

"But Maurice knows it's Dumont Day. He's not expecting to work."

If Claude and Jean-Pierre suddenly showed up at the Gagnon's this morning, would they suspect we knew something about the crash after it happened? I didn't want to put them in that position.

I thought out loud. "Daniel has to return to his practice today," I paused. "Legrand. He can run back to Nairn Centre."

Claude's features relaxed. "He's going to be part of this family, so he might as well become acquainted with our eccentricities."

"J.P., Marie, and the children are coming for breakfast. I'll explain it to the girls once you three leave."

* * *

Evie-Jayne descended the ladder while I was making coffee and stoking the fire in the kitchen stove. Geneviève played with a spoon and cup in her highchair.

"*Bonjour,* maman." She kissed me on the cheek from behind and yawned loudly as she ran her hand over Geneviève's head.

I turned. Her eyes were ringed by dark circles. "Sweetheart, didn't you sleep?"

She grimaced and shook her head. "I kept having terrible dreams, hearing screeching like train wheels, and people screaming," she shuddered.

Sophie waddled up behind her sister. "Me too." Sophie's eyes were hollow. "It has something to do with the crash, right, maman?" She picked Geneviève up out of her highchair and cuddled her.

I nodded. "Come." I put my arms around the girls' shoulders, steering them to the table. "Coffee will be ready soon. We'll talk after breakfast."

The door flew open. "*Bonjour* everyone." Étienne's energy filled the room. "What a glorious morning!" He turned to Sophie. "Daniel just left, but he asked me to give you his love and tell you that he'll be back in three days." He rubbed his hands together. "That coffee smells terrific. Madame Dumont, may I help with breakfast?"

He moved to the kitchen. "My specialty is pork slices with eggs and biscuits, but I am a fair hand at pancakes as well."

I gave my girls' hands a squeeze and joined Étienne in the kitchen. Claude emerged from the bedroom, kissed each of his daughters, and then picked up a cup of coffee before heading to the barn. "I'll wait for J.P. out there," he said.

Five minutes later, we heard Jean-Pierre call, "Whoa!" Then, two pairs of feet pattered across the veranda, excited voices calling, "Mamère, mamère." Two fists pounded on the door.

Laughing, I ran to open it and scooped the two little girls into my arms. When five-year-old Rita caught sight of Sophie and Evie-Jayne, she ran, trying to embrace them both at the same time. "*Mes tantes.*" Her voice was muffled by their skirts.

Three-year old Cécile clutched my hand as I drew her into the house. Her eyes as blue as her father's, stared uncertainly at the two women. I pulled off her hat and smoothed back her blond curls. I never stopped marvelling at the wonder of genetics. Cécile looked like Jean-Pierre when he was her age, and her character was reserved, like his, but her stature came from the shorter, stockier Lemieux side.

373

Rita, with her bubbly personality and unruly corkscrew black curls, was her mother's daughter, but in the long, lanky Dumont frame.

"*Bonjour,* maman Catherine." Marie stood on tiptoe to kiss my cheek while I pulled baby Jacques from her arms.

"How are you, my *grandpère?*" I whispered against his cheek. Most people would think it strange to be holding their grandfather when he was an infant, but for me, it was just part of life. I'd left the luxuries of my own time behind long ago, but the people who mattered stayed with me. I saw Gran in the eyes of the grocery clerk of Mr. Hall's store and *grandpère* in the manner in which Mr. Edwards held his back as he walked. It was Amelia's hands I glimpsed wrapped around a cup in the cafe of The Klondike Hotel.

"You look exhausted," I said.

Marie's eyes filled with tears. "Jacques is up every two hours."

"Poor you." I forced a smile. "But you can rest today. There are plenty of us to keep the children occupied."

Sophie had managed to cajole Cécile onto her lap beside Geneviève while Rita regaled Evie-Jayne with tales of school and her pet rabbit.

"Go, sit," I said to Marie. "Breakfast will be ready soon."

* * *

Breakfast was a boisterous meal. Étienne had outdone himself as chef, producing fried pork strips, toasted bread, fried eggs, and pancakes. "For the little ones," he said.

While conversation zigzagged in the air above the table, Evie-Jayne's eyes darted to her father's, but he avoided her glare. She tilted her head at me, mouthing the question, "Well?" I shook my head and raised my hand, palm outward. When she gave an exaggerated, "Huff," Sophie put her hand on her younger sister's knee.

With the plates empty and the last of the coffee swirling at the bottom of the cups, Claude turned to Jean-Pierre. "*Bon, mon fils*, we should be on our way."

"Where are you going?" Sophie asked.

"You can't work. It's Dumont Day," said Evie-Jayne.

Claude looked around the table. "There's something we have to do. Your mother will explain." He rose. Jean-Pierre followed.

"But, *papa* . . ." Evie-Jayne's chin began to quiver. Her eyes darted between her father and Étienne, who had begun clearing the plates.

"Legrand, since you are soon to be part of the family, you're with us today."

The young couple stared at each other. Realization dawned on both their faces at the same time. Étienne dropped the plates back on the table and pulled Evie-Jayne into his arms. When Evie-Jayne ran to her father, Étienne hugged me. Then, his arms dropped, and he moved to offer Claude his hand. "Monsieur Dumont, *merci beaucoup*. I promise I will love and care for your daughter—" The rest of what he had to say was cut off as Claude pulled him into his embrace with Evie-Jayne. The whole family crowded around the young couple until they were squeezed into a giant Dumont hug.

The clock struck ten. Claude pushed backward. "*Bon*. We need to be on our way."

As soon as the door closed behind the three men, Sophie and Evie-Jayne turned inquiring looks on me. They knew to keep their silence in front of Marie.

"Evie-Jayne, why don't you take the little ones to the outhouse. I'll clean up."

"I'll help you, maman Catherine."

Baby Jacques squalled.

"Marie, why don't you feed him in our bedroom. Then, stretch out on our bed and have a nap."

Marie threw me a grateful smile and disappeared.

I sent Sophie to put her feet up on the settee while I cleared the table and poured the hot water into the basin. I'd just begun washing the dishes when Rita and Cécile bounded through the door, followed by Evie-Jayne.

"Mamère, we fed the chickens. I gave Étoile an apple," Rita said.

"I gived Beau *une carotte*." Cécile demonstrated how she'd held the carrot up to the horse.

"*Bravo, mes filles.*" I gathered the two girls to me. "Your basket of toys is waiting for you by the fire. Go play. Your tantes and I need to talk." The little ones scurried to the hearth.

Sophie lifted a sleepy Geneviève out of her highchair and barricaded her with pillows on the settee to nap. Then, she joined Evie-Jayne and me at the table. I'd made tea to accompany the conversation we were about to have. The dishes could wait.

"Who's teaching your school today?" Evie-Jayne asked Sophie.

"Celestine."

Evie-Jayne raised her eyebrows. "I thought she was teaching in our schoolcar?"

"Her husband, Joseph, stopped carrying his goods around the homesteads just after they got married last spring. He said peddling was no life for a married man, so they opened a store in Espanola." Sophie gestured to her abdomen. "Celestine took over my school in September."

"But what about our little school?" Evie-Jayne's face dropped.

I jumped in. "Now that there's a bridge across the dam to Espanola, few children were still attending Stanley Station schoolcar. It made sense to close it at the end of the last school year."

Evie-Jayne's brow furrowed. "What will Celestine do when you return?"

"I'm not." Sophie sat back with a sigh of contentment. "Daniel's practice is growing. We don't need the money, so I'll stay home with the children."

"That's why I'm never having children." Evie-Jayne folded her arms. "No one is stopping me from fulfilling my career."

Sophie's eyes darkened. She leaned toward her sister.

I pushed my arms across the table between them. "And that's the end of this conversation."

The girls held their stare for a moment before leaning back into their chairs.

I spoke quietly into the silence. "Today, is the day the train will crash." For the next hour, I recounted what would happen and explained the role their father, brother, and Étienne would play in history.

WILLOWS

Chapter Thirty-Seven

The morning passed like syrup through an hourglass. Evie-Jayne took Cécile and Rita tobogganing while Sophie washed the lunch dishes. I cubed pieces of moose and beef, browning the chunks in butter and diced onions on the wood stove before dropping them into a beef broth laced with red wine simmering in the iron pot over the fire. Once the dishes were done, Sophie sliced carrots while I cubed potatoes to add to the meat. The Dumont Bourguignon was a favourite, and on Dumont Day, we spoiled ourselves by igniting a cup of whiskey over the whole thing before serving.

The clock struck the half hour. Twelve-thirty. Sophie and Evie-Jayne swung their eyes to mine across the lunch table. I stretched out my legs, and wrapped my hands around my half-empty mug.

"Maman, can I go play?" Rita asked.

"*Moi* too?" Cécile chimed in.

Marie took in their empty plates. "*Oui, mes filles*, but stay quiet. Geneviève and Jacques will be sleeping soon."

Sophie murmured under her breath, "God willing."

As if on cue, Jacques began to fuss. Marie sighed.

"Poor little guy," I said. "A strange place, all these people. It's a lot for a two-month old."

"But, I feel like I'm not doing my part for Dumont Day." Tears spilled over the dark circles under Marie's eyes.

Sophie put her arm around her sister-in-law. "It's okay. We've got it under control." She gently steered her toward the bedroom. "Jacques needs quiet, and you need rest."

Marie's mouth twitched into a grateful smile. "*Merci.*"

"Whew!" Sophie exhaled as soon as the bedroom door closed. "It's almost time."

The clock struck twelve forty-five. Distant clickety-clacking of train wheels. The train was right on time.

My granddaughters continued to play in front of the fire.

My daughters' eyes widened. Their chests rose and fell with quick shallow breaths. I pressed my hands over my ears, even though the screaming came from inside my head. It had never been this loud before. Sophie hugged Geneviève against her chest. Evie-Jayne bent double, chest on her knees, and wrapped her arms around her head. Just when I was sure my legs were about to collapse, the sound drifted into the distance and our frozen tableau melted. Evie-Jayne and Sophie circled their arms around me.

I lowered myself into Claude's chair, my heart still hammering like a runner's at the end of a hundred-yard dash.

Sophie stretched out on the settee, cuddling her daughter on her chest.

"I need fresh air," said Evie-Jayne. She took the two little girls outside. Fortunately, they'd been so absorbed in their imaginary play that they'd remained oblivious to our reactions.

I leaned back into the chair, comforted by Claude's scent embracing me. A sharp snap came from the fire. I bolted upright. Echoes of the screams filled my head. Those poor people, battered and crushed by pieces of broken railcar, consumed by roaring flames, or trapped beneath ice in the frozen river. Please God, I prayed, keep Claude, Jean Pierre., and Étienne safe. Sophie dozed on the settee with Geneviève on her chest.

My feet began to shimmy against the floor. The vibrations travelled up my legs. I popped to my feet and walked to the kitchen window, knowing it was too early to see the men, but hoping that my looking might speed their return. Rita saw me and waved as she and her sister emerged from the barn. Evie-Jayne started a snow fight and soon the girls were screeching with delight. She was so natural with children, treating them as reasoning equals. I admired her commitment to a career, proud that she was a woman ahead of her time, but I hoped that one day she'd find the space to also enjoy the bliss of motherhood. If anyone had asked, I'd have picked Sophie as the daughter that would push the boundaries of social norms. Growing up, she'd always been the adventurous, curious one, precocious and thirsty for knowledge while Evie-Jayne had lived within the lines. Unexpected outcomes kept motherhood interesting.

A few stray crumbs caught my eye on the kitchen work top. As my hands brushed them to the edge, I became mesmerized by the dark grain of the oiled pine surface. Every January 21st, I thought of Ida and wondered what had become of her. And then there was Hannah. A flush of warmth embraced my heart knowing that she was reunited with family. I found comfort in knowing there were others like us, that we weren't alone.

Turning, my eyes travelled through the open living space. The front entry with its double row of wooden dowels and bench where Claude had flipped and thrown three-year-old Jean-Pierre out of his clothes. The cedar blanket box beside the settee where Sophie had first pulled herself to her feet, gracing me with a wide grin before dropping backward onto her bottom. The hours of lessons at the scarred pine table. A six-foot Christmas tree each year in the corner, all of us singing carols accompanied by Claude on the guitar. Claude had shown me how to love and accept myself because he loved and accepted me.

I pulled my shoulders up to my ears and then dropped them forcefully to shrug off the blanket of thoughts. The clock chimed three, and there were voices outside. A fist clenched in my stomach, then released at the sound of little-girl boots pattering along the veranda. It was Evie-Jayne, back with Cécile and Rita.

I heated milk and set out a plate of cookies to the accompaniment of shrieks and giggles as Evie-Jayne helped the girls out of their winter clothing.

Sophie slipped into her chair at the table. Geneviève still drowsing in her arms, she wrapped her hands around the mug of hot chocolate and inhaled deeply. "Mmm. No one makes *le chocolat chaud* like you, maman."

"It's the cinnamon stick." Evie-Jayne smiled saucily as she revealed my secret.

Once Rita and Cécile had drained their hot chocolate and depleted the plate of cookies, they began squirming in their chairs.

"Grandmaman, can we play in the loft?" Rita asked.

"Of course, *mes filles.*"

Evie-Jayne helped the girls select two toys each from the box, which she carried up for them before she supervised each of them mounting the ladder.

I refilled our mugs, pausing to look out the window. No sign of the men. "Let's sit at the fire," Sophie said. She settled in her father's chair, sighing as she took advantage of its width to spread the weight of her pregnant belly.

With one ear, I tuned into my daughters as they distracted themselves by planning Evie-Jayne's wedding. The other ear scanned for the arrival sounds I was frantic to hear. It was after four o'clock.

At five o'clock, I rose to light the lanterns, taking the opportunity to check out the window. Violet twilight was already too dense for me to see clearly. Suddenly, three slumped purple silhouettes interrupted the shafts of silver moonlight filtering through the trees. They trudged in single file across the pasture, lifting their snowshoes with slow deliberation.

I gasped. "They're back."

Sophie and Evie-Jayne crowded beside me at the window. Both caught their breath.

"I'll put on the coffee," said Evie-Jayne.

"I'll get the whiskey," said Sophie.

I flung the door open and leapt into Claude's arms. He pulled my head against his chest. The smell of smoke assaulted my nose. "We're okay," he whispered against my hair. I felt his shoulders shake as his grip tightened around me.

Jean-Pierre and Étienne walked past us without a word.

Claude pushed backward. "It was just as you described." His eyes blazed. "I always believed your story, but . . . you carried *this* . . ." He shook his head. " I had no idea . . .your strength . . ." His hand squeezed mine as if he could make our bones meld together. We followed the others into the house.

Sophie stood wide-eyed at the table, the whiskey bottle in her hand. Evie-Jayne was frozen at the kitchen work top, brow wrinkled as her gaze met her father's. Marie was a statue in the bedroom doorway, head tilted toward Jean-Pierre.

"Papa!" Rita's call broke the trance.

The girls clambered down the ladder and into Jean-Pierre's arms. He buried his face in their hair, beckoning for Marie to join the embrace. Evie-Jayne rushed to hug Étienne. Sophie ran to her father.

Claude cleared his throat. "Let's sit."

The girls and I finished setting glasses and mugs on the table while the men shed their outdoor clothing. Rita and Cécile were soon back in the loft. Marie returned to the bedroom in response to Jacques's urgent cries.

Evie-Jayne pressed against Étienne, brushing back his sticky hair, wiping smudges of blood from his cheeks.

Claude white-knuckled the bottle as he poured shots of whiskey. "It was horrible. The screams. The fire." He lowered his face into his hands.

"I had one man by the arm, pulling him from the water. Blood poured from his head." Etienne gazed at his trembling hands " Then he let go . . . slipped under the ice. Gone."

Claude pushed a glass of whiskey across the table to him. "You need this. It'll stiffen your spine."

"You did well, today, *mon frère*," said Jean-Pierre. He raised his glass and the two young men downed the liquor with one swallow.

"I was carrying a little boy wrapped in a blanket." Jean-Pierre shuddered. "His blood seeped through to my mitts. The cuts on his body were so deep . . ." Silent tears left tracks in the soot on his face. "He just stared at me with his deep blue eyes. He was no bigger than Rita."

I saw the ghosts in Claude's eyes when he raised his head. "I could only grab one little girl and her mother from the second-class car before the flames took over. I threw the mother to the snow and rolled the child to extinguish their clothing." He threw the whiskey in his glass down his throat. "I hope they make it."

"Three men from the train worked with us, freeing survivors that were pinned under metal and inside cars." Jean-Pierre said. That fit, I thought. Conductor Reynolds, Brakeman Morrison, and Passenger Robert Burroughs from the Bell Telephone Company.

"We carried the survivors to a car where two women were cleaning and bandaging wounds as best they could, tearing shirts and petticoats, whatever they could find.," added Claude.

"Two?" I asked.

He nodded. "Mrs. Linall and . . ." He looked at his son.

"I didn't hear her name." Jean-Pierre shrugged. "I better go to Marie." He rose and walked slowly to the bedroom. "She knows nothing about your past, *maman,* but I need to tell her about the crash."

I turned to Claude. "And you were the three men referred to in the report?"

"Yes." Claude put his hand on Étienne's shoulder. "And this young man covered the five miles to Nairn in record time. Then, he had the presence of mind to bring the doctor and several men back by hand car."

Evie-Jayne squeezed Étienne's hand. The bite of the whiskey was chasing the pallor from his face, but his eyes remained sunken. His grip on the glass was more steady. "I don't understand. It was like you all knew it was going to happen?"

Evie-Jayne rubbed at the smudges on his cheeks. "I'll explain later."

At the sound of a hesitant tap, our heads swivelled toward the door. Claude rose and opened it at the second, more assured knock.

"*Bonsoir, Monsieur. C'est la maison de Catherine et Claude Dumont?*"

I whirled toward the door. The voice awakened a deeply buried memory.

Claude took a sharp breath as his eyes met those of the stranger. "*Oui.*" He stepped back. "You're the woman from the train?"

She nodded.

"*Entrez.*"

I stifled a scream with my hand over my mouth.

Everyone's eyes flicked from me to the stranger.

Yellow lantern light glowed along the strands of her long blond hair spilling over her shoulders as she unwrapped the woollen scarf. My mind registered the smudge of dirt, or perhaps it was dried blood, across her cheek. It felt like the room had emptied of air. My heart dropped.

Our gazes met, and I tumbled into the familiar deep ocean blue of her eyes.

"I found your letters." Her voice was loaded with accusation and longing.

"Amelia?" I croaked and stood.

She moved into the room. " Tante Cath . . ." she swallowed loudly. "Maman?"

"Amelia!" I pulled my daughter into my arms.

Ballad of the Spanish

*Up north of Biscotasing
The mighty river is born
Through rock cuts, ov'r lowlands
Her southward path is worn*

*Home to beavers, geese and otters
Ducks, bass, pike, and the bear
Paddlers love her beauty
You can hear the loon call there*

Chorus
*Loggers may have jammed her
Miners they have dammed her
But the Spanish keeps rollin' along
Her tea waters mirror
Birches, pines and poplars
And the Spanish keeps rollin' along.*

*Voyageurs they had travelled
The river called Sagamak
Came across a Spanish captive
Told the tale when they got back*

*Since early eighteen hundred
The tale then it was told
Sagamak became the Spanish*

And the region Espagnole
Chorus
Once a highway for lumber
Choked with ice and logs in spring
All winter lumberjacks work
You could hear their axes ring

The miners needing power
Dammed the river, flooded land
The railways opened westward
Across this river bridges spanned
Chorus
No one saw it coming
When the train went off the track
A hundred souls went in her waters
Forty-eight did not come back

Now we sail upon her waters
Build our homes along her shores
We know her tranquil nature
Our spirits will restore
Chorus

The *Ballad of the Spanish* was written to accompany the novel. The music was written by Ron Whitman, lyrics by Sylvia Barnard.

You can listen to Ron perform the song at SoundCloud Ron Whitman Ballad of the Spanish.

Author's Notes

When I retired, my husband and I moved from Sudbury, Ontario, to live on the shores of the Spanish River near Nairn Centre. We spent many summer evenings fishing from our small motorboat and soon learned that the stone piers where the first rail bridge crossed the river could always be counted on for bass or pickerel. When my husband and I commented on our success at the piers, our neighbour, who had fished the Spanish for decades, told us that locals attributed the abundance of fish at that spot to the remnants of the train derailment mired in the river's bottom.

Intrigued by his comment, I combed through news reports about the crash. The Espanola Public Library contained a goldmine of documentation, and the staff could not have been more helpful in guiding me through their collection. Thus the novel was born, with the 1910 Spanish River train disaster as its inciting incident.

As a writer, I am interested in people and how they are formed by their choices in the face of adversity. I spent hours on our deck, imagining life on our property a hundred years in the past. How did the hopeful settlers make a life in this harsh landscape? While the Dumonts are a fictional family, their circumstances and struggles are drawn from journals, photos, and historical texts describing the life of settlers in Northern Ontario during the late 1800s and early 1900s. And what better location for the Dumont home than on the property where they came to life in my mind. Gran's bungalow was modelled after our home. Like Catherine, when I needed inspiration or simply wanted to reflect on my writing, I snowshoed to the bridge piers in winter, and paddled my kayak there in summer.

Rhubarb, Strawberries, and Willows is a work of fiction, but the descriptions of the early logging industry, the building of the transcontinental railway, and the development of Nairn are based on fact from history texts, news articles, maps, and historical documents.

Whenever I read historical fiction, I wonder which characters are real, so I offer these details to readers:

Who is Real in *Rhubarb, Strawberries, and Willows*?

    Lois Maxwell who had a summer home on Faraway Road in Espanola

    Abe Obey (his name was believed to be spelled Aubé, but became anglicized)

    William Cornelius Van Horne

    Joseph and Margaret Edwards, Joey Jr. Edwards

    Richard and Eleanor Fensom

    Andrew and Mary Dever

    John and Clara Hall

    Hector and Anne McLean

    James and Flora Hammond

    Robert Bell

Acknowledgements

This novel would not have achieved its final form without the thorough, honest input from my editor, Maggie Morris (The Indy Editor), who challenged my character believability, smoothed my descriptions, brought authenticity to dialogue and helped me find the ending for the novel.

I'd like to acknowledge the contributions of the following people who walked this journey to my debut novel with me.

Thank you,

Alyssa York, (*Effigy, The Naturalist*) my first mentor on this project, who showed me that less can be more by making every word earn its spot on the page, during my coursework in the Humber College Creative Writing Graduate Certificate.

Catherine Graham, (*The Celery Forest, Quarry*) who awoke the poet in me to bring rhythm and lyricism to my prose during our week together at the Haliburton School of Art and Design: Fleming College

The writers of the Niagara Branch of the Canadian Authors Association who gave generously of their time, helping me strip out and tighten my narrative through their detailed critiques.

My friend and fellow writer, Susan Doornbos who untiringly read, reread and reread yet again, various sections and versions of the novel as it evolved, poking holes in my timelines and catching the incongruities.

Special thanks to my husband, Ron Whitman, who was my biggest supporter, believed in me through the ups and downs, and was always ready to offer advice and encouragement.

All of you helped me write a better book and I give you my heartfelt thanks.

Lightning Source UK Ltd.
Milton Keynes UK
UKHW040639271022
411161UK00008B/126/J